W9-BNO-333

The White League

Thomas Zigal

The White League

The Toby Press

First Edition 2005

The Toby Press LLC
POB 8531, New Milford, CT. 06676-8531, USA
& POB 2455, London WIA 5WY, England
www.tobypress.com

© Thomas Zigal 2005

The right of Thomas Zigal to be identified as the author
of this work has been asserted by him in accordance
with the Copyright, Designs & Patents Act 1988

All rights reserved. No part of this publication may be reproduced,
stored in a retrieval system, or transmitted in any form or by
any means, electronic, mechanical, photocopying or otherwise,
without the prior permission of the publisher, except in the case
of brief quotations embodied in critical articles or reviews.

This is a work of fiction. The characters, incidents, and
dialogues are products of the author's imagination and are
not to be construed as real. Any resemblance to actual events
or persons, living or dead, is entirely coincidental.

ISBN 1 59264 115 6 *hardcover*

A CIP catalogue record for this title is
available from the British Library

Typeset in Garamond by Jerusalem Typesetting

Printed and bound in the United States
by Thomson-Shore Inc., Michigan

In memory of Rick Roderick
1949–2002
Rest easy, old friend

New Orleans only has thirty families. Everyone else is there to work for them.

—*A local adage*

Behind every great fortune lies a hidden crime.

—*Honoré de Balzac*

New Orleans, 1990

Chapter one

Mistah Paul, two callers waiting to see you," Rosetta said, taking the briefcase from my hand as she greeted me at the door with my afternoon gin and tonic. There was nothing inside the case except my earphones and a half-dozen blues tapes. "I hesitate to call them gentlemen because I reco'nize the one of them from the news."

She gave me a look, brow furrowed, clearly disapproving of whomever it was. Her worn eyes held a hint of accusation, as if I myself had summoned these suspect visitors to my home. I had seen that look on Rosetta's face many times when I was growing up, usually when I'd disappointed her by doing something thoughtless or hurtful. It was a look that said, *You better than that, child. I expect more out of you.*

"I had them wait by the patio," she said, slowly shaking her head. "Don't want their kind in this house while we're setting up for Miss Julie's birthday party."

She turned and walked away down the long entrance hall, her bony shoulders protruding sharply through the white uniform dress, the briefcase wagging at her side. I sipped the drink and watched her disappear into the late afternoon shadows near the stairwell. Rosetta had completed chemotherapy only two months earlier for cervical cancer and her full weight had not yet returned. I was concerned about her. She had always been a large woman, with a soft round copper face, bright dancing eyes, and a quick laugh. The cancer had diminished her, shrinking the woman who had nurtured us as children, whittling her face into a gaunt, shocking study of the grave. Her legs were stick thin now, her dress draped loosely on her frame, and the light had vanished from her eyes. She was only sixty-four years old, but she appeared ancient and doomed. It was difficult for me to watch my old nanny slowly fading into the darkness. She had joined the Blanchard household when I was five months old and had remained with us, in one capacity or another, for the past forty years. I was closer to Rosetta Jarboe than I was to my own difficult aunts.

I removed my business jacket and dropped it on a Queen Anne armchair in the parlor. Loosening my tie, I walked back into the foyer and made my way down the hall. I could hear the clinking sounds of dinner preparation behind the kitchen doors and I waved at Dell and Corinne, who were placing formal settings around the long dining room table with a practiced perfection.

"Everything okay, ladies?" I asked them. "How many are coming?"

"Twenny-two," Dell responded with a harried smile. She was a tall, rawboned black woman, early fifties, who had been with us for nearly fifteen years. "The *big* family plus three of Julie's friends from school."

"Are y'all going to survive this one?" I asked, grinning sympathetically. There was a secret to treating one's employees with respect and appreciation. You had to mean it. They knew when you didn't.

"Ax us tommawra mornin'," Corinne said in her thick Creole accent. The two women laughed and continued with their work.

When I opened the beveled French doors at the end of the hall and stepped out onto the patio in the gray winter light, I saw the two untimely visitors sitting at a table by the pool. They had been offered no refreshment, a further sign of Rosetta's disapproval. It was one of those temperate February days when the clouds settle low and heavy over the city, a tropical depression causing a dull ache in the temples. Perhaps seventy degrees, no need for an overcoat. Even so, sending the visitors outside unattended, with a moist Gulf wind scurrying dead magnolia leaves across the lawn and tarp-covered pool, was an undeniable message of scorn. *Please wait in the rear of the premises, where you belong.* When I saw who the two men were, I realized Rosetta's decision was an old black woman's revenge.

At my arrival, one of the visitors stood up formally, buttoned his dark western-cut jacket and hitched his wide shoulders, crossing his hands over his crotch like an undertaker at a funeral. He was a tall, thick-necked white man with a shaved head and a heavy black mustache. His rigid posture, dark sunglasses, and the grim expression on his face suggested that he was in the protection services; law enforcement or personal security. I turned my attention to the man who had remained seated, although for an instant I didn't recognize him. His features had been altered cosmetically over the years, a subtle reshaping of flesh and bone, enough to throw me whenever I saw him on television or in newspaper photos. But now here he was in person. He smiled and spoke my name, and the scenario I'd been dreading for so long was suddenly unfolding, here on the secluded grounds where it had all begun. Until the moment I saw Mark Morvant sitting at my patio table with a sly smile on his face, the recurring nightmares had all but vanished and I had nearly convinced myself, with considerable effort as the years crept by, that my past was finally dead and buried.

"Hello, Paul," he said with that memorable southern lilt. In college he had worked studiously on the timbre of his voice, practicing for the day when he would address larger audiences. "Long time no see, *cuño.*"

I sipped my gin and tonic and smiled at the word. *Cuño* was a term of endearment from the Spanish *cuñado,* meaning "brother-in-law." Or possibly a dirty word, *coño.* Nobody knew for sure. It was like calling an old friend *cuz.* Somehow the appellation had been appropriated by the Cajuns and the Y'ats—the white trash New Orleanians who always greeted you with *Hey, man, where y'at?* instead of the usual *How's it going?*

"Hello, Mark," I said, trying to sound calm and cordial. "Yes, it has been a long time."

"This is my associate, Louis Robb," he said, gesturing with a long white hand at the hulking presence standing beside his chair. "Louis is a retired police officer from Shreveport. We go back a long way." He smiled darkly. "Though not as far back as you and I."

Louis Robb and I approached each other across the patio flagstones and he shook my hand with a silent nod. His grip could have broken my fingers, something I was sure he wanted me to understand from the outset. He was much taller than I, maybe six-three, the deep cleft in his chin measuring exactly at my eye level.

"Can I offer you gentleman some refreshment?" I asked, resisting the temptation to rub my sore hand. "Coffee? We have a shipload." It was an old family joke that no one ever laughed at except the Blanchards themselves. "Or would you care for something stronger?" I raised my gin and tonic.

"No, thank you," Morvant answered for both of them. There was an almost feminine grace in the way he gestured with his long hands. I remembered that several of our fraternity brothers had speculated that he was gay. "We won't be long, Paul. But I appreciate your hospitality. That old mammy of yours seems to have forgotten her manners."

I shrugged. "She's been very ill," I said by way of apology.

"And how is her boy?" he asked. "The one in prison."

It had taken him less than five minutes to raise the question. First blood was drawn.

"Well, Mark," I said, "he's still in Angola. Close to twenty years."

The Louisiana State Penitentiary at Angola was a penal hellhole spread along the banks of the Mississippi River in West Feliciana Parish, north of Baton Rouge. Tomorrow there was a parole hearing for Jaren Jarboe, and Rosetta had asked me to attend the proceeding with her and our attorney. I wondered if Morvant knew about the hearing and if that was why he was here.

"Twenty years," he said, shaking his head as if the figure was beyond comprehension. "Wonder if he's got any asshole left."

Louis Robb snorted and looked me over, head to foot. What had his boss told him about me?

"Did you drop by for my views on prison reform, Congressman Morvant?" I asked. I didn't want this discussion to go any further than necessary. "To what do I owe this privilege?"

He was pleased that I had called him *Congressman*. His cornflower blue eyes shone appreciatively, their color enhanced by the tinted contact lenses. That wasn't the only glamorous improvement to his appearance. At some point during the past few years an implant had strengthened his weak chin, rhinoplasty had reduced and straightened his nose, and a facelift had removed those puffy bags under his eyes that I remembered from our drinking days at Tulane. But the most dramatic alteration was to his hairline and coiffure. I remembered a pasty forehead receding high into his thin, boyish blond thatch, but now the line had been lowered and his refashioned hair was uniformly silver and as stiffly sculpted as an evangelist's. Mark Morvant was a remade man. A new and improved face and wardrobe to match the new political image. The white supremacist had become a respectable Louisiana state congressman representing the white-flight suburbs of St. Tammany Parish across Lake Pontchartrain in Covington and Slidell.

"I'm going to run for governor, Paul," he said without a trace of irony, "and I'm here to call on your help."

I wasn't surprised by this declaration. Two years ago, when he was first elected to the statehouse, the news media had speculated that Morvant harbored ambitions for the governor's mansion or the U.S. Senate, but needed experience in the legislature to give him credibility. It hadn't taken him long to make his move. Two years in elected office and he was ready to run the state of Louisiana.

"I'm always happy to help an old friend, Mark."

It was a lie in his case, of course, and I suspected he knew it. I had avoided him for years and hadn't contributed a cent to his extremist causes or his congressional race.

"I appreciate your support, Paul," he said, lacing his long fingers and smiling through even white teeth. "I'm glad you're in a generous mood. I haven't heard from you in a long time, and I was beginning to wonder if you'd forgotten your old fraternity brother."

"I watch the news," I said. "You're hard to miss."

His smile spread wider. This pleased him, too. He'd craved attention and acceptance since his days at the TΣK house in the late sixties, and in spite of his notoriety he still seemed to require validation on a daily basis.

"I've always placed a premium on friendship," he said. Something darkened in his eyes, as if a shadow had passed above the towering oak at the edge of the patio. "Allegiance, loyalty, the common cause. These are the foundation stones of any civilization, Paul. Honorable men are obliged to uphold the social contracts between them. I do something for you, you do something for me. I'm sure you agree with that."

I knew where this was going.

"Old favors," he said with a distant look in his eye. His thoughts were focused on another time and place. "Hell, let's call it what it is. You owe me one, brother," he said, "and I'm here to collect."

I watched Louis Robb for his reaction. He remained standing, implacable, an exemplar of the warrior's body language. I wondered again how much he knew.

"I'm prepared to help you, Mark," I said. There was no point in prolonging this charade. I wanted him out of my hair as soon as possible. "How much are we talking about?"

He stood up and stared across the covered pool toward the guest cottage set back under the oak trees near the far wall. The cottage had served as slave quarters before the Civil War and as a home for domestics long afterwards, until the 1930s when my grandfather had found the close proximity of black people too disagreeable and had reclaimed the small stone structure for personal family use. When I was growing up it had provided the perfect children's playhouse and a changing area for swimmers.

I knew why he was looking at the cottage. He'd been inside it one dark night many years ago when we were fraternity brothers.

"You have any idea how much money it takes to win a campaign for governor in this state?" Morvant asked, still facing the cottage. He cut a tall, lean figure in his charcoal gray Brooks Brothers suit.

"I couldn't begin to guess," I said.

"That sorry bastard Edwin Edwards spent ten million in his last race and *lost*," he said. "Most of it on bribes and kickbacks. Ten million dollars."

He turned and stared past me toward the ivy-covered wall of the manse, his eyes ranging upward to the row of second-story windows. The circumstances of his last visit had prevented him from fully appreciating the magnificent structure itself, one of the many visual splendors along St. Charles Avenue. He seemed to notice my home's mass and distinction for the very first time.

"Beautiful place you've got here, *cuño*," he said. "Be a damned shame if something happened and you…well, we don't want to think bad thoughts, do we now?"

He was threatening me, the son of a bitch.

"You've done a fine job of carrying on the Blanchard tradition, my man," he continued. "I admire you for that. When we were in college I used to ridicule you and your prissy Uptown ways behind your back. Envy, I suppose. You had it and I didn't."

Morvant had grown up in the tough working-class neighborhood of Arabi, the ugly edge of urban sprawl downriver across the line in St. Bernard Parish, and he'd attended Tulane on a scholarship he'd earned from his public high school. Though he'd spent most of his time in the bars, like all good Tulane frat boys, he'd maintained a respectable 3.0 average until he was expelled in his senior year for wearing black face to class and disrupting a Julian Bond speech on campus with his racist diatribe.

"I didn't think you'd ever live up to the family name," he said, glancing at me, three distinct lines etched across his cosmetically lowered forehead. "But I can see you've done all right, after all. CEO of the coffee business. Quite impressive," he said, studying my features. "I'm sure it's what your father always wanted, rest his soul."

Yes, I had certainly changed since my fraternity days.

"And you married a Jew, I hear. Ida Benjamin's daughter. Very good career move, *cuño*. You know what they say about New Orleans. 'The Catholics built it, the Jews own it, and the niggers enjoy it.'"

Louis Robb snorted and worked his jaw.

I checked my watch. My daughter, Julie, had turned thirteen today and her birthday party was set for this evening. I wanted to get this over with and send them on their way before company arrived.

"I appreciate your compliments, Mark. I think we've established that we're both doing well," I said. "So how much do you need? I don't think the election commission will allow me to give you the entire ten million."

It was intended as a joke, but neither man laughed.

"Let your conscience be your guide." The honeyed lilt to his words carried a hidden mockery. "I know you'll be generous with your own money—for old times' sake," he added with a wry smile. "But you're right, one man can't fund an entire governor's race. Certainly not with the new finance restrictions. I'm going to need more help than just you, Paul. I'm going to need the support and endorsement of the White League."

I stared at him. The tumbler had grown cold in my hand and I wanted to get rid of it, along with these two intruders. "The White League?" I asked. I wasn't sure what he was talking about. And I wasn't sure he knew what he was talking about, either. "Do you mean the old White Citizens Council? That outfit run by Leander Perez?" They had been the outspoken enemy of the NAACP and New Orleans school integration back in the late fifties and early sixties.

Morvant smirked at my confusion. But then his smirk turned cruel. "Please don't play games with me, Paul. I've never played games with you. When you needed me, I was there. So don't jerk me around, *cuño*. That's not very good manners."

"I really don't know what you're talking about, Mark. The only White League I've ever heard about was that gang back during Reconstruction—the one in the shoot-out on Canal Street. There's a monument down near the Riverwalk."

My great grandfather had fought in the battle. As I remembered the history lesson, an organized group of local white citizens had clashed with the carpetbagger police, a troop of freed slaves and ragtag Yankee sympathizers who had replaced the regular New Orleans police force after the Civil War.

"If you think pleading ignorance is going to help you, Paul, you're sadly mistaken. I know your family has been White League since the beginning, and I know you grew up around their activity. I'm betting that when your daddy died, he passed his colors on to you."

I was so surprised by his remark that I couldn't contain my amusement. "If you're trying to join the Krewe of Jove, Mark, you're wasting your time."

Jove was one of the oldest Mardi Gras organizations, dating back to before the Civil War, and its membership was a closely guarded secret. It required being born into the right family. I was a member, all right, but I avoided the old farts in the krewe as much as possible and only participated once a year in the Carnival parade and evening ball.

"You can't buy your way into Jove," I said, still amused by his mythical White League. "And take my word for it, you don't want to. It's a pack of crusty old dinosaurs whose only pleasure in life is to get shit-faced one weekend a year and throw plastic beads from a parade float. The krewe doesn't give money to politicians. They'd rather waste it on a good party."

Morvant slid his long, elegant hands into his suit pants and ambled toward me until we were close enough to embrace like old friends. But we didn't. He was slightly over six feet tall, and he peered down at me with an air of disappointment.

"I'm not talking about a fucking Mardi Gras krewe or Leander Perez and a bunch of irate old ladies walking a picket line in front of a niggerfied school," he said, irritation mounting in his voice. "The White League, Paul. I know your great grandfather was with them from the start, and so was his son later on, and then your father. For nearly a hundred and twenty years you people have been pulling the strings in this town. It used to be the cotton brokers and bankers and mercantile big-wigs. Now it's fat cat lawyers and coffee barons and oil and gas men. The deal-makers, Paul. The ones who decide who's in and who's out. Thumbs up or thumbs down." He knitted his brow. I remembered that intense, driven expression from when he was in college and beginning to voice his militant views around the frat house. "If somebody poses a problem to the common good, they're the ones who eliminate the problem."

I realized he was under some strange misconception about the way things operated among the old New Orleans aristocrats. "You're talking about the old boys in the Magnolia Club and the Pickwick Club," I said, still somewhat puzzled.

The gentlemen's clubs had existed in downtown New Orleans since the 1840s, and some were associated with Mardi Gras krewes. Their stately quarters had always provided a cloistered place where upper crust business leaders could gather and chat amiably and strike lucrative deals over cigars and brandy.

"But you're making them sound like some kind of organized cabal, Mark. I assure you they're not. I'm a member of the Magnolia Club and I've been to lunch there many times and watched those clowns trying to agree on a salad dressing. They blabber about stocks and the Saints' season and rising crime. On their own they couldn't organize a two-car funeral. They may've been powerbrokers thirty years ago, but right now they're palsied old geezers drooling in their bread pudding."

Morvant cut his eyes toward the bodyguard and shook his head in disgust. The gesture said, *What am I going to do with this guy?* Louis Robb moved his jaw slightly and cracked his neck, a menacing sound. He had the practiced glower of a professional wrestler.

"I'd hoped we could be straight with each other and discuss this like gentlemen," Morvant said, losing patience. "We go back a long way, Paul. You did a careless thing that got you in deep shit, but I always liked you, man. I thought we were friends. I remember that phone call like it was last night." He glared at me, a disappointed father scolding his son. "How about you, Paul? Do you remember how it was that night you called me? You were falling apart and crying like a titty baby and you didn't have anybody else to turn to."

"I remember," I said, taking a long swallow of my gin and tonic. How could I have forgotten? I had relived that scene in a thousand sweaty nightmares.

"And I came to your aid."

"You did," I said, acknowledging what we both understood.

"And afterwards—did I ask for anything?"

"No."

"Did I want money?"

"No, you didn't."

"All these years, have I ever asked for a favor?"

"No," I said. I could feel a trickle of sweat under my shirt collar.

"Then why do you want to treat me this way, Paul? I come to your home with a simple request and you jerk my chain. Is that any way to treat an old friend who saved your ass?"

I turned and studied the French doors to see if anyone from my family was within earshot. "Why don't we discuss this somewhere more private?" I suggested. I didn't want Louis Robb to be a party to our conversation, either.

"It looks like I'm not welcome in the big house, *Mistah Paul*," he said, exaggerating the name, mimicking Rosetta's voice. "So I'm perfectly happy to discuss this problem out here in the open, where the whole world can participate." He looked at his bodyguard. "Don't you want to hear what *Mistah Paul* has to say for himself, Louis?"

Louis Robb smiled darkly but remained silent.

"What exactly do you want from me?" I asked Morvant, lowering my voice. This conversation was beginning to come unraveled. I could see that he was working himself into a heated confrontation, and my home was the last place on earth I wanted that to take place.

"I'm willing to make a significant contribution to your campaign, Mark. As much as the law allows. But I don't have any juice with the old boy network—and I sure as hell don't know anything about a White League. I stay pretty much to myself and my family." The absolute truth. "If you're looking for somebody plugged into the network, you're talking to the wrong guy. I'm considered a loner in most Uptown circles, and I like it that way."

Morvant was undeterred. He crossed his arms over his suit jacket and questioned my sincerity with narrowed eyes. "You underestimate me, Paul. Have you forgotten that I'm a student of history?

I always do my homework." He had begun to raise and lower the heel of his right shoe in an impatient rhythm. "I know all about the White League. If a man wants political support in this city, he goes to the League with his hat in hand and asks for their blessing. So that's what I'm doing here, Paul. I'm asking for their blessing and their financial backing. I know they already appreciate what I've done for Louisiana politics. I'm balancing the power for white folks. I'm their kind of candidate. We believe in the same principles. But I can't win this election without their help, and that's where you come in, my friend. You're going to be my go-between. You're going to represent my interests in their circle. And when the time is right, you're going to introduce me to the League leaders face to face."

I studied his overheated features, the wrinkled brow and strong jutting chin, and wondered if I was witnessing a seminal episode in American political history, the exact moment the infamous Mark Morvant had gone mad. Ever since our college years he'd been a raving paranoid, like all the angry militants and antigovernment conspiracy theorists of our time, and it occurred to me that his obsessions may have now reached some irreversible stage of emotional damage. Perhaps the demons had whispered one too many dark secrets in his ear and his mind had finally snapped.

"Mark, I will be happy to write you a check," I said, eager to dispose of this matter and see these men out the gate. "But I can't introduce you to a group that doesn't exist. There is no White League. You're living in the past. That was ancient history."

I remembered an old book in my father's library. I had skimmed through its pages when I was a teenager but hadn't seen it since. There was a photograph of my great grandfather and several other stern, white-bearded Confederates posing at a plaque dedication ceremony in front of a monument, sometime in the 1930s, if my memory was correct. They were the last survivors of the White League battle on Canal Street. Sixty years later, there they were, New Orleans aristocrats dragging their beloved Dixie flag with them to the grave.

"Ancient history?" Morvant smiled caustically. He reached into the vest pocket of his suit jacket. "Then how do you explain this, *cuño*?"

He produced a folded white page and handed it to me. At some point the paper had been wadded up and then straightened, a vein work of wrinkles like an old man's face. When I opened the creases I saw that it was a note handwritten on my father's distinctive private stationery—*From the desk of Charles M. Blanchard*—which he used only for his most personal correspondence:

> *Henry,*
> *Willie gaining ground. Things getting out of hand.*
> *Must get the League together and discuss what to do. Are*
> *you available this week?*
> *Warm regards, Charles*

I was stunned. It was certainly my father's peculiar, ornate handwriting. "Where did you get this?" I demanded. The page looked as if it had been retrieved from the trash.

Morvant was elated by my reaction. He could see that the note troubled me and he could hardly contain his joy. "I have operatives everywhere," he said, laughing at my confusion. He glanced at Louis Robb, who worked his iron jaw and returned a knowing smile. "I may be a Y'at from Arabi, Paul, but over the years I've learned a thing or two about gathering intelligence."

Even in our benumbed fraternity days he had been a fierce, unyielding competitor. He wanted nothing more than to win every argument, humiliate his opponents, and gain the approval of those who had doubted him. And here was his vindication—solid evidence for the existence of some sort of League. Evidence that I was at a loss to explain. I had no idea what my father was talking about in the note.

"Willie?" I said, perplexed.

"Wilhelmina Phillips," he said. "That uppity black bitch on the city council. The one making noises about shutting down Mardi Gras."

Wilhelmina Phillips was an outspoken city councilwoman who had been trying for several years to pass an anti-discrimination ordinance aimed at racially integrating the Carnival krewes and Mardi Gras organizations.

"Sounds like I'm not the only one who'd like to see her career come to an end," Morvant said.

I studied the note in my hand. Surely there was a simple explanation. My father had belonged to the Krewe of Jove and the Magnolia Club, but I had never heard him mention membership in any sort of League. Was this one of his dry jokes? The late Charles M. Blanchard had been a private man not given to lengthy discussion or frivolous distractions. He'd spent long hours at the coffee offices on Magazine Street, six days a week, and he'd enjoyed few hobbies or passions outside of family and work. He could be ill-tempered and strict and uncompromising, but he was also a zealous protector of his children and the sheltered world in which we lived. I wondered how many secrets he had kept from me.

"I'm not sure who this *Henry* is," I said without raising my eyes from the note.

Morvant didn't hesitate. "Henry Lesseps. Good old Henry the Fifth. Your father's drinking buddy."

He was beginning to read my mind. The attorney Henry Lesseps was the first name I had considered.

"The Lesseps family is deep in the White League," Morvant said, as confident of his facts as an archive librarian. "They have been for generations."

My irritation was reaching surface level. "You know a helluva lot more about this group than I do, Mark. I should be asking *you* the questions."

He smiled at the backhanded compliment, but the smile faded quickly into suspicion. "Have you forgotten who I am, *cuño?*" he said with one well-groomed eyebrow raised defiantly. "I'm the guy who knows where all the bodies are buried."

I heard the French doors open and turned to find my daughter crossing the flagstones toward our conversation. I tucked the note into my shirt pocket.

Even in her prim school uniform, with her white blouse hanging haphazardly out of her skirt and her long dark hair bunched to one side and frizzed by the humidity, she still carried herself with a buoyant grace and her mother's composure. She also had Claire's deep inviting eyes, the prominent Benjamin nose and firm jaw, and a bright smile miraculously free of braces. A recent interest in soccer had trimmed off her youthful baby fat and hardened her thighs, and her calves were now lean and muscular under the knee-length stockings.

"Hi, Dad," she said, throwing her arms around me in an affectionate hug. I could see she was excited about her birthday party tonight. "I just wanted to say hello."

"Hello, sweetie," I said, pecking her on the forehead. She was already as tall as her mother and growing like a stalk.

She regarded Morvant and Louis Robb with a shy smile, then dropped her eyes and blushed. She was at that age when older men made her uncomfortable.

"Hello, Miss Blanchard," Morvant said, stepping forward with his hand extended. "I'm an old college friend of your father. My name is Mark Morvant."

He didn't expect her to refuse his hand, and neither did I. Nor did I expect her to express such a vocal opinion. She was certainly her mother's daughter.

"I know who you are," she said, leaning against my shoulder in a lazy slump, grappling my arm. "You're the racist from St. Tammany. You don't like Jews and black people."

Morvant grinned at her remark. "I no longer feel that way, young lady," he said. "Many years ago I said and did some foolish things." He looked at me and aimed his words like a shaft. "I hurt people and caused a lot of anger and confusion, and I'm sorry I did that. But I'm a different person now. I've tried to make things right with God and my conscience. I don't hate anybody anymore."

He was good, the delivery rehearsed and skillful. Perhaps it was this Biblical repentance that had convinced the gullible, forgiving folks in his district to vote for him. But I didn't believe his transformation for a heartbeat, the East Coast media didn't believe him, and I could tell by the skepticism in my daughter's eyes that she didn't believe him, either. She had heard her mother rail against Morvant since the day he'd won office in St. Tammany.

"Don't be late for the party, Dad," Julie said, giving my arm another squeeze before releasing me. She turned and walked back toward the house without acknowledging Morvant's homily or excusing herself, and her dismissive attitude clearly annoyed him. He wasn't used to being ignored.

"Delightful girl," he said, his gaze following her past the planted jungle of tall leafy ferns and banana trees. "She seems to love her father dearly. It would be a shame if she ever heard something that would change all that."

He was trying to provoke me, the bastard, but I wouldn't give him the pleasure. "I'm sorry, gentlemen," I said, struggling to remain untouched by his threat. "I have to get ready for a birthday party. How can we conclude this meeting to everyone's satisfaction?"

Morvant smiled roguishly. I sensed that he'd been waiting me out, biding his time like a veteran salesman, softening me up for his best offer. "In three weeks I'm going to announce my candidacy for the governor's race," he said. "To win, I need big contributions and the promise of more down the road. I can't raise ten million dollars from my usual constituents. They're all working stiffs who send me twenty bucks after the rent check clears. Fifty if some homeboy has just broken into their crib."

He made a half turn toward Louis Robb as if to indicate the kind of people he was talking about. Rednecks from northern Louisiana, poor white trash from the Cajun bayous, a handful of car dealers who still told nigger jokes at their Lion's Club luncheons. They couldn't buy him an election.

"You've got three weeks to deliver the White League, Paul. I want their patronage in this election. I want cash up front and payouts on a regular basis. And as soon as possible I want a clear picture of our long-term financial relationship—with guaranteed future security. Do we understand each other, *cuño?*"

He laughed at the shock registering on my face. I hadn't expected him to be so brazen. I looked deep into his blue contact lenses. "There's a name for this kind of pressure, Mark. Ask your cop friend, Mr. Robb," I said, nodding at the ex-police officer standing at attention behind him, "if he's ever heard the word *extortion.*"

Louis Robb didn't appreciate my remark. He left his post by

the patio table and moved toward us with a loping, equine movement of his shoulders. He was all heavy muscle and upper-body strength, and I suspected he had no natural speed. Morvant raised a hand, signaling him to keep his distance.

"*Extortion* is an ugly word," he said, returning my stare. "Do you really want to play word games with me, *cuño*? I can think of some ugly words myself. How about possession of narcotics, concealing a crime, obstruction of justice?"

I did not want to battle with him and capitulated with a weak wave of my hand and a long weary exhalation.

"But we can go beyond words if you want to, Paul," he said, pressing his attack. "We can examine historical artifacts. Like I told you, I'm a student of history. I've always collected souvenirs."

He reached into the outside pocket of his suit jacket and withdrew a beaded object that he held out in his palm, his body positioned to obscure it from Louis Robb's view. Morvant displayed the long dangling earring, then quickly concealed it in a closed fist and returned the earring to his pocket. I had seen enough to know what it was. The earring was unforgettable. Wooden beads and cowry shells from the Ivory Coast. I'd bought the gift in an exotic African import shop in the French Quarter.

"You kept one, goddamn you," I said under my breath.

Morvant stepped closer. "For sentimental reasons," he said with a cunning smile. "I imagine the police have the other one buried away in some evidence drawer. Do you suppose that nosy colored cop—what *was* his name?—is still looking for a match after all these years?" He reached out and squeezed my shoulder. "It'd be a shame if this thing found its way to his mailbox, now wouldn't it, *cuño*?"

He could see that I was stunned by the revelation of the earring and incapable of locating my voice. He stepped back, measuring me with a triumphant smile. He seemed enormously pleased with himself. I fit his portrait of the pathetic Uptown rich boy, pampered and inept and morally weak. A necessary piece in the Mark Morvant grand scheme of things, perhaps, but on the most fundamental level, an object of pity and scorn.

"Louis," he said, still appraising me in that judgmental

19

gaze, "would you give Mr. Blanchard a handful of those brochures, please."

The tall bodyguard walked toward me while reaching into his jacket. His stolid face had become animated with a ruthless devotion to duty and for an instant I thought he might produce a leather sap and strike me on the head.

"Please pass these out among your brethren," Morvant said to me. "I want them to know where I stand. They can count on Mark Morvant to speak for them in Baton Rouge."

Louis Robb handed me a small stack of red, white, and blue political brochures. There was a handsome, smiling photograph of Morvant on the cover, surrounded by glossy slogans:

A Real Choice for a Change
The Time Has Come
Mark Morvant for Governor

"In three weeks, Paul," he said, "I make my official announcement. Don't disappoint me."

I opened a brochure and scanned Mark Morvant's political agenda. I didn't need to read the fine print to get the picture. The one-time extremist was now a respectable, conservative Republican. No more nigger-baiting, no more night-riding. The man had seen the light and it wasn't from a burning cross.

"We'll stay in close touch," Morvant said. "I'll call you every couple of days for a progress report."

I stood helpless like a mute delivery boy with a stack of grocery flyers in his hand. "Mark—" I said, unsure where to begin. There was no way to meet his expectations. I had never heard of this latter-day White League he was certain existed, and I couldn't produce any financial support beyond my own, which would be a tricky business in itself, given my wife's contempt for Morvant and his beliefs, reformed or not.

He saw the exasperation on my face and raised a hand to prevent any more excuses from me. His patience was clearly exhausted. "Don't bother to summon the help. We'll find our way out," he said, cutting me off. "I don't want that old mammy washerwoman to go to any trouble on my account."

He nodded to Louis Robb that it was time to leave, then gazed off toward the guest cottage and the spreading oaks near the far wall of our property. "There's a gate back there, if my memory serves," he said, one final reminder of the dark bond that had sealed us together on that night long ago. "It's been a long hard road—right, Louis?—but we don't mind the walk."

The bodyguard laughed at something that passed for a thought. "You're startin' to sound like old Martin Luther Coon, boss."

Morvant laughed at the idea, too, and clapped his man on the shoulder. They set out together past the edge of the pool, across the long green expanse of lawn. The south breeze mussed a stiff silver wing of Morvant's hair and he patted it neatly into place. I watched them until they disappeared behind the cottage, and then I followed to make sure the gate was bolted shut. You couldn't be too careful in New Orleans, even in the opulent splendor of the Avenue. Violence was never more than a block away, coming your direction, and an open gate was an invitation you would live to regret.

Chapter two

My parents called it the *garçonnière*. We children called it the *playhouse*. My wife, Claire, humorously referred to the small stone structure as the *cabana*. I unlocked the door and stepped into the quiet enclosure, the natural light made dusky by drawn drapes. I hadn't been inside for several months. We rarely used this place during the winter, so the air felt thick and stale, a breeding culture of molds and fungal growth. I smelled wet plaster and wondered if the roof had leaked during the January rains.

We had remodeled the cottage ten years ago, altering its purpose from guest quarters to fitness area, with treadmill and rowing machine and of course a wet bar, in compliance with the New Orleans building code: *Where two or three are gathered together, liquor shall be required.* I walked over to the bar, removed a tumbler placed upside down amongst a neat row of glasses, and blew into the wide mouth, dispersing a film of dust. In the small refrigerator below the bar I found a chilled blue bottle of Bombay Sapphire gin and poured myself an inch of syrupy white liquid. It went down smooth and settled nicely over the first drink I'd had. But I knew I had to pace myself or I wouldn't make it through the long evening ahead.

The treadmill, a cumbersome motorized contraption seldom used anymore, occupied the space where a stately queen-sized bed had once floated on brass legs. In spite of my regrets, I still took guilty pleasure in remembering the great sex I'd had on that bed as a randy Tulane college boy. In those days we got high on reefer instead of this expensive gin I was drinking. Reefer and sometimes a harder rush, as I discovered later on. But I was by no means the first Blanchard to enjoy the carnal comforts of that bed. Once, when I was only nine years old, I peeked through the dust-caked window and caught my sister doing something naughty with Rosetta's son, Jaren. I didn't snitch on them because Jaren was my friend.

Jaren Jarboe. *Two J*, his black schoolmates had called him when we were kids. Midway through his teen years the nickname had taken on another meaning. By then he'd cultivated a reputation for carrying two joints in his pocket at all times. Jaren was the one who'd turned me on to marijuana and Motown and to many of life's forbidden delights. My mentor and oldest companion.

Jaren had grown up in our household on St. Charles Avenue. He was always visible in my favorite childhood photographs, occupying the margins of the frame. When Rosetta came to work for us he was two years old, and my parents allowed her to bring him into our home when child care proved too difficult and too costly for her to manage. Forty years ago, that arrangement was highly unusual. The children and husbands of domestic employees were expected to remain outside the residence, rain or shine, hats in hand, shuffling their feet and staring at the ground. They never crossed the threshold. I can't recall any other Uptown family granting such permission. In their social circle my father and mother were often chided for this decision. At Mother's weekly luncheons her sisters would tsk and tease her: *My word, Doris, is that a real live Little Black Sambo in the nursery? Don't your children have* toys *to play with?*

My earliest memories of Jaren were of our playground escapades at the little park on the corner of Octavia and St. Charles, a few blocks from our home. Rosetta would turn us loose on the merry-go-round and amble off to visit with the other nannies on a shady bench. My brother, Perry, was in school by then, so my sister,

Kathleen, took his place screaming and running wild with the boys. She was Jaren's age, two years older than I, and watching them rough-house together, even in those innocent pre-kindergarten years, made white passersby uneasy.

So for the first ten years of my life I had had a black friend who spent more time with me than my fussy older brother. Jaren and I played army together, we glued model airplanes, we traded superhero comic books and baseball cards like any two white kids in suburban America. But all of that came crashing down in 1960, when the public schools erupted in those infamous desegregation battles and white people turned against the blacks they'd known for years. Even the well-educated Uptown whites divided militantly on the issue. Resistance or crafty compromise? My parents were by no means liberal and accepting, but they were disgusted by the coarse, confrontational methods of Judge Leander Perez from Plaquemines Parish and the so-called White Citizens Council. They hated his vulgarity and the shocking spectacle of angry, overweight Y'at women wearing muumuus and carrying illiterate placards in front of the schools. New Orleans had become a laughingstock on the national evening news.

Such tacky glasses, I remember my brother saying at the time, referring to the swoopy harlequin frames worn by all the picketing housewives. *Those women look like Martians at a 3D movie.*

Overnight the decision was handed down that Jaren could no longer spend his after-school hours at our home or eat supper with us every evening. I was confused and angry. Best friends for our entire lives, and I didn't even get the chance to say goodbye to him. One day he was there, playing football with me and the Delery boys on the side lawn, doing his homework on the floor of my bedroom, the next day he was gone. I protested vehemently. *Jaren is not like other Coloreds!* I called upon every argument an intelligent ten-year-old could formulate. I cited the contradictions, the hypocrisy, the unfairness. It didn't matter. In the end my father assured me that I had not comprehended the full scope of the issue. And as it turned out, I hadn't.

I didn't see Jaren again for five or six years. No one in our household talked about him or mentioned his name. I asked Rosetta about her son from time to time, and she always stiffened proudly when she said, *Doin' good. The boy's doin' good, child.* But I sensed her reluctance to speak freely, to elaborate with her usual warm effusiveness. I knew she'd been hurt by my parents' decision as well, but had outwardly, stoically, maintained her professional composure. For me Jaren's absence was a small stone bruise that ached for a while but eventually healed. For Rosetta, the change had torn something essential from her heart. She wasn't the same afterwards. A coldness crept through her. I felt it, and I think Kathleen felt it, too. The trust was gone, a subtle, immeasurable dimension of respect. To our dear nanny we had become just another typical New Orleans white family, loyal only to our own kind.

I finished off the gin and splashed a little more into the tumbler, gently swirling the cold liquid as I walked over to the bathroom door and leaned against the jamb. This bathroom had been much simpler before the renovation. In the old days there was no shower with Jacuzzi tub, only a toilet and a boxy porcelain sink jutting from the wall. I stared at the tile floor, still the original checkerboard pattern of small black and white squares. Despite my tight grip on the glass I suddenly felt the same electric surge of panic I'd felt the night I discovered her naked body curled around that commode.

"Do you remember how much she loved this old cabana?"

I hadn't heard my wife enter the cottage. She was standing near the treadmill, gazing about the room as if looking for lost memories tangled in the cobwebs.

"It was her favorite hidey place. Remember when she liked to sneak out here and bounce up and down on the old bed?"

I was slow to realize she was talking about our daughter as a toddler.

"And now she's a tall skinny teenager, Paul. My God, where did the time go? She's so damned sophisticated these days. Violin... makeup...Tom Cruise. I miss the little imp that used to run around half-naked on the lawn with a wicked grin on her face."

I smiled at the memory of chasing down Julie at playgrounds and City Park and the zoo, an active child always trying to escape from us. "She gets better with age," I said. I'd been partial to the ten-year-old Julie. So curious and wise, and yet finally open to reason.

Claire had apparently just returned home from her afternoon of charity work. Today's objective: teaching pregnant teenagers in the St. Thomas Housing Project how to make a grocery list. She hadn't yet changed out of her jeans and running shoes, and she was sporting a neatly cuffed denim jacket, a replica of the one she'd no doubt worn at Brandeis in the early seventies. Only this version cost considerably more at Gae-tana's on Maple Street and featured a pair of yellow roses femininely embroidered above the pockets.

"I see you're getting a head start on the evening," she said, studying my gin tumbler with a disapproving air. "Don't overdo it, please. The guests are arriving at six-thirty."

"I'll be fortified and full of my usual charm, darling Claire."

"Every time you're full of charm, darling Paul, you end up saying something you shouldn't. Usually to my brother."

I never knew which Claire I was getting at any given moment: gracious, enchanting wife or scolding shrew. She externalized her stress more than anyone I'd ever met. *Keep your own counsel,* the Blanchard family motto, was not in Claire's nature.

"Your brother is an arrogant prick," I said. "He expects to be insulted, and I hate to disappoint him."

There was the slightest trace of a smile around her pretty mouth. Since the beginning of our relationship she had fiercely upheld her own blood loyalties and family pride, but on the subject of her brother the orthopedic surgeon she remained artfully ambiguous.

"Julie said you had a peculiar visitor a short while ago. Your old fraternity brother." The thought of Mark Morvant in our home actually flared her nostrils and ignited a fire behind those deep brown eyes. "What on earth was he doing here?"

"Just in the neighborhood, he said. He dropped by to see if I wanted to suck down some suds and go burn a cross at the synagogue."

"Not funny, Paul. What was that asshole doing in my house?"

"Actually, I'm not sure he made it into the house. Rosetta shooed him off to the patio."

She smiled with a sly appreciation of Rosetta's skills. "Go ahead, girl," she said.

Claire and I had known each other since we were children. Our families were drawn together by business rather than friendship, although we did socialize on occasion, usually during the Carnival season. For three generations the Blanchard Coffee Company had supplied our trademark Creole blend to the Benjamin grocery stores in New Orleans. Claire and I had often joked that ours was a marriage made on aisle four.

Because she was two years younger than I—a chasm of differences when you're growing up—I hadn't really noticed the comely dark-haired Benjamin daughter until she was a teenager, when we were awkwardly matched for a dance at the Rex Ball one rainy Mardi Gras evening. Her father was one of three Jews in the Rex Krewe, an historical anomaly in this city, and their family remained in town during the Carnival season, unlike the other prominent Jews who had always left for New York or Sun Valley to avoid the social awkwardness of being shut out of the grandest celebration of the year.

My dance partner at the ball had been friendly and charming and well-bred, and she'd laughed at my nervous attempts at humor. Even at fifteen she'd cut a shapely figure in her Renaissance gown, with believable cleavage and flawless skin, and when she finally lowered her mask at the end of the dance I was left speechless by the dark beauty of her eyes and her exquisite bone structure. It was possibly the first time in my young life that I'd understood how sexual the female eyebrows could be, a suggestion of something secret and fine.

There was little I could do about my tumescent interest in Claire Benjamin. I was at Jesuit High and she was at Newman, a former Jewish orphanage converted into a snooty Uptown private school for wealthy non-Catholics. Our worlds didn't intersect. Besides, she was too young for me. And Jewish. My friends would have ridiculed my taste. But I had a driver's license and a cherry red '66 Ford Mustang, and I drove by her house on nearby State Street every night for a year, hoping desperately to catch a glimpse of her. It was an exercise in futility and I eventually grew interested in other girls. But I never forgot Claire Benjamin. And when I returned to New Orleans in 1973, having dropped out of Tulane and run away to California for three years to escape what I'd done, I found her slumming at the F&M Patio Bar on Tchoupitoulas Street one summer evening after her junior year at Brandeis and fell in love all over again and knew that one day I would ask her to marry me.

"You're not going to get out of this one, darling Paul," Claire said, unpersuaded. "What was Mark Morvant doing here?"

I walked over to the bar and splashed more gin in my glass. She took the icy blue Sapphire bottle from my hand and replaced the cap, then returned the bottle to the mini-refrigerator. I sipped and smiled at her, trying to deflect her silent disapproval. Her arms were folded militantly across her denim jacket and she wore the devoted, wind-blown look of a marathon runner, her face ruddy from some recent physical exertion, possibly a tumble in the sack with that Christian Brother she worked with in the St. Thomas Project. Her hair was still as black as it had been as a child—without artificial help, as far as I knew—only bobbed short now and parted down the middle and fingered back behind her ears, the hairstyle of choice for Uptown women past thirty-five. She was glaring at me in her defiant mode and would not let up until I told her a convincing lie.

"He said he was passing down St. Charles on his way back from some Republican luncheon, saw the old manse, and wondered how I was doing these days. It sounded like a spontaneous act of nostalgia. He's a mellow Unitarian now, you know. Aren't they the ones with the wholesome singles mingles?"

"Hah hah."

"He's expanding his constituency."

"Julie said he had a bodyguard."

"He figured he might need one if you were at home."

She smiled reluctantly, pleased with my compliment. "This isn't going to become a habit, is it?" she asked. "I don't want that man to set foot on our property ever again. And I hope you have the good sense to avoid him in public. He's poison, darling Paul. If you get linked to him in any way, it's bad for business."

The Blanchard coffee business. Her family's grocery chain. *It's bad for business* was her father's favorite war cry.

"Worry not, darling Claire. I don't like the bastard any more than you do. He was a grandstander in college and he's a grandstander now. I promise not to join his church."

"He's a card-carrying Republican now, Paul," she said with a caustic smile. "Do you promise not to join the Republicans?"

I sipped gin and returned her smile. "You know me," I said with an affable shrug. "The very definition of bipartisan. Always fair-minded, always accommodating. It's good for business."

Her eyes brightened with the mischief of my sarcasm. She stepped forward and kissed me affectionately on the cheek. "I'm going to go shower and get ready for the party," she said. "You should do the same."

There was an unsettling finality about her turning and walking away from me. I was overcome with a momentary anxiety, as if we'd had a fight and everything was finished between us and I would never see her or our children again. I don't know why I felt that way. Bad memories lingering in the room, perhaps. Morvant's sudden appearance after all these years. The possibility that I might lose the only things I cherished. I started to say something clever to detain her, to give her a parting hug and hold her in my arms. To my amazement she turned abruptly and smiled at me, as though reading my thoughts. The smile was naughty and knowing and totally unexpected. "It's too bad we got rid of that bed," she said, glancing at the place where the old frame had once been moored like a regal barque. "We could sneak out here some night, when the kids are asleep, and put it to good use."

I was surprised by her remark. I thought she'd given up such longings for me. We hadn't made love in months.

"I would like that," I said, finishing off the gin, desperately needing another one.

"I almost suggested it back when we were dating," she admitted, her eyes glowing with fond recollection of those simpler times. "This old cabana seemed like the perfect hideout for all our misbehaving. I'm surprised you didn't think of it yourself."

I had considered bringing her here, of course, but the idea had frightened and repulsed me. I couldn't face what had happened in this cottage. I wouldn't enter the place at all for many years afterwards.

"I have a feeling you had your share of fun in here before you met me," she said, looking about the room with a foxy smile. "Did you ever bring a girl here, darling Paul?"

"Unchaperoned?" I asked, feigning astonishment. "Why, darling Claire, that would've caused a family scandal."

She laughed. "Somehow I don't believe you," she said, giving my face a firm pat. Her hand was warm and moist. "Don't lose track of the time reliving old conquests, dear. Remember, guests at six-thirty."

Once she was gone I opened the refrigerator and retrieved the gin bottle, helping myself to another generous sample. Nudging aside one corner of a drape, I peered out the water-stained window. The light was gray and heavy, dulling the tropical green garden of elephant ears and lush banana stalks bordering the patio. I thought I could smell the rendering plant across the river, a hint of burning horseflesh. These low stagnant clouds threatened to smother the city for several days until something broke, a cold front moving southward with sweeping rain.

I watched Claire cross the long green lawn toward the house, her ass shifting with a graceful rhythm in those tight jeans. I wondered if she knew I was watching her.

When she reached the patio flagstones, our son Andy raced through the French doors to greet her with a bounding exuberance. He hadn't seen his mother this afternoon and nearly knocked her over in his enthusiasm. They embraced and swung around the patio like dancing lunatics, and I was delighted to hear his laughter, the carefree sound of an eleven-year-old, and the rising cries of their horseplay.

They loved each other very much. We had a good family and a good life together. I couldn't imagine hurting them. I couldn't imagine losing all of this.

But I took Mark Morvant at his word. I believed he was capable of malice. I had witnessed his behavior back in our fraternity days and knew that his mean streak ranged far beyond ideology into the gleeful, adolescent sadism that certain young men enjoy and carry into adulthood like a dead bird hidden in their vest pockets. He had exalted in our Greek initiation rites, brandishing a cattle prod and zapping naked pledges in the bed of the house pickup as we careened down dark River Road at high speed, making them urinate on car batteries for the pleasure of seeing them moan, inducing them to chug liquor until they passed out in their own vomit. Morvant certainly wasn't the first frat brother to haze a pledge, but he prided himself on subtle, ingenious tortures and relished the results with a dark delight that caused many of us to wonder about him.

And I had seen other things, too. I had driven with him on joy rides into the housing projects late at night, throwing paint balloons into scrubby yards, screaming *Niggers go home!* at the top of our lungs. I knew it was wrong and immature at the time, but we were usually drunk and bored and brimming with vague resentments and misplaced hostility. After the second or third foray I grew ashamed of myself and stopped going. But Morvant and two other TΣKs kept it up for months, bragging about pranks more serious than paint balloons. There was a nasty rumor of gasoline and a house fire. Which is why I had phoned Morvant that horrible night, and no one else. I knew he would know what to do. And he would never judge me or succumb to an attack of conscience. Because he had already done unspeakable things that no sound conscience could abide.

I walked over to stare again at the bathroom tile. I wondered when he had taken the earring. She had always worn them while we were making love, and though my memory of those final hours was less than reliable, I was reasonably sure I'd noticed the cowry shells dangling from her ears when I'd dropped to my knees, opened her mouth, and tried to breathe life into her.

I downed the last of the gin and left the tumbler unwashed on the bar. Outside the cottage I stood for a moment in silence, surveying the quiet grounds. Claire and Andy were no longer frolicking on the patio. I could hear a streetcar rumbling down St. Charles Avenue, clanging its bell. The air felt still and trapped beneath the gray dome of sky. I was having trouble breathing now myself. It was nearly impossible to take all of this in.

I began to weep in broad daylight. I couldn't control myself. The nightmare had returned and I was crying as hard as I had that night when Morvant had knelt over her naked body, running his hands along her bare shoulders and neck, searching for a pulse. *Shut the fuck up, Blanchard,* he'd scolded me. *Nobody needs to know a damned thing about this.* And then he turned and looked up at me and laughed like a deranged man. *As long as we stay friends. Right, old buddy?*

After all the countless days and sleepless nights since, I still hadn't forgotten that laugh and the wild look on his face. Mark Morvant had meant every word he'd said to me this afternoon. I had three weeks to give him what he wanted or he would destroy my life.

Chapter three

My brother was probably the only person in New Orleans with whom I could discuss the White League without fear of ridicule or offense. It was conceivable that he could clarify the note written by our father. And if the secret organization truly did exist, Perry might be willing to share what he knew. In exchange for favors, of course. For him, life was a matter of banter and barter. The former he'd inherited from our mother, the latter from dear old Dad.

Perry played happy-hour piano and sang cocktail songs at various hotel lounges around the city, and sometimes at a gay bar in the Quarter. This was not exactly what his graduate music professors at Tulane had promised him by age forty-four. For a number of years he'd taught piano at a small private college in Mobile, Alabama, but as with many of Perry's stories, that had ended badly in a hushed scandal involving male students, and he'd returned home to New Orleans to give private lessons and live out of the Blanchard coffee jar. He hadn't disgraced himself in at least five years, for which the family was exceedingly grateful, and he seemed to have settled down with a younger man named Nico, a research historian of some sort who owned a beautifully renovated upper apartment on Royal Street.

Today was Thursday, which meant that Perry was playing at the Royal Orleans Hotel, thank God, and not the Sticky Wick. I changed out of my Frost Brothers business attire and dressed casually for a New Orleans evening of leisure: cotton slacks and a light blue shirt (instead of the usual starch white), with a boldly patterned tie Julie had given to me on my last birthday. The temperature still lingered around seventy degrees even at five o'clock, so I satisfied my sartorial sensibilities with the navy blue blazer that had always made me feel like the captain of a collegiate rowing team. Despite Claire and Julie's efforts to dress me in studly *GQ* fashions, I resisted such pretensions and maintained a traditional—they called it *stodgy*—appearance that didn't draw attention to itself. I had long stopped trying to build an image. In my circle, image and status were byproducts of your family name, a coin toss of birth, and not dependent on how you dressed or even how much money you were worth.

The Royal Orleans was a massive, elegant hotel that occupied an entire block in the Quarter and had once been the site of the Louisiana State House, before the capital was moved to Baton Rouge. The poet Walt Whitman had written about a slave auction he'd witnessed in the hotel, which was called The St. Louis in those days. Although New Orleans was extremely slow to change, I presumed that slave-trading was now prohibited in the Royal Orleans, although I wasn't so sure about high-class prostitution.

I left my BMW in the dark, grease-stained hotel garage and paid an elderly black attendant handsomely to keep an eye on it for me. The piano lounge was located in a spacious wing of the grand lobby, and I could hear Perry's languorous tinkling of the keys as I stepped out of the elevator. The notes plinked through the staid, palatial air of the hotel in a lazy mood, sounding to my ear like a parody of a Las Vegas nightclub routine. Like everything Perry did or said, it was impossible to determine if he was serious or putting his listeners on.

The floral green carpet felt like crushed velvet underfoot as I ambled past a long, sumptuous hors d'oeuvre table and made my way toward one of the many intimate seating arrangements in the lounge, two unoccupied armchairs and a settee lit by matching amber candle-lamps. I sat down and smiled at Perry, who held forth twenty feet away at the piano. More than anything else I felt like a gentleman caller at a tony French bordello, awaiting my summons to a room.

Perry noticed me immediately and returned my smile with an expression of surprise followed by sardonic humor. He rolled his eyes in that typical Perry gesture of mortification and self-mockery. *What the hell am I doing here, brother Paul? How did it come to this?* The look caught me off guard and I stifled a laugh. Even though he'd lost a step to age and worldly disappointment, my brother was as ever the wryest wit in town and could make me laugh with only the slightest effort.

High Carnival season was still a week away, so the lounge wasn't packed with tourists this evening and there was a collective countenance of boredom and quiet desperation among those who were killing time before their dinner reservations at Antoine's or Galatoire's. In the seating cluster next to mine, a late middle-aged couple drank silently and stared at Perry, who provided them the excuse they needed to avoid conversation. They seemed the very definition of torpor, their years together like a glacier that had slowly worn them down to bedrock. The gentleman dropped his hand-tooled leather boot to the plush carpet and leaned forward, requesting a song. "Somethin' coon ass!" he said with a beery laugh. Typical Texan weekender, a large red-faced man with graying sideburns and a car dealership bravado. "Somethin' from ol' Satchmo. You know that one about Basin Street, don'tcha, son?"

Without so much as a glance in the man's direction, Perry spidered into an elaborate intro, a flurry of chords and bluesy runs, then began singing the song. Only he didn't sound like Louis Armstrong. He sounded like Bill Murray performing a *Saturday Night Live* skit. Judging by the happy smile on the auto dealer's face, he either didn't care or he didn't understand that my brother was playing him for sport.

I hadn't seen Perry in at least six weeks, and in spite of his vamping animation during the old New Orleans classic, he didn't look well. Kathleen had phoned me sometime ago to say she thought our brother had AIDS, and when I pressed her about it—Had he said so himself? Was there a rumor floating around?—she'd said, "No, he just doesn't look healthy. And with a gay man these days, if there's *any* doubt—there's *no* doubt. I'm worried about him, Paul."

This evening I understood why she was concerned. Perry had always battled a weight problem, the pounds fluctuating wildly from season to season, depending on the passing fads of exercise and dieting. I had suspected that he might suffer from some subtle form of anorexia. But I could see he'd clearly dropped weight, maybe twenty pounds, within a few short weeks. He no longer filled his stylish Italian suit. The jacket hung loosely across his shoulders, reminding me of Rosetta in her baggy dresses, and I didn't like what that might signify. As he'd grown older, his plain round face had jowled slightly, like an English barrister's, but the usual fleshy softness had disappeared now and his bone structure was apparent for the first time since his college years. What disturbed me most was his hair. Perry had always been vain and fastidious about his hair. When we were school children he'd primped for half an hour every morning in front of the mirror, oiling and parting and combing his thick dark hair to perfection. But this evening, as I stared at Perry's salt-and-pepper hair lying flat and lifeless like a bath cap around his scalp, I had a nagging suspicion that the anemic wave on top was a hair weave and not the real thing. I couldn't imagine Perry with a bald patch, and I'm sure the idea horrified him as well.

My brother concluded the song with a flourish of cheesy scat singing and then stood up, bowing gracefully to the distracted applause of the Texan couple and maybe three other occupied tables scattered about the lounge. "Thank you so kindly, ladies and gentlemen," he said, pressing his hand against his heart. "Your enthusiasm has given me encouragement and the will to go on. With your permission I will return after a short break. Please leave your gratuities inside my piano bench. I will see to it that the funds are forwarded to St. Rock Hudson's Orphanage for wayward boys."

He yammered on in his usual speedy fashion, but his words drew no response from the listeners, who had returned to their private miseries.

"Brother Paul, my beloved sibling," he said, embracing me,

holding me against his loose suit jacket. His hands were warm, and wet with perspiration. In spite of the tongue-in-cheek greeting, he seemed genuinely pleased to see me. "Such an honor to share this moment with you." His voice dropped and his tone changed instantly. "What the hell are you doing here, silly man? Don't we have a birthday party to attend in a little while?"

"Six-thirty," I said, tapping my watch to remind him.

"I've already told the lovely Claire I'll be half an hour late. My people need me. God's work is never done," he said with a fluid gesture toward the piano, like Vanna White revealing a new refrigerator. "So what brings you here, buckaroo? Please don't tell me the bottom has fallen out of the coffee business again. I've just leased a Porsche."

"The business is fine. In fact, we're thinking of starting a new line of gourmet products."

"Wait! Stop," he said, holding up his hand. "Don't say another word. All this corporate talk is confusing me."

"I forgot. You're the artist of the family."

"You know the rules."

I smiled and offered him a seat. "Can I buy you a drink, Wolfgang?"

"My, this must be a serious visit," he said, loosening his silk tie and sitting down on the forest green settee. "You wouldn't have a cigarette, would you?"

I ordered a gin and tonic and he asked for Perrier and a pack of whatever cigarettes the waitress could rummage.

"Have you been on another diet, Perry?" I asked, trying to breeze past the subject. "You look a little thin."

He raised an eyebrow at me. He knew what I was thinking. What everyone in the family must be thinking by now.

"I needed to lose some cellulite," he said with a barb to his words. His dapper kid-skin shoes were crossed at the ankles and an arm rested along the low, brocaded back of the settee. "Please tell dear nosy Kathleen that I'm hunky-dorey. Ship shape. Top of my game. And tell anyone else who's so deeply concerned about my welfare that I will outlive them all."

I was encouraged to hear him speak with such conviction. At least Perry hadn't lost confidence in himself.

"Is that why you came to see me?" he asked suspiciously. "You want to make sure I don't sneeze in the punch bowl at your daughter's birthday party?"

"You're always the cob in the punch bowl, Perry. We wouldn't have it any other way."

"Asshole," he laughed.

"Actually, I came to ask you about something else."

"As long as it's not the stock market, sports, or the Middle East. I don't keep up with any of them."

"What about southern history?" I asked. "You were the know-it-all when it came to Civil War trivia. What do you remember about the White League?"

He looked at me as if I'd spit up on my new tie. "You *can't* be serious," he said, exaggerating the droll affectation. "You drove into the Quarter, paid Negroes good money to park in a garage, and plopped your ass down in a fruity piano lounge just to ask me about Civil War history? Now I'm worried about *you*, Monsieur Le Fou."

I should have known this wouldn't work. When was the last time I'd had a serious conversation with my brother?

"In Dad's library there was a book about the Crescent City White League and that gun battle on Canal Street during Reconstruction," I said, pressing on, hoping to capture his attention. "We both read it in high school, I think. Don't you remember talking about it? I looked for the book in the library a little while ago but couldn't find it."

"I have the book. I've had it for ages."

This didn't surprise me. He had pilfered books from our home library now and again, without telling anyone, and after our father's death a few years ago I'd caught him raiding the shelves, carting off his favorite volumes.

"May I borrow it?"

"Certainly." He arched one eyebrow. "Why the sudden interest in New Orleans history? You've never cared a fig about ah beloved Ole South," he said in an imitation of the cartoon character Foghorn

Leghorn. "You with your Cali*fornic*atin', cannabis-smokin', degenerate ways."

The waitress arrived with drinks and set the glasses atop coasters on the marble coffee table, allowing me time to compose a plausible strategy. She'd also brought a pack of cigarettes and Perry thanked her profusely while breaking open the seal in a desperate rush for nicotine.

"A rumor's been floating around for years that the White League still exists in secret," I said. The rumor was only a few hours old, as far as I was concerned, but I wanted to give it a seasoned credibility. "Do you know anything about that?"

Perry forked his fingers and slowly withdrew the cigarette from his lips, closing his eyes briefly as if to savor the moment. He blew smoke out the side of his mouth like one of our prissy aunts, a small, tight frown hardening his jaw. "Dear Lord, the White League," he said with a sip of Perrier. "The White League *moderne*. This is quite a concept. Where did you hear such a rumor?"

"Don't tell me you haven't heard the rumors yourself," I said, bluffing. Trickery, inversion, deceit—these had been my only effective weapons against the far more duplicitous Perry Blanchard. "I'm told that the League never disbanded. Four generations and still going strong. Maybe some of our old family friends—who knows?" I smiled at him. "Maybe one of *us*."

He didn't seem amused. The frown had sharpened his entire face. His reaction was more serious than I'd expected. "For what purpose is this League supposed to be leaguing?" he asked.

"Oh, the usual reasons," I said, tasting my gin and tonic and studying his strangely nervous response. "Social order. Financial gain."

He tapped his cigarette into an amber ashtray on the coffee table and spoke without meeting my eye. "Why ask me? This is your territory, my brother the CEO. It sounds like Magnolia Club shenanigans." He drank Perrier with a deep thirst and retrieved a handkerchief from his pocket to mop his forehead. "You're the club member in good standing, *pas moi*. The last time I was in the club was Mardi Gras twenty-odd years ago, when an elderly gentleman who shall go unnamed went down on me in the kitchen pantry. Needless to say, they've never seen fit to offer me a membership. I'm not exactly their idea of social involvement."

Hearing about his sexual escapades had always made me uneasy. I never knew whether to believe Perry or not. And I cringed every time he revealed something sordid from his past.

"The White League isn't Magnolia Club. It isn't old krewe, either, as far as I can tell," I said. "I've been around the old boy network long enough to know a few things, and the White League hasn't shown up on my radar screen."

He gestured languidly with his cigarette hand. "If you haven't met this creature face to face, dear boy—what with your status as heir to the Blanchard throne and all—then why in heaven's name are you giving serious credence to such a silly fairy tale?"

I could hear the resentment in his voice. He was the oldest male child and as such should have inherited the mantle of authority and leadership in our family. But things hadn't worked out that way. Father had entrusted the coffee business to me, in large part because I had worked for him down at the company office for the last twelve years of his life. Perry had never shown an interest in the family enterprise but *I* had, if only because working for my father had been easier than pursuing a real profession where effort and ambition counted.

"Take a look at this," I said, removing the note from my blazer pocket.

I handed him the sheet of stationery that contained our father's handwriting. He unfolded the page and read in silence, the smoldering cigarette lodged between his fingers only inches from the paper. I thought Perry might laugh it off or make one of his sarcastic comments. He took his time reading the short passage, perhaps twice as long as it should have taken, his eyes moving across the words. Then he let out a deep breath and crushed the page in a tight fist.

"So," he said, looking away, tapping his cigarette with irritation against the ashtray. "It *was* him, after all."

I had no idea what he meant. I waited for my brother to say something more. When our eyes finally met I noticed a tear glistening on one of his lashes. I was taken aback by his sudden emotion.

"Dear old Dad was behind it, goddamn him," he said, his voice unexpectedly hoarse. "Just as I suspected all along."

"What are you talking about, Perry?"

He wiped the tears from his eyes with the handkerchief and then focused on me with a harrowing intensity. His expression was so fierce and unforgiving it made me squirm uncomfortably in my armchair. "Did they send you to deliver another message, Paul?" he asked, leaning closer, speaking in a raspy stage whisper. "Is that what you are now, little brother? Their messenger boy?"

"Perry, what the hell are you talking about? You're starting to scare me."

"You tell your butch friends that I have a gun now," he said, his eyes blazing with a disquieting madness. "A sweet little Ladysmith nine-em that fits very nicely in the coat pocket. And I'm going to start carrying it everywhere I go. If they try to do what they did to me the other time, I'll use it on them. Is that clear, brother messenger boy? You tell them this faggot ain't gonna play the little girl anymore."

I was shocked by the maniacal look on his face and the fury of his words. I couldn't remember the last time I'd seen my brother this overwrought.

"Jesus Christ, Perry, I don't have a clue what you're talking about."

He mashed out the cigarette with a trembling indignity and then stood up. "I should've known they would get to you sooner or later, Paul," he said, dropping the wadded note into the smoldering ashtray. "But frankly, I'm disappointed in you. We were never that close as kids, but I've always loved you and tried my best to protect you. I want you to remember that. I would throw myself in front of a bus for you and Kathleen. I would give up my life for you. If something happens to me, you remember that, Paul."

I reached down and plucked the note out of the ashtray before the paper caught fire. "Perry, you're being melodramatic," I said. "Sit down and tell me what the hell you're talking about."

He gazed about the nearly empty lounge. The Texan and his wife had left for dinner, and only isolated individuals remained here and there, drinking in silence and waiting for the music to begin again. "I am who I am," he said without a trace of irony, "and this is what I do. I may not be executive timber, Paul—I may not be in your League—but I won't be treated with disrespect. You tell Dad's old friends that for me. I know I've never been the boy they wanted me to be, but it's too late in the day to live a lie. If they try to humiliate me again," he said, his eyes afire, "I won't scare this time. You tell them that."

He turned and marched toward the piano and settled himself on the bench with a brittle elegance. For several minutes I listened to him sing an old Randy Newman song about Louisiana washing away in a hurricane. He sounded positively inspired. But I was still shaken by his anger and couldn't finish my drink. I soon left the lounge and returned to the hotel garage to see if my BMW was in one piece.

Chapter four

The birthday dinner included twelve adults and ten children, half of them Julie and Andy's cousins. The older guests were arranged by place-cards around the long dining table, but a separate table had been festooned with party decorations in the *grande salle*, on the other side of the opened pocket doors, where the youngsters could carry on without fear of parental disapproval. Julie had chosen the evening's menu, four of her favorite courses plus dessert, with her first official splash of red wine in the bottom of a tall-stemmed glass. She downed the wine in one mouthful before the soup was served, a sure sign that the Blanchard genes were taking effect, like a secret, time-released implant.

Kathleen had brought Mother from the senior apartment fortress down near Lee Circle, where she lived under round-the-clock professional care. The old girl hadn't spoken a word since her stroke last year, but she could scribble a few shaky words and communicated primarily with her eyes, which remained remarkably clear and expressive despite the neurological damage. Her attendants had dressed her nicely in a dark evening gown and had arranged a black lacy shawl around her shoulders, adding a string of pearls below the sagging wattles of her neck. Her hair had been washed and styled in a stiff white meringue, and lipstick gave her small pale face a touch of color. She sat regally erect in a wheelchair at one end of the table, an ironic smile permanently fixed to her lips. Her expression never changed now, only the cryptic messages in her eyes. There was something unsettling about that smile, as if she could read everyone's most intimate thoughts but was keeping them to herself.

Kathleen remained at her side the entire evening, assisting with the meal, the awkward negotiation of spoon, fork, and water glass. Mother could feed herself using her one good hand, but it wasn't always a pleasant sight. And she sometimes grew frustrated with the tedious concentration required and would sweep aside a napkin or butter knife with an impatient spasm of the wrist.

She had always been the center of conversation in our family and among her friends, so her present condition was no doubt unbearable to her. As dinner progressed and the wine flowed and tongues began to wag, she issued a wistful moan from time to time, perhaps in response to something said. It was difficult to tell. Sitting beside her, dabbing her powdered chin with my napkin, I felt the presence of a proud, loquacious woman trapped inside herself, like a suffocating crustacean eager to crawl out of its brittle shell.

Claire's parents were seated across from each other at the other end of the table. Hillis Benjamin was a cantankerous old character I liked very much, and his courageous wife, Ida, was an outspoken Civil Rights advocate from the earliest days of what bigots had angrily called the Second Reconstruction. Ida had worked quietly and effectively to integrate the libraries, the YMCAs, the city parks—and she'd been reviled by the white population of New Orleans for doing what she deeply believed in. She'd been spat upon while shopping, cursed at in restaurants, and burned in effigy from a tall oak tree on St. Charles Avenue. Her tires had been slashed in the driveway of their State Street home. "Of course I was frightened, Paul," she'd once confessed to me when I asked about those days, the late 1950s. "I was constantly worried about Hillis and the children. But if you let bullies scare you into giving up, then they win. And I wasn't going to let them win."

I admired her because I'd never possessed any real convictions myself, or the slightest desire to make a statement of public consequence. My few principles had always been deeply private and manifested on a personal level. But Ida Benjamin was a remarkable woman who didn't fear her own inner voice.

Claire's brother and sister were also present with their spouses, and it didn't take long for Dr. Marty Benjamin, an obnoxious and obscenely wealthy orthopedic surgeon, to introduce the topic that every Uptown New Orleans dinner conversation inevitably turned to, usually well before the main course was served—*The Crime Problem.* Meaning White People victimized on the street by Black People from the projects.

"Who wants to begin?" Marty asked with a wine-flushed grin. He was a large, fleshy man who customarily perspired after his first drink. He had an enormous head, disproportionate to his body, and his wet hair curled in boyish locks around his ears and temples but had thinned to near baldness at the crown. He was only forty-three, but looked ten years older and carried himself with an authoritative heft. His chin was as soft as tapioca and he wore thick horn-rimmed glasses, which made me wonder how he performed his famous reconstructive surgeries with the necessary delicate precision. I suspected that he was quick to take credit for someone else's work, probably a team of brilliant and underpaid assistants.

"It's been a particularly bad season," said Creed Brossette, sighing like a defeated farmer who had lost his entire spring crop. Creed was the dark, handsome son of an established French family, an earnest malpractice attorney married to Nina Benjamin, Claire's younger sister. "I'm aware of eight muggings since Christmas. *Eight!*" he repeated for emphasis, "all within the Uptown area. All *our* social set, naturally. Judith and Ken Mentel were held up getting into their car over near Carrollton by the same animal who shot that Tulane girl."

A black male, of course. That was always understood. Profile: sixteen to twenty-five years old, usually from one of the projects hulking along the outskirts of small, splendorous Uptown New Orleans.

"He would've killed Judith and Ken, too, but a car alarm went off close by and he panicked and ran off. But the moron tossed

Ken's wallet out in his front yard over in Gert Town and a neighbor kid found it. The kid tipped Crimestoppers for the reward, and the police busted down Bright Boy's door. Looks like they arrested the girl's murderer."

There was a collective groan. *Sad, sad,* as the Cajuns liked to say.

"Did you hear about Karen Jaubert?" Kathleen chimed in before the reactions had abated. Two weeks ago on Neron Place, a quaint renovated street too close to the Claiborne thoroughfare. Karen couldn't remove her earrings fast enough for the mugger. He pulled a knife and threatened to cut off her ears if she didn't hurry. Then he forced her to undress on the dark front gallery of her home and would have raped her had not her German shepherd begun to bark inside the house, scratching and pawing the window.

"They don't like police dogs," Marty observed. He was a library of strongly held observations.

And so the flood of stories began....

Emily Frater had been pistol-whipped in front of her six-year-old son while removing grocery bags from her car. A young man broke into Dan Levine's house on Adams Street and stuffed him into a closet before cleaning out the place. Three elderly friends we all knew well—Sonny Donaldson, Maria Gelpi, and George Scanlan—were accosted at gunpoint after a gallery opening on Julia Street, and Sonny's car was stolen. Poor Terry Trahan, ex-Marine and Vietnam POW, returned home late one night with too many bourbons under his belt and was thrown to the ground by two teenagers as he crossed his lawn. Creed Brossette related the incident with gallows humor: "Terry told me, 'Goddammit, Creed, I had a .45 in my car, a .38 just inside my front door, and a whole damned arsenal in my den—but I couldn't get to any of them with my face full of lawn!'"

The guests laughed heartily. I glanced at Claire, who was seated at the far end of the table next to her parents. She had managed only a polite smile. She didn't like this kind of talk and had clearly reached her limit. "I'm sorry, y'all, but this gets so tedious," she declared impatiently. "Haven't we heard enough of these urban horror stories?"

"Oh, come on, Claire. This is very instructive," laughed Marty. He was sweating with great authority and only marginally serious. "We need to discuss the do's and don'ts of Uptown survival. How else are we going to avoid the same fate as all those other poor bastards?"

Dell and Corinne were working their way down the long table, systematically removing plates and used silverware, preparing to serve a wonderful bread pudding for dessert. They'd listened to white folks complain about crime for years, damning black perpetrators who might've been their own sons. On many occasions I had discussed this very problem with the women in our employ and knew that they didn't tolerate violence and crime any more than Marty Benjamin or Mark Morvant. They abhorred what had befallen an entire generation of black youth, but they trusted in God and prayed every day that His will would prevail over evil and adversity.

"I agree with Claire," said Ida Benjamin, visibly irritated by this litany of recent offenses. She was a small shrunken woman now, silver-haired and wrinkled, with an arthritic bow in her posture. But I could still see remnants of the beauty she had once possessed, eager eyes and an engaging smile that lived on in her daughters. "Everyone in this town is obsessed with crime. We complain about what's happening in the streets, but nobody is lifting a finger to change the cause of these problems."

"Here we go," Marty said with a coarse laugh. "Get out your violins, ladies and gentlemen. Mom's going to sing her usual tune."

"That's not a very nice thing to say, Martin." His wife, Laura, was an untalented dilettante artist but a decent person, if somewhat bossy by temperament. When she spoke it was usually with a grim moral supremacy. Over the years I had found that whenever I kissed her cheek in greeting at one of our infrequent family functions, her tight skin tasted like vitamin B.

"Poverty and discrimination," said Hillis Benjamin, his first words in half an hour. He had been uncharacteristically quiet the entire evening. "This is always the Ida Benjamin party line, isn't it, dear? The excuses we've heard lo these many years." The natty little man seemed exasperated with his wife, as if they were midway through an argument they'd been waging for forty years. "But my question is the same, yesterday and tomorrow: Whatever happened to individual responsibility? What makes one of these kids become a goon and another one become a millionaire basketball star?"

While the Benjamins began to take sides and argue among themselves, my mother moaned for attention and her left hand flailed spasmodically near her wine glass, like a live fish on a cutting board. Her eyes darted at me, then at Kathleen, with what I interpreted as either panic or concern.

"She wants to say something," Kathleen observed, digging into the handbag at her feet for a pad and pen.

Mother pointed feebly at the empty chair beside Kathleen and grunted again. *Where was Perry?* she seemed to be asking. And sure enough, when the note pad was produced and Kathleen placed the pen in Mother's hand, she scrawled Perry's name followed by a wobbly question mark.

"I spoke with him earlier and he said he'd be a little late," I explained, checking my watch. "I'm surprised he's not here by now. He's missed the main course."

In fact, Perry was more than an hour late.

"All those encores of 'Scotch and Soda'," Kathleen said with a wicked grin.

My sister was our very own Queen of Jove, the belle of the ball at age forty-two. Although she had always been an attractive brunette, in the Blanchard fashion, Kathleen had transformed herself into a flashy blonde these days, as blonde as a high school cheerleader. She wore her hair shoulder length with a slight inward flip, like most of her girlfriends out in deep Metairie, the soulless suburb where she met them for lunch in shopping centers and afterwards tortured her once-perfect body in a mall health facility, sweating and pumping iron and dancing to aerobics tapes. I had to admit that she looked fit and energetic, and it was perhaps this vigorous new mind frame that had led her to assess poor Perry's current physique with a critical eye. Tonight she was wearing a silky maroon dress belted casually with a thin gold braid, showing off her hourglass figure. A small beaded gewgaw was pinned near her low neckline, something crafted by one of her Newcomb artist friends. There was an air of revived sexuality about her, a sense that she wanted to be noticed and touched. I couldn't imagine why she'd gone to such effort at a family birthday party where all the men were taken. Perhaps she regarded the occasion as a safe trial run. She'd divorced her petroleum geologist husband about five years ago and had experienced her share of amorous losers in quick succession, but she hadn't dated anyone in months, as far as I knew, and appeared a little hungry for male attention.

"I'm sure Perry will be here any minute," I said to Mother, patting her inert right hand. "He never misses a dessert. He knows we've stolen the recipe for bread-pudding sauce from Commander's."

She stared at me with those intensely questioning eyes, slightly moist now after a glass of wine. There was something on her mind, but it would take a skillful round of charades to puzzle it out.

"Sounds like the natives are getting restless," said Claire's sister, Nina, nodding toward the *grande salle*, where the children's boisterous laughter was threatening to overwhelm our own table talk.

"I'll take point on the first scouting party," I volunteered, relieved to have an excuse to sneak away for a few moments. "If I'm not back in five minutes, Nina, call in the Rangers."

The children were indeed having a merry time in the adjoining room, raising the decibel level to an ear-piercing soprano pitch. Julie was pretending to be drunk from her nip of wine, much to the amusement of her school friends, and Andy was entertaining the older girls with his comic repartee. "So what's the deal with this *mock* turtle soup, Dad?" he asked as I bent down to kiss his sister's sweet-smelling hair. She was distracted by all the attention and had hardly touched her *boeuf Bourguignon*. "Who's getting the last laugh?" Andy asked. "Us or the lucky turtles?"

"Please make yourself useful, Andy dear, and go steal me some more wine," Julie said, with a queenly gesture. "Dad, when do I get to open my presents?"

I glanced through the open doorway at the grownups still arguing *The Crime Problem*. "As soon as the old geezers finish coffee and dessert," I said, squeezing her shoulders affectionately.

A girl named Erin McCall shrieked at my choice of words, and this set off a gale of teen giggling. I was beginning to enjoy my new company. I looked at the grownup table again and realized that the old people were sucking all the fun out of the house. If I could, I would've stayed in here the rest of the evening, helping Andy entertain the troops with our lame jokes.

The children's laughter had grown so loud I didn't hear the doorbell. Rosetta was standing in the foyer, waving her bony hand, summoning me with a beleaguered frown. Someone was at the door. My brother at last, I thought, making his late entrance like a spoiled diva.

"Mistah Perry's friend want to speak with you," she informed me once I'd joined her in the hallway.

A young man in his early thirties was standing alone on the portico with two neatly wrapped presents in his hands. I had met Nico only once before, which is why I didn't recognize him at first. He was a short, olive-skinned Latin fellow, either Italian or Cuban, with a shadowed young face and stylishly gelled black hair, absent any sideburns. He was wearing an expensive suit beneath his unbuttoned herring-bone overcoat, but his tie was loose, the collar slightly askew, and he looked like a disheveled law student after two scotches at a bar.

"I'm sorry, Mr. Blanchard, but Perry can't make it tonight," he said, handing me the presents. "He asked me to deliver these for him."

A violet envelope addressed to Julie had been slipped underneath one ribbon. The other present contained a card with my name on it.

"Is everything okay, Nico?" I asked, both surprised and irritated that my brother had canceled without notice. "I saw Perry earlier. He said he was coming."

Nico was clearly embarrassed by this assignment. He had trouble meeting my eye. "He isn't feeling well," he said. "He came home from playing at the hotel and collapsed on the bed. I think he has a fever."

"I see. Maybe I should give him a call."

"That sounds like a good idea," Nico said, adding, "In a few days. When he's feeling better."

He thanked Rosetta, who had remained at the door by my side. "Good night, Mr. Blanchard. Perry sends his best to the birthday girl."

He turned and made his way across the bright-lit gallery, passing between the tall white columns and disappearing down the stone steps leading to the front grounds. "Just a minute, *Nee-co*," I called out, pronouncing his name with more spleen than the poor young man deserved. "I want to have a word with you."

I left Rosetta at the door and strode across the gallery to speak with him in private. He was waiting near the circular lily pond below, his hands in the pockets of his overcoat.

"What the hell's going on?" I said as I approached along the brick walkway. The night was damp, with a slight chill in the air. Moisture dripped from the dark canopy of oak limbs overhead. "Perry was fine two hours ago. Is he having one of his famous tantrums?"

Nico's handsome face shone like polished bronze under the security spotlights blazing from the second-story balcony. "You'll have to discuss that with him, Mr. Blanchard," he said. "He asked me to bring the presents and make excuses, so I have."

"Please stop calling me 'Mr. Blanchard'," I said, my patience drained by the gin in my system. I was growing annoyed with the way this entire day had turned out. "I'm not your employer, for Chrissake."

"Yes, sir," he said with an indifferent shrug.

I sighed and rubbed my face. This was one time I wished the person I was scolding would fight back, show some backbone.

"If Perry thinks he's hurting me by acting this way, he's mistaken. The only person he's hurting is himself. I don't even know what he's so upset about."

Nico shrugged again, ill at ease and looking for the quickest way out.

"If you know what's eating him, Nico, I wish you would tell me. Because I don't have a clue."

The young man raised his chin and stared me in the eye. We were the same height, I realized as he straightened his posture. He seemed to be gathering himself under the many layers of expensive clothing, girding for the full force of my anger. "That's interesting, Paul," he said with a cynical edge. "Because Perry thinks *you're* the one who knows everything now that your beloved father has departed."

I didn't appreciate his tone. It brought the ire into my voice. "First of all, my brother has no business discussing our family with a—a—"

"Faggot boyfriend?" he said, his eyes narrowing darkly.

"A total stranger," I said with a sudden urge to slap his arrogant face. "Whatever his issues are, he needs to discuss them with me. Face to face," I said, adding for emphasis, "Like a man."

Nico smiled at my remark. The demure, well-mannered courier was beginning to discover his talent for sparring. "With you two, I picture more of a cat fight," he said with boyish insolence.

"Listen here, young man," I said, taking a step closer to him, "I'm looking for some answers myself. So if Perry gets in a weepy confessional mood, tell him to give me a ring. He knows more than I do."

I looked around for the off-duty police officer we'd hired as security to watch over the cars in the parking circle, but the guard was nowhere in sight. I wanted him to escort our visitor off the premises.

"So long, Paul. It was special sharing these family concerns with you. See you again soon, I'm sure." Nico's demeanor had crossed the line from acerbic to hostile. "Maybe someone will invite me to the next Blanchard potluck. I make a mean *paella*."

Hands stuffed in his overcoat pockets, he ambled off down the walkway toward the gate and the limb-shrouded darkness of the Avenue. I watched him vanish into the night shadows and wondered again where our security guard was. Armed protection was standard procedure now, even behind closed gates and within the wrought-iron confines of one's own property. Every respectable restaurant in town posted an off-duty policeman in the parking lot to escort diners to and from their vehicles.

I was returning along the brick path when I saw him approaching across the grounds. "Hello, Mistah B., it's Officer Junius," he called, a tall black man in uniform, waving his flashlight and identifying himself to allay any suspicion. We had used Officer Junius on other occasions and had found him to be reliable and uncommonly courteous.

"Is everything okay, Officer?" I asked.

He could no doubt hear my concern that he'd deserted the automobiles—two Volvos, a Mercedes, and a Lincoln President—the combined net worth of a Third World country.

"Needed to check out a vehicle parked on Arabella by the fence. Man's been sittin' there all evenin'," he said, turning to look back toward the side street. "Seem like he's scopin' the place."

I could see the binoculars strapped around his rain poncho.

"I went over to have a talk with him, check what he's up to," the officer said. "Man has a serious attitude problem. Give me 'It's a free country' and like that. I ran his plates and the Olds is registered to…" He shone the flashlight on the note pad in his hand. "Louis A. Robb of Shreveport. That name ring a bell, sir?"

I feigned ignorance, shook my head. "Not that I recall," I said.

"Big ugly white man, if you don't mind me sayin' so. Shaved head. Heavy mustache. Maybe done some time. You'd know if you seen him before."

I wrinkled my mouth. "I'm drawing blanks, Officer."

"I'll radio a unit and ax my buddies to drop down on him. They pat him down, run him through the computer, his attitude might improve."

"You don't have to do that."

"It's no problem, Mistah B. He got no business sittin' out there, scopin' your house. And he got no business talkin' to me thataway."

I borrowed his binoculars and tried to find the car in the darkness sixty yards away. The ancient oak boughs were dense and the lawn sloped gently toward the street. Fingering the adjuster I could make out the wrought-iron rods of the fence and a dark car hiding outside the weak orb of streetlight. Why was Louis Robb spying on my house? Had Morvant assigned him to keep track of my visitors? Did they think this was the Thursday night poker game for the White League?

"The man's right," I said, handing the binoculars back to the officer. "It's a free country. Don't hassle him unless he comes on my property."

"Just gonna teach him a little respect, Mistah B."

"Please call off the patrol unit, Officer Junius," I said in a firm voice. "It's my daughter's birthday party. I don't want a flashing police car and some bad street scene going on right next to my home. We're trying to enjoy ourselves tonight."

There were other reasons not to harass Louis A. Robb of Shreveport.

The officer agreed reluctantly to cancel the call and we shook hands. I reached into my wallet and gave him an extra twenty for being such a conscientious guardian of the realm. I remembered something my mother had said to me when I was a child: *Always, always tip Negroes well, son, so they won't harm you the next time you cross their path.*

Did we ever truly escape our parents and who they wanted us to be? The older I got, the more I became like them in small hideous ways.

Chapter five

hile Julie opened her presents, juvenile pandemonium broke loose in the *grande salle*, a flurry of expensive wrapping paper and girlish screeching and sarcastic commentary by Andy. Envy was the ruling passion, a raw, ugly exhibition of adolescent jealousies and venal desire. The grownups huddled in guarded camps on the periphery of the melodrama, like baffled missionaries observing a savage ritual. Using the chaos as my cover, I slipped out of the room and stole down the hallway to the library, a resplendent Victorian chamber where my parents often spoke in whispers in deference to some quaint notion about the sanctity of reading. I closed the double doors behind me, anxious to unveil my own present from Perry.

I had already guessed what he'd sent. The old book was covered in green cloth that had frayed with age, like a tattered canvas vest. The loose spine bore the title *The White League and the Battle of Canal Street*, with the author's surname underneath. I remembered the small line-drawing of the monument spire on the front cover. Opening the book, I found the familiar illustration from *Harper's Weekly* pasted across the inside board and endpaper, a dramatic battle scene raging in the downtown business district in the early 1870s. Noble, whiskered men wearing tailed morning coats and top hats were attacking the mostly black Reconstruction police force under clouds of cannon smoke. Sabers cleaved the air, rifle butts flailed, bodies sprawled across the cobblestones, horses fell broken and bleeding. The particulars of the history lesson, registered and forgotten so long ago, were beginning to come back to me.

The book had been published in 1939. I turned a few pages, amused by the subtitle—"The Overthrow of Usurper Rule in New Orleans, September 14, 1874." The author's dedication read: "To the White League, for their heroism on the fourteenth of September. Their courage and patriotism serve as an inspiration to their descendants, to those who struggle for State's Rights, and to Louisianans dedicated to the Common Cause."

The Common Cause, of course, meant the restoration of white supremacy in Ah Beloved Ole South. Mark Morvant had used the phrase himself. It was astonishing to realize that a hundred and twenty-five years after the Civil War, this sentiment still ran deep in certain circles, finding new hope from time to time among the deluded mossbacks who clung to their dark schemes. I wondered if this pompous book had fueled my old fraternity brother's misguided assumptions about the White League.

I opened the envelope addressed to me. There was no salutation, no signature, only Perry's gothic calligraphy rendered with machinelike precision: *You can have this back. I don't want it on my shelves. I am done with the family and its whole sorry charade. I won't let you people hurt me anymore.*

It was the most beautifully printed rebuke I had ever received.

I set the book and note on the teakwood writing desk and gazed at the shelves of rare, specially bound editions encased behind the glass doors of a wall-length mahogany cabinet. These were my parents' prized possessions and the likely source from which Perry had pilfered the volume. I was still trying to understand what he'd meant by his accusation—*Dear old Dad was behind it, goddamn him*—and why he'd turned on me with his paranoid suspicions, when the library doors opened and Kathleen appeared in a sudden rush of noise channeled down the hallway.

"You're always sneaking off and having all the fun, Paul," she said, closing the doors behind her and sealing us in silence. "I thought I saw you come down here."

Drinking burgundy from a long-stemmed glass, she sauntered over to the white marble fireplace and leaned against the mantel for support. She had had her share of wine tonight and her face was flushed and daring. A sexy blonde wave hung low and out of place on her forehead. Clearly my sister was no longer the virgin Queen of Jove. Still, I had always been proud of her beauty and grace, even after I'd discovered that she'd been the source of the trouble with Jaren and the real reason my parents had put an end to his presence in our home.

"You look foxy tonight," I said with an admiring smile. "Are you trying to seduce Marty away from Laura?"

"Hah hah," she said, making a face. Then she dropped her eyes and grinned like the proverbial cat with a mouthful of feathers.

"Uh-oh," I said. "There *is* somebody new."

"Maybe," she said, peeking at me through the hair in her eyes.

"Please tell me he's more interesting than that last guy. Whozzit?—the dentist." I shook my head. "What on earth was the attraction there? All those free samples of floss?"

She ignored my sarcasm. "I ran into an old acquaintance at lunch the other day at the Upperline," she said. I surmised by her tone that it was someone I knew as well. "I hadn't seen him in years. We talked. He asked for my phone number."

"Are you going to tell me who it is, or do I have to hire a detective?"

Her coy demeanor suggested something naughty and forbidden. A married man.

"If anything comes of it, you'll hear the rumors," she said. "This town can't keep a secret."

I wasn't so sure I would agree with that.

"So where the hell is Perry?" she asked, her mood turning sour. "I don't really give a damn but Mother wants to know."

"He's in a Perry snit," I said, one of our sibling code phrases to describe a specific nuance of his temper. We'd seen him act this way so often we had created a shortcut vocabulary. "Some perceived offense. I think I may be the culprit this time. Or maybe Dad and the ghosts of the Confederate past. I honestly don't know."

"Gawd," she said, rolling her eyes. "His snits never cease to amaze me. How did he look to you this afternoon?"

"You were right. He's lost weight," I acknowledged. "But he assures me it's nothing more than health consciousness."

She grimaced and sipped the last of the wine. "That's crap and we both know it," she said. "Christ, I could use a cigarette. Doesn't anyone smoke in this house?"

I shook my head. She and Perry were the only closet smokers in our family.

"What are we going to do, Paul? I'm really worried about that poor crazy boy."

I sighed, longing for another gin and tonic. "He's not a boy, Kathleen. He's a grown man, and by now he ought to know the rules of safe sexual behavior."

"What if it's too late? What if he's already sick and he doesn't know it yet?"

"Then we'll take care of him." I had already considered that. "We'll spend every dollar we have to make him well."

Suddenly her eyes were red and glassy. "I can't abide the idea of Perry suffering through this," she said, sniffing, running a finger across her nostrils like a socially awkward child. "He's suffered enough for one lifetime. He's had more than his share of emotional pain."

I walked over and offered her a clean, pressed handkerchief, which she accepted gratefully. "It's 1990, Kathleen. Things are different now. He's been out of the closet a long time and we all accept him for who he is," I said. "Every Uptown family has at least one. Why do you think Tennessee Williams loved this place?"

As she daintily blew her nose I realized she was gazing aslant at me through the tangle of hair in her eyes. "What did he say about Dad?" she asked, suspicious and defensive.

I shrugged, unprepared to show her the note that had upset Perry and launched his rant. If there was something to this White League business, I doubted that Kathleen would have insider knowledge or be involved in any way. Women weren't players. The New Orleans power structure had always separated gender roles as assiduously as they segregated race.

"He blames Dad for being behind something that happened way back when," I said. "It sounded personal. But maybe it's just another one of Perry's oversensitive reactions. Whatever it is, he still holds a grudge."

Her chin dropped and she looked away, upturning the empty wineglass in search of the last drop. "Jeezum, don't you keep a bottle of brandy in here anymore?" she asked, suddenly agitated. "I would kill for another drink and a cigarette."

"Kathleen," I said, striving to focus her attention. "Do you have any idea what Perry was talking about?"

She propped her elbow high on the mantel and pressed a fist against one eye. "Oh fuck, Paul, let's not go into this," she said, her head canted away from me. I thought one of her migraines might be coming on. "He's never gotten over what happened to him back during that David Ferrie thing. And I don't blame him. It must've been horrible."

I hadn't heard David Ferrie's name mentioned in years. The bizarre pedophile had been one of the principal suspects in D.A. Jim Garrison's infamous investigation of the John Kennedy assassination. I knew that Perry had served as a student cadet in Ferrie's unit of the Civil Air Patrol out on Lake Pontchartrain, and that there had been scandalous rumors about Ferrie's sexual misconduct with the boys under his tutelage, including my brother, who was seventeen at the time. I had seen photographs of Ferrie, with his scroungy, rat-like toupee made from floor carpet and his fake eyebrows fashioned from a grease pencil. The man in those pictures repulsed me. I couldn't imagine his appeal to such clean-cut, All-American boys. But I still remembered the secrets and innuendo that floated about our home in those days, my parents repressing their rage, struggling to deal rationally with the profound shame they'd endured because of Perry's association with that vile creature. At the time I was Julie's age, thirteen, and they all did their best to keep the scoldings and punishment out of my sight. I knew something serious was happening, but Perry moped about in his bedroom so humiliated and withdrawn that I'd avoided him for days on end. And even in our twenties, during those rare moments of candor between us, when Perry was finally revealing his homosexuality and the torments of his clandestine life, he never once mentioned David Ferrie's name and I didn't care to bring him up. I didn't want to know.

"So Mother and Dad were bent out of shape about it," I said, shrugging, still puzzled by Ferrie's elusive charm. "What did Perry expect would happen when they found out? He was under age and getting blow jobs from a dirty old man with a hair-loss disease."

Kathleen released the fist from her eye and slowly turned to study my face in a stricken silence. She and I had never openly discussed Perry's sexual habits, so I wondered if my comment had offended her. But then she sighed and sank against the mantel and her expression softened. "Christ, Paul," she said, her dark eyes revealing a rare vulnerability she reserved for her two children and few others. "You don't know the whole story, do you? You were too young."

"I'm not too young anymore," I said, an inexplicable anger creeping into my voice. "Now why don't you tell me what I should've heard a long time ago."

She continued to study me, and for an instant I felt the older sister at work, maternal and protective. "Do you remember what came out about David Ferrie in the Garrison investigation?" she asked, raising a pencil-thin eyebrow. "He and two of his young men drove to Houston on the day President Kennedy was assassinated. Ferrie was a pilot, and Garrison tried to prove that it was Ferrie's assignment to wait down there for the shooters to arrive from Dallas by car so he could fly their getaway plane."

The Garrison inquiry had taken place more than twenty years ago and seemed like ancient history to me, but I remembered this aspect of the probe because our family knew the family of one of the young men in question. He was an Uptown boy who later attended Tulane with Perry.

"Well," she said, chewing her bottom lip, a nervous habit since childhood. "There weren't *two* young men with Ferrie that day in Texas." She hesitated, then said, "There were three."

I stared at her, my mouth going dry from the sudden realization of what she was telling me. "Oh Jesus," I muttered.

Her cheeks had turned blotchy crimson, like a heat rash. She toyed with the empty wineglass, swirling invisible burgundy. "Dad knew the Garrison people extremely well," she said, "especially his old friend Henry Lesseps. Somebody kept Perry's name out of the investigation. Read any history book about the assassination—read Garrison's own book!—and you'll find the names of the two young boyfriends who rode with Ferrie on that car trip. But you won't find any mention of Perry Blanchard."

I didn't know whether to believe the story. Not that Kathleen would lie. But she was describing something that had happened nearly thirty years ago, under monumentally convoluted circumstances, and the information from that incident had a way of twisting into knots.

"How do you know this, Kathleen?"

A small sad smile crooked her mouth. "Trust me," she said. "I know."

"Then why is he pissed off at Dad?" I asked. "It sounds like Dad saved his sorry ass from public embarrassment and a horrendous legal investigation that ruined everybody connected to it. Why isn't Perry down on his knees every night, lighting a candle to his dear dead father for sparing him from the Garrison circus?"

Kathleen set her glass on the mantelpiece next to the ornate silver base of a candelabrum, then glanced at the double doors as if making sure we were secure in our privacy. "Something did happen to Perry back in those days and he's never gotten over it," she said. "If I tell you about it, Paul, I want your solemn promise you won't ever utter a word. You can't tell Perry you know this, or anyone else. Is that understood? You can't even discuss it with Claire."

I nodded. "Understood."

"Cross your heart and hope to die?" She sounded like Kathleen at ten years old.

"Cross my heart and hope to die," I said, gamely making the mark.

She was not only biting her lip now, she was nervously rubbing her hands, as if removing something unclean. I couldn't imagine how she'd withstood the pressures of being a Mardi Gras queen.

"A good ten or fifteen years went by before Perry could bring himself to tell me what had happened to him," she said, her shoulders hunching as though the memory still left her cold. "Do you remember when he was at Tulane and he had that terrible car accident and his face was cut up and bruised and his arm was broken?"

"Of course," I said. I had been in high school at the time and visited him at Touro Infirmary every day for a week, until he was finally released in a plaster arm cast.

"It wasn't a car accident, Paul. He was beaten up."

The surprise must have contorted my features, because she gave me a strange, sympathetic look.

"He'd gone to one of those gay bars in the back of the Quarter, near Rampart, and picked up two men who were drinking there together." She rolled her eyes, critical of his behavior. "I have a hard enough time picking up one man, but there was Perry, making it a threesome. Only things didn't go well after they left the bar."

She said that the two men walked Perry over to nearby Congo Square, which was what we old timers still called the park where slaves had congregated in the nineteenth century to dance and beat their drums and swoon in voudou ecstasy. By that time the square had become a dangerous place, especially at night. It was too close to the Iberville Housing Project and the rough black neighborhood of Tremé. Three white men had no business there after dark.

"Perry thought they were going over for a quickie—or whatever it is they do in a park at night—I don't even want to know," Kathleen said, holding up her flattened palms. "But the two men weren't gay. They got Perry off into the bushes and beat him up pretty badly. You remember what he looked like. He tried to fight back and they broke his arm." She took a deep breath, forcing herself to finish. "He told me that when he was down on the ground, pleading for mercy, they urinated in his face."

I was angry now. At my brother, for leading such a careless life. At the bastards who had done that to him. At everyone who had kept these things from me.

"Rednecks rolling a queer," I said, almost to myself. "I hope to God he wised up and that sort of thing never happened again."

"No," Kathleen said, impatient with me, grabbing my blazer sleeve. "No, Paul, it wasn't a random pickup. They'd stalked him. They knew who he was and where he hung out, and they'd set a trap for the silly fool. They were there to deliver a message."

I wasn't following this. "What kind of message?" I asked.

"Somebody hired them to teach Perry a lesson. They made that perfectly clear," she said. "That's why he can't forgive or forget. The bruises went away and his arm eventually healed, but he's never gotten over what they said to him."

My heart was racing. "And what was that?"

I could see Perry's indignation reflected in her face. I could hear his resentment in her voice. She had appropriated his anger.

"They told him there were people who didn't approve of his behavior," she said, her words low and bristling. "Good upstanding people who wanted him to stop smearing his family name. These good people had already helped him out of one jam, they said—and Perry knew they meant the David Ferrie thing. But he was still hanging out in the wrong places, running with a bad crowd, doing things he shouldn't be doing. They told him he had to change his ways or else."

I felt a shiver run through my body. "Or else what?" I stared at her, waiting. She lowered her eyes, finding it difficult to verbalize the rest of it.

"They threatened to castrate him, Paul. At least that's what Perry told me. If he didn't clean up his act they were going to hunt him down again and—" She closed her eyes, unable to complete the sentence.

I'd always figured that every homosexual had at least one

nightmare encounter to report. This one seemed to take on a larger, more sinister significance. "I'm guessing the little lesson worked," I said, ashamed of my own cynicism. "That happened over twenty years ago and Perry still has his family jewels, as far as I know."

Kathleen folded her arms and hunched her shoulders again. "He tried to be a good boy as long as he could," she said. "He stopped going to gay bars and picking up strange men. He even dated a couple of Newcomb girls."

I smiled at that picture, pitying the proper young women who had endured Perry's duplicity and biting wit.

"But in the end we are who we are," she said, shrugging hopelessly. In spite of her outspoken conservatism in other matters, she had been the first family member to accept Perry's homosexuality without conditions. "He knew he couldn't fake it for the rest of his life. So he took that teaching job in Mobile, hoping to escape this goddamned city and whoever was watching him."

Perry had taught there for fifteen years, an exemplary music professor, by all accounts, before his affairs with several male students were exposed and he chose to resign.

"But apparently Mobile wasn't far enough away," Kathleen said. "He started getting phone calls. Maybe twice a year. 'We understand you're behaving yourself, young man. Keep up the good work.' That kind of thing."

He didn't recognize the voice, she explained. It was always the same avuncular old gentleman with a classic Uptown accent. *Noo Or-li-yuns.* On the surface the caller seemed sincere and caring, but there was a queasy implication of high moral judgment and enforced supervision lurking around the edges of his message. *We're still keeping an eye on you, boy.*

"Perry eventually had one of the calls traced," she said. "It came from a pay phone at the Columns."

No surprise there. The Columns was a venerable landmark hotel on St. Charles Avenue, its gallery dining tables a convenient rendezvous for avuncular Uptown gentlemen in dinner jackets.

"The man always spoke in the royal *we*," she said. "'*We* are pleased that you've straightened out your life, son. *We* will be in touch again.' You know Perry. Everything's a plot. He was convinced there was some organized conspiracy of decrepit old Uptown bluebloods breathing down his neck."

"The beloved brethren of the Magnolia Club?"

"The Magnolia Club. The krewe captains of Momus, Jove, Proteus, and Rex. The Knights of Columbus and the Daughters of the Confederacy," she said, shaking her head at Perry's paranoia. "As far as he was concerned, *everybody* was in league against him."

In *league*, I thought, considering that word. I glanced over at the writing desk, where the cloth-covered book lay next to Dad's old-fashioned quill-like pen slanted in its ink well. "He didn't mention any specific names?" I asked, ambling over to the desk.

"He was sure it was some of Dad's friends," she said, lowering her voice as if our father were in the next room. "Some of the old boys who knew Dad was unhappy about his son's lifestyle and wanted to do them both a favor. He didn't think Dad was involved." She fingered the hair out of her eyes and sent me a cold, sobering look. "He didn't think Dad would have his own son peed on and beaten to a pulp."

I opened the cover of the old book and fanned through several pages, skimming past photographs of the White League's leaders, cartoons by Thomas Nast, and a battle map marking the various skirmishes and the sites where "heroes and martyrs" had died on Canal Street and the levee area.

"What about you, Kathleen? What do you think?" I asked, my eyes drifting up from the pages. "Do you think Dad could've done something like that to Perry?"

Her lips parted to answer my question but she hesitated, remaining mute for quite some time. Her reticence surprised me. Kathleen was not one to withhold her opinion on any subject. She always knew her own mind. But this response seemed to require all her powers of deliberation. I could see the conflict and confusion roiling behind those troubled eyes. For once she wasn't dead certain of the truth, or even where she stood amid her own torn allegiances.

Before my sister could answer the question, the double doors opened dramatically, the wing-shaped handles releasing with a loud brassy echo, and Claire entered the library, exuding irritation from head to toe. "So here you are," she said, directing her annoyance solely at me.

She and Kathleen had always maintained a cool distance, opposites in politics, fashion, and astrological compatibility—Perry's explanation. They often ignored each other on social occasions, and that seemed to be their unstated agreement this evening.

"I can't believe you're hiding in here while your daughter is opening her birthday presents," Claire complained, her beautiful brown eyes flashing their disappointment. A faux smile was fixed in place, as if she were needling me all in good fun, but I felt the nasty sting of her reproach. I knew this reaction all too well. Claire was one of those competitive parents who kept score with her spouse. And in her mind she was always ahead.

"I doubt very much that anyone missed me in all that racket," I said sheepishly. "I'll get her to show me her gifts tomorrow, when things calm down."

Claire folded her arms and stared at me. "She asked where you were," she said, unwilling to forfeit the final parry. "It's her *birthday party*, Paul."

Kathleen retrieved her empty wineglass from the mantel and crossed the room toward the double doors. "Claire dear, this is my fault," she said, her voice sweet in all its southern-belle innocence. "I dragged him away to find out why Perry didn't come tonight. I'm a little worried about our brother's *condition*," she said, emphasizing the word.

She stopped, looking Claire straight in the face, two women the same physical size but otherwise worlds apart. "AIDS," Kathleen said, tsking with a theatrical shake of the head. "A crisis of epidemic proportions. We've all got to pull together and do something about it while we still can."

Claire was not amused. She glared at my sister, fully aware that the homily was intended to replicate one of Claire's own.

"Come along, Paul," Kathleen said, glancing over her shoulder at me. "Let's go visit Julie and put some fun back in this party before the Benjamins stage a sit-in."

She breezed past Claire and disappeared down the hallway. My wife glowered at me, her nostrils flaring. "Some day," she said, "I'm going to strangle your sister Scarlett with that tacky curtain cord she's wearing for a belt."

Chapter six

The party broke up around ten o'clock and I escorted everyone to their guarded automobiles. Officer Junius took great care to ensure that the guests were seated safely in their locked vehicles before he opened the wrought-iron gates. He wasn't the only armed citizen in the entourage. My father-in-law, Hillis Benjamin, always carried a nickel-plated .32 automatic in his jacket after dark, and he wasn't afraid to use it.

Julie had invited her three girlfriends to sleep over because tomorrow was a teacher in-service day without classes. After establishing the ground rules with the girls camped in Julie's bedroom and the guest room down the hall, Claire returned to our bedroom suite, still silent and angry at me for my perceived offense. She shed her clothes quickly in the dressing area, slipped on her silk nightgown, and crawled into bed without so much as a *Fuck you, good night*. I was well acquainted with this behavior by now. It had happened all too often over the past few years.

Even though I had consumed enough gin to drop a Gurkha, I was restless and wide awake. I went downstairs for a final nightcap to slow my racing mind. Rosetta and the two cooks had gone home, leaving Dell and Corinne to clean up. They were working diligently in the kitchen, wiping counters and loading the last coffee cups into the dishwasher. I thanked them again, gave them each a fifty-dollar cash bonus, and poured myself a stiff cognac.

"Rosetta was awfully quiet tonight," I said to the two women. "Is she feeling poorly?"

"Got that boy on her mind," said Corinne, hand-drying a wine-glass. "She don't like goin' up to Angola and hear them parole people talk about him the way they do. She be awright after tommawra."

"One way or the other," added Dell.

"Mmm hmm," Corinne agreed. "One way or the other."

I took my cognac across the hallway to the library. The house seemed remarkably calm considering the number of children on the premises. I didn't trust the silence. At this late hour the high-ceil-inged room was as chill and inhospitable as a museum at midnight. I picked up the book Nico had returned this evening and opened the cover. It would take all night to read *The White League and the Battle of Canal Street*, maybe longer, and I didn't have the energy or the patience. I set the book aside and reached for the telephone on my father's writing desk. No one in this town knew more about Civil War history than my old high school history teacher, a Jesuit priest named Father Joseph Dombrowski, and I felt certain he could tell me everything I needed to know about the origins of the White League. Father Joe had returned to New Orleans after a long absence up north and was now living with three other Jesuits in a community house only five blocks from here. The children and I usually attended his Masses at the Loyola University chapel, and he'd come to our home for dinner. I recalled his admission that he was a lifelong insomniac who spent his nights in reading and meditation. Despite the late hour, I gave him a call.

"Yes, Paul, I'm awake," he said in that clear authoritative voice that had never lost its Chicago edge. "How is my favorite C student?"

"Struggling with the material as usual, Father. I've got some questions and I need your academic advice. May I come over? I'll bring a small token that should make it worth your while."

He and I shared a deep appreciation for Bombay Sapphire gin, something I'd discovered on his dinner visit.

"In that case," he said, "how can I refuse? Knock lightly, the other monks are getting their beauty sleep."

Their community house was a smartly refurbished two-story residence on Calhoun Street across from the Loyola campus. I arrived in less than ten minutes and found the aging priest waiting for me at the door. I handed him the bottle of gin packaged in a gift box and he smiled, shaking my hand firmly and showing me to a small visitors' parlor near the front entrance.

"It has to be *somebody's* feast day," he said, rubbing the box affectionately. "Let's celebrate, shall we?"

"Only a small one for me," I said, more than a little high from my day of steady drinking.

He disappeared down the hallway and returned promptly with two thick tumblers, the gin cut with ice and tonic water and squeezed limes. "Cheers, Paul," he said, tapping his glass against mine and sitting across from me on a velvet Victorian love seat. The parlor was small and furnished with weighty antiques, the built-in bookshelves lined with leather-bound volumes that bore a distinct ecclesiastical brawn.

"So what brings you out at this time of night, my friend?" he asked, tasting his drink with visible delight. "Did you forget to study for your mid-term again?"

Father Joe Dombrowski was a large, shambling man in his late fifties now, with the same crew cut he'd worn in the 1960s when he'd been my history teacher at Jesuit High. Only now his hair had turned steel-bristle gray and naked scalp peeked through in a patch the size of a Gulf sand dollar on the crown of his huge head. Although he possessed the hulking build and rugged, acne-scarred face of a football coach or Marine drill sergeant, he was a kind and noble soul who had been the most patient teacher I'd ever had. Unlike several other Jesuits I could have named, he'd never humiliated me in class.

"I should've paid more attention when you were covering that unit on Reconstruction," I said, smiling at him. "Who knew it would come back to haunt me twenty-five years later?"

"My goodness, Paul. Reconstruction? We're not talking about knee surgery, are we?"

I grinned at his joke. "No, Father. It's a long story, but I need to learn everything I can about a New Orleans group called the White League. I have a feeling you're the place to start."

His bulldog face grew somber and he stared at me as if offended. "The White League?" he said, pondering the words. His brow creased as he consulted his wrist watch. Something wasn't right. I had the impression he might end our conversation abruptly and send me home.

"You once said if I ever needed to speak with you about any-thing—"

He continued to stare at me for several awkward moments, lost in thought, and then suddenly he shook himself out of it, took a long drink of gin and tonic, and cleared his throat. "Yes, of course, Paul. I did say that and I meant it. I was thinking more along the lines of spiritual counsel."

I shrugged. "It's personal, Joe, if that's what you mean."

"The White League is personal? This is starting to get interest-ing," he said. His smile was attentive and shrewd. "Go ahead, my friend, you've got my attention. What the hell's on your mind?"

"Tell me about them. Tell me everything you know."

He relaxed against the stiff-backed love seat. He was wearing a bulky purple sweatshirt that covered his wide upper body, and his feet, encased in suede house slippers, were crossed at the ankles. I was trying to remember why they'd transferred him out of Jesuit High and sent him back to Chicago at the end of my freshman year. He'd been too outspoken, as I recalled, on the subject of Catholic school integration in the city.

"Well, young Blanchard, why don't we see how much you've retained from my class," he said, clearing his throat again. "First of all, to understand the White League, you have to understand Reconstruction and white outrage. In my view, Reconstruction was even more fascinating and complex than the Civil War itself. It was like this time warp in which incredible social progress was made and then scrapped. It didn't work because the changes were imposed by

Paul

force. White southerners hated what was shoved down their throats after losing the war, and there was no way, ultimately, to make such radical social changes stick."

I added all that I remembered from his class. "Slavery was abolished and the South had to put up with an occupying army that enforced law and order."

"Bravo," he said, clapping one hand against his tumbler. "I'm encouraged to hear that you didn't sleep through the essentials."

He continued, explaining that any man who fought for the Confederacy, and anybody refusing to sign a loyalty oath to the Union, couldn't vote or hold office. Beginning in 1865, only carpetbaggers, Yankee sympathizers, and freed slaves were elected to public office across the South. Mayors, state legislators, even governors of the southern states.

"All these illiterate Negroes and white opportunists from north of the Mason-Dixon were taking charge down here and telling the homeboys what to do. The new legislatures started passing reforms, spending public tax dollars coughed up by wealthy whites, and generally controlling the way things were run."

He drained the glass and sat forward, moving his hands as he spoke, growing more animated by his favorite subject. "For the first time in the history of this country, the South became racially *integrated*," he said with a sense of moral excitement. "Everyone forgets how remarkable that was. Public accommodations and services, like saloons and street cars, were open to black people. Even the schools were integrated. Black kids and white kids sat side by side in classrooms. This was in 1870, Paul. Think about it. You didn't go to school with black kids until you were in high school and L.B.J. signed the Civil Rights Act. But during Reconstruction, for about twelve incredible years in the nineteenth century, the races rubbed shoulders in a way they hadn't before—and wouldn't again for another ninety years."

"And it drove every single white person in the South bat-shit crazy."

"Right you are, my friend. Louisiana whites retaliated against Reconstruction by electing their own representatives and working behind the scenes to unseat the *impostors*, as they called the people who'd taken over state government and city hall. The only thing that prevented violence and an armed overthrow by whites was tough little Phil Sheridan and his federal troops garrisoned right here in the city of New Orleans."

He shook the ice in his tumbler and considered the ill effects of an empty glass. "Enter the White League," he said, pouring more gin. "They predated the Klan in Louisiana. The group was founded by New Orleans plutocrats—merchants, bankers, defrocked politicians, cotton and cane planters. Wealthy executives with brushed goatees and soft hands and all their teeth intact. The same ones who'd formed the city's social clubs and secret Carnival balls. They rode in the Jove and Comus parades during Mardi Gras."

The leaders were all articulate, well-educated spokesmen for the Lost Cause, and many of them had been officers in the Confederacy. As opposed to the anti-papist Klan, most of the White Leaguers were good practicing Louisiana Catholics. They dressed in spiffy cravats and tailed coats and rode in surreys to Sunday Mass at the cathedral. Their Garden District homes were filled with books and fine china and family portraits with the children.

"But being executive types," Father Joe said, "they were a little spongy around the middle, and long of tooth, so they relied on the loyal young clerks and rising managers who worked for them. Their young protégés became the foot soldiers who would do their fighting."

He stood up and turned to the bookshelves behind him, searching for something among the intimidating volumes.

"By the summer of 1874, after nine years of federal occupation, they'd had enough of the Union military presence in New Orleans and all that political misrepresentation. And oh yes, *Negro insolence.* You can bet that was at the top of their list. So a handful of League officers got together in the library of the Magnolia Club downtown and wrote a public call to action. Ah yes, here it is."

He had found a book that looked very familiar. The same book, with the same fading green cloth cover that was resting on my father's writing desk at home.

"You've got to hear this word for word, Paul. It's a priceless piece of rhetoric," he said. Standing behind the love seat, he began to read.

"'Fellow citizens!'" he intoned with a melodramatic flourish of his free hand. "'Love of liberty and honor, a proper respect for our families, and the hope of retrieving the fortunes of our state and people—physically and morally—demand in tones that no *true man* can disregard—that our sloth and indifference be cast aside—that we be up and doing!'" His voice was Shakespearean turned Colonel Sanders. "'The experience of the past nine years has demonstrated that those who now hold the government are incompetent to rule—that from their rule can come but corruption and degradation. Look about you, and what do you behold?'"

He waved an arm at his surroundings.

"'Alas! Naught save abandoned and uncultivated fields—a disheartened and disgraced people—Louisiana bankrupt in fortune and in name. Can you bear it any longer? *Negro ignorance*—solidified in opposition to white intelligence and led by carpetbag and scalawag villainy—continues to hold the state, your fortunes, and your honor by the throat. They perpetrate upon you indignities and crimes unparalleled. Will you permit this without a fight?'"

"Nay!" I exclaimed.

"'For years the Negroes have been organized in the interest of their own race,'" he continued. "'For years they have mocked the legitimate interests of white people. You know the truth. You cannot have been blind to it. *What shall you do?*'"

"Rise up!" I said, lifting my glass high.

Father Joe pumped a power fist in the air and raised his voice in mock southern heroism. "'We shout to the heavens, dear brothers of the true South—*Organize the White League!*'"

He and I laughed as he snapped the book shut.

"By damn, that's oratory!" I said. "They don't write 'em like that anymore."

He sat down, slightly winded, the book in his lap, and drank his gin like a preacher drinking water after a long Sunday sermon. "The truth is, the message worked, Paul. The Crescent City White League, as they officially called themselves, soon claimed three thousand men," he said. "A former Confederate general named Fred N. Ogden—a pompous old goat who'd made a fortune in men's ties—and several of his cronies organized themselves into military units, with White League officers commanding battalions in neighborhoods all around the city. Throughout the summer of 1874 they marched their young recruits through residential streets and parks, drilling them in the art of war." He raised his coarse gray eyebrows. "Although they denied this in congressional hearings later on, the White League was preparing to overthrow Union rule and take back the city of New Orleans from federal troops."

But it seemed Ogden and his captains realized that their militia lacked adequate firepower. They had no artillery, and their weapons were limited to shotguns, pistols, and outdated muzzle-loaders, with ammunition in short supply. So to solve the problem, the League started buying guns and ammunition from dealers in New York and Pennsylvania.

"And this, as they say, is when the shit hit the fan."

He explained that several cases of rifles, revolvers, cartridges, and bayonets purchased by the White League were transported by steamer to the port of New Orleans. In early September 1874, the Metropolitan Police confiscated a furniture wagon loaded with these arms as the driver made his way from the wharf up Canal Street. Detectives arrested several prominent leaders of the White League.

"As you can imagine, the arrests ignited a firestorm of protests," he continued. "The city was ready to explode."

Four days later the steamer *Mississippi* reached New Orleans with another shipment of weapons purchased by the League, and this time the authorities were forewarned.

"The official governor of Louisiana was a hated Republican carpetbagger named William Pitt Kellogg. He issued an order to seize the cargo. In retaliation, the White League organized a noon rally on September 14th at the statue of Henry Clay on Canal Street," he said. "The League officers saw this as the moment they'd been waiting for—the answer to their prayers. They organized their squadrons throughout the warehouse district above Canal. Armed men were spread out from Lee Circle down to the levee."

The hapless Metropolitan Police Force, he explained, was stationed in the French Quarter below Canal Street, and they had no idea that a disciplined army of insurgents lay waiting for them in the city streets only a few blocks away.

"You see, the Mets were a shaky bunch of freedmen and white Unionists. A poorly trained outfit, and pretty ragged, but nevertheless they became the official law enforcement in the city after the all-white New Orleans police force attacked and murdered thirty-four black delegates at a political convention."

Canal Street itself, one of the widest, most prominent boulevards in the country, extended from the batture of the Mississippi River upward past the boundary of the old city, and it would serve briefly as a demilitarized zone between the two opposing forces.

"The noon rally drew six thousand raging New Orleanians," Father Joe said. "Speakers demanded the resignation of Governor Kellogg and the end of federal interference in Louisiana. One rabid orator even called for the city to become an armed camp until Kellogg and his *hirelings* were thrown out." My old teacher seemed to appreciate the populist fervor without agreeing with its politics. "While the rally was reaching a fever pitch, White League soldiers were sneaking around two blocks away, building barricades and breastworks from those old iron street-crossing plates and anything they could get their hands on. They were even derailing streetcars and pulling up pavement stones."

Another group of armed Leaguers surreptitiously took over City Hall and the telegraph office, shutting down all municipal communications. When word of these actions reached General James Longstreet, a repentant, repatriated Confederate officer now serving as head of Kellogg's state militia, the general issued orders for his Metropolitan Police to advance on Canal Street and regain control of the city.

"Longstreet and his right-hand man, Algernon Badger—the police chief of the Mets—led five hundred of their troops and several rolling artillery pieces from the French Quarter to Canal Street and created a long picket that stretched all the way to the railroad depot on the river levee."

Longstreet and Badger were intent on preventing the White League from commandeering the cache of weapons aboard the steamer *Mississippi* docked at port.

"The general sent a dozen police officers to break up the rowdy crowd at the Henry Clay statue, but the officers were jeered at and fired upon, so they hightailed it back to their picket line. Ready to rumble, Fred Ogden led two hundred of his White Leaguers down to the levee to ambush them, and he ordered his troops to take cover behind freight and cotton bales stacked along the riverbank."

When Police Chief Algernon Badger discovered that a sneak attack was under way, he ordered his men to wheel out their Gatling gun and two twelve-pound Napoleon cannons and open fire on the hiding Leaguers.

"And that's how the famous Battle of Canal Street erupted," Father Joe said with an elated smile. "The cotton bales were battered and went up in flames, but the White Leaguers held steady and returned gunfire, killing the police gunners and their guards. When all hell broke loose, the Metropolitans broke ranks and ran. Poor Badger was shot four times and fell off his horse. The Leaguers overtook his position and captured the artillery weapons. The fight was on, and other White League units attacked the Metropolitan line from side streets along Canal. Those untrained bastards didn't know what hit 'em. A wounded General Longstreet had no choice but to lead their retreat back to the French Quarter."

Fred Ogden's horse was shot out from under him, but the old Confederate survived the spill with only minor damage to his person. Realizing that their efforts were futile, Met stragglers soon surrendered. The Battle of Canal Street was over.

"The entire skirmish lasted only fifteen minutes," Father Joe said, "but there were quite a few casualties." He consulted the book in his lap and found the battle stats. The White League sustained sixteen deaths and forty-five wounded. The Metropolitan Police suffered eleven dead and sixty wounded.

"By late afternoon on September 14th, 1874, Canal Street and downtown New Orleans belonged to the White League and the citizens of the Old South. They declared victory and promised a new beginning for the white people of Louisiana. They were convinced that Yankee tyranny was gone for good and things would return to the way they'd been before the Civil War."

At noon the next day, two thousand cocky White League troops marched up Canal Street displaying confiscated weapons and flags and the artillery pieces they'd taken from the Mets. Women and children cheered along the route. A telegram was sent immediately to President Grant in Washington, informing him that the Kellogg government had been deposed.

"Let me see if I can find what they wrote," he said, paging through the book in his lap. "Oh yes, here it is: 'We feel that we are free once more, and thank God for the calmness and courage of our citizens. A load of degradation and oppression has been lifted from our people, and we are now hopeful for the future. We businessmen are greatly encouraged. As citizens of the United States, we confidently rely upon you for your recognition and guarantee of the new State.'" He glanced up at me. "They wanted Grant to accept their victory and recognize a free white state. The message was signed by two dozen presidents of New Orleans banks and insurance companies, the ruling elite of the city. You can bet they were all White League."

But Ulysses S. Grant was not persuaded. He saw this as outright rebellion and quickly sent Union troops from as far away as Detroit. Five days after the battle, twenty-five companies of federal infantrymen marched into New Orleans, escorted by four companies of heavy artillery. Five U.S. Navy gunboats and two warships docked in the harbor, their cannons trained on the city.

"Grant and Phil Sheridan were ticked off big time and ready to kick some serious ass. The leaders of the White League understood that they were vastly outgunned and about to be pounded into sawdust. They returned the State House to carpetbagger William Pitt Kellogg and withdrew from the streets. The restoration of the Old South had lasted less than a week."

Quite an amazing episode. "And that was that?" I asked.

"No, not by a long shot. The White Leaguers had tasted victory, however short-lived, and were feeling their oats. During the next few months they continued to resist Reconstruction laws and went so far as to launch guerrilla raids on the integrated New Orleans schools, chasing black children out of classrooms. Black parents were outraged and fought back. A group of black men with straight razors and bricks faced down the Leaguers and killed one of them. Mobs of armed whites and blacks started roaming the streets at night, fighting like gangs, until the federal military authorities finally stepped in and took control of the situation."

"Did Grant arrest any of the League leaders?"

He smiled and began flipping through the book again. "If General Sheridan had had his way," he said, "they would've all been rounded up and shot. He called the White Leaguers *banditti* and wanted to punish them severely. Here's what he wrote to the Secretary of War in Washington: 'I think the terrorism now existing in Louisiana could be entirely removed and confidence re-established by the arrest and control of the ring leaders of the armed White Leaguers. The banditti who murdered men here on the 14th of September should be punished in justice to law and order in this southern part of the country.'"

"That word *banditti* has a nice ring to it."

"No one took the general's suggestion. Over the next several months two congressional commissions couldn't agree on which side was to blame for the Battle of Canal Street, and which individuals should be punished. Not one member of the White League was ever convicted of a crime. Fred Ogden walked free. I suppose Grant and his people figured it was better to let a sleeping dog lie. Things had settled down and he didn't want to inflame the situation."

"So that was the end of Fred Ogden and his boys?" I asked, eager to confirm that the White League had died off in the 1870s. "Their moment in the sun was over?"

"Not quite yet," Father Joe said, reaching for the bottle and splashing gin over ice. "For the next two years the city was relatively quiet and Ogden's name virtually disappeared from the newspapers. Sheridan suspected the White League was still training in secret, against his orders, and kept them under surveillance. His federal troops searched the city for months after the battle but couldn't locate that Gatling gun and the two twelve-pound Napoleans the White League had captured. Little Phil wanted revenge, but his hands were tied."

He stirred his drink with a glass rod. "With Sheridan around, things were fairly stable for Reconstruction New Orleans. But then the election of 1876 came along and it was déja vu all over again."

The election of 1876 caused the usual political turmoil in Louisiana, he said, with both sides declaring victory—S.B. Packard, the Reconstruction Republican, against Francis T. Nicholls, a Confederate brigadier general who'd lost an arm at Winchester and a foot at Chancellorsville. The rival candidates were inaugurated separately, each insisting that theirs was the legitimate authority.

"And in the middle of all that chaos, guess who reared his big bearded mug?"

"Fred the Men's Tie Maker?"

"You got it," he said. "Ogden assembled six thousand White League soldiers overnight in January 1877 and seized the courts, the police station in the Cabildo, and the arsenal. The League was ready and able to repeat the violence of September 14th."

"So Sheridan was right. The League had been drilling in secret."

"Yes indeed. They were even stronger than before. And so the Republican Governor Packard quickly surrendered everything except the State House, where he holed up for four months while federal troops and White League volunteers patrolled the French Quarter in an uneasy truce. Packard pleaded with lame duck President Grant to recognize his Republican administration in a show of force, begging the old man to send in more soldiers. But poor drunk 'Unconditional Surrender' had grown weary of the vagaries of Reconstruction and informed the besieged governor that public opinion no longer supported the use of U.S. troops in the Deep South. He wouldn't lift a finger."

Rutherford B. Hayes was inaugurated as president of the United States in March of that year, Father Joe said, and the new president ordered federal troops to withdraw from the State House in New Orleans. Packard had no choice but to relinquish the government of Louisiana to Francis Nicholls, General Ogden, and the White League.

"It was the nail in the coffin for Reconstruction, I'm sorry to say. The Yankee dogs were finally sent packing, uppity Negroes were silenced at long last, and life returned to the good old days of segregation and racial intolerance," he said with grim sarcasm. "And that was how the South was restored to its full glory, my friend. That's how it became the hateful place we've known all our lives. Separate and unequal once again. Defiant, violent, ignorant, and backward. Civil rights wouldn't return for another eighty or ninety years, and the black community would be forced to live like second-class citizens, or worse. You know the story. You've lived it yourself."

He set the book aside on the love seat and smiled at me, a tired, defeated smile that said the hour was late and there were heavy burdens on his soul. I didn't want to bother him any longer, but I had one more question before I left his company.

"And so when Reconstruction ended, Father, did the White League disband?" I asked him. "Was that the end of the fight for them, too?"

He shrugged. "I've never found a reference to the Crescent City White League being active after 1877," he said. "And believe me, I've done my homework."

I settled my tumbler on a tile coaster on the rosewood side table. "One day they've got six thousand men playing soldier in the French Quarter, the next day the whole gang disappears. It's a little hard to believe."

He seemed to appreciate my observation. "You know, young Blanchard, I may have underestimated your academic potential."

I had to be sure of my facts. It was the only way to hold my own against Mark Morvant.

"What if the White League didn't disband a hundred years ago?" I asked him. "What if they went underground and kept on going in secret, just like they'd done when Sheridan was trying to bust them? Is that possible, Father?"

He measured me through those kind, aging eyes. Sympathetic, as always, yet circumspect.

"Is it possible that the White League never broke up and that they still exist to this day as some kind of secret organization?" It was time to lay all my cards on the table. "That's the reason I came here tonight, Joe. I've got to know if these people are still around."

He raised an eyebrow. "This is all very interesting speculation, Paul. What makes you ask that question?"

"I've got my reasons."

He inhaled deeply and splashed more gin into his tumbler, then a handful of ice. "Why don't you ask someone in your family?" he said matter-of-factly, a friendly suggestion without a hint of malice. "I believe there's a Blanchard mentioned in the book. One of the men who shot Algernon Badger off his horse, as I recall. He might've been your great grandfather."

No doubt he was.

"I'm not much on family history, Father. And there's nobody left who would know."

Sipping his drink, he sat back in the love seat and studied me. There was a pensive expression on his pocked face in the dim nocturnal lighting of the parlor. Was he disappointed in me, the C student who had never changed the world or succeeded at even the smallest endeavor? Time passed in which he seemed to be lost in weighty consideration. Then he stood up slowly, stiffly, and replaced the old green book on the shelf.

"I'll be back in a moment," he said, excusing himself to leave the room. I thought he might have needed the toilet after an hour of steady drinking. I heard his footsteps creak up the stairs out in the hallway, and in a short while he returned with something in the palm of his hand. From a distance, in the subdued amber light, it looked like a dead butterfly.

"Have you ever seen one of these?" he asked, sliding the soft spidery object into my hand. It was a small black velvet bow with a dotting of white silk on each wing.

"No," I said, examining the fabric. "What is it?"

"It's what some good old boys stuffed into my mouth one

night about twenty-five years ago after they dragged me out to the levee for a beating."

I felt my jaw drop. "Jesus, Father," I said, shocked. "You were beaten?"

He gave a low, tight laugh at my surprise. "Paul, do you have any idea why my Order transferred me out of New Orleans back in the sixties?"

"I've always heard it was because you were in the bishop's face about civil rights."

"Yes, partly," he said, nodding. "I was pushing the old codger to integrate the Catholic schools in town, which were even farther behind than the public schools, if you can believe that. The bishop didn't like me—didn't like the fact that I was vocal and making waves—and that was a problem for the Order. True. But then something happened that put the hair on the toast for breakfast."

Twenty-five years later the memory was still painful and he had considerable difficulty telling me. Pacing back and forth behind the furniture, he spoke with a solemn reluctance. "I was jogging through Audubon Park one evening when four men wearing those damned Mardi Gras float masks rushed out of the bushes, knocked me senseless, and dragged me to their car."

He explained that they'd put a hood over his head, drove him out to River Road, and marched him to the top of the levee that walled back the waters of the Mississippi.

"My name had been in the newspaper for pushing the integration issue. At first I thought they were Klansmen or maybe some of Leander Perez's redneck goons from down in Plaquemines Parish. Those three civil rights workers had been murdered in Mississippi not long before and I was scared shitless, I don't mind telling you. I didn't know what to expect, but I prayed to our merciful Savior to make it swift, whatever they had in mind. I didn't want to be tortured for hours before they killed me."

I listened in horror as he described how the men had forced him to kneel in high grass with his hands tied behind his back and the hood over his head. He heard shells being loaded into a shotgun, and then a rapid pump action.

"They called me a nigger lover and every other name in the book," he said, nervously pacing the parlor. "And they told me I'd better start praying, which I had no trouble doing. Somebody gave the signal to shoot me, and when the shotgun went off I was splattered by stinging pellets."

I held my breath.

"I fell over in the weeds and crapped my pants. I heard them laughing their asses off. But I wasn't dead. I wasn't even hurt. It was an old southern schoolboy initiation prank—you shoot the shotgun off in the air and your buddy throws a handful of rock salt against the paralyzed victim. You think you're shot, but it's only a cruel joke."

Speechless, I rubbed my chest as if I'd been shot myself.

"They told me I'd better stop making trouble. The usual racist diatribe. They said they'd let me live for now, but if I kept being a problem they'd find me again and the next time they'd kill me. Then they pulled the hood off my head and stuffed that thing in my mouth."

I studied the small black velvet bow in my hand.

"At first I thought it was some kind of big tree roach or something. Another one of their vicious pranks. But they told me it was a message from the men they were working for. The men who'd sent them to rough me up. And if I knew what was good for me, I'd go on back up north and never come down here again."

The bow had a loop on the back, fashioned to hook around something, probably a button. I pictured it worn on a shirt or jacket, like a boutonniere.

"How did you get away?"

I was thinking of Perry now and his ordeal with those men that night in Congo Square.

"They kicked me in the ribs for good measure and drove off, and I stumbled down the levee and caught a ride with an old black man puttering along in a rattletrap pickup," he said. "My Father Superior thought it was time to get me out of New Orleans. I argued with him about it. I wanted to stay on and fight it out with the bigots, but he was insistent and arranged my transfer. I was a young hothead and really didn't understand the extent of the danger I was in."

I remembered that my entire freshman class had been heart-broken when we learned of his departure. We had adored our big shambling iconoclastic history teacher.

"So what the hell *is* this thing?" I asked, handing the bow back to him. "Did you ever figure out who those guys were and what this meant?"

He examined the bow for probably the ten thousandth time since that terrible night in 1964. "Several years later I was down here visiting the monks and decided to go see the Civil War exhibit in the Cabildo museum," he said, pausing to pour another drink from the gin bottle. "I was walking through the Reconstruction wing, doing my usual history buff routine, and lo and behold I came across one of these damned things in a display case."

He turned the bow over in his palm and then placed it delicately on the side table beside the ice bucket.

"It was in the White League display, Paul," he said, giving me a chilling stare. "These discreet little bows were worn on the button of a man's suit coat, sort of like a secret ring worn by a Mason. The museum card said that White Leaguers wore them for decades after the fourteenth of September. If you met a man on the street, the bow let you know he was in the brotherhood."

Now *I* was ready for another drink. "My God," I said. "Do you suppose it was *them*? Do you think they were still going strong in 1964?"

He savored his drink and looked away. His huge shoulders shuddered underneath the loose sweater. "I don't know what else to believe," he said, his speech now showing signs of alcohol.

We finished our drinks in silence and he walked me to the front door, his heavy hand on my shoulder, guiding my steps like a sight instructor escorting the blind. Out on the small brick landing he embraced me fraternally, a forceful, righteous presence engulfing my own wide dimensions within the ample folds of his sweater. I thanked him again, shook his firm grip, and said good-bye. But when I turned to depart down the steps, he grabbed my arm.

"Hold on a second," he said in a low voice, and I realized that two dark figures were loping down the sidewalk in front of us. "Let them pass."

It was two young black men, I saw now, one wearing a hooded jogging jacket and the other a knit cap. They slowed down and stared back at us, exchanging a few hushed words between them, then kept moving swiftly in the direction of Audubon Park a few blocks away. I remembered the story of poor inebriated Terry Trahan eating lawn in his front yard while two muggers went through his back pockets.

"Go in peace, Paul. Believe in a protective God," Father Joe said, releasing my arm, "but don't forget to lock your car doors, okay?"

Somewhere up the street an alarm was whooping a familiar tune. The National Anthem of New Orleans.

Chapter seven

I returned home well past midnight, but before going upstairs to bed I slipped into the library to satisfy my curiosity about something I thought I remembered seeing in the old green book.

The heavy velvet drapes were drawn across the French doors leading to the patio, sealing in a damp musty odor emanating from the hundreds of old volumes that were moldering on the shelves. I found *The White League and the Battle of Canal Street* where I'd left it on the writing desk and took the book to my favorite armchair, in the corner near the drapes. Skimming the pages, I eventually located the battle description where Metropolitan Police Chief Algernon S. Badger lay in the street with a broken arm, a mangled leg, and gunshots through his hand and body. The White Leaguers would have finished him off with a *coup de grace* to the head, the author maintained, were it not for the intercession of one Adam D. Blanchard, described as a conscientious young clerk for Kurscheedt *&* Bienvenu's hardware store on Camp Street. Apparently my great grandfather had convinced his comrades that Badger would serve a greater purpose if they spared his life and held him for ransom as a prisoner of war. Adam Blanchard and his unit fashioned a makeshift stretcher out of a saloon door and spirited away the police chief's wounded body under their armed protection to Hotel Dieu hospital, where the doctors amputated a leg but saved the man's life.

I had no memory of my great grandfather. He died when I was two years old, having survived nearly a full century, living most of those years as a grocer who had started his own coffee company in the late 1890s, the source of our family wealth. Mounted on the wall in my office on Magazine Street was a prized photograph that had appeared in the *Times-Picayune* in 1952, a few weeks before his death. Four generations of Blanchard men stood in a stiff row, my father holding me, a puny baby, Perry gripping his pant leg, and grandfather and Great Granddad positioned next to us. The bespectacled, stoop-shouldered old man leaned on a walking cane for support. Shorter than the other men, he looked like an ailing Sigmund Freud, with his white hair and neatly trimmed white beard. He was wearing a bow tie and rumpled white Panama suit, which signaled the season as late spring or summer in New Orleans. The spirit had already left his countenance and his expression was dour, as if he were in considerable physical discomfort and wanted it all to end. By that time, his wife had long passed and so had all his friends, the passionate young firebrands who had fought in the streets to overthrow Yankee tyranny. I had always been told that Great Granddad died peacefully in his sleep—no doubt content, in 1952, knowing that insolent black people knew their place and the good families ruled the city once more, as they had on that glorious day in September 1874. In his final doddering repose, sleeping soundly in his bed, dreaming whatever last blue bird dream, he surely could not have imagined what would transpire in this country over the next two decades.

I thought I heard a rebel yell somewhere in the distance, and for a moment I wondered if the old man's ghost was floating down the hallway in search of cowardly stragglers of the Metropolitan Police.

Thumbing to the end of the book, I read the author's final summary of the events of September 1874: *"The courageous actions of the White League had led directly to the end of Reconstruction, the South's darkest era of humiliation, greed, and injustice,"* he stated with pride and passion. *"And though the League never again assembled as a body of armed troops zealous to defend the city's honor, there have been numerous indications that their prominent members have continued to exert influence over municipal decisions and the social well-being of our people, and have passed their leadership and wise counsel on to subsequent generations. For their mantle of protection and guiding spirit, the citizens of New Orleans are most grateful and indebted forever. Long live the White League!"*

There it was, set in print in 1939. *Numerous indications* that the White League still existed at that point in time. The author seemed convinced of it. *Passed their leadership and wise counsel on to subsequent generations.* And if the League was continuing to exert influence in 1939, why not in 1964? Or for that matter, why not today?

I found the author's zeal to be quaintly amusing. Dixie flags and rattling sabers no longer swelled my heart. Ever since the liberal Jesuits had opened my eyes, I had shunned the myth and melodrama of my southern heritage. It was a hateful legacy, and I had faced that fact long ago. Slavery was abhorrent. Racial intolerance was wrong. I had done my best to avoid the ridiculous people who still believed that the South would rise again. And perhaps that was why I had never encountered the White League. If they lived on in secret, carrying out their forefathers' vendetta of supremacy and political control, then they surely understood that I was not their boy. No more than Perry.

I continued to page through the photographs in the green book and found the one I'd remembered after all these years. Great Granddad Blanchard and the last eight survivors of the Battle of Canal Street posed in front of the Liberty Monument, as the spire was now called. The caption revealed that the monument had been erected in 1891 on the site where Algernon Badger had been shot from his horse. The photo was dated 1934, and the wizened old survivors had gathered to place wreaths for their fallen comrades, listed by name in stone, and to dedicate a new plaque at the altar-like base of the tall narrow pinnacle. The plaque read like an explanatory footnote to the entire White League episode: *"United States troopers took over the state government and reinstated the usurpers, but the national election in November 1876 recognized white supremacy and gave us our state."*

I recalled that about ten years ago, Dutch Morial, the first black mayor of New Orleans, had attempted to remove the monument, but his action was prevented by the majority-white city council. As a conciliatory gesture they allowed him to pave a smooth granite slab over the offensive language about white supremacy.

I studied the gaunt faces of the old coots in the photograph, read their names in the caption below. These New Orleans surnames were as familiar to me as my own. I had gone to school with their great grandchildren, attended endless boring social engagements with Frerets and Plauchés and Angells. Over the decades their families had grown and prospered, becoming the civic fodder that filled our social clubs and carnival krewes and captained the banks and law firms and petroleum home offices. A slow recognition took hold of me. My peers were the descendants of the White League. I knew them all by name.

And then I noticed something else in the photograph. Great Granddad and his mummified comrades were all wearing small dark boutonnieres in their suit lapels—what looked like the unblossomed buds of a black rose. The same velvet butterfly bow that those good old boys had stuffed into Father Joe's mouth that night on the levee. The gentleman's symbol of the White League.

Another shout brought me out of my reflection, only this time I was certain the sound had come from outside the French doors a few feet away. I heard a girlish squeal of pleasure and bare footsteps running across the patio flagstones, and then a young male voice, slightly deeper and more aggressive, in hot pursuit. It wasn't Andy, I was sure of that, but someone older. I stood up and pushed aside the heavy drapes, peering through the cold glass door. Burglar floodlights illuminated the pool area. The blue plastic tarp over the swimming pool was undulating above disturbed waters. Had one of Julie's girl-friends gone for a moonlight dip? Something had been tossed across a patio chair, either a towel or underclothing.

"Who's out here?" I said, opening the French doors and stepping into the damp night air. I caught a glimpse of two figures dashing into the darkness beyond the light's outer reach, one chasing the other in a ribbon of fading laughter. The girl's luminous afterglow disappeared beneath low black oak limbs at the far boundary of the grounds.

"What the hell's going on out here?" I said, raising my voice despite the decorous silence of the hour.

I lifted the article of clothing from the chair and discovered that it was a cotton pajama top patterned with innocent pink flowers. Underneath lay a simple white training bra with cups the size of a child's fist. I did not recognize the top as Julie's. This gave me some relief. On the other hand I didn't relish the idea of explaining such behavior to the guilty girl's parents. That would be Claire's job.

I walked quickly to the end of the patio flagstones and called into the darkness: "Hello out there! Come back inside immediately, young lady!"

I noticed a faint flicker of light through the curtained windows of the cottage. After a few moments of hushed quiet I thought I heard voices down there, then a high tittering female sigh. What the devil was going on? I abandoned the light and security of the patio and marched off across the dewy St. Augustine lawn, wetting my new dress shoes and the cuffs of my trousers, a cold, unpleasant sensation.

As I approached the small stone structure, a boy's voice erupted excitedly and was quickly shushed, and then others suppressed their laughter. A more calculating father would have waited outside the door and listened, collecting incriminating evidence to build his case against the accused. But I was too irritated to strategize intelligently. I barged through the cottage door without warning and glared down at the guilty parties, two girls and two boys sitting in a circle on the floor. Julie's friend Erin McCall gasped and grabbed her pajama shirt and covered her budding breasts. No one else dared to move.

"What in God's name is going on?" I demanded, a question intended for all of them at once.

A candle flittered in its saucer, the only source of light in the room. My mini-refrigerator had been raided, and three bottles of liquor, including my favorite Bombay Sapphire gin, were lying half empty within the ring of accomplices. The dealt cards and heap of clothing in the center of the circle gave away their game of strip poker. Twelve, thirteen year old girls and a couple of boys I had never met before. One of them had quickly snubbed out his cigarette in a bottle cap.

"Where's Julie?" I barked, trying to contain my anger.

They were too embarrassed to speak. All eyes were cast to the carpet.

"Erin," I said, addressing the girl who had slipped her pajama shirt back on. "Is that Julie running around outside?"

She shook her head but refused to meet my fierce gaze. "No, sir," she said. "Julie's not feeling well."

At that moment I heard a retching noise in the bathroom. The door opened cautiously and a clean-cut, dark-haired boy of fourteen or fifteen stepped out. He looked Italian, or possibly Middle Eastern. "I'm very sorry, Mr. Blanchard," he said. "Julie's in here and she's pretty sick."

I grabbed the boy's shoulder and shoved him aside. On the floor of the cramped bathroom my daughter was kneeling over the toilet bowl, clutching the rim with both hands and vomiting long burgundy strings into the water.

"Julie!" I gasped. "What's the matter, darling?"

My head reeled. She was kneeling in precisely the same place where I'd found that other girl a hundred lifetimes ago.

"She's had too much to drink," the boy offered.

I whirled around, my voice so furious they all recoiled in fear. "I want you boys off my premises in two minutes or I'm calling the police!" I said. "And you girls had better go find whoever is running around the yard like a wild banshee and take her back inside the house. Do *not* leave your rooms for the rest of the night! *Do you understand me?* I will deal with this in the morning."

There was a mumble of respectful *yes sirs* and the cottage cleared in seconds. I grabbed a face towel and wet it in the sink. "Julie, sweetheart," I said, kneeling down to wipe her face. "Are you okay? Let's get you cleaned up and back in bed."

"I'm sorry, Dad," she said, turning her pale, stricken face to stare at me. Her eyes were swollen and wet and barely able to focus.

Vomit had greased her chin and the front of her pajamas. "I guess I messed up my birthday pretty bad."

As I cleaned her tender face she closed her eyes and began to cry, but her tears were soon interrupted by another wave of gagging.

"It's all right, baby," I said, gently rubbing her arched back. "Don't worry about it, okay? Everything will feel better in a little while, I promise you."

Watching her body convulse over the toilet, I suddenly remembered something Mark Morvant had said this afternoon. *She seems to love her father dearly. It would be a shame if she ever heard something that would change all that.* I rubbed her back and realized how much I loved my daughter, and how much I detested the son of a bitch who would destroy what I had unless I paid his price. He had no money, no worthy attainments, no children to hold in his arms. He resented the good fortune that had befallen me. He knew I didn't deserve these many blessings. Without his favor—and his silence—my charmed life would have turned out altogether different.

Mark Morvant had me exactly where he wanted me, the bastard. If he couldn't have his share of good fortune, he would stop me from having mine.

Chapter eight

W hen I wandered down to the kitchen at half past six the next morning, in search of strong Blanchard coffee, Rosetta had already let herself in and was making grillades and grits for our breakfast. Over the past forty years she had rarely been involved in the family meals, but on occasion she cooked a pot of red beans or skillet-stewed pork chops for her own enjoyment, and the food was always a culinary delight. This morning the buttery aroma of sautéed onions, sweet peppers, and thinly sliced beef, and the ritual of brewing fresh coffee, seemed to mobilize her spirits. She worked with determined purpose, hands busy over two burners and a coffee maker, fortifying us for the long day ahead.

"Morning, Mistah Paul," she said, dishing grillades onto two plates. "It's ready. Pour your own coffee, child."

The once-robust Rosetta was now stork-like in her movement, with sharp elbows and bony shoulders and a stringy neck half the size of its original soft, fleshy mass. I had seldom seen her wear anything but a white domestic's uniform, but today she was attired in an old-fashioned Sunday church-going dress that fell below her knees, navy blue with a white lace collar, belted at the waist, the material too bulky for her emaciated frame. She clomped around the stove in low black patent-leather heels. A matching patent-leather purse, nearly the size of a mail pouch, rested next to a gray overcoat and ladies' hat in the kitchen nook across the room. A casual visitor might have wondered if we were attending a parole hearing or a wake.

"How are you feeling this morning, Rosetta?" I asked, taking our plates to the table. "Did you sleep well?"

"Feelin' a little puny these days," she said. "But I be fine once I get a little food in me."

I complimented her on the breakfast and we ate in a stilted silence. It wasn't like her to go for long periods without talking. She had always been a lively, entertaining conversationalist, especially when we were children. We'd loved her many stories about the old New Orleans of her childhood, scary memories of the frizzly rooster man and black cat bones and corners of the city that seemed as mysterious and far away as Port-au-Prince. But she hadn't been the same person since the chemotherapy, and privately Dell had confided in me that she believed Rosetta was preparing to meet her Lord and Savior.

She raised the wide coffee cup to her lips with two unsteady hands, sipping like an invalid with a soup bowl, then rattled the cup back on its saucer. "Will you pray with me this morning?" she asked, fixing her sunken eyes on me with a grave intensity. I could see a small strip of adhesive tape peeking from the hairline of her wavy black wig. "Before Mistah Gautier come by and we get all caught up in lawyer words," she said. "Will you join me in prayer, Paul?"

"Of course, Rosetta," I said, reaching over to touch her gaunt hand.

"The good Lord is the only one that can save him today," she said, worried about her son at the hearing. "Cain't expect a miracle from them hard white folk that runs the parole board."

"Let's not get discouraged," I said. But I knew that Rosetta had been disappointed too often to feel any buoyant optimism. Jaren had twice been denied a motion for retrial, and his last parole hearing, five years ago, had resulted in denial as well.

She clutched my hand, bowed her head, and offered a prayer to

Our Merciful Father. I closed my eyes and held her fragile hand and prayed that an innocent man would be released today. In our silence together I remembered the time this dear woman had tried her best to teach me how to throw and catch a baseball. I was nine years old and wanted to try out for Little League, because all my friends at Holy Name were trying out, but I didn't know the first thing about the techniques of the game. The day before try-outs she marched me out to the lawn with Jaren, two old beat-up baseball gloves from their house, and a grass-stained ball. When Jaren proved to be an ill-suited teacher—a bit too rough and cocky—she took the glove away from him and played catch with me herself. *Step into your throw with that lef' foot, child,* she'd instructed, showing me how it was done. *Put your whole body into it.* Master of so many of life's mysteries, she also knew how to throw a baseball like a man.

I was miserable at the try-outs on that crisp spring Saturday morning, rejected by every team. Rosetta and Jaren were standing by the cyclone fence when I moped off the field. *A little more practice this summer,* she'd said, full of wisdom and solace, wagging my small hand as they walked me back to the car, *you be ready for nex' year, Mickey Mantle.*

Thirty years later, her strong throwing hand had grown tender and frail, but as we prayed together at the kitchen table I held that hand reverently, like a supplicant holding a sacred relic. I was a guilty sinner unworthy to touch the hem of this woman's long navy blue garment. All I could do now was to offer small comforts in her life and pray for forgiveness.

After we stacked the dishes, Rosetta roamed through the stately grand room, cording open the drapery and tying sashes. Misty gray daylight crept through the window glass. The house remained still and undisturbed by voices, the children all asleep. At seven o'clock sharp I left a note for the slumbering Claire. Without being specific, I told her that she should speak with Julie about her behavior last evening, but recommended only light punishment for this first offense. I was leaving it up to my daughter to tell the truth about what had happened in the cottage. The irony did not escape me.

Rosetta and I walked down the damp brick pathway to the

gate, the morning air saturated with the odor of wet garden soil. My old school friend, the attorney Eric Gautier, was waiting for us in an idling Mercedes parked on St. Charles Avenue. By my arrangement he had been Jaren's lawyer for the past six or seven years, and this morning he was chauffeuring us to Angola.

"Good morning, Miz Jarboe," he said with a cheerful smile when I opened the front door for Rosetta. "You ready to give 'em hell today?"

"No, Mistah Gautier," she said, smiling slyly in response. "I'm gonna give 'em a strong dose of *heaven* instead."

She opened the rear door for herself and insisted on sitting in the back seat. "You boys go ahead and visit some," she said. "I might want to catch up on my sleep."

"You don't have to sit in the back of the bus anymore, Rosetta," I said, teasing her.

"Want to stretch my legs in this fine car," she said with a dismissive wave of the hand. "You sit up front, child, and make sure the lawyer don't run us into a swamp."

Eric had been reading the morning *Times-Picayune* and drinking coffee from a plastic travel mug, the car's heater set at a soothing hum. As soon as I fastened my seat belt he handed me the newspaper and pulled slowly onto the narrow, oak-shaded avenue, where light traffic was moving along at a somnolent pace. It was half an hour too early for the Tulane and Loyola secretaries who cruised around Audubon Park every weekday morning, competing for the few vacant parking spaces.

"Willie's at it again," he said, nodding at the paper's headline. "And it looks like she may have the votes this time."

Councilwoman Wilhelmina Phillips had revived her anti-discrimination ordinance once again. She seemed damned determined to integrate New Orleans' most famous attraction. The old-line Mardi Gras krewes, especially the big three stalwarts—Momus, Jove, and Proteus—had limited their membership exclusively to white men of good breeding for nearly a hundred and fifty years. No women, no people of color, no Italians, no Jews. The Krewe of Rex attempted to be more considerate and civic-minded, and a handful of prominent

Jewish business leaders had been accepted into the club, my father-in-law among them. During the Great Depression, Hillis Benjamin's father, the founder of the family grocery chain, had agreed to bail out the bankrupt Rex Krewe, financing their float constructions and elaborate costume ball in exchange for his son's membership in perpetuity. But despite his wealth and eminent status in Rex, Hillis remained excluded from Jove, the oldest and most prestigious krewe, and he'd never been allowed through the doors of the powerbroker Magnolia Club downtown. He resented this deeply, as he'd informed me on several occasions in his own oblique fashion. Although we hadn't discussed my father openly, Hillis knew that Charles M. Blanchard was one of the Neanderthals who'd been unwilling to accept Jews in Jove and Magnolia.

The odd thing about Dad was that he'd genuinely approved of my marriage to Claire, had loved her dearly and doted on our children, and had treated Hillis and Ida like kin during our occasional inter-family dinners. So it was difficult to comprehend why the old boy refused to stand on a float next to someone of the Hebrew persuasion, disguised by a mask, wig, and silly tights, for the sole purpose of throwing cheap plastic crap at throngs of begging tourists.

"She's certainly on a tear," Eric said, glancing over at the newspaper article I was reading. "I respect her principles, but I'm not sure how she expects to enforce a statute like that."

The article explained that Wilhelmina's ordinance would punish any organization found guilty of violating the Civil Rights laws in the selection of its members. In Willie's brave new world, guilty krewes would be banned from parading on public streets and assembling in municipal buildings, and the responsible leaders would be fined $3,000 and sentenced to five months in jail. I laughed aloud at the thought of my father or Henry Lesseps wearing neon orange parish prison uniforms and eating mystery meat from a tin plate.

"How can you force a group to socialize with people they have nothing in common with?" Eric asked rhetorically. "Busing didn't work, and neither will this. You can't just ram this thing down everybody's throat. Does Willie really think she can wave a magic wand and reverse two centuries of New Orleans tradition?"

"I'm not sure I'm with you on this, Eric," I said. "Zulu has been parading for eighty years and they don't have any problem letting white people ride on their floats and dance at the Zulu ball."

The Zulu Social Aid and Pleasure Club was the premiere black Carnival organization and the sponsors of the liveliest and most entertaining Mardi Gras parade. They had originated as an alternative to white Carnival and a satire of the Rex parade. But in recent years their traditional costumes, including cartoonish black face, African spears, and grass skirts, had elicited criticism from progressive black leaders and accusations of Uncle Tomfoolery. Still, the scolding objections had not thinned the wild Zulu parade crowds, or diminished enthusiasm for the most revered catch of the Carnival season, the gold-painted coconuts tossed from Zulu floats.

"I think Willie just wants to see the old honkies squirm a little," Eric said with a tight smile. "She knows she's got a black majority on the city council for the first time in history, and she figures it's time to make a power move. Mardi Gras is the most obvious target. What better way to remind the white patricians that they're outnumbered in this city and that times have changed?"

My old friend was a small wiry man in impressive physical condition. Every day at lunchtime he worked out at the New Orleans Athletic Club on Rampart Street, a palatial facility where those very same patrician gentlemen swam nude in the days before women were allowed membership. I joined him whenever the spirit moved me, usually twice a week, but I was no match for his energy and dogged discipline on the bicycle and Cybex machines. He played tennis competitively in the under-forty league at the country club in Old Metairie, and he coached his sons' soccer and baseball teams to frequent championships. No matter what time of day or night you crossed Eric's busy path, he looked as if he'd just stepped out of a gym shower. His short auburn hair was usually slick-wet and combed straight back, his fair face aglow from heat and exertion, his closely trimmed red beard, now dusted with gray, curled damply along a Van Gogh wedge of chin.

His father was a founding partner in the esteemed law firm of Glynn, Gautier *&* Lesseps, and at age forty Eric had become a junior partner as well, following in Russell Gautier's footsteps. The older attorneys had been personal associates of my father, and the firm represented the Blanchard Coffee Company whenever we needed counsel. But my friendship with Eric went back to elementary school at Holy Name, and later at Jesuit High, where we'd belonged to the same insular Uptown clique. From the earliest years he'd distinguished himself as a conscientious student and determined athlete, while I struggled to discover whatever small talents God had given me. As a teenager he'd won regional tennis tournaments and excelled as a skillful second baseman on the Jesuit Blue Jays varsity baseball team. He graduated near the top of our class while I clawed my way to the middle, and he'd earned an academic scholarship to Georgetown and then had studied law at the University of Virginia. In contrast, I was accepted at Tulane as a "legacy admission," thanks to my father's influence, but dropped out before my junior year and fled to the anonymity of California. Yet regardless of the gaping chasm between us in natural gifts and ambition, and our occasional differences of opinion, Eric and I had remained good friends. Like me, he was something of an impostor in Uptown social circles, preferring to smoke dope and listen to the Rolling Stones on a head set rather than attend a den meeting of the Mystick Krewe of Jove. We were kindred screw-offs who often covered for each other. I knew many of his innermost secrets. He knew one or two of mine.

"If Willie's new ordinance passes, the krewes will be forced to go public with their membership process," Eric continued, "and that will destroy the whole tradition of secrecy. Hell, half the enjoyment of Carnival is that nobody knows who the maskers are on the floats, or who's asking your wife to dance at the ball."

Although the morning light was the dismal color of pewter, and river fog drifted up through the oak arcade in Audubon Park, Eric was wearing small round sunglasses and squinted into the windshield as if hindered by a blinding glare.

"I'm always surprised at how serious the old guys are about hiding their identity," he said. "If they bust this whole membership thing wide open, the masks will come down and the magic of Carnival will disappear forever."

Until Mark Morvant's appearance yesterday, I didn't care about secret identities or clandestine organizations. I certainly didn't care about the so-called magic of Carnival. As far as I was concerned, the tiresome controversy was much ado about nothing. But expressing that attitude in public could ostracize a person from certain New Orleans circles.

"You sound like an attorney talking himself into a law suit," I said. "Ah, yes, I can picture it now—Eric Gautier defending the poor downtrodden Krewe of Jove and their right of privacy and freedom of association." I waved my hands like a theater director setting a scene. "I'm seeing a long line of stooped old codgers appearing on the stand, wearing ski masks, their voices electronically altered for television."

I was relieved to hear Eric laugh at himself. He was taking this issue far more seriously than I'd expected. He and I had always maintained an irreverent distance from the snooty class struggles of our fellow New Orleanians.

"How do you feel about this, Miz Jarboe?" Eric asked, stealing a look at Rosetta in his rear-view mirror. "Do you think Wilhelmina Phillips is right?"

At first I thought Rosetta hadn't been listening to our conversation. She took her sweet time in consideration, and I wasn't sure she'd heard the question. But then she spoke finally, her voice slow and deepened by age.

"I think everybody getting too agitated about silly nunsense makebelieve," she said. "Folk want to play king and queen—styling around and all—that up to them, mmhmn. You ax me, they wasting good money. Oughta be fixing up the city, but what you gonna do? I always enjoyed Carnival—took you kids down to Napoleon to catch some throws when y'all was young. Didn't much matter to me who was on the floats, long as things went peaceful and everybody was passing a good time."

I turned in my seat and smiled at her fondly, remembering those chill Mardi Gras days and the police motorcycles speeding near the curb to keep the crowds at bay. Rosetta held our hands, three white children and her own small son, all of us cheering wildly, our nanny bouncing up and down on her toes, waving frantically at the floats, *Throw us somethin', mistah!* I remembered scrambling under grownup legs for the hail of beads and doubloons that had fallen to the ground. *Stay close, now, chirren!* she'd always instructed us. *Make sure you keep your eye on me.*

"Willie cain't change people and their ways," Rosetta added with a thoughtful grunt. "They have to change their own selves."

Eric smiled and glanced again at the rear-view mirror. "If you ever decide to run for office, Miz Jarboe, you've got my vote," he said. "I'll even run your campaign for you."

Rosetta grunted again, a bubble of weary skepticism. "What makes you think I need a lawyer to run my election, Mistah Gautier?" she said, chuckling. "I'm used to doing for myself, young man."

I laughed and clapped my hands, applauding her remark, and Eric laughed, too, aware that his condescension had been slammed back in his face by an ailing old black woman with attitude.

The climate-controlled Mercedes purled past Gibson Hall, the venerable Romanesque administration building at Tulane University—"the streetcar academy," as my father's generation had called the place. It had always been a provincial intellectual cloister for smart Uptown boys until the Jewish kids started flocking in from the East Coast in the 1960s, the ones who couldn't get into Ivy League schools. *Jewlane*, the cynics at the Magnolia Club had dubbed the university now. The current university president was a liberal New Yorker much maligned by the alumni old guard, who were withholding pledges and donations to their alma mater until after he was gone.

"Rosetta, I don't want to build up a false sense of hope," Eric said, "but I think we have a good shot at it today. Jaren's been a model prisoner, which is why they made him a trustee. Everybody likes him, even the warden."

St. Charles curved into Carrollton Avenue at River Bend, near the famous Camellia Grill, where for decades the Negro short-order cooks had conducted their flamboyant omelet ballet, a graceful choreography of sizzling eggs and hash browns and whirling spatulas staged for the amusement of tourists sitting at an open counter. For the next few blocks we cruised alongside a streetcar, rumbling and clanging its way up the grassy neutral ground beneath Carrollton's vaulting oaks.

"We've worked up a new strategy for today's hearing," Eric continued, sounding somewhat tentative, as if he were trying to convince himself. "Don't be surprised by what you hear. It may seem like a big gamble, but we figure we've got nothing to lose."

As Eric had told me many times, nobody ever won a pardon or parole in Louisiana. The procedure was an exercise in futility. But I was aware that he'd been in close contact with Jaren through phone calls, letters, and occasional visits, working assiduously on his case. I admired my friend's tenacity and perseverance, especially because I knew he had no real hope for a release.

He accelerated the Mercedes, guiding us toward the shabby concrete on-ramps of the Interstate, which in recent years had begun to resemble the despoiled ruins of an ancient forum. Beneath the shadowy overpass, a purple K&B drugstore cart had been abandoned in a sea of broken glass. Fading graffiti smeared the pillars and cement slopes. *Curb your nigger*, one message suggested, defiant and unscathed after all this time.

"So you gonna get my boy out today, Mistah Gautier? Is that what you're telling me?" Rosetta asked. I could hear the skeptical amusement hidden underneath her question. She was holding back a wary smile.

"I'm going to do my best."

"Did you say your prayers this morning, like I axed you to?"

"Yes, ma'am, I did," he said with a straight face. He patted the tasteful tie hanging over his white starched shirt. "I'm even wearing a scapula the nuns gave me in third grade. The good Lord owes me a favor for keeping this thing. If my count is correct, I've got about ten thousand years of Indulgences accrued. Are you wearing your scapula, Blanchard?"

"I traded mine for a Little Richard record."

"You're a fine lawyer and a good man, Mistah Gautier," Rosetta said, yawning, already worn out before the trip had begun. "I'm gone say a short prayer for you right now. I'm gone pray that you've read a few more lawyer books since the last time we went up to Angola and you didn't get the job done."

Eric smiled wickedly. "This time," he said, "we'll tell them what they want to hear."

On I-10 the lanes heading downtown were clogged with rush hour traffic, but our side was sparse and quick-moving. After Metairie Cemetery, with its elegant stone mausoleums and Confederate memorials and crypt tableaus, we sped westbound, past long murky drainage canals and the bleak roadside detritus of Metairie and Kenner, anywhere suburbs with generic warehouses and office buildings lining the access roads, and a shopping mall spreading halfway to Lake Pontchartrain. As Eric and I made small talk, he kept glancing furtively in the rear-view mirror at Rosetta, and I sensed that he was eager to tell me something confidential.

In another quarter hour we had reached the marshes and clear sight of Pontchartrain, morning vapor wisping off its still gray surface as if the lake were a smoldering cauldron. The interstate slowly elevated onto thick concrete pilings above the Bonnet Carré Spillway, a wide flood-control canal connecting the lake and the Mississippi River a few miles to the south. Soon we were floating high above the water, only two other vehicles in sight and a sixteen-wheeler far in the distance, the gloomy morning to ourselves and the white egrets sitting stoically on grass islands near the shoreline.

Rosetta began to breathe deeply, a ragged catch in her chest, and I looked back and realized she'd fallen asleep. Eric had noted this as well. "The city council is holding a public hearing tomorrow afternoon," he said, staring forward into the monotonous miles of interstate ahead. The marsh had vanished and we were riding level with an unbroken wall of thick green treetops entangled by climbing vines. "Anyone can get up and address the proposed discrimination ordinance. The council plans on voting on it by the end of the day."

"So I've read," I said, dropping the folded newspaper onto the floorboard by my shoes.

"The captain wants us all to be there," he said in a near whisper, inclining his head to see if Rosetta was truly asleep. "A silent show of numbers. You need to come."

The krewe captain of Jove was a septuagenarian bank president, and all his lieutenants were well-known doctors, lawyers, and CEOs. This was going to require a clever sleight-of-hand, the members sitting together at a public hearing without giving away their secret identities.

"You know how I feel about these things," I said quietly. "I really don't care."

"I know," he said, patting my knee as if calming a disturbed child. "I'm just passing along information. The captain asked me to contact you personally. He wants some younger blood in the audience."

I smiled wryly. "He doesn't expect me to get up and speak, I hope."

He smiled at the idea, too, his rakish beard stretching toward his ears. "No, he's not *that* senile," he said, his eyes darting mischievously behind the sunglasses. "But you'd better show up and keep me company, dude. You and I are a hundred light years more open-minded than our aging brethren, and somebody's got to keep the discussion rational. Especially with hotheads like Basil and Claude in the house."

"I'm not sure we'll be sitting on the same side of the aisle, Eric. I like Willie. She's a little strident, but I know where she's coming from and I respect her for it. I actually voted for the woman."

He looked at me and laughed incredulously, then held himself in check. "You're serious, aren't you?" he said, lowering his voice.

"Dead serious."

"You're the first white person to admit that out loud."

"Which is why I'll probably skip the hearing. I don't care one way or the other about the ordinance, but I don't want to line up with a white lynch mob."

We both fell silent for a moment. Eric seemed annoyed by my indifference. I stared out the window at the endless guard rail whizzing past, an emergency phone box stationed every few miles on this desolate freeway through the wetlands. A sudden breach in the heavy greenery exposed the bayou off to our right, an ancient cypress swamp with gnarled trunks spaced far and wide in the deep brown water. I could see a dilapidated shack high on stilts, the boards bare and rotting in the fetid air. It may have been an abandoned duck blind, or a refuge for fishermen and nutria trappers. One more hurricane would scatter that feeble pile of lumber for ten miles across the bayou.

"You *like* her," Eric said, shaking his head. "I don't know why that surprises me. You've always been that way."

I wasn't sure what he meant. "What way, Eric?"

"You know," he said with a nonchalant shrug. "You've always been…" He hesitated, groping for a word, a phrase. The exercise frustrated him and he grew slightly agitated. "Hey, you sit around your office all day listening on headphones to Muddy Waters and the Neville Brothers, for Chrissake. You've always been into that whole funky black music thing."

"Yeah? So?"

"So I don't know why I'm surprised you voted for her. I mean, look where we're going," he said, extending an open palm at the windshield and the jungle-bound interstate rushing toward us. "The friggin' heart of darkness." He glanced over his shoulder at Rosetta, whose body had slumped into a peaceful repose. "You're the Lord of Lost Causes, man. I don't know anybody else who'd put themselves out like this."

"*You* are," I retorted.

"I'm getting well paid, remember? I'm the hired gun. You've got more noble reasons, I imagine."

"I've known him since I was a baby. We grew up together, Eric. For a long time he was my best friend."

After Jaren disappeared from my life, I didn't see him again until we were in high school. I remembered crossing his path by accident in the madness of Bourbon Street one Mardi Gras Day. He was running with a tough black Fortier High crowd and acted distant and combative when I said hello, but I wasn't convinced it was anything more than a pose. A couple of years later, when I was a freshman at Tulane, I wandered into a Decatur Street club called The Bank and discovered Jaren playing bass for the house band. He was a very different person by then. Off-kilter Afro, headband, sweat-drenched dashiki, Jimi Hendrix cool. He had mellowed considerably, no doubt because of the constant weed use. During the break he embraced me like a long lost brother. The hostility of a few years earlier had evaporated, and we were childhood friends again.

At that time he was house-sitting someone's party boat docked at the West End Marina on Lake Pontchartrain, and I began to hang out there on weekends, smoking dope and listening to records and babbling incoherently with his strange assortment of friends, black and white, musicians and dopers and street artists he'd met around the Quarter.

Jaren's party boat became notorious—legendary—and there were weeks at a time when he wouldn't go aboard because he was certain the marina was under police surveillance. When cops swarmed the deck a year later with an arrest warrant for homicide, they also recovered thirty pounds of marijuana and a dozen dime bags of Laotian brown heroin in the cargo hold.

The District Attorney's office charged Jaren with criminally negligent homicide in the death of his Creole girlfriend, Nola Guimont, who had overdosed from the same Laotian brown heroin found on his boat. Two flatbottom gator hunters had discovered her body floating in the Barataria swamp, south of the city, and a grandstanding D.A. was convinced that Jaren had dumped her there.

Out of respect for Rosetta, my father hired Glynn, Gautier & Lesseps to defend Jaren. Unfortunately they assigned an inept young criminal lawyer on his way to another career, and I watched the bumbling rookie sleepwalk through the trial without enthusiasm or clear focus. Jaren testified under oath that he hadn't seen his girlfriend for two weeks before her disappearance and that the dope belonged to the boat's owner, a shady Costa Rican businessman who refused to be deposed or return to Louisiana and reclaim his confiscated vessel. The jury didn't believe his story. The prosecutor portrayed him as a drug dealer guilty of supplying his girlfriend with deadly smack, and he piled on another charge for possession of narcotics with intent to sell. *That lowlife drug pusher sitting over there in his comfortable chair may not have put a bullet in her head, ladies and gentlemen of the jury,* the prosecutor had said in his summation, *but he killed that young woman with his dope, all the same. And then dumped her body in a swamp as if she were nothing more than a load of garbage.*

I was the only Blanchard who attended the trial. I sat next to Rosetta and held her hand. When the verdict was read and the judge issued his sentence, she swooned and began to weep, and a deputy was obliged to assist us. He brought her a cup of water and helped me seat her upright in a chair.

Thirty years in Angola penitentiary. A white college boy like myself wouldn't have survived a day. The very thought of it had frozen my blood.

"I guess what I'm saying is I respect you for standing by your man," Eric said. We had descended from the elevated interstate over the bayous and were sailing through lush delta countryside a few miles east of the bending Mississippi River. "Some people—like me, specifically—talk the talk. In fact, I do it for a living. But you, my friend, have walked the walk."

I turned and looked at him, somewhat apprehensive about where this was going.

"You've walked in some pretty heavy places," he said with a respectful nod in my direction. "Taken chances. I've never had the stones to go where you've been. But I'm impressed with your spirit of adventure. You've been out there on the edge, man, and you're still standing."

I did not consider myself an adventurous man. It was unclear to me what he was referring to, but there was a dark implication that left me uncomfortable. Was he talking about my lost years in California? Or did he know the secret that had caused me no end of anguish and regret? I couldn't imagine how. I hadn't breathed a word to any living soul. Only one other person knew what had happened that night—my old fraternity brother who'd shown up yesterday with blackmail on his mind.

Chapter nine

The Louisiana State Penitentiary at Angola sprawled across eighteen thousand acres of fertile bottomland along the east bank of the Mississippi River, fifty miles north of Baton Rouge, in the crook of the L shape that Louisiana forms. The prison farm was originally three cotton plantations worked by slaves from Angola—thus its name. I had been told that until 1901 the convicts were leased to private farm operations along the river, producing free labor for wealthy planters. In those days, brutal treatment and deplorable work conditions had led to two hundred inmate deaths every year. Some of the victims were as young as twelve years old.

We turned off famous old Highway 61 onto a two-lane country road that delivered us past poor rural settlements named Solitude and Retreat to the steep Tunica Hills overlooking the river. Even in early February the surrounding wilderness was deeply green, and thick with oaks, beech, and magnolias. I remembered my last trip through this area five years ago, when the dogwood and azaleas had been in bloom. Along the route, crude homemade signs advertising hen eggs and rabbits for sale had been nailed to telephone poles. Two miles from the penitentiary gate someone had erected a hand-painted billboard:

> *Do not despair*
> *Jesus is there*
> *So keep up your fight*
> *Day and night*
> *He shall be free*
> *Some day*

"That's what I'm sayin'!" Rosetta hummed and rocked when she read the words. "Jesus, be there with us this day, Lord!"

At the entrance to the prison grounds we stopped at the small glass guard booth positioned underneath a high-arching shed roof. The words *Louisiana State Penitentiary* were displayed high above. Off to the left, a line of heavy trucks idled next to a cinder-block outbuilding, waiting to enter with their day's delivery. On the right stood a tall guard tower whose occupants were perched in the glass viewing box with binoculars and scoped weapons. Eric presented his Bar card and driver's license to the guard at the booth, and after checking his sheets to make sure we were scheduled for an official appointment, the man asked us to step out of the vehicle. He and another officer wearing a dark blue uniform searched the Mercedes thoroughly—the trunk, underneath the hood and seats, the glove compartment. They confiscated Eric's road maps and told him he could retrieve them when he departed.

"What's that all about?" I asked my friend in a quiet voice as we stood side by side, waiting for the search to conclude.

"They're afraid an inmate might get his hands on a map and plan an escape route," he said with a skeptical grin. "They don't want them to know where they are."

I watched the guard paw through the pockets of our suit jackets hanging in the back seat. "They know where they are," I said out of the side of my mouth. "About eight miles past the shit end of nowhere."

"So far from God," Eric said. "So close to Mississippi."

The second guard was a no-nonsense black man, maybe fifty years old, with a weathered face and an institutional swagger. He set Rosetta's large handbag on the trunk of the Mercedes and probed its contents. "Gotta keep your meds, awnty," he said, placing two of her plastic containers in a clear baggie. "Here, write your name down on this label, please ma'am. You won't be needin' these in the next two hours, will ya?"

"Might," Rosetta said defiantly. She was not happy that a man was looking through her handbag.

"If you run into a problem, tell the cap'n to call up here and we'll bring what you need. Have a good day, ma'am."

The prison was composed of six camps, as the compounds were called, plus a heavily fenced residential area where the warden and many guards and LSP personnel lived with their families. The safest neighborhood in America, they claimed, although in the late 1940s a warden's wife had been murdered in her home by a trustee housekeeper, who dressed in her bloody clothes and tried to escape by swimming the river. Legend had it that when the warden was shown the drowned body, he emptied his revolver into the corpse.

Eric knew where he was going and drove us down a dirt road bordered by neatly tended flower beds and a prim white picket fence. Off in the fields I could see hundreds of silent inmates marching in clusters to their work assignments. They all wore jeans and white button-down shirts, instead of traditional prison stripes, and carried long-handled hoes across their shoulders like soldiers with rifles. Armed guards dressed in cammo jackets and baseball caps rambled alongside them on horseback. LSP Angola was the largest maximum-security prison in the country. Eighty percent of the inmates were black. Eighty-five percent of the men who entered Angola would die here. I considered it my personal mission to save Jaren Jarboe from becoming another statistic.

We drove past the prison hospital to the yellow cinder-block building called the Visiting Shed, a waiting room attached to the office complex where the parole hearings were held. More than a dozen cars were parked out front—other attorneys, family members, and victims prepared to testify for and against. From my last visit I remembered that the board scheduled multiple hearings on the same day and passed quickly through each case as if these proceedings required no more deliberation than traffic court.

The visitors' room resembled a grade school cafeteria, vintage 1960, with a buffed lime-green linoleum floor, low folding tables and bolted-down benches, fluorescent lights, and hinged windows opened by rusty hand cranks. Several glowing machines provided soft drinks, coffee, and snacks. When we arrived, the place was already packed with teams of grim-faced participants in this parole charade. In yet another cruel irony of the penal system, victims of the crimes these men had committed were stuck in the same room with the loved ones who had come to support their boys. The victims waited nervously, in self-imposed isolation, to explain why their assailant should not be released. A heavy sense of despair permeated the common air we all breathed. No one was happy to be here in this sorry collection of broken lives. I knew that most of these families would walk away from today's hearing in tears. I only hoped that Rosetta wouldn't be one of them.

The three of us shared a table with the assistant D.A. from Bossier Parish, who was with a young white woman drinking a Barq's Root Beer and staring sullenly at the water stains on the Formica surface. She was well dressed and attractive, but something had hardened inside her and the anger she carried was palpable. Her body was so tightly wound, her demeanor so focused and intense, I thought she might begin to scream at any moment. Clearly someone incarcerated in this place had harmed her beyond forgiveness or restitution.

Rosetta appeared physically uncomfortable in these environs. The bench provided no back support, and she shifted about with a pinched expression, gripping her handbag close to her as if the security guard roaming the room might try to seize it from her. Finally she declared she had dry mouth and requested a Coke. When Eric rose and ambled toward the soft-drink machines, counting the change from his pocket, I followed him.

"So what's this secret strategy you have in mind, counselor?" I asked in a low voice as we faced the row of selection buttons. "Aren't you going to share it with the guy who's footing your bill?"

My remark was taken more seriously than I had intended. His eyes narrowed slightly behind the round-rimmed glasses. "If I tell, you won't enjoy the melodrama," he said.

"Come on, Eric. I hate surprises."

He trickled quarters into the slot. "Like I said, we're going to give them what they want. Last time, we tried to argue his innocence. If you recall, I prepared a point-by-point refutation of the charges. I had an air-tight alibi for his whereabouts on the day the young woman disappeared. I had sworn affidavits from known drug dealers saying the pot and heroin belonged to the asshole Costa Rican who owned the boat. I would've won that debate before the Supreme Court. But the parole board didn't care. That's not what they wanted to hear. I only managed to piss them off. They don't believe that any man inside these walls is innocent. So this time," he said, punching a button with a stiff jab, "Jaren is going to make a full confession and plead for mercy."

I groaned. "Jesus Christ, Eric. That's your winning strategy? It sounds like Nixon's secret plan to end the war before Christmas."

"You want something?" he asked, pointing to the machine. "Look at this. It can give change for dollar bills."

"A confession ought to earn him a one-way ticket to spend the rest of his sentence in this hellhole."

"They've got NuGrape. This place is caught in a time warp. When was the last time you had a NuGrape?"

"You were right the first time, man. He didn't do it. I've known him since we were rug rats and I believe him when he says he didn't kill that girl and dump her body in the swamp. Don't make him say he did."

He flattened a dollar bill into the changer. "What makes you so sure of that, Perry Mason? You got a surprise witness for me today?" Change rattled into the slot. "If you've got a signed confession from the *real* perp, I'll be happy to share it with the parole board."

The Coke can rumbled down through the innards of the machine. I jerked it out of the tray before he did. "Let me go tell Rosetta to cheer up," I said. "Your secret strategy is fucking *inspired*."

He clutched the sleeve of my suit jacket, detaining me. "It's our only chance, Paul," he said, his voice suddenly soft and revealing. I could see the desperation in his eyes. He knew he was going to lose again.

"Listen, Eric. She almost died of that cervical cancer a few months ago. She's with us on borrowed time," I said. "His sentence is up in ten years, but she isn't going to live that long. You get him out of here today, goddammit. I don't care what it takes—you get him out of here. I don't want her to die knowing her boy's still in Angola."

"Calm down," he said. "People are starting to look over here."

I took a deep breath and released it slowly. "Buy me a NuGrape," I said. "I need some comfort food."

He smiled awkwardly and jangled more change into the machine. "We've got one other thing on our side today," he said.

"Don't talk to me about scapulas and Jesus, okay?"

He thumbed a button. "That man over there speaking to Rosetta," he said.

I turned and saw a tall distinguished black man standing over her, the two of them conversing amiably, like old friends. He was wearing a handsome blue suit with a corduroy vest and a conservative tie. I hadn't spoken to him in twenty years, but I knew who he was.

"Nola Guimont's uncle," Eric said. The dead girl. "A New Orleans police lieutenant, one of the few black men with thirty years' service. He's here to represent her family."

Police Lieutenant James Castle smiled at me from across the room. He was a large man, well over six feet tall and still built like a defensive tackle, but his hair had receded dramatically into a short crop of tiny gray coils. I remembered the patient, almost scholarly manner of his interrogations, and how he had seemed more like a dapper jazz saxophonist than a cop.

"You two have something in common. He's never believed that Jaren did it, either," Eric said, "and he's here to ask the parole board to set him free."

I offered Lieutenant Castle a weak smile in return, but felt incapable of moving my feet toward the table. He was the one man

I'd always feared back during the investigation. He'd contacted me soon after the gator hunters had found the girl's body and requested a meeting to ask routine questions about Jaren and Nola. He explained that his interests were personal, as her uncle, and that he was not officially involved in the case. I cooperated admirably, answering his inquiries like an innocent choir boy. I admitted that I'd visited Jaren's boat on several occasions but denied witnessing drug use of any kind—a blatant lie. I denied seeing them fight or threaten each other, which was true. I explained that I'd known Jaren since childhood and enjoyed hearing his band play, but I wasn't aware of any drug dealing from the boat—another brazen lie.

We met three times over the course of a month. Officer Castle was still in uniform at the time, and I always drove to his squad car parked near the tennis courts at the Audubon Zoo, where he asked me questions as I sat beside him in the front seat of the cruiser. He didn't want to embarrass me by showing up at the fraternity house or my family home, he explained, and he didn't want me to appear at the precinct station because that would have constituted official business, which he wanted to avoid as much as I did. His method of interrogation was polite, friendly, non-threatening. He plodded along at a slow, deliberate pace, establishing chronology and personal connections, scratching his heavy chin with a blunt thumbnail, a puzzled crease etched in his wide forehead as he worked through the details of who Jaren was and why he might've done such a thing to his niece. He didn't take notes and he never once asked if I knew Nola or had done drugs with them. In fact, he didn't seem interested in me at all, which gave me some small relief.

I'm gonna tell you something, he confessed on one of our visits. *I feel very bad about this whole thing myself. The girl's mother—my sister—had a rough time, raising them kids by herself, and she asked me to keep a special eye out on her daughter. I didn't do my job, son. I let my sister down. I shoulda spent some time with that girl and seen where she was headed. Now she's dead and my sister's tore up about it and I don't know how I'm gonna make it right by everybody that's hurting.*

I was extremely nervous during those sessions and sweated profusely. I felt stifled and claustrophobic inside his cruiser, with its trapped odors of greasy seafood and human funk. At some unpredictable moment, usually twenty minutes or so into the questioning, my voice would begin to quaver. He was aware of my discomfort and assured me that there was no need for anxiety or alarm. But underneath his paternal solicitude I sensed the workings of a streetwise investigator with a suspicious mind. There was nothing brilliant about him or his lumbering search for answers, but he seemed to be concealing a deeper knowledge behind that disarming smile. I'd felt as if I were being stalked by a very cunning adversary.

By our third meeting I had finally summoned the courage to ask him the question that had been on my mind from the very beginning. Why me? There were others who could tell him more—Jaren's band buddies and the other riffraff who crashed on his boat every night. How had he gotten *my* name and tracked me down?

I could still remember the watchful look he gave me, his eyes gone hard and his head drawn back as though squinting at an object too small and distant to decipher. *I talked to the young blood himself,* he admitted matter-of-factly. *Your name came up. He figures you and your family might know something to help him out of this jam.*

At the time I thought Officer Castle was speaking about legal counsel, which my father had already arranged for Jaren. Twenty years later I still flinched trying to understand his underlying implication. Had the entire cross-examination been a routine shakedown for cash by yet another dirty New Orleans cop?

"You're going to crush Rosetta's drink if you keep squeezing it like that," Eric said. "Let's go say hello to the lieutenant. He may be our angel of mercy today."

James Castle shook Eric's hand first and greeted him cordially. They had obviously been in contact over the past few months while Eric prepared his parole argument.

"Been a long time, young man," Castle said to me, gripping my hand a beat longer than necessary. More than any other reason, I'd fled to California twenty years ago to escape Officer James Castle and his probing eyes. "I almost didn't recognize you all spruced up and such. You look a damn sight better with a haircut, Mr. Blanchard."

Rosetta, still seated, chuckled at the remark. Her thin body was slumped forward against the table, her hands clasped and resting on the Formica. "I've had my worries about this boy," she said with a shrewd smile, "but he turned into a proper gentleman after all."

"Don't be deceived," Eric warned them. "He still hasn't done an honest day's work in his life."

The three of them laughed, and I laughed along with them, demonstrating what a good-natured fellow I was.

"The lieutenant tells me he's gonna ax the parole board to let Jaren go," Rosetta said, reaching over to pat his large hand. "That's the Lord workin' over-time. Thank you, Jesus. And thank you, Mistah Castle."

He smiled at her and squeezed her hand affectionately. "Like I explained to Mr. Gautier," he said, looking directly at me, "just before my sister died last year—that's the girl's mother—she told me to get that man out of Angola, he's serving hard time for something he didn't do. My sister wanted me to come up here and tell Parole she never believed Jaren Jarboe was to blame. So that's why I'm here this morning."

Tears flooded Rosetta's eyes and she dug through her bag for a tissue. I placed a comforting hand on her shoulder.

"My sister and me, we spent a lot of years chewing this thing over and looking square at the facts. Whatever happened to my niece, there's one thing we know for sure," James Castle said, staring at me with those deep-set, accusing eyes. "Young Jarboe didn't take her life."

My palms were perspiring now. I was beginning to feel as trapped and edgy as I'd felt back when he was grilling me in his squad car.

"Truth is, my *niece* was to blame for what happened to her. Nobody forced the girl to run with that crowd or shoot a needle in her arm. We all have to live with the choices we make in this life. And sometimes," he said with sadness in his voice, "a grown child dies because she takes a wrong turn."

I looked around the visitors' tables at the sad brood of lost and damaged souls. Simple people whose loved ones had taken a wrong turn.

"They were young," I said, my fingers still pressing Rosetta's shoulder. I didn't know why I was challenging the lieutenant. I should've kept my mouth shut. "Young people make mistakes, Lieutenant Castle. But one mistake shouldn't ruin somebody's whole life."

The man smiled patiently. He had been a police officer for thirty years and had booked more than his share of ruined lives. "Some are fortunate enough to survive their mistakes, Mr. Blanchard, and some aren't," he said. "What I've seen in my job, the ones that survive usually have somebody in their corner. Somebody with a good name and deep enough pockets. The unfortunate ones get cut loose with the gators."

I felt the barrel of his comments aimed directly at my heart.

Eric seemed uncomfortable with the drift of Castle's conversation and interceded. "Lieutenant," he said, checking his watch, "they're going to call you first for your statement. That should be in about fifteen minutes. You'll go in alone and stand before the board."

The police officer consulted his watch as well. "I need some time to collect my thoughts," he said. "God willing, I'll see y'all afterwards and we'll have cause to celebrate."

He shook Eric's hand and bent down to hug Rosetta, his thick suit sleeve wrapped around her shoulders. Then he straightened his posture to full height and shook my hand. "I'm glad you've made something of yourself, young man," he said. "Every morning when I have my cup of coffee, I think about you."

An awkward moment lapsed until I realized he was referring to Blanchard Coffee. "It's a pleasure seeing you again, sir," I lied with a perfect smile. "We can't thank you enough for coming today and doing this."

He was a much larger, more physical man than I, still robust in his mid-fifties. I could feel his formidable strength in the handshake. "I've lived with my own guilt over that child's death for twenty years," he said, refusing to release my hand until he was ready. "I just want to see that right is done, so we can all get on with our lives. Especially Jaren Jarboe and his mother."

The words were gracious and touching, but the cold accusation in his eyes chilled me to the bone. Nothing had changed in twenty years. He knew I was lying about everything.

Chapter ten

The parole hearing took place in a small airless office with faux wood paneling and Danish Modern furniture, the décor reminiscent of the parlor in our church rectory when I was growing up. Three board members sat behind a long polished table and greeted us with tepid smiles as we were led into the room by a guard and ushered to the turquoise-cushioned chairs arranged in the rear. I remembered two of the members from my last appearance here—the chairman seated in the middle, a tough old poker buddy of the former governor, and the ex-cop to his right, a crusading law-and-order bully who had once been chief of police in Morgan City. The new member was an elderly black man who seemed more interested in scribbling notes and signing the forms in front of him than in making eye contact with the supporters of Jaren Jarboe.

There were seven members of the Louisiana State Parole Board altogether, but only three appeared for any given hearing. I made a quick appraisal of these hard-bitten men, sitting magisterially behind stacks of yellowing, unread files, and realized that Eric was right. They would not be persuaded by paper arguments or the weight of evidence.

Mercy was theirs to give or withhold, depending on their moods and blood-sugar levels at the moment of deliberation.

"Good mornin'," the chairman said, peering at us over the frames of his half-moon reading glasses. His eyebrows were tangles of coarse gray hairs as thick as a mustache. "I wanta thank y'all for coming here today."

Eric crossed the cramped room and shook the chairman's hand, then the others'.

"Are we ready fuh—" The chairman glanced down at the file in front of him. He spoke with a mush-mouthed cracker accent from one of the northern parishes, possibly Monroe, and there was an adenoidal whistle after every sentence. "—Inmate Jah-boh?"

Eric nodded and we all turned toward the adjoining chamber, a break room with a small round dining table and hot coffee steaming from a Mr. Coffee. From the aroma, it smelled like a cheap brand of Community Coffee with chicory, and I wondered what it would take for Blanchard to win the LSP contract. It had to be a monster account.

A door opened in the break room and Jaren was escorted by a guard into the hearing office where we waited. His wrists and ankles were manacled with only a foot of chain, but he shuffled along in a graceful rhythm, well practiced at this routine by now. Wearing jeans and a pale blue button-down shirt, freshly ironed, his sleeves rolled neatly above the stainless steel cuffs, he carried in his bound hands an ordinary blue photo album, the kind you could purchase at any pharmacy or department store. I hadn't seen Jaren in five years and he'd aged noticeably, a light frosting of gray in his short-shorn hair and trim mustache. He wasn't a tall man, maybe two inches under six feet, but he carried himself with authority. Twenty years of prison muscle filled his shirt and his pant legs, bulging his shoulders and thighs, but despite his impressive build, he looked older than his forty-two years, the youthful mischief gone from his eyes. His once-chiseled face had begun to bloat slightly, and loose flesh sagged beneath his chin. He smiled at his mother and then acknowledged me with a solemn nod. I wondered if I had aged poorly in his estimation as well. We were no longer the barefoot boys who'd once fished together along the riverbank behind the zoo.

"Hello, child," Rosetta beamed, pulling herself awkwardly from the turquoise seat cushions and starting toward him.

"No physical contact, ma'am," the guard reminded her with an outstretched hand. "Please take your seat."

She stopped abruptly, chastened by the command, and stared down at her heeled shoes. Her sudden shrinking response appeared bred in the bone, a reflex harkening back to an earlier time when she'd been scolded in that same voice by other white men in charge of the world she inhabited. I stepped forward, took her limp hand, and walked her back to the chair.

"Mornin', Mistah Jah-boh," the chairman said, quickly skimming Jaren's file. "We understand you would like to be considered for parole at this time. Why don't we go ahead and get started, then. Do you wish to make a statement?"

"Yes, sir, I do." Jaren sounded like a Yale graduate compared to the peckerwood in charge of his release.

"Proceed, then."

Standing with his back to us, Jaren placed the blue photo album on the table in front of the three parole board members and then paused dramatically, with a deep inhalation that flexed his shoulder blades, as if he were preparing for a long breathless oration. "I was gonna show you gentlemen the scrapbook I've been keeping for the last five years," he began, "because I've got some recommendation letters from the warden and my chaplain and the senior deputies that know me well. And I've got some other letters from the teachers I've worked with in the anti-drug programs I visit in the schools. The letters all say Jaren Jarboe is a good, hard-working, rehabilitated man who's served his time on the Farm and deserves a second chance on the outside. I also kept a collection of stories I wrote in the *Angolite* newspaper," he said, nudging the album cover with his spidery fingers. "They'd give you a pretty good idea of how Jaren Jarboe's attitude has changed about things in general since he been here."

He gazed at the scrapbook in a long thoughtful silence, then pushed it aside. "But I'm not gonna trouble you gentlemen with this. It's all just words on paper. You know, and I know, that I been a model prisoner for most of my time here and everybody respects me. That's not the problem. The problem is there are two Jaren Jarboes, the one now and the one that got himself in trouble twenty years ago. And the Jaren Jarboe of today can't expect to be paroled unless he takes responsibility for what he done to a young girl back in those days." He paused again to let his words take effect. "A man doesn't deserve mercy until he seeks forgiveness for the old life that led him to such a bad end."

His last sentence could have been addressed directly to me.

"So I stand here before you gentlemen," he said in a firm voice, "to face the sins of my past and ask you to forgive the old Jaren Jarboe for his transgressions. And I'm asking you to please give the new man one more chance to make it right with those he hurt." His wrist manacles rattled as he turned halfway around and looked dolefully at his mother. "And those he let down."

Rosetta choked up and began to sob quietly. She opened her handbag in search of another tissue, and I gave her my pressed handkerchief and gently rubbed her shoulder.

Jaren's admission sounded sincere and convincing to me, although I still felt uneasy about this new strategy to confess to a crime he hadn't committed. I glanced at Eric, who sat stoically beside me with his freckled hands crossed over one knee. His confident expression showed that he was pleased with his client, who had obviously responded well to weeks of coaching.

Jaren spoke for perhaps five minutes more. He acknowledged that his drug lifestyle in the late sixties had resulted in the tragic death of Nola Guimont. He confessed to using heroin with her, explaining that her death had been an accidental overdose, and he told them he'd transported her lifeless body to the bayou south of Lafitte and had dumped her there in the middle of the night. Eric was an effective instructor, the shameless bastard, but Jaren's graphic description left me queasy and lightheaded. Was this humiliating shine-show the only way to win our man's parole?

Hearing her son confess to these crimes after so many years of believing in his innocence, Rosetta lost her composure and began to weep inconsolably. I put my arm around her shoulders and held her close, feeling a sudden desperate need for a straight shot of Bombay Sapphire.

"The last time you appeared before this board, you insisted you were an innocent man," interjected the ex-police chief from Morgan City. Everything about him suggested an earlier era—the drab brown suit and thin tie, the oiled crest of hair. "You said you had no part in that poor girl's death. Am I correct about that, Mr. Jarboe?"

"Yes, sir." Jaren held his head high, his broad shoulders straight, prepared for the inevitable grilling.

"You have denied your involvement in this crime for twenty years, isn't that correct, Mr. Jarboe?" the old cop persisted.

"That's correct, sir. Until recently I wasn't strong enough to accept responsibility for what I done."

"And now you want us to believe you're a responsible man," the cop said, his voice reeking with contempt. "Overnight you got religion and you see the light."

"Not overnight, sir. I've been bothering on this a long time."

The black parole board member looked up from his notes. "Are you aware that the young lady's uncle was here a few minutes ago, Mr. Jarboe, testifying on your behalf? He believes you had no involvement in his niece's death."

"Yes, sir. I know Lieutenant Castle. I know how he feels about this."

The old black gentleman spoke in a slow, articulate manner. "Then how are you going to explain yourself to him and his family, young man? He's been on your side all these years. Are you going to tell him the truth now?"

"Yes, sir, I'll tell him the truth. He's a fair man and he'll understand."

The chairman shifted about in his seat, adjusted the reading glasses that had slipped to the tip of his nose. "What I don't understand, Mistah Jah-boh," he said, "is why you didn't tell us these things the last time you stood before this board. You woulda saved everybody considerable time and effort, and our decision mighta turned out otherwise in your favor. You see what I mean?"

"Yes, sir. I apologize for that."

"Un-hunh. Well, suh, I admire you for having the courage to finally face up to your misdeeds and get this off your chest. I truly do," the chairman said, glaring sternly over his glasses at Jaren. "Most of the men in this institution never show remorse for what they've done. They live in denial of the truth. They appear before this body and try to con us into believing they're innocent. They lie and make excuses and try to twist the law to their advantage. I appreciate the fact that you've been honest with us today, Mistah Jah-boh. That tells me something about your present character."

"Thank you, sir."

The chairman glanced at his watch and shuffled through the papers piled in front of him. There was a long uneasy silence while his two colleagues did the same.

"Does your legal counsel have anything to say at this time?" the chairman asked.

Eric rose to his feet and buttoned his suit jacket. "Yes, sir. May I address the board?"

"Go ahead, Mistah Gautier," the chairman said. "I know you're a lawyuh, but make it brief, if you pl*eee*ze."

Eric stepped to the table and stood shoulder to shoulder with Jaren. They made quite a contrast, the prisoner in jeans and manacled wrists, and the dapper, well-barbered attorney in a five-hundred-dollar tailored suit the color of a mourning dove.

"Gentlemen," Eric began in a personal, engaging tone, "the most significant question we're asking you to consider today is, 'How long is long enough?'" He smiled warmly at the three men as if they were members of his country club. "Fifteen years? Twenty? In my client's case, twenty years *is* enough. You won't hear any argument about that from the warden or the prison personnel he comes into contact with every day. They know he's been here long enough. He's paid his debt to society. He's a completely rehabilitated man. And so I'm here this morning to appeal to your sense of fairness and to ask you to grant Jaren Jarboe his freedom."

As Eric continued to speak, I studied the faces of the men listening to his plea and saw in their cold, dead eyes the abhorrence they felt for Jaren and every wretched soul inside these godforsaken walls. These three individuals were chosen to make crucial parole decisions because they had no sympathy whatsoever for misfortune and human weakness—no tolerance for liars and cons—and absolutely no respect for expensive New Orleans lawyers who would try to persuade them otherwise. I listened to Eric speak, and I watched their terse expressions, and in the back of my mind I heard the heavy iron bars slamming shut on Jaren's future.

"Mistah Paul Blanchard? Would that be you, suh?"

The chairman spoke my name. Eric and Jaren had turned and were staring at me. The parole board members gazed across the small room in my direction.

"Yes, sir?" I said, rising to my feet. Eric must have told them something to arouse this question, but I hadn't been paying proper attention.

"You, suh, have caused a serious problem in my marriage for many years," the chairman said. After a tense moment his flaccid face broke into a craggy smile. "She prefers your family's brand of coffee, I drink CDM. If you'll pardon the pun, Mistah Blanchard, it's almost *grounds* for divorce."

There was a smattering of weak laughter all around.

"Your wife is a wise woman," I said.

"She would concur with that statement," he said, grinning slyly. "Now Mistah Blanchard, you have agreed to employ Mistah Jah-boh at your coffee plant in New Orlyuns if the inmate is released, is that correct, suh?"

"Yes, sir, it is," I said.

"Tell us more about that, Mistah Blanchard. Why are you willing to employ this man?"

I looked at Jaren and smiled. He did not seem especially receptive to my gesture of friendship.

"Jaren Jarboe and I grew up together. We were childhood friends," I said, glancing down at the sniffing Rosetta with my professional smile firmly in place. "I would trust him to *run* my company,

Mr. Chairman. He's highly intelligent and hard-working, and I'm certain he'll do an outstanding job at his assignment. We'd be proud to have him on board at Blanchard Coffee."

The chairman asked me what kind of work I had in mind for Jaren, and I mentioned several possibilities in the warehouse, including shipping clerk.

"I admire your willingness to offer an employment opportunity to an ex-convict, Mistah Blanchard," the chairman said. "I may have to change my mind about your coffee."

Eric's laughter sounded hollow and forced. The old chairman regarded him with a jaundiced eye and asked what provisions would be made for Jaren's place of residence, should he be released. Eric showed him the letter from a halfway house near the St. Thomas Housing Project offering Jaren a home during his parole period. My attorney friend had certainly done his homework.

"Thank you, Mistah Gautier. I see we have one other guest who has made the trip from New Orlyuns," the chairman said. "You are Mistah Jah-boh's mother, am I correct?"

Rosetta raised her eyes for the first time in several minutes. My handkerchief was wadded in her fist, and I could read the force of anger and disappointment in the knotted cords of her wrist. "I am," she responded in a hoarse voice.

"Before we terminate this hearing and make our decision, would you care to say anything, Missus Jah-boh?"

Eric tried to signal her with his eyes. I could see that he didn't want her to speak and possibly jeopardize the delicate stratagem he had set to work. But Rosetta stood up, despite the attorney's body language of imploring alarm, and faced the three parole board members with her chin lifted high. The tears were dry now and there was a ringing admonition in her words. "God forgives the sinner who repents," she said. "How can *we*—sinners all—not do the same?"

She worked her dry mouth as if chewing something stale. "Mistah Chairman," she said, "my boy has paid a heavy price for what he done. Twenty long years inside this terrible place. That's long enough. Now I ax you to please let me take him home. Maybe I didn't do such a good job when I was bringing him up, but I've always been a working lady and I had my hands full making a living all by myself. This time I will watch after him and see that he live a Christian life till my last dying breath on this earth. I promise you that, gentlemen. You have my word. Jus' gimme my boy back."

Her statement caught me off guard and a hard lump swelled in my throat. Her words must have broken Jaren's heart as well, because when I glanced over at him, he was biting his lip like a penitent child.

Chapter eleven

Rosetta, Eric, and I were asked to wait in the wood-paneled corridor outside the hearing room. Eric reminded me that ten minutes was the average time it took any parole board to reach a decision.

Ten minutes passed, then fifteen. After twenty minutes he stopped pacing and whispered, "This is probably good news. They aren't rubber-stamping this thing yet. I'm guessing the black guy is holding out on our side."

Five minutes later we were summoned into the chamber. Jaren reentered from the break room with the guard at his side and stood rigidly at attention before the polished table. The chairman read the board's decision. They commended inmate Jarboe for his honesty and for taking responsibility for the crime he committed. "I'm sure God has forgiven you," the chairman declared in a flat voice. "And so has Miss Guimont's family."

But the Louisiana State Parole Board had not forgiven him. The chairman reprimanded Jaren for wasting twenty years in denial, at the expense of the courts and the penal system. The board had determined that he should serve the remainder of his original sentence—ten more years—in reparation for his deceit.

Eric's legal strategy had been a horrendous miscalculation. I glanced at him and saw that he was shaken, the ruddy color drained from his boyish freckled face. He lowered his eyes, humbled by defeat.

"It's your right to petition for parole again in the future, Inmate Jah-boh," the chairman announced as he glowered over his reading glasses, the handwritten decision still clasped between both trembling hands like a papal decree. "Perhaps the board will have a more lenient disposition at that time."

Rosetta moaned and her frail body went slack. Eric helped me hold her upright in the chair as she gasped for breath, her eyes fluttering as if she were having a seizure.

"Mama, you all right?" Jaren said, his voice raised in alarm. He moved toward her but the guard seized his arm.

"May we please have some water?" I said.

The elderly black parole board member hurried into the break room and returned with a paper cup filled with cold water from a bottle dispenser.

"Fan her, Speed!" Jaren instructed. "Give her some air."

He was standing only a few feet away, forbidden to touch his mother, his broad shoulders squared and the foot of manacle chain stretched taut between his clenched fists.

I waved my hand frantically back and forth in front of Rosetta's damp, angular face. When I glanced over at Jaren again, he was staring at me with a fierce unforgiving resolve.

"You better keep looking after her," he said directly to me. I could feel the full brunt of his anger at everything that had happened here today, and at everything that had gone wrong over the past twenty years. "You hear me, Speed? Make damn sure she's taken care of. You owe me that much, boy."

I stared at him, speechless.

"It's time, Two J," the guard said, grasping Jaren's elbow. "We gotta book you back inside."

"Gimme another minute," Jaren said, anxious to see his mother recover first.

The guard took his instructions from the chairman, who issued a subtle shake of the head. "'Fraid not, bro'," the man in uniform said. "Your mama be awright. These folk got it under control. Come on, now. Time to go back to the house."

His leg chain rattling in choppy steps, Jaren watched his mother over his shoulder as he was guided out of the room. She opened her eyes and knocked the cup of water out of my hand in a flailing spasm of limbs. "*Lord, don't take him!*" she cried, calling her son's name while he was being led away.

Chapter twelve

I found Eric loitering under a covered walkway outside the Visiting Shed, resting his shoulder against a support pole and gazing blankly down at the cultivated flower beds that skirted the walk. He looked forlorn and dispirited and mentally absent from his surroundings. My words startled him out of his reverie.

"Ahh, my clever friend," I said as I approached. "I thought that new legal strategy worked well, didn't you?"

His eyes settled on me with an angry heat. "I'm in no fucking mood, Blanchard," he said.

I had no genuine taste for sarcasm, either. My heart felt heavy and worn.

"How is Rosetta?" he asked, trying to deflect the bitter disappointment we were both feeling.

"The prison doctor and a couple of medics are with her," I said. They were keeping her under observation in a small First Aid room. "She seems to be okay. Just a little overwrought."

"Jesus," he said with an irritated sigh. "Mercy means nothing in this goddamned place. Those pricks had made up their minds before Jaren walked in the room. He was dead meat before it ever got started."

"I'm sure you're right."

"It was a desperate gamble, I admit. But we tried arguing the case last time and they didn't listen. It took them five minutes flat to turn us down."

It was shortly past noon but there was no sun, only steel gray cloud cover above the vast open fields that stretched from this congregation of buildings to the tree line along the Mississippi River far in the distance. I could hear the thunk of hoes in the humid air, hundreds of silent men chopping the soft black earth a half-mile away. A lone guard on horseback, rifle slung across his saddle, was returning across the green pasture like a weary messenger with a dispatch from the battle front.

"I'm not a lawyer, Eric," I said, watching the rider rein the horse and take a long drink from his canteen, "but I can't believe it's ever a good idea to confess something you didn't do."

My statement aroused his indignation. "You know what, Blanchard? You're the only white man in the state of Louisiana who believes he's innocent," he said. "Maybe you need to find yourself a lawyer who agrees with you. Or a psychiatrist to help you work out your personal investment in this case. I've wasted enough time on this obsession of yours." He shoved off from the support pole and elbowed me out of his way. "I'm gonna go check on Rosetta. We need to get out of here," he said. "I have a court appointment in New Orleans at four."

After he walked away, I stood staring out at a thousand acres of flat verdant field that had once grown cotton and sugar cane for the plantation masters. A troop of convicts was shuffling down a dusty road to the west, their long-handled hoes rising above them like wicked scythes borne by death figures in a medieval landscape. A pickup truck crawled toward the group, its tailgate swinging loose, a slew of ancient Igloo water coolers crammed in its bed.

I had noticed the well-dressed black man sitting at a concrete picnic table outside the cafeteria, but he was facing away from me and I wasn't sure it was James Castle until he stood up and ground out his cigarette on the lawn with his large shoe. There was a pained look in his eyes as he strode toward me, tromping through the azaleas planted beside the walkway.

"Bad news, Lieutenant," I said.

"I heard," he said, halting in front of me with his suit jacket drawn back behind the huge hands stuffed into his pants pockets. I was having a difficult time meeting his gaze and instead peered down at his polished wingtips and the clod of garden fertilizer clinging to the round toes.

"We'll try again," I said in a timid voice. "As soon as he's eligible. We're going to fight this thing until we win."

He studied me for a long, uncomfortable interval without speaking a word. When I finally found the courage to look at his wide brown face, I felt terrorized by the penetrating judgment in his eyes.

"I loved that girl like my own daughter," he said. "I don't suppose you saw what she looked like after a week in the swamp."

I shook my head.

"It's hard to forget something like that, son. It stays with you a long time."

I took a silent breath, searching for the right words. "With all due respect to you and your family, sir," I said, "I think Jaren's done enough time for what he did."

He laughed at me. "Take that slick bullshit somewhere else. You're wasting it on me."

Although we were outdoors in an open breezeway, I felt the same clawing sense of claustrophobia I'd felt earlier in his presence. I began to perspire heavily under my suit jacket.

"At least you show some conscience," he said. "I give you credit for that. Most white folk would walk away clean and let it slide. Maybe someday that conscience will stick you hard enough to do what's right. Someday before his mama dies," he said. "If you love that ol' lady like I think you do, before she pass, you'll tell her the whole truth, son."

I put on my office face, the impassive mask I wore when addressing my staff. "I don't know what that is anymore, Lieutenant."

He narrowed his puffy eyes. "Don't play with me, son. You know exactly what I'm talking about. The courts and parole board might be satisfied with theirselves on this one," he said, "but you and me, we're not through yet, Mr. Blanchard."

I saw now what I should have understood long ago. It meant too much to him. Family heartache, loyalty to his people, maybe even a rare sense of justice. He couldn't let it go. Not this time, not ever.

"So long, Lieutenant," I said, smiling that false smile I had practiced over the years. "Thank you for coming up here today and speaking on Jaren's behalf. We appreciate your support."

He was no longer the patient cop who had grilled me in his squad car twenty years ago. Long days and nights wearing a badge in a dirty town had hewed him a sharp edge. "Pass on my regrets to Missus Jarboe," he said. "I hope she gets to feeling better. Tell her I'll call on her one of these days."

I didn't like the idea of him discussing these matters with Rosetta. "Have a safe trip back, Lieutenant Castle," I said, still smiling pleasantly. "There's a lot of bad road between here and New Orleans. You be careful, now."

I stepped around his hulky body and returned along the walkway to the administration building. With every step I could feel his eyes on the back of my head.

Chapter thirteen

On the return trip to New Orleans, the mood in the car was solemn, and for the most part, silent. Rosetta had recovered from what she called her *church spell*, but she slept a good deal of the way and spoke only when she needed to stop for a restroom. Eric and I exchanged few words. He seemed annoyed with me for involving him in this hopeless case. For the first time in my life I wondered if our friendship would last.

Back on St. Charles, I made sure Rosetta ate something before driving her home to her renovated shotgun on lower Arabella Street, a comfortable place she had owned for fifteen years. She usually walked the five blocks to and from our house, but today I insisted on transporting her myself.

"Rosetta, there's something I've got to explain," I said, escorting her slowly up the front walk with my arm interlocked in hers. "Jaren really didn't do those things to that girl. He was in love with her. There's no way he'd treat her that way. You know him better than that."

She stopped abruptly and I felt the tug of her full weight, raw bone and rustling dress and heavy handbag, as she turned her gaze on me with the correcting look I had known since I was a toddler.

"He said so hisself, Mistah Paul," she said. "You heard him plain as day. He told those men he done it. That's why they come down on him so hard."

I shook my head, remembering what James Castle had said: *Tell her the whole truth, son.*

"The confession was Eric Gautier's bright idea," I said. "He thought it would work, the fool. He figured if Jaren went ahead and confessed, they'd be satisfied with time served and let him go."

I urged her along and we walked up the steps to her narrow porch, an impeccably swept space with wrought iron railings and a wood-slat swing hanging from two long chains.

"I should've learned my lesson from what my father taught me in the coffee business," I said. "Don't ever leave the tough decisions to lawyers. They always compromise when they should fight—and fight when they should compromise."

The sun had relinquished its presence today in south Louisiana and the sky remained as gray and shabby as field cotton. I always associated Rosetta's house with the smell of hydrangeas and sweet olive, which she grew in her small yard, but it was still winter, despite the warm afternoon, and the blooming season was six weeks away.

"You mean to tell me my boy say such things in front of those men and they not even true?"

"Not a word of it was true," I said.

She glared at me in disbelief, as if I were the one who'd convinced her son to confess. "I never believed he did," she said in a strong voice. "Not my boy. Mm-mnnh, not Jaren. I never believed it was him."

She dug into her handbag for a ring of keys, then began the elaborate ritual of unlocking her burglar door, screen door, and the two locks on the reinforced wooden door leading into her prim living room.

"I see that Mistah Gautier again," she said, muttering to herself as she fumbled with the keys, "I'm gonna whip his scrawny tail end."

At home I mixed a gin and tonic at the bar in the den, where I found a note from Claire saying she and Andy had gone clothes shopping.

I was slightly irritated that she'd chosen the bar as the most reliable place in which to communicate with me. Other wives would have left a note on Daddy's workbench.

Julie is grounded in her room for the weekend, the note stated. *We will discuss when I return.* So much for the gentle reproach for a first offense.

I knocked lightly on my daughter's bedroom door. "Julie, I'm home," I said. "May I come in?"

A long silence ensued. I thought she might have fallen asleep. Or escaped out the second-story window and down the roof.

In time there was a stirring in the room. The doorknob rattled. "Hi, Dad," she said, opening the door only a few inches. She was wearing an old white t-shirt that reached her knees and her dark hair was unbrushed and uncharacteristically greasy. She peered out at me through swollen eyes, as if she'd been crying all day. "I've been busted," she said, trying to hold back the tears. "The whole damn weekend."

"So I hear. I'm sorry," I said with a sympathetic smile. "Does that mean you can't hug your dad, either?"

She opened the door wide and threw both arms around my chest, pressing the side of her face against my loose tie, squeezing with all her might. A few months ago my ribs would not have ached when she did this. I was impressed by her growing strength.

"I guess you told Mom what happened," I said, laying my hand tenderly on the back of her head.

"Most of it," she mumbled into my tie.

"Whaaat did you leavvve ouuut?" I asked in a childlike sing-song.

She considered my question and took a deep breath, the air whistling in her nostrils. "The blooooow job," she sang back.

Shocked, I grasped her shoulders and held her at arm's length. She began to laugh. "Gotcha, Dad," she chortled, slapping me on the chest.

"That's real funny, Julia," I said, addressing her by her formal name.

"You should see your face," she said, laughing harder and backing into the room.

"Well, I do have some concerns about you hanging out with older boys I don't know."

She folded her arms and smirked. "Oh gee, Dad, have we come to the father-daughter discussion when you warn me about sex, drugs, and rap music?"

Her sarcastic tone of voice sounded exactly like Claire's when she was annoyed with me.

"Just this. Don't go in the cottage with boys," I said, hearing more than a simple parental admonition in my words.

"Those boys go to Newman, for Chrissake." The same wealthy private Uptown school Claire and her siblings had attended. "They're not crackheads from the projects, Dad. Their parents drive Volvos and go to stupid art openings, like you and mom."

"Fine," I said. "But I don't know their names. I don't know who their parents *are*."

As soon as I'd said it, I realized that that was the exact response my own father would have had. And anyone in his social set. Was I becoming one of them?

Julie cocked one hip and focused her teenage insolence on me. "They're white and they live Uptown," she said defiantly. "Isn't that pretty much all that matters to you and your friends, Dad?"

I stepped into the room and engulfed her in my arms, feeling the tension and resistance in those gawky limbs. She was maturing so quickly, already separating from Claire and me, finding her own voice and attitude. Confronting, disputing, ignoring. This behavior was new to me. My own adolescent rebellion had been secretive and cerebral, for the most part. Flight rather than fight. But at this moment, holding my daughter in my arms, I faced the sad realization that she was no longer the same sweet child who had always searched for my hand at every crosswalk.

"No, that's not what matters to me," I said, kissing the top of her oily, unwashed hair. "*You* matter to me. And Andy," I said, adding as a prudent afterthought, "and Mom."

For a precious instant she returned the affection, embracing me without restraint.

"But do stay out of the cottage with Newman boys, okay?" I said. "And stay out of my gin."

Downstairs in the library I phoned my assistant at the office. It was nearly five-thirty on a Friday afternoon, but I had asked her to remain at work until I checked in.

"Sorry, Angie," I said. "It's been a long, crazy day. I had hoped to call sooner."

"It's okay, boss," she said. "I needed to catch up on a few things. And this gives me a chance to miss the traffic."

Her name was Angelique Foucher Thomas and she was a Creole of Color—*gens de couleur*, as they were called in the old days—a light-skinned black woman from an established Creole family in the Seventh Ward near the Gentilly neighborhood. Stylish, intelligent, and sweet-natured, Angie was an attractive twenty-eight-year-old Xavier graduate who could *passe blanc* anywhere but in New Orleans. She was married to a Negro named Gary Thomas, an intern at the Tulane Medical Center, and they had a three-year-old son. She had worked for me since I'd taken over as CEO two years ago, and our relationship had slowly evolved into a personal friendship.

"What's going on in the bean world?" I asked her. "Did you miss me?"

"*I* did," she giggled. "But the invisible hand turns the page whether you're here or not."

This was not a sardonic exaggeration and we both knew it. Angie understood the coffee business better than I did, and she certainly possessed a sharper mind for accounting, sales, and the details of employee relations. In spite of my father's tutelage and his attempts to apprentice me with various managers, I had no leadership skills and even less interest in the family enterprise. The truth was, I didn't care. I didn't want the company to fail, of course, and I didn't want to let down the hundreds of people who depended on me for a livelihood, but I had no passion for the business and spent most of my days avoiding executive responsibilities. Blanchard Coffee was very fortunate to have Angie and several old-timers who had worked for my father. The company ran itself, with or without me.

"Did the invisible hand answer my phone calls?" I asked.

"I think I handled all of them except one," she said in a voice as soft as a ripe plum. "Some guy named Mark called. He wouldn't give me his last name or leave a number. He said he was an old frat brother from Tulane."

The bastard had called me at my office. "What did he want?"

"He didn't say. It sounded personal. Did you two once have a special relationship you've been hiding all these years?"

I swallowed a mouthful of gin and tonic, furious that he'd tried to contact me at my place of business. It was his way of reminding me that the pressure was on.

"Am I wrong about this? I've always suspected that frat boys are running around naked and servicing each other in those big houses they live in," she said.

"My *brother* was the one interested in frat boys," I said, trying to smooth the anger out of my voice.

She had never met Perry, but she'd certainly listened to me vent about him from time to time.

"I think that's all, boss. Unless you're interested in a blow-by-blow of the marketing meeting we had this morning about the new gourmet line."

"It can wait till Monday. Why don't you get out of there and go start your weekend?"

There was a short pause on her end. "I'm joining Jane, Alex, and Marcia at the Columns for a quick one on the way home. Why don't you come by?"

"A quick *drink*, you mean?"

"Yeeees," she said, her voice deepening into a throaty laugh. "What else would I mean?"

I smiled at the idea of getting pleasantly looped with her and three of my young bean counters at happy hour. I had joined them once or twice, but my presence seemed to dampen their spirits.

"Will you give me a rain check?" I asked. "I have to be somewhere in a few minutes."

The Magnolia Club, in fact. The pressure was indeed on. The clock was ticking.

"Oh dear, I'm such a bubble head," she said, suddenly exasperated with herself. "I haven't asked about Angola."

I sighed. "It didn't go well. He was denied parole."

Another awkward pause. "Damn. I'm sorry, Paul. You must be disappointed. How is Rosetta?"

"She almost fainted when they read the decision, but she's okay now. She's at home, resting."

"Bastards," she said. "You sure you don't want that drink? Sounds like you could use some company."

I could have used *her* company. Just the two of us. A deluxe corner suite at the Columns, candlelight and a bottle of wine, a warm soaking bath together in a claw-legged tub. This was not the first time I had fantasized about such a scenario with my assistant.

"I can't think of a nicer offer, Angie," I told her. The absolute truth. "But I have to take care of some personal business that's starting to rattle my chain."

Chapter fourteen

I t was often said that New Orleans has only thirty families, and everyone else was here to work for them. Unfortunately, there was more truth to that sly old crack than anyone cared to admit. And if you wanted to find one of the scions of the elite thirty families, the first place you would look was the Magnolia Club at five o'clock on any given weekday.

The club was located downtown on Canal Street in a narrow Georgian residence designed by the distinguished local architect James Gallier in the 1840s. Gallier had built the three-story home for a wealthy doctor, but during the Civil War the elegant domicile was confiscated by occupying Union forces and served as their naval headquarters. Club leaders had purchased the mansion after the war, and with only minor alterations and additions, the structure and its Old World furnishings had remained untouched for nearly a hundred and twenty-five years. Seat of the New Orleans power structure, the Magnolia Club had hosted American presidents, grand dukes of Russia, and industry tycoons in the courtly southern splendor of an *ancien régime*. Every year on Mardi Gras, special parade bleachers were erected in front of the building to accommodate the club's favored families, and King Rex himself traditionally stopped his float there to toast the Queen of Jove, who always greeted him with a deep curtsy from her royal balcony. I remembered how beautiful my sister Kathleen had looked in her virginal white gown and tiara, waving with refined grace to the passing crowds, and how proud of her we all were on that crisp Fat Tuesday morning two decades ago when she was Queen of Jove.

These days, foot traffic on busy Canal Street—roaming packs of black teenagers from the Iberville Housing Project, lost Midwestern tourists, homeless panhandlers—took little notice of the innocuous old landmark, dwarfed as it was by the brand-name athletic shoe emporiums, fast-food restaurants and glass storefronts crammed with the latest electronic gadgets. In the modern city center, dirty and generic and doomed, the Magnolia Club appeared quaint and out of place, a monument to the past, with its genteel side garden of fruit trees behind a wrought-iron fence and a discreet residential front door whose etched glass contained the image of a magnolia blossom, the only hint to the building's identity. There was a simple button doorbell, but it had been disconnected decades ago, because members never entered from the plebeian sidewalk of Canal Street. Anyone impudent enough to ring the bell had no business here.

I left my BMW with a valet in the cavernous old parking garage on Common Street, directly behind the club, and took the private elevator to the rear entrance. At this hour I knew I would find Henry Lesseps in the club library, sipping scotch and reading *The Wall Street Journal*. Like all of us, Henry was a creature of habit and had maintained this routine for fifty years, at one time in the fraternal company of my father, who used to meet him every afternoon for a whisky sour and idle conversation about their day.

Hoping to avoid contact with the more loquacious club members, I walked quickly down the long corridor that dissected the old residence, passing through a gallery of fading oil portraits of the Magnolia Club presidents from its earliest days. They eyed me with stern reproach, those mustachioed men wearing high winged collars and cravats, staring down at me with the fierce, appraising gaze of predatory birds. They knew I was a prodigal son, uneasy here in my father's house of many rooms. They were not deceived by the false smile disguising the lie in my heart.

I hurried past the billiards room, where several gray-haired gentlemen stood chatting amiably around the card tables, attended to by elderly black waiters dressed in white jackets and bowties. When I entered the library I was surprised to discover only two members sitting in the heavy leather reading chairs: Henry, and the old Fifth Circuit Court magistrate who had rendered the legal decision to integrate New Orleans public schools in 1960. Nearly ninety years old now, the judge could still dominate the most casual debate, political or literary, and for three decades had steadfastly refused to apologize for his historical desegregation rulings from the bench, much to the dismay of fellow Magnolia Club members. Like my mother-in-law, Ida, an old friend of his, he had endured numerous personal attacks in the press and under the cover of darkness. Two of his dogs had been poisoned, his car had been vandalized several times, a cottonmouth water moccasin had been hidden in his mailbox, and his hedges had been set ablaze one evening in a roaring arson fire. But in spite of the constant threats, he wore a dashing smile at all times, like someone who appreciated a good paradox. He simply refused to be intimidated.

I said hello to the old man and he responded with a gnomish twinkle in his eye. I knew he couldn't remember my name, but he offered an avuncular nod, our bond the membership we shared in this august body of men. There was a famous story that one day an outspoken member of the club had been reading the *Times-Picayune* in this very library, complaining bitterly about recent desegregation decrees, when the judge walked in with a volume of Elizabethan poetry tucked under an arm. *I see you're still a nigger lover,* the man said, pointing to an article about the judge in the newspaper. *I see you're still a buffoon,* replied the judge. *But tell me—how is the roast beef today?*

At the other end of the narrow room, Henry Lesseps sat reading *The Wall Street Journal* in a nimbus of silence under a magnificent old Louis xv chandelier. I regretted that I might be interrupting his sacrosanct routine, but nevertheless I cleared my throat as a warning of approach and sank down in a deep leather chair across from him. It was the same chair my father had occupied at this hour of the day for the latter part of his life.

"Afternoon, Henry," I began, searching the mahogany coffee table for reading material to occupy my hands. "How is life treating you?"

"Well, my goodness, *Paul*," he said, acknowledging my sudden appearance with surprise and affection. "What an unexpected pleasure. It's been a long time. We never see you around these parts anymore."

Anymore was a generous misreading. I had never been a regular attendee at the club. I searched my memory and couldn't recall a single lunch or cocktail hour since Mardi Gras Day a year ago.

"The company's got me running nonstop. We're launching a new gourmet brand, so I'm practically sleeping at my office these days," I said, a shameless lie.

He smiled at me, gallant and restrained. "Very good," he said with an approving blink. "Charlie would be pleased that you're taking your responsibilities so seriously."

He said this with cautious optimism, as if responsible behavior was a shocking turnabout for me.

Henry Lesseps was now in his mid-seventies, a tall dapper man wearing a silver-gray suit with a black and red striped tie. He kept trim by playing eighteen holes of golf every weekend at the country club in Metairie. He and my father had been classmates at Tulane in the 1930s, but Henry had grown more vigorous with age while my father's health had declined into obesity and heart disease. Dad had always been jealous of his friend's vitality and good looks, and he would call him Hollywood Hank whenever the attorney appeared at our swimming pool wearing his sunglasses and sporting a stunning tan. His most popular nickname was Henry the Fifth, although the origin of the moniker was uncertain and a source of whispered dispute. Some said it was because his clients were notorious for taking the Fifth Amendment on the stand, others insisted it was because he held the record for most challenges to the Fifth Circuit Court of Appeals. Still others joked that he could put away a fifth of scotch and still recite entire statutes of the Napoleonic Code in French.

Whatever the reason, whether endearment or derision, his peers in the Magnolia Club and the mandarins of Uptown society treated him with the highest respect and deferred to Henry Lesseps as the most intelligent and articulate living defender of their interests.

"How did the hearing go?" he asked. "I haven't had a chance to speak with Eric yet. Did our man win parole?"

He was the named partner in the law firm of Glynn, Gautier & Lesseps.

"I'm afraid not," I said glumly.

"I'm sorry," he said with a resigned shake of the head. "I knew the odds were against him. If Eric couldn't convince those gentlemen, they must be a tough bunch to please."

"They're impossible," I said. I was tempted to complain about Eric's strategy, but I didn't want to get him in trouble with the firm.

"No need to punish yourself, Paul. Your family has done its best by that young man," he said, as if Jaren was still the same druggy twenty-two-year-old scruff wearing an off-kilter afro. "Your father, rest his soul, spent a considerable amount of money on the boy's defense when his mother couldn't afford a good attorney. If Charlie hadn't come forward, the case would've gone to a public defender."

Henry's longish hair was wavy and white, with faint yellow streaks the color of stained chicken feathers in the combed-back wings above his ears. He spoke through a thick-set jaw that sometimes obstructed his tongue and teeth, one of the few signs of his aging, but his blue-green eyes glowed with a youthful exuberance.

"You Blanchards have taken very good care of Rosetta," he said. "Her life has been quite comfortable. Far better than others of her station. There's some consolation in that, Paul. You've gone well beyond what anyone expected," he said, raising a hand in an obliging gesture. "My advice—let it go. He'll be out when he's out."

Henry and I clearly did not shoulder the same burden of conscience.

"We need to take some time to rethink our approach," I said. I had no intention of dropping the next parole petition, with or without the help of Glynn, Gautier & Lesseps. "And then decide whether or not we've got a chance."

"Good man," he smiled.

A corpulent old waiter named Walter materialized between our chairs and offered a cordial greeting. "Afternoon, Mistah Blanchud. Haven't seen you here in much too long. Gin and tonic, is it?"

"Yes, it is, Walter."

He had served drinks at the Magnolia Club for thirty-five years and was a master of memory and charm.

"A fresh scotch, Mistah Leh-sups?"

"Yes, thank you, Walter. Mighty fine."

The old waiter retrieved Henry's empty tumbler and slowly made his way toward the door. I could hear a growing hum of voices down the corridor, the hour luring more members to the club. Soon the library would be overrun with drinkers, their conversations loud and gregarious. I had little time to ask Henry Lesseps the question I had come to ask.

He set aside his *Journal* and nodded at the *Times-Picayune* spread across the coffee table between us. "Can you believe that woman?" he said. The front-page photograph of the ever feisty Wilhelmina Phillips stared at us with a mocking defiance. "She's been pushing that foolish agenda ever since she took office. And now she's managed to drag the whole thing into a public debate. Dammit, I can't believe she's forced our hand on this."

He formed a fist and dropped it like a gavel against the soft leather arm of the chair.

"I wish it were otherwise, Paul, but we have no choice but to gird our loins and go into battle. I tell you, sometimes I wish we could...." He hardened his jaw and clenched both fists, then quickly calmed himself. "I hate to admit it, but this gets my blood boiling."

I had rarely seen him so agitated. He was known as a man of patience and dispassionate deliberation. Ages ago there had been talk of him running for political office, but his short stint as assistant district attorney had apparently put an end to that ambition. He'd clashed with his boss, Jim Garrison, during the infamous JFK assassination investigation and eventually resigned. According to my father, the experience had discouraged Henry of any further interest in public life.

"I hope you'll join us in the council chambers tomorrow afternoon," he said, his eyes fixed with a steely concentration. "I've agreed to represent our side of the argument, but I'll need all the support I can get. The blacks will be there in force to make their case. We've got to put bodies in the chamber and mount serious resistance or we're beaten."

I smiled at him. "That'll be a dead giveaway, won't it, Henry? A phalanx of white businessmen in three-piece suits pretending to be concerned citizens? Willie and the whole town will know we're krewe."

He shrugged and placed his long bony fingers in his lap. "They don't know one krewe from another, Paul. And we'll never tell them." A small roguish smile tugged at the corners of his mouth. "Tomorrow afternoon a white contingent will be there *en masse*. That's all they'll see, and all they need to know. We'll spread out around the chamber in case they've got a grenade."

I smiled. The door had opened for my purposes. "An unaffiliated white delegation?"

"Exactly." This devilish subterfuge seemed to animate him.

"A white league," I said, waiting for his reaction.

He shrugged again, revealing nothing. "If you will," he said.

"The White League attacks the usurpers," I said with a wry grin. "Our forefathers would be proud."

The rogue's smile was there again, dueling with his natural restraint. "I didn't realize you were a student of local history, Paul," he said.

I gazed around the old library at the lace curtains and pier glass mirrors and delicate gilt trim, absorbing the fact that this was the very room where Fred Ogden and his gentlemen colleagues had formed the Crescent City White League. In these ancient leather chairs a dozen defeated, disgruntled Confederates had gathered to vent their rage about the Reconstruction government and insolent Negroes, and to devise a plan to amass weapons and throw the oppressors out. This was where they'd penned their call to arms in the summer of 1874, according to Father Joe and that frayed green book, and where the officers had retreated for brandy and Havana cigars after the Battle of Canal Street had ended and the White League had claimed victory.

Walter returned with our drinks and I tipped him handsomely, then waited for him to limp away before I spoke again.

"Willie's an ambitious lady," I said, shuffling through the news pages on the coffee table until I found the sidebar article I'd read in Eric's car. "Did you see that she wants to remove the old White League monument as well?"

"Par for the course," Henry said, taking comfort in his single malt scotch. "She won't rest until she destroys every last vestige of Civil War history in the city."

"Tomorrow's going to be a long day," I said. "Mark Morvant's organized a rally to save the monument."

He sighed, worn down before the battle had even begun. "I wish that fellow would stay out of it."

"Morvant?"

"He pushes everything to the extreme. We don't need a showboater taking up our cause. He makes us all look like raving baboons."

I was sorry to hear he had so little regard for Mark Morvant and his politics. I had hoped to call on Henry for a private donation to the Morvant campaign.

"I guess I'm still naive enough to believe we can preserve our southern heritage without the tar and feathers," he said.

The voices were growing louder in the corridor. I was running out of time.

"Do you suppose the White League will show up at Morvant's rally?" I asked, forcing the issue into the open.

He raised the scotch to his lips and peered at me over the rim of the glass, indulging in a long silent drink. The hardness in his narrow eyes left me unsettled, and I felt as if I were being spied on through a sniper's scope. He seemed to be buying time, considering how to respond. When he lowered the glass finally, he worked his thick jaw in a subtle chewing motion, savoring the drink.

"Lesseps *grandpère* fought in that battle," he said with a proud smile. "If he were around today, the old boy'd be out there tomorrow morning with his seven-shot Spencer carbine, defending that monument with his life."

"I've been told that the White League still exists, Henry, and that they're very much in charge of things," I said. "I hear they haven't lost a step since the good old days."

He made a soft clearing noise in his throat and smiled at me with what seemed like sympathy. "The White League?" he said, amused. "Going strong after all these years? That's an intriguing idea. Where is this coming from, Paul?"

I glanced over at the old judge seated at the other end of the library. He was deaf as a post and absorbed in his Shakespeare. Feeling momentarily immune from exposure, I withdrew the crumpled stationery from the inside pocket of my sport coat and stood up, handing Henry the note without explanation. He slipped on his bifocals and quickly read my father's message, then stared at me over the top of the glasses.

"How on earth did you get this? Have you been digging through our dumpster, you rascal?" he asked with equal portions of astonishment and good-humored razzing.

"It turned up," I said, shrugging indifferently. "What does it mean, Henry? 'Must get the League together.' What League was my father talking about?"

He looked me over, a critical assessment of my slumped posture and crossed legs, and for a moment I thought he might lecture me on proper comportment, as my father had done from time to time when I was younger. But suddenly he burst into laughter, his entire body shaking as he removed his glasses and wiped his eyes with a handkerchief.

"My God, I miss Charlie," he said, wiping the lenses as well. "He had a wonderfully dry sense of humor, didn't he? I could always count on him to raise my spirits when things were grim. If he were still alive, he'd be sitting right next to me tomorrow afternoon in the council chambers, passing me sarcastic notes while I'm standing there like a jackass arguing against the ordinance."

He tossed the stationery onto the coffee table with an air of dismissal, as though it were the prosecutor's weak exhibit at trial. "He was joking, Paul," he said, chuckling to himself. "That foolish woman was stirring up trouble again and Charlie wanted to know 'Where is the damned White League when you need them?' That's all it was, son. One of Charlie's dry jokes. Goodness, he could make me laugh. I miss him more than you can imagine."

A joke between old friends. It made sense. But I could already hear the ridicule and doubt in Morvant's voice. He wasn't going to buy this simple explanation.

"Henry, I know the White League met secretly for years—and well into the twentieth century. They were always working behind the scenes," I said, an artless bluff and my parting attempt to find out the truth once and for all. "I've seen a photograph of my Great Granddad Blanchard at the monument ceremony in the 1930s. Your grandfather was there, too, and a dozen old Leaguers with one foot in the grave."

"Oh yes, I remember that ceremony, Paul. I was in college, then, and I went down to watch their last hurrah. Those poor old duffers couldn't remember their own names," Henry said with sadness in his voice. "Their best years were far behind them."

I uncrossed my legs and sat up straight. "Had they kept the White League going?" I asked. "You know—passed it on to another generation?"

He nodded once, with an emphatic blink. "When your father and I were growing up, we heard stories about the League and what they were capable of. Workers would go on strike at the docks or shut down a cigar factory owned by one of the families, and sure enough the labor instigators would be dragged out in the middle of the night and beaten, their meeting hall burned to the ground. If a black man tried to register to vote, his house was bombed. People knew that the White League could make anything happen. When I was ten or twelve years old I asked my dad about them and he told me I would learn such things in due time." He paused and smiled at me. "But only if I proved myself worthy of their trust."

I had the distinct feeling his remark was aimed at me.

"And did you earn their trust?" I asked. "Did they ever invite you in?"

He opened his mouth in a silent laugh, his formidable jaw

hanging like a lowered bridge. I could see silver fillings in his molars.

"Yes, they did, Paul. But under very peculiar circumstances," he said. "One day when I was studying at Tulane, Dad phoned me long distance from Baton Rouge. I believe it was January or February of 1935," he said, his eyes shining with the clarity of that moment. "He told me to find your father, Charlie Blanchard, and a couple of hunting rifles, and to meet him at the Baton Rouge airport. This was it, he said. My initiation into the League. We were going to kill Huey Long."

My shocked reaction gave him great satisfaction and he laughed.

"He was involved in something called the Square Deal Association. They were furious with Huey and his political corruption. About three hundred of them had armed themselves and taken over a courthouse in East Baton Rouge Parish, but the National Guard had shown up and chased them all out. He called to tell me they were reassembling at the airport, where Long was supposed to be landing in a few hours. He wanted Charlie and me to join their hit squad."

I knew that the Uptown aristocracy had despised the Kingfish and his mentally ill brother Earl Long, who became governor later on. I had heard my father rail against the Longs my entire life, even though Huey was assassinated before I was born and Earl had died pathetic, powerless, and insane. The blue bloods hated those two populist crackers as much as they hated conniving Italians and loud-mouthed blacks. Huey Long, in turn, had felt socially ostracized by the snobbish Mardi Gras crowd and had punished them by cutting off state funds to New Orleans, taking control of various municipal departments, siphoning city tax revenues into the state coffers, and sending fully armed National Guardsmen into New Orleans from time to time in a demonstration of power.

"They called themselves the Square Deal Association, but the White League was behind it all the way," Henry said. "Didn't your father ever tell you this story?"

"Not a word," I said. My father had rarely shared a childhood or college memory. He wasn't a man who volunteered personal information.

"Charlie and I were barely twenty years old and full of piss and gunpowder. We drove up to Baton Rouge in my family's Touring Car, loaded with a couple of rifles and Colt pistols and an old Confederate saber that hung in my father's study. We didn't take the phone call seriously and indulged in a few snorts of brandy along the way. I thought Dad might be pulling my leg, but when we got to the airport we saw their automobiles circled out by the runway. There were probably a hundred men with weapons, and they were in a sour mood after being routed by Huey's guardsmen. By then they'd worked up more courage and were mad as hell. You have to understand that most of them were educated gentlemen, bankers and lawyers and insurance brokers from the city, and they looked like English gentry out for a hunt with their hounds. My father was walking around with a twelve-gauge shotgun tucked against his ribs and Charlie's daddy—your grandfather—had some kind of World War One carbine. It was a cold winter's day and we mostly sat in our cars and smoked cigarettes and passed the brandy flask. I'm not sure what the plan was. Nobody seemed to know what to do. I guess we were all supposed to open fire when Huey stepped off his plane."

He laughed, acknowledging that the incident had been a ludicrous, poorly conceived idea. The scotch had loosened his tongue and he was in an ebullient mood.

-Telling the story clearly delighted him. His face was animated by a stately smile.

"Your daddy and I hid out in the woods till dark, then came on back in. Oddly enough, they didn't confiscate the Touring Car. We hopped in that baby and roared over to the Baton Rouge parish jail. The arrested men had already made bail and were gone. I don't think Huey intended to prosecute them—just let them know who was boss in Louisiana. A few weeks later he dropped the charges and nobody was ever indicted."

I was amused now myself. I couldn't picture my genteel father hiding on his belly in the wintry woods.

"The irony is, we didn't have to go to so much trouble," Henry said. "Less than a year later that Dr. Weiss fellow shot Huey Long in the state capitol building. The sorry bastard's days were numbered."

I noticed several club members outside the library doorway, drinks in hand, greeting one another with brotherly cheer. They would be upon us at any moment.

"And that was your initiation into the White League?"

"My first and last encounter," he said, his eyes dancing around the memory. "I never heard another word about the League after that. The Battle of the Airport was their final humiliation."

I took a long needy drink of gin and tonic. "Quite a different experience than the Battle of Canal Street," I said. "Where were Fred Ogden and his troops when you needed them?"

He smiled at my remark. "Precisely," he said. "And that's all your father was saying in the note." He gestured to the veined page of stationery lying on the coffee table. "Lord, I could use him and his sense of humor tomorrow afternoon."

The first two members to invade the quiet library were Basil Parker and Claude Villere, highly opinionated men whose audacity and rudeness usually swelled with each glass of sherry. They were both around sixty years old, indolent and excessively indulgent, and had managed to avoid any semblance of professional duty all their lives. I didn't like either one, although we had a great deal in common. All three of us were living off someone else's industry.

"Look who's here!" Basil effused as he bobbed across the carpet on oxblood penny loafers. "Are my eyes deceiving me, Claude, or is that Blanchard *fils* sitting in his daddy's old chair?"

I retrieved the note, folded it, and stuck it inside my jacket. "Hello, gentlemen," I said, raising my glass. "Cheers and chin-chin."

"Let's wave to the judge, everyone," Basil said, waving theatrically at the old man. The judge looked up from his pages, smiled open-mouthed, and returned the wave. He couldn't hear a word Basil was saying.

"What's he reading, *Othello?*" Basil asked. "We don't want him ruling on miscegenation or the sodomy laws, do we, boys? Hello, Judge! Good to see you. Thank you oh-so-much for the mess we're in, you commie shit."

Basil Parker was a short, fat man with a coal black toupee, jowled features, and a deep dimple in his chin. He dressed stylishly—some would say foppishly—and despite his two marriages and four children, I had always thought he was gay. Today he was wearing a charcoal gray blazer with a maroon turtleneck, and I could smell his cologne from ten feet away. Basil's year-round parties were the talk of the town, and he was much beloved by his friends in the Uptown social set. No one knew the exact source of his income. Family money, of course, in something as mundane and unsavory as insurance or real estate. His grandfather had been one of the most virulently racist governors the state of Louisiana had ever produced.

"I've been trying to talk young Blanchard into joining the fun tomorrow afternoon," Henry said, smiling at me. "Perhaps you gents can twist his arm."

"You'd better be there, Blanchard," Basil said, one hand cocked on his wide hip, "or we'll tell everyone your coffee is made from ground-up pickaninny hair."

Claude Villere found this enormously funny. He laughed so hard the cabernet sauvignon sloshed in his glass. "Basil, how crude," he said.

Claude was the Mutt to Basil Parker's Jeff. Tall and angular, with the ruddy, venous skin of a freckled boy turned sixty, his most distinguishing feature was a silver mustache whose choppy shape resembled a well-worn toothbrush. He sported large horn-rimmed glasses that were out of proportion to his birdlike head and the silver hair that rose stiffly like a waxed tuft from it. Claude had married wisely, into the Whitney Bank family, and had managed one branch or another when he was younger, but it was widely known that he'd shown no aptitude for banking, and in time his in-laws had paid him generously to stay out of the office.

"Paul thinks the old Crescent City White League may show up tomorrow—with their bugles blowing—to rescue us from Willie Phillips and her cohorts," Henry said with a mischievous grin.

The three men exchanged laughs. I was mortified that Henry had revealed our conversation.

"The dear old White League certainly had the right idea,"

Claude said, making a pistol with his free hand. "Shoot first and cast your ballots later."

For the usual corrupt reasons, the current governor had appointed Claude as chairman of the board of the Louisiana State Museum, and the silly man was known to wander about the Cabildo uninvited, lecturing tourists and shamelessly bossing the employees.

The library was beginning to fill with other members and the murmur of many voices. I had wanted to tell Henry about what had happened to Father Dombrowski in 1964 and gauge his reaction, but I'd lost my chance. I finished my drink quickly and stood to leave.

"Don't hurry off, Blanchard," Basil said. "We haven't called the League to order yet. The night is young," he said with a wicked gleam in his eye, "and we may vote to go out and lynch some Italians."

I thought about my brother Perry and wondered which of these men had been making those phone calls to him over the years. The calls that said, *Behave, young Blanchard, we've got our eye on you.* Could it have been Basil or Claude or even Henry Lesseps?

"Nice to see everyone," I said. "Good-bye, Henry."

Henry pulled himself out of the leather chair and shook my hand. "You'll join us tomorrow afternoon, I hope," he said, his hand as cold and rigid as a cadaver's. "Don't disappoint us, Paul."

Don't disappoint us. The same message my brother had heard all his life.

I bid a brisk hello/good-bye to a handful of my father's old friends as I made my way down the corridor through the gallery of dead presidents. Ghostly eyes followed my every footstep in this haunted mansion, giving me an unsettling sensation of always being watched. I didn't know what gave me pause to glance up at one of the portraits—a bearded dandy who looked like an urbane version of George Armstrong Custer, his flowing cravat as silky as a woman's scarf. Something about the man had caught my attention and I saw now what it was. A familiar dark butterfly bow sat on his upper lapel, the sign of the White League. I ambled along the row of presidential portraits, looking for others with the telltale bow. How many were there?

"Hello, young Blanchard!" someone called from the dark end

of the hall. He was standing in the twilight shadow with two other tall figures. I could hear the ice clinking in their glasses. "What are our coffee shares going for today?"

I waved at them without responding and hurried on toward the garage elevator. For a fleeting moment I thought I heard them all laughing behind my back.

Chapter fifteen

I phoned Mark Morvant at both his home and his office and received the same recording of his honeyed baritone voice assuring me that my message was important and promising a prompt response. I was eager to tell him I'd spoken to Henry Lesseps and to relate Henry's explanation of the note from my father, but I found myself in the uncomfortable position of defending an account I didn't quite believe. What about the black velvet bow stuffed into Father Joe's mouth? Still, I wanted Morvant off my back as soon as possible. Despite my own doubts, I needed to convince him that the White League had dissolved in the 1930s and he was chasing after phantoms. I couldn't abide the idea of spending the next three weeks running around in circles trying to satisfy his desperate hunger for campaign support.

The telephone rang around ten o'clock, while I was reading that old green book in the family library. I lifted the receiver, prepared to deliver the long oration I'd been rehearsing all evening. But it wasn't Mark Morvant.

"Collect call from the Louisiana State Penitentiary," the operator announced in a brittle clip of syllables. "Will you accept the charges?"

I was caught off guard. In the twenty years of his incarceration, Jaren had never spoken directly to me by phone. The idea unnerved me. I didn't know what I could possibly say to him after what had happened at Angola today.

"Yes, I accept," I managed to respond.

"Go ahead, then," the operator instructed.

There was a long faltering pause, as if the connection required more technical service. I waited, my palms beginning to perspire. A recorded message informed me, "This call may be monitored for your own protection." It did not make me feel any safer.

Then finally Jaren's serene voice, unchanged after all these years: "Sorry to bother you so late. I didn't know who else to call."

"No problem, Jaren. Anytime," I said, rushing nervously into an apology. "I'm sorry about the hearing. I don't know what it's going to take to get you out of there."

A weighty silence. I could hear him draw a breath before he spoke again. "That's not why I'm calling," he said. "I'm worried about mama."

"She's fine, Jaren. The prison doctors examined her thoroughly and kept her under close observation for a good long while, and she rested all the way back to New Orleans. When I left her at home she was her old self again."

"I've been calling her all night," he said. "She ain't answering."

I didn't like the sound of that. "Maybe she went to bed early."

"I call her every Friday night. She lives for it, Speed. She wouldn't crash without talking to me. Especially after what went down today."

He'd called me Speed since we were kids. And not because I was swift and athletic, but because I wasn't.

"I'll drive over there and see what's going on. Give me a number where I can reach you and I'll call you back in half an hour."

"I appreciate it," he said.

He seemed remarkably calm for a man who had been denied his freedom only a few short hours ago.

"We're going to get you out of there, Two J," I said. And I meant it.

"Yeah, unhunh. You and that brilliant lawyer friend of yours," he said. "Only do me a small favor first. Go check on my mama."

The night was damp and still, the neighborhood as morbidly quiet as the small old Jewish cemetery I passed on my short drive down Arabella Street to Rosetta's bungalow. Safety spotlights blazed from the peaked roofs along the row of renovated shotguns, but Rosetta's place was dark, both outside and within. I knocked hard and rang the doorbell several times, but there was no answer. Fortunately she had given me a key during her chemo sessions a few months back, when I was chauffeuring her to the clinic, and I used it to let myself in.

"Rosetta, it's me! Paul! Are you here?"

I called her name again, repeating myself louder and louder as I plodded cautiously through the unlit living room full of old lady furniture. I didn't want to startle her. And I certainly didn't want her to shoot me as a burglar.

I found her lying face down on the floor near her bed. The television was playing softly, its gray light flickering across the tidy room. She was wearing a heavy bathrobe and only one slipper. I knelt quickly, checked her pulse, and discovered she was still alive—but her breathing was shallow and labored.

"Rosetta, can you hear me?" I asked, patting her wan cheek. She had placed her wig on a head mannequin atop her dresser, and without the hairpiece her scalp was covered in a coarse gray stubble that made her look masculine and very old.

"Don't worry, darlin'," I said, "I'm going to get us some help."

I dialed 911 and then sat on the floor, holding her head in my lap, waiting for EMS to arrive. I stroked her arm and told her how much I loved her, and how much Perry and Kathleen and Claire and our children loved her, and how Jaren had loved and missed her every day. My mind was afloat with memories of her warm laughter at the little playground a few blocks away and those cold Mardi Gras mornings when she'd held our hands among rowdy strangers, protecting us through the showers of beads. I was overwhelmed by the prospect of losing her and my body went numb and all I could feel was her presence next to me, then and now and forever. I could almost hear her heart beating slower, fainter. I didn't want her life to end this way.

When the attendants finally appeared in the bedroom with their stretcher and oxygen equipment, I was in tears and unwilling to let go of her. Only later would I remember the strong young medic who had lifted me up and walked me out of the house into the cool night drizzle. The EMS van lights were flashing and neighbors had gathered along the sidewalk and I found myself sitting on the curb across the street, clutching my trembling knees. The minutes dragged on while they ministered to her in the house. When I realized they might be bringing her out in a body bag, the darkness felt like my only friend in this whole messed-up world.

I didn't hear him walk up, but suddenly there he was, standing over me, his hulking physique stuffed into jeans and a hooded running jacket. I didn't bother to look up until the man spoke and I recognized his voice.

"You figure it was the stress?"

"I don't know, Lieutenant Castle. I'm not a doctor."

"She seem all right when you brought her home?"

I nodded. "I should've checked back with her a while ago. This is my fault."

He lit a cigarette and took a long drag, staring toward the house and the flashing EMS van. "Got a call from Angola," he said. "Two J told me you were coming over here. He said you were s'posed to call him back."

I didn't want to talk to Jaren right now. In my emotional state I really couldn't face him. "Why don't you make the call," I said. "Tell him what's happened."

"Let's see how this comes out, first."

We didn't speak for several minutes. He finished his cigarette and mashed it underfoot on the damp pavement. I could hear the neighbors conversing quietly, concern etched in their faces. Mostly older people, black and white, folks who had known Rosetta for ten or fifteen years. No one was leaving yet.

"Did you tell her?" Castle asked, his deep voice penetrating the silence.

I knew what he was talking about and I just wanted him to stop. I was in no condition to play games with him anymore.

He peered down at me and repeated himself, as if he thought I hadn't understood the question. "Did you tell her, son? Is that what did this to her?"

An EMS attendant banged open the screen door and the gurney was wheeled onto the porch. Rosetta was swaddled in a white sheet, her thin body strapped to the table. I stood up from the curb and stared at the police lieutenant. "Leave me alone," I said. I could hear the anger shaking my voice.

He stared back, his fleshy face pinched and weary in the flashing red light. "I'll make your phone call for you, son. But sooner or later, you'll have to make that call yourself. It's long overdue."

I was angry enough to curse him. But I knew better than to do that. "Leave me alone, Lieutenant Castle," I said through clenched teeth. "Do you understand me? I don't want to hear this shit right now."

I walked away from him and crossed the street to hold my nanny's hand.

Chapter sixteen

I called Claire from a pay phone in the hospital waiting room. It was nearly midnight, but she was still awake, and worried. I had told her I was going to check on Rosetta, and when I didn't return within the hour she'd phoned Rosetta's place and received no answer. She knew something was wrong.

"What are the doctors saying?" she asked, her voice as tight as a platinum wire.

"Her blood pressure's weak. Could be a heart attack or stroke. She's definitely dehydrated and they're pumping her full of liquids. They've got to stabilize her before they run any tests."

"Poor woman. She's had a miserable day," Claire said. "I would come down there but the kids are asleep."

"No, it's okay. You can see her tomorrow."

"What are you going to do?"

"I'll stay here a while longer," I said. "Until they tell me she's out of danger."

"Do you need anything? I can send something by cab."

I needed her love and understanding. I needed to hear the joy in her voice the way it used to sound. I needed to hear her laugh again. I needed to turn back the clock and face my own duplicity and free a frail old woman from her grief. None of these things were available by cab.

"No, sweetheart," I said. "I'll be fine. Just send nice thoughts our way."

I was allowed to look through the glass panel into Rosetta's room in the Intensive Care Unit, but not to go inside. For two hours I made periodic visits to her door. She was sleeping in a tangle of tubes and monitor cords, surrounded by IV stands and electronic screens blinking and tracking graphs. An oxygen mask covered her mouth and nose. I didn't know if she was conscious of where she was and what had happened to her. I wondered if she could hear my voice if I snuck inside the room and spoke to her. *If you love that ol' lady like I think you do,* James Castle had said, *before she pass....* Would she understand my words if I bent down close to her ear and confessed the whole awful truth?

Shortly after two A.M. I conferred with a night nurse who assured me that Rosetta was stable and showing signs of improvement. "She won't be going home anytime soon," the woman said, "but she'll be released from ICU in a few hours and placed in a regular room."

The nurse was a solid-built black woman in her mid-thirties. She looked up from her chart. "Is Mrs. Jarboe your—"

She stopped herself, searching for a way to properly frame the question. There was a disarming innocence about her curiosity.

"My aunt," I said. Down here we pronounced the word *awnt.*

"Un-hunh," she said, nodding, understanding instantly that I'd meant long-time nanny, housekeeper, or cook. A word from the unwritten code of the city, a private vocabulary we all shared. It wasn't so much a lie as an honest attempt by good people to show respect.

"Is she covered under your insurance?" she asked, jotting something on the chart.

"Yes, she is."

"Okay, thank you, Mr. Blanchard." She glanced up, catching my eye. "You related to the people that make the coffee?"

I nodded. "I run the place."

She looked me over and shook her head. "You owe me stock

options," she said, narrowing her eyes. "You got any idea how much of your product I drink just to keep myself awake on this job?"

I tried to smile. "I'll send you a case on Monday. Compliments of the family."

She peered through the glass door panel at Rosetta lying in bed. "Why don't you go on home and get some sleep, Mr. Blanchard. Your aunt's in good hands tonight. We'll see what the doctors tell us tomorrow."

Outside, in the early morning darkness, a windy norther was sweeping cold rain across the silent city. I drove home beneath the swaying oak limbs of Prytania Street, my windshield wipers fighting the steady downpour. Just before I turned into the driveway and signaled the electronic gate-opener, I noticed a car parked on the side street in the same spot where Officer Junius had confronted Louis Robb. Was it Morvant's man again, watching my home at this late hour in the shivering rain? What in God's name was the point?

I circled the block and slowed down as I approached the Oldsmobile's rear end, flaring my bright lights to read the license plate and shake up the lone figure slumped behind the wheel. I idled alongside the driver's door and whirred down my window, struggling to see through the rain.

"Hey, you!" I shouted. "What the fuck are you doing here? Taking names? Tell your boss they don't march around my lawn when it's two in the morning and pouring down rain!"

There was no response from inside the big Olds, no movement, only the sound of heavy rain beating on its roof. I couldn't tell if the vehicle was occupied or if I was seeing shadows.

In the comfort of my home I crawled quietly into bed next to Claire, trying my best not to wake her. But she moaned and rolled over to face me, her breath against my cheek, and for the first time in many months I felt her slender arm around my body.

Chapter seventeen

Breakfast was a dismal ordeal around the kitchen table. I explained Rosetta's condition to Claire, the two children, and Dell and Corinne, who floated about near the service island in an emotional silence, unable to keep still or meet my eyes. Andy appeared the most shaken. His soft, androgynous face lost its color and his eyes grew moist as I described finding Rosetta on her bedroom floor. She was like a grandmother to him and Julie, especially since my mother's stroke. He loved Rosetta because he was supposed to, and because she was good to him. And she loved him because he was another innocent child who needed her attention.

"Does this have anything to do with the cancer?" Julie asked, chewing a mouthful of toast.

"I don't think so," I said. "I think it's something else."

Claire looked sleepless and slightly frayed, as if she'd been the one waiting in the hospital half the night. "She had a very rough day. It was probably just too much for her," she said. "She'll be on her feet in no time, guys. You wait and see."

At ten o'clock I phoned the hospital and was told that Rosetta was alert and improving steadily, and that the staff was beginning to run a series of tests. I was advised to delay visiting until the afternoon.

I called Morvant's office again, and this time a young female aide answered in person. "This morning Representative Morvant is leading a rally to support keeping the Liberty Monument right where it is," she reported.

The Liberty Monument was what smug white diehards had always called the White League memorial at the base of Canal Street.

"There's going to be a battle reenactment, which should be good family fun. Sons of the True South, I think the group is called," the aide said. "I'm sure the congressman would love to see you at the rally."

She sounded reasonably intelligent and competent. I wondered how *Intern with white supremacist* would look on her résumé.

"I left a message for him last night," I said, adding that I was an old fraternity brother and this was a personal matter.

"Why don't you go by the monument and give him your support? Mr. Morvant is working hard to preserve our history," she intoned, with a subtle emphasis on the word *our*. She knew she was speaking to a white person. "But he's run up against a lot of angry opposition. He would appreciate you being there."

There was no way to avoid what I had to do. It was in my best interest to speak with Morvant as soon as I could. He would have to be satisfied with a generous campaign contribution from me and me alone. The White League did not exist anymore. That was Henry's story and I was sticking to it.

I struggled with the idea of throwing on jeans and a sweatshirt and sneaking through the crowd incognito. But I didn't want to be mistaken for a crackpot Confederate sympathizer, so I dressed in cotton slacks with a tweed sport jacket and tie. When I consulted my image in the mirror I saw an aging preppie who could stand to shed a few pounds and get a sharper haircut.

The rain had lasted only an hour during the night but the streets were still wet and puddled with murky water. Drainage was always a problem in a city six feet below sea level. The mild norther gusting toward the Gulf had left behind a crispness in the air, and the sky was clear and blue above the wilting date palms. Except for the faint dead-dog odor of decay, the morning felt hopeful and as light as the Mediterranean coast in spring.

I drove downtown along Magazine Street, where cans and paper debris had collected in the gutters like driftwood at low tide. An elderly Cuban grocer was sweeping the sidewalk in front of his store. Young bohemians wandered sleepy-eyed into the bistros with newspapers lodged under their arms. Narrow, dilapidated Magazine Street was the last refuge of the barber shops, drugstores, and five and dimes that had closed their doors a generation ago in upper America.

Many things had changed downtown since General Fred Ogden had led his White League troops on horseback to the cotton bales stacked along the Mississippi wharf. The tall masts had disappeared on the river, the cargo ships and passenger steamers were all gone, except for a frilly white paddle-wheeler employed as a tourist attraction, and the wharf had been transformed into a convention center, hotel, and long narrow shopping mall called the Riverwalk. A colossal new aquarium was under construction only a brick's hurl from where Metropolitan Police Chief Algernon Badger had been shot from his horse. There was serious talk about building a Las Vegas-style casino across the street to lure more tourist dollars to the city. The entire basin of Canal Street, where the famous boulevard deep-ended into the Mississippi River and the White League battle had claimed twenty-seven lives and left a hundred men wounded, was now a prime commercial location, towered over by chain hotels and parking garages and the sturdy steel beams of new construction projects rising into the sunlight. The only reminder of what had once taken place here, the teeming trade along the river and the battle to restore a way of life destroyed by war and Reconstruction, was a modest marble obelisk bearing the names of the dead white men who had fought for fifteen minutes in a fleeting moment of glory. The last time I had actually stopped to view the monument, while touring a group of Colombian coffee growers through the Riverwalk, I'd been struck by how slight and shabby the edifice appeared, like an old rock shard kicked loose amid the shiny glass and brick architecture surrounding it. If not for the fact that traffic had to detour around the spire, no one would have noticed it at all. A small, inconspicuous memorial by any measure, it hardly seemed worth the rancor it had aroused in New Orleans political circles for the past twenty years.

To accommodate the rally and battle reenactment, police barricades had routed traffic away from the monument. As I cruised down Canal Street in my BMW, I saw the TV satellite trucks and a cordon of uniformed officers and realized that the event had taken on more significance because of tensions between Wilhelmina Phillips and the white establishment. I could drive no closer than Fulton Street and was forced to detour through an industrial warehouse area, where I circled back and found the parking lot for the Riverwalk mall. While setting my car alarm, I noticed a Confederate general astride a white stallion in an empty handicap parking space near the ticket arm. With a long waxed mustache and chin whiskers, his saber drawn, he gazed like a stone sculpture toward the Liberty Monument another fifty yards beyond. Two dozen cotton bales had been dragged into the parking lot to create a wall of defense, and a hundred of the general's White League troops huddled behind the bales with their Winchesters and flintlock Prussian muskets. A rough-looking bunch, all middle-aged or older, their beards authentic, they were costumed in CSA grays and partial uniforms scrapped together for the occasion. More than anything else they resembled an aging biker gang playing make-believe soldiers. I knew that these fringe-element Confederate reenactors drilled in secrecy, like the original White League itself, marching and firing cannons out in the woods and debating failed Civil War strategies like a klatch of garden club matrons discussing a romance novel. Rare invitations like these, maybe four times a year in outlying corners of the Old South, summoned them to blow their bugles and wave the Dixie flag and lumber into action. They were all barefoot twelve-year-old boys at heart, living in their heads, fantasizing the way it should have happened on the distant smoky battlefields of Antietam and Gettysburg.

Horns were honking in the lot, irate drivers backed up to the ticket booth, their public parking spaces occupied by cumbersome cotton bales. The rag-tag soldiers held their positions with a fearless resolve. They'd come from as far away as Hattiesburg, Pine Bluff, and Ville Platte to stage a battle and they weren't giving ground to weekend shoppers driving Suburbans.

Louis Robb was the first person I recognized near the monument. His shaved head, like a leathery aviator's cap, stood out above the other men standing in a small group next to the speaker's platform. They looked like redneck deputies out of uniform from backwater St. Bernard Parish. Potbellied, mullet-haired Gomers, all wearing sinister wraparound sunglasses and scowling at the television cameras. Robb noticed my approach and gave me an ominous smile. I wondered if he'd heard me screaming at his Oldsmobile last night in the pouring rain.

Mark Morvant was speaking into a microphone set up on the wooden platform at the base of the Liberty Monument. I walked up in time to hear him utter the words *ancestry* and *preservation* and *First Amendment rights protected by the Constitution*. Three grim-jawed flag bearers stood at attention behind him, proudly displaying the American, Louisiana, and Dixie flags above their heads. The crowd numbered less than fifty, by my rough count, but they applauded Morvant enthusiastically and carried signs expressing their outrage that the monument might be taken from them. DON'T MESS WITH MY HERITAGE! WHITE PEOPLE HAVE RIGHTS TOO! News reporters ambled through the audience, interviewing onlookers and scratching notes on their pads.

I stood in the back of the assembly, perhaps sixty feet from the microphone, and listened to my old frat brother prattle on about *courage under siege* and *defending our birthright* and how the Battle of Canal Street had overthrown tyranny and oppression. I didn't want to be here, but it was the one sure place I could find him today. I intended on drawing him aside after the rally and discussing our business in private.

As I watched him work the crowd, I realized that years of addressing church socials and Kiwanis luncheons had polished his style. I appreciated the skills he'd developed as a public orator. He had presence, he projected well, he looked relaxed and in control. I couldn't welcome my own company managers to a working lunch without breaking into a cold sweat.

Mark Morvant had succeeded in capturing the media's attention because his Hollywood makeover contrasted so dramatically with the knuckle-dragging cretins who usually represented violent hate groups in the Deep South. With his blow-dried silver hair, handsome smile, and verbal acuity, he had become the JFK of white supremacy, confident and compelling and dapperly turned out. He had a clever wit and an ability to debate his opponents intelligently. He was in command of facts, figures, and historical anecdote. As a rule he'd never pounded his fist or spewed invectives, even in his most aggressive diatribes, and he'd charmed many a female interviewer with that *je ne sais quoi* animal magnetism that many of the best politicians possessed. Watching him mesmerize this audience now, with bold declarations and a charismatic smile, I asked myself what secret wound was driving all that repressed anger and need for revenge? What had caused a man with such raw natural appeal to take the low road of bitterness and retaliation? I wondered if there was some deep personal scar, something that had bruised him as a child, a fistfight or a shattering humiliation suffered at the hands of a black person or Jew.

I myself had never forgotten an incident from my own childhood, a memory that had surfaced from time to time throughout my life whenever I was pondering these things. Rosetta had taken Kathleen and me grocery shopping at Winn-Dixie, where there was a wonderful mechanical horse at the entrance, a galloping, gold-maned beauty that looked like Roy Rogers' Trigger. It cost a nickel to make the horse rock up and down, and Rosetta usually gave me one nickel to ride the animal while she pushed her basket through the aisles. After the ride was over I would sit on the horse and make shooting noises and fantasize about killing Indians and outlaws until another little boy or girl came along with their nickel, and then I would relinquish the saddle and watch their smiling faces as the magical horse rose and dipped across the western plains. One day a black boy about my age had walked up and rudely told me to get down off the horse, he had a nickel and wanted to ride. He was a skinny burr-headed kid with a runny nose and holes in the knees of his jeans, and a belt so long the tongue drooped down to his thigh. He had showed up eating a head of raw cabbage with both hands, pausing only to wipe snot on his shirt sleeve. An ugly brown scab on his ear had cracked and was threatening to bleed. I reluctantly dismounted the horse and watched him climb up onto the plastic saddle. He made shooting noises and spurred the horse with his heels and yipped wildly as he ate his cabbage and laughed down at me. *Where is your nickel?* I asked him. *You have to put your nickel in the slot.* He cackled and said, *I ain't got no nickel, you stupid white boy. Hah hah hah. You so stupid you give up yo' horse and I ain't got no nickel. Hah hah hah.*

I despised him for laughing and pointing his mess of cabbage at me. I despised him for lying and cheating and having no regard for manners and common decency. I despised him for being a nigger boy with a runny nose and holes in his pants and a hand-me-down belt. My sister Kathleen had materialized beside me and remarked, *Why don't you drag him off that horse and beat him senseless and teach that boy a proper lesson?*

I was thinking the same thing. I was thinking I shouldn't let a snot-nosed nigger boy disgrace me in public. I stepped forward to grab his leg and yank him off Trigger. I was worried that he might fight back and beat me up and add to my humiliation, but I knew that was the chance I had to take to defend my honor. But before I could do anything at all, his mother appeared suddenly and slapped him hard on the wounded ear. *Whatchou doin' eatin' that cabbage, boy?* she said, grabbing his arm and violently yanking him from the horse. *You got money to pay fuh dat? Git your ass down off dat thing and come on wit' me. We gotta pay fuh dat cabbage, now, fo' we leave this sto'. You li'l shit turd!*

I watched him slink away, his angry mother dragging him meanly by the wrist. He glanced back at me and smiled slyly, triumphantly, as if his free ride on Trigger had been worth all the trouble he was in. I suddenly felt sorry for that poor boy. His life was very different from mine, and would be, forever after. I would always have a nickel in my pocket, and he would always have a bleeding scab somewhere on his frail body.

That little nigger boy is gonna get a bad whippin' when he gets home, Kathleen had said that day. Over the years I had remembered that boy and Trigger and the incident in the Winn-Dixie. He would have been about forty years old by now, my age, if he was still alive.

Maybe something like that had happened in Mark Morvant's life. And maybe he'd remembered the mocking laughter of the sassy little boy, but not his bleeding ear.

When I looked up toward the platform, Morvant seemed to be staring directly at me as he spoke: "And so, my friends, this monument honors the White League not only for the bravery they showed in 1874, but for the impact their actions have had on our lives even today in 1990. The White League is not dead and forgotten—they live on!"

Raising a hand in the air, warding off the applause, he continued to stare at me with that winning smile, his words seemingly framed for my benefit.

"They inspire those of us who work for a stronger future for New Orleans and the state of Louisiana. Their spirit ennobles us, and we are proud to be their grandchildren and great grandchildren. Under their guiding hand, we will build a better tomorrow for our people."

The audience cheered energetically. I searched for familiar faces, looking for Uptown Brahmins of my father's generation, but I couldn't find a single withering soul who might remotely qualify for membership in the White League. He was wasting his breath on this crowd. These people were alienated white trash—gun freaks and grease monkeys and retired military folk—the same angry Y'ats who'd swung protest signs at little black girls trying to enter a school house in 1960. The white ruling elite did not attend high-profile media events with toothless rednecks.

A TV cameraman swept the crowd with his video rolling, and in a panic I turned my back and walked quickly away, mortified that I might be captured in background footage. I couldn't afford to show up as a Morvant supporter on the ten o'clock news.

That's when I noticed the blue-clad Union officer sitting atop his snorting steed. A serious-minded fellow with dark circles around his eyes and a bushy mustache and goatee, he was surrounded by a company of armed soldiers dressed in Yankee uniforms. A small crew of cannoneers attended what appeared to be an antique Civil War mountain howitzer, which they were aiming toward the White League reenactors hiding behind those cotton bales in the hotel parking lot. The two opposing forces were preparing to attack one another in mock battle, with television news cameras filming the staged melodrama.

"And now I will turn the program over to Yankee Police Chief Algernon Badger," Morvant said with a game smile, pointing toward the officer sitting on horseback, "and he will commence today's honor ceremony. Take it away, Chief Badger!"

The audience booed the Reconstruction police superintendent. The bearded actor ignored the insults and saluted Morvant with his saber, then turned to the cannoneers and slashed the air, commanding them to fire on the cotton bales. The old howitzer exploded with black smoke, an ear-ringing blast that echoed off the buildings nearby. Badger's horse whinnied and danced nervously, its shod hooves clacking on the pavement. The White League troops returned rifle fire. I could see their commander astride his stallion—the old tie maker Fred Ogden, I surmised—waving his sword and entreating his men to rush the Yankee dogs. Almost immediately the Met policemen began to fall. Their comrades dropped their weapons and retreated down the small side street next to the new aquarium construction, fleeing back to the French Quarter. When the actor playing Algernon Badger slipped from his saddle and sprawled on his back in the street, the audience cheered heartily and applauded the attacking White Leaguers, who by now had reached their enemies with bayonets flashing.

In the midst of the booming gunfire and shouting and orchestrated mayhem, I didn't notice the band of protesters making their way from a parking garage toward the battle scene until they were nearly upon us. There were about forty black people marching defiantly and chanting with placards raised. TEAR DOWN HATE! SAY NO TO RACISM! WHITE SUPREMACY MUST GO! I recognized the leader of the group as the Reverend Calvin Frazier, pastor of the New Zion Baptist Church, at eighty years old still the most passionate voice of the New Orleans civil rights movement. He was a short, stout man with heavy jowls and a soft waistline bulging generously against his white Sunday shirt and suspenders, his gray-white hair bushed stiffly upward like boxing promoter Don King's. Thirty years ago the Reverend Frazier had led a sit-in at the cafeteria in the basement of City Hall, and television cameras had exposed policemen beating him and dragging him bodily up two flights of stairs to throw him in a patrol car. At the time, many Uptown whites, including my parents, had been alarmed to see the respected minister treated with such brutality.

I watched Reverend Frazier and his protesters file around the Liberty Monument, clapping and chanting, and then advance directly toward the platform where Mark Morvant stood watching the reenactment with his flag bearers. These black marchers appeared to be middle-aged professionals wearing respectable office attire, but Morvant looked horrified by their sudden appearance, as if he were under attack by machete-wielding Bantu warriors. There was a momentary lull in the battle noise and the audience turned and recognized what was happening. Louis Robb and the other bodyguards rumbled toward the stage, shouldering bystanders out of their way. Sensing a confrontation, the squadron of New Orleans policemen stationed on the outskirts of the rally moved forward into the crowd. I heard the Reverend Frazier shout in his hoarse pulpit voice, "Will you grant me the microphone, please?"

"No, I won't, sir!" Morvant replied over the loud speaker. "This is *our* rally. You people obviously have no respect for what we're doing here today. We may be the minority in this city, Reverend, but we still have the right to assemble. And you don't have the right to disrupt us."

"This monument is a symbol of humiliation for the black people of New Orleans!" the minister shouted, his ancient face growing flushed and indignant. "We won't tolerate it any longer. So we're here to oppose you, Mr. Morvant. We're here to condemn racism and injustice. May I please be allowed to address these citizens, sir? I want to explain why this monument should be torn down!"

The whites jeered him.

"Come back when it's Black History Month," Morvant taunted. "We'll schedule a debate—just you and me, Reverend."

Angered at this remark, the black marchers heckled him. One of them hurled a placard at the stage. Reverend Frazier tried to mount the steps, apparently to seize the microphone, but Louis Robb grabbed the old man by the collar of his suit jacket and flung him to the ground. This ignited an ugly fistfight, black against white, a flurry of punches and ripped clothing and yanked hair. I was delighted to see Louis Robb take one on the chin from a tall well-dressed black man who looked as if he might've played college basketball in his prime.

As the police struggled to break up the brawl, separating fighters with mace and nightsticks, I found myself weaving closer and closer to the platform. I wasn't sure what was drawing me into the center of the storm. Perhaps it was seeing Reverend Frazier thrown to the ground. He was Rosetta's friend and pastor and maybe that was why I felt a sudden and inexplicable need to protect the old man. My adrenalin was pumping and my nerves were on edge but I was alert and unusually light and graceful on my feet. When I reached the stage, where the scuffling was most intense, I discovered a young muscle-jawed white police officer with a chokehold around Reverend Frazier's fleshy neck, attempting to drag the elderly minister, kicking and thundering, away from the scene. Blood was running down the old man's ear. Another officer kept jabbing the eighty year old in the ribs with a nightstick and ordering him to stop resisting arrest.

"*Let go of that man!*" I shouted at the two cops, surprising myself with this outburst. I couldn't believe what I was doing. I had never confronted authority in my life. But once I opened my mouth and started shouting, I felt a stone wall crumbling somewhere within me. "Did you *understand* me? Let go of him! *Do not treat this man with disrespect!*"

"Yo, mister, *back off*!" the cop with the nightstick said.

Reverend Frazier was gasping for breath. Foam bubbled from his mouth. He coughed and sputtered like a drowning man desperate for air. They were choking the life out of him. A sudden image of Rosetta raced across my mind, the poor woman lying on her bedroom floor, unable to breathe.

"You're hurting him!" I yelled, clutching the shoulder of the cop administering the chokehold. Red-faced, his jaw flexing, he swung an elbow and cursed me. In my anger I gripped the back of his gun belt and tried to pull him off the Reverend. I didn't see where the blow came from, but it knocked me to my knees and I couldn't focus my thoughts for several excruciating moments. I may have blacked out, I don't know. The pain was intense. I heard my name called and gazing up into the sunlight I saw a girl I had always known and another worried face glowering down at me, but they soon disappeared in the chaos. I wasn't entirely aware of my situation, or where my rubbery legs were taking me, until two policemen shoved me into the back of a squad car with handcuffs clamping my wrists. I closed my eyes and rested my head against the seat, trying to stay awake and quiet the ringing in my ears. The side of my head felt numb and I suspected there was a lump there the size of an ice cube.

"You all right, young man?" asked a deep, hoarse voice from somewhere close by.

When I opened my eyes and glanced sideways, still dizzy from the blow, I realized that I was seated beside the Reverend Frazier. His tie was unknotted, his white shirt hung out of his pants, one suspender flapped loose, and his hair swooped upward like a troll doll's. The foam had caked on his lips and he appeared exhausted and dehydrated. He smiled wearily at me and raised his wrists, showing me the handcuffs. "The great common denominator," he said with an old man's chuckle.

"Did they hurt you, Reverend?" I managed to ask.

"Just a little winded is all," he said. "I've had worse. You look like you got knocked around pretty good yourself."

The sealed squad car reeked of day-old vomit. "Jesus, it smells bad in here," I said, dropping my head between my knees to keep from throwing up all over myself.

"Don't blame me," the minister said. "I'm wearing my Depenz."

I smiled and tried to sit up straight. "My name is Paul Blanchard, sir," I said by way of introduction. "I believe Rosetta Jarboe is a member of your church. She's worked for my family for forty years."

"My goodness, yes. I know who you are, Mr. Blanchard. I knew your father. Your people have been awfully generous to Miss Rosetta through the misfortune she's borne."

He was unaware of what had happened to Rosetta last night. I told him she'd been admitted to the hospital for tests.

"Thank you for telling me, Mr. Blanchard. I'll pass by and visit her as soon as I get out of these bracelets," he said, jiggling the handcuffs with a jaded laugh. Then he looked at me strangely and his face grew solemn. "You're the young man who's been trying to get her boy released from Angola."

I nodded, uncertain whether to feel pride or shame.

"Miss Rosetta tells me you're a good man," he said, his slack old smile filling the entire back seat of the squad car. "'Blessed are they who hunger and thirst for justice,' Mr. Blanchard. Your reward will be great someday."

His praise only made me feel less worthy. "Don't canonize me yet, Reverend," I said. "I'm just a common sinner trying to help out an old friend."

"Thank God for the common sinner," he laughed. "Where would I be without you?"

He glanced over his shoulder out the back window. The altercation had finally ended, courtesy of a dozen New Orleans police officers who had dispersed the crowd with their nightsticks and now roamed the area ordering stragglers to move on. Two black protesters, a man and woman, were being escorted to another squad car in handcuffs. I didn't see Morvant or Louis Robb anywhere, or the woman who had spoken my name. The blow to my head had scrambled my faculties and for a crazy moment I'd thought it was...my sister.

"I know how *I* got here, young man," the Reverend said, rattling his handcuffs, "but what brings you to these parts? You're not White Power, are you? I've heard the Blanchards used to be, but you don't seem like the type."

Gazing out the window, wondering if it could really have been Kathleen out there, I noticed that several Morvant supporters had gathered with the Confederate soldiers at the Riverwalk parking lot and were taunting the police.

"No, Reverend, I'm not with them," I said. "I just came down to buy some slacks at the mall and I heard that cannon go off and saw the soldiers. I guess my curiosity got the better of me and I wandered too close to the front lines."

He clucked again, Solomon-like in his judgment and wisdom. "Well, son, I'm glad you did," he said. "You provided a welcome distraction. The only thing that kept those devoted public servants from breaking my windpipe was them taking a breather to bust you upside the head."

The vehicle's door lock popped and the door creaked open, letting in blessed fresh air. A large man wearing a blue police uniform crouched down on Reverend Frazier's side of the car, peering in at us. "You all right, Rev?" he asked.

I recognized the voice before I made out his features. It had been a long time since I'd seen James Castle in a cop uniform. Twenty years, in fact, since the time I'd sat in his squad car answering questions about Jaren and Nola.

"If any of my men hurt you," he said, "I'm gonna kick some rookie ass."

"I'm fine, James," the minister said. "You cain't hardly damage an old saddle horse like me."

Castle reached in with a key and unlocked the Reverend's handcuffs. "Come on outta there," he said, offering his hand for assistance. "They had no right roughing you up like that. I'm gonna suspend their butts for a week without pay."

Reverend Frazier rubbed his freed wrists and smiled haggardly at the police lieutenant. "Uncuff my friend here, too, James," he said.

James Castle stared at me as if he hadn't yet registered my presence in the car. "My, my, what have we here?" he said in mock surprise. "I b'lieve I recognize this gentleman, Rev. He's one of those big Uptown CEOs with juice, idn't he? Wonder how he got himself pitched in the back of a police unit? Heard he tried to take down one of my men. Bad executive decision, mister. Don't matter how much juice you got in the boardroom. A citizen could get hisself in serious trouble for that kind of behavior. Maybe spend some quality time in the parish jail."

He was squatting back on his haunches, glaring into the back seat at me. "I thought you already figured out that jail's no place for a man like you, my friend? Some people go to jail, they never come out again. Innocent don't make a damn bit of difference these days."

Reverend Frazier interrupted him with a gentle admonishment. "Brother James, this fella was just trying to help an old man out of a sorry predicament. Do me a favor and take off his cuffs."

Castle extended his hand again. "Come on out, Rev," he said, offering to assist the old man. "You don't belong in there."

The minister refused the invitation. "Not till you unlock his cuffs," he said, nodding at me, stubbornly declining to budge. "You take off mine, you take off his. This gentleman saved my windpipe."

Castle expelled an impatient breath and regarded Reverend Frazier with exasperation. Then suddenly he seemed to find the humor in the episode. He shook his head and laughed a deep tolerant laugh, as if this wasn't the first time he'd encountered the minister's obstinacy.

"One of these days, Blanchard, you're gonna run out of friends in high places," he said, staring at me through those small hard eyes as he leaned across the Reverend Frazier to unlock my cuffs, "Then where you gonna be?"

Chapter eighteen

The ICU nurse at Touro Infirmary told me they'd moved Rosetta into a private room on the fifth floor. As I left the elevator and made my way down the polished tile corridor, I saw my brother come out of a room just beyond the nurses' station. He didn't look happy to see me and may have walked on past without acknowledging my presence if I hadn't stopped him.

"How is she doing?" I asked.

"Sleeping," he said, failing to meet my eye. "I sat with her for about an hour but she didn't seem to know I was there."

He'd never been as close to Rosetta as I had, but he loved and respected her and appeared depressed after finding her semi-conscious in a hospital bed.

"Did you speak to any doctors?"

He shrugged aloofly. "A smug little prick named Abramowitz," he said. "No bedside manner whatsoever. Why don't his people stick to selling suits?"

"What did he say, Perry?"

He cocked his head to one side. "Don't use that impatient tone of voice on me. I'm not one of your bean grinders," he said, eyeing my pants. "What happened to your knees? You're a mess, dear boy. You look like a gay car mechanic. Is that blood on your collar?"

I peered down at my knees. I knew I hadn't been in complete command of myself since the nightstick blow to my head. In my dazed condition I'd overlooked the grease stains on my chinos.

"And you need to drag a comb through your hair, for goodness sake. What would our old Dad say if he saw you like this in public?"

I could feel the tender lump swelling under a thatch of hair. The entire incident seemed so surreal now, and far away, a foggy nightmare dissolving in the light of day.

"Perry, we're off on the wrong foot here. Let's start over," I suggested. "Hello, my brother. It's so nice of you to stop by and visit Rosetta. I understand you've spoken with one of her doctors. What did he tell you?"

"Keep that up," he said, raising a single eyebrow, "and I *will* slap you, Paul."

Perry didn't look so great, either. His face was taut and sallow, his eyes weary and receding into dark sockets. There was indeed an air of illness about him, as if he were recovering from a nasty bout with the flu.

"The scintillating Dr. Abramowitz believes that she's suffering from stress-related exhaustion," he said, after a pause for theatrical effect. "No indication of stroke or heart attack. No measurable neurological damage. No symptoms related to her recent cancer. No negative reaction to medication." He waited, studying me with critical appraisal, as if deciding whether to continue or walk away. "The subject appears to have collapsed due to fatigue, dehydration, and indeterminate emotional distress. In other words, dear boy, they don't have a fucking clue."

An orderly pushed an ancient black man past us in a wheelchair. He was toothless and emaciated and barely capable of holding up his head. I promised myself that the Blanchards were never going to allow our old nanny to deteriorate like that.

"I spoke to Claire. She told me that Jaren was denied again,"

Perry said, his mood shifting to an unexpected concern. "I imagine Rosetta was terribly disappointed."

I sighed, absently rubbing the sensitive knot on my head. "She had a fainting spell at the prison," I said. "My guess is she didn't fully recover from that. I should've had her examined when we got back to town."

He raised his chin imperiously and leveled me with that silent, haughty reproof I had fallen victim to over the years. I thought he would say something characteristically snide, but to my surprise he softened his expression, with something akin to sympathy. I could feel the older protective brother somewhere inside those hollow eyes.

"You're important to her," he said. "Go sit with her awhile. She'll know you're there."

He brushed past me, walking on. I turned and watched him trudging down the brightly lit corridor. "Perry," I said, wanting to finish that business between us. "The note wasn't for real. Dad was just joking around."

He slowed his pace but didn't stop. I noticed how badly the Italian sport jacket fit him across his shoulder blades, the material bunched where it had once spread evenly.

"I spoke with Henry Lesseps," I said to his back, raising my voice. "He told me there was nothing to it."

My brother halted. A long interval passed, as if he were rehearsing lines in his head, and then he turned to face me again. A cruel smile crept across his face. He marched toward me with strong, measured purpose in each stride, quickly closing the distance.

"My foolish little brother," he said, lowering his voice to a confidential whisper that sounded eerie and gruff. He was close enough to deliver that slap he'd promised. "There is so much you don't understand. Mother and Father did a fine job of keeping you in the dark."

"There is no *League*, Perry," I said, dropping my own voice so only he could hear. "Once there was, a long time before we were born, but not anymore. Dad wasn't part of some great secret conspiracy, and neither am I. His note was a tongue-in-cheek remark between old friends. They were kidding around, man. You shouldn't have given that message a moment's thought."

He issued an impatient, open-mouthed sigh. I could smell the sherry on his breath. His eyes jittered strangely as he studied my face. "You really don't know anything about them, do you?" The question had a peculiar resonance, part criticism, part disbelief. "You truly are as ignorant as you seem."

He and Mark Morvant were beginning to sound alike.

"It was a stupid note and I made the mistake of taking it seriously and asking you about it," I said. "I'm sorry I did. Henry straightened the whole thing out, as far as I'm concerned. It was all a waste of time."

He narrowed his deep-set eyes and his smile turned to acid. "It's no fairy tale, Paulie boy. I've been an observer of the White League for many years now. Spectator and spectacle. I'm a little surprised you've never been invited to the game," he said. "What evil deed could you have done to get yourself blackballed from the club, too? Is there some dread secret you've been keeping from me all these years?"

I glared at him, utterly surprised, my mouth as dry as meal. Was it possible that these shadow men, if they truly existed, had found me unworthy because they knew what I'd done?

"Don't look so glum, chum," he said, giving my shoulder a friendly swat. "Now that you've cleaned up your act and taken over Daddy's company, they might change their minds about you. Things are looking up for you, little brother. Your stock is on the rise. One of these days you'll get a phone call late at night. They'll take you for a ride, welcome you into the fold. Maybe it'll be a nigger roast out in the sticks." I felt the white heat of his mockery. "Or maybe a queer roll back o' town. Daddy's old pals showing you their manly love."

I gazed down at my dirty knees and the gleaming tile floor. I couldn't bear to look at him. A lifetime of repressed anger exuded from his every pore.

"Some sons they're proud of," he said, "some they're not."

He waited in silence until I raised my eyes. I was surprised to find that his anger had suddenly vanished and his voice was no longer trembling. He'd taken a deep breath, composed himself. "Which one are you, Paul?" he asked in that husky whisper.

He smiled sadly at me and turned to walk down the corridor without another word, and this time I didn't try to stop him.

When I entered the room, Rosetta was sleeping soundly on her back, the covers drawn up to her chest. Absent the wig, her hair looked like Gertrude Stein's, a close, mannish crop of black and gray. The monitors and IV stands were gone. Perry had left behind a beautiful flower arrangement with a get-well card signed by him and his friend Nico. I felt thoughtless and ill-mannered for not bringing something myself. Standing at her bedside I touched her cool forehead and cheek, speaking her name in a low sing-song the way a mother might wake her child. *Ro-seh-tahhh.* Her eyes fluttered and she looked up at me with a blank faraway stare, then a slow recognition took hold and she smiled. It lasted only an instant before she lapsed into sleep again. I arranged the covers around her bare arms and sat down in a chair beside the nightstand. A headache was building in the deep cavity behind my eyes and I still felt weak and out of sorts. The exchange with Perry had certainly not improved my disposition. Now I was curious to know what solid evidence he had, beyond vague late-night phone calls and the assault in Congo Square twenty-five years ago, that an organized League was behind the harassment.

After a short while a nurse swept into the room on those squeaking soft-soled hospital sneakers. "Hello," she said, an attractive young white woman not many years out of nursing school. "How is this good lady doing this afternoon?"

"I was going to ask you the same thing."

She smiled professionally but didn't offer an opinion. A textbook lesson in quick, efficient motion, she fussed with Rosetta's bedding, examined a tray of uneaten food, and scribbled something on a chart.

"How did you get that bump on your head?" she asked, adjusting the room's thermostat. I was impressed that she had noticed.

"A policeman took exception to my behavior."

She threw me a watchful look. My explanation had made her nervous.

"When did it happen?" she asked. I couldn't decide if she was questioning my veracity or formulating a medical diagnosis. I clearly didn't match the profile for a police beating.

"A little over an hour ago, I think."

"Let me get you some ice," she offered. "It'll stop the swelling. Would you like a doctor to look at it? You may need some attention."

"No, just the ice, please. I'll be fine."

I sat in the chair, holding the ice pack to the side of my head, and closed my eyes in the cool antiseptic silence of the room. The stinging in my scalp eventually gave way to numbness. Fatigue and a long sleepless night were beginning to catch up with me and I felt as if I could doze here for hours while pretty young nurses tended my wounds and brought me trays of microwaved dinners. I must have nodded off because at some point I believed I was riding a mechanical horse, my stomach churning wildly as gold-maned Trigger bucked up and down in the bleak fluorescence of an old grocery store. Then suddenly I was awake and sick to my stomach. I rushed into the bathroom and vomited in the toilet. Maybe the nurse was right, I thought as I knelt over the commode. Maybe I needed medical attention. A doctor's clearance. But after vomiting several times, emptying my stomach, I felt much better, as if my body had finally purged itself of every rank disappointment it had endured over the past forty-eight hours. I was cupping water into my mouth, spitting into the sink, when I heard Rosetta's voice calling.

"*Jaren!*" she said when I opened the bathroom door. "You gotta stop doin' that, baby boy. That stuff poison. It gonna kill you."

Her eyes were open but she was unaware of her surroundings. She didn't respond to my voice or the touch of my hand rubbing her shoulder. Within moments her eyelids had closed again and she was lost in troubled dreams.

Chapter nineteen

I hadn't set foot in City Hall since my Cub Scout den had trooped through its labyrinthine corridors on a field trip when I was eight years old. Constructed in the early 1950s, City Hall was said to be modeled after the United Nations building in New York and certainly reflected the generic faux-moderne municipal architecture of its era, in marked contrast to the classic European grandeur only a few blocks away. As unattractive and poorly conceived as the structure appeared from the outside, the interior was even worse. When I entered the place, looking for the city council chambers, I had the distinct feeling I'd wandered by mistake into the Central Registry of Births and Deaths in some struggling banana republic. The carpet was threadbare, the ceiling water-stained, the fluorescent lights buzzing and sputtering. Knobs were missing from office doors. A sullen young civil servant sitting at the information desk directed me to the basement of the building, where the city council chambers had been set up temporarily while pest control exterminated upstairs. As in much of New Orleans, there was a post-colonial ambience about the place, as though the brilliant, cultured people who had founded this city and once lived here in idyllic splendor had abandoned everything quickly after some great cataclysm and disappeared. Where once were giants now dwelled a lesser race paddling about in lost waters.

I was in no position to complain, of course. I knew all too well that every generation was weaker than the last.

Downstairs, the meeting room had already filled to capacity. A score of people, most of them black, stood in the corridor near the open doors, listening to the proceedings. I pushed through the crowd, excusing myself to unfriendly stares, and made my way into the chamber. The windowless space was crammed with metal fold-ing chairs divided by a narrow aisle, and I was not surprised to find one side occupied solely by whites, the other by blacks. No one had crossed over. This promised to be a long, bitter battle.

With a furrowed brow and grim determination in his voice, the mayor sat in the center of the long makeshift conference table, speaking into a desk microphone, offering introductory comments. The seven council members were stationed to his right and left—four blacks and three whites—with feisty Wilhelmina Phillips seated next to him, adjusting her glasses and studying the audience with a severe expression. The black-majority voting bloc included the mayor as well, and their solidarity was impenetrable. For the first time in the his-tory of New Orleans, black politicians had the power to accomplish anything they desired.

Uniformed police officers were planted throughout the room to keep the peace. The tension was palpable, a pressure of simmering hostilities and jangled nerves. I took one look around and realized that a small incendiary remark could set this entire gathering ablaze.

"...and so to make sure that everyone understands this ordi-nance clearly and objectively," the mayor was saying, "I will ask Councilwoman Phillips, the sponsor of the resolution, to read the wording at this time."

The mayor was a Creole from the Seventh Ward, a tall digni-fied businessman with wavy silver hair and coffee-colored skin, his features more Hispanic than Negro. He had once studied for the priesthood. In his first term he'd built a reputation as a conciliator, a reconciler, a moderate voice of reason. As a man of mixed heritage, he was admired and distrusted by both black and white voters, which seemed the perfect balance of power in New Orleans.

"Thank you, Mayor Lalande," Willie Phillips said, sliding the microphone closer as she began to read her proposed ordinance.

I searched for an empty chair among the white audience on the left side of the aisle. Spotting Eric Gautier's wet, slicked-back hair and J. Crew polo shirt, I stumbled over several pairs of shoes to get to the vacant seat next to him.

"Hey," he said with a terse nod, clearly not overcome with brotherly love for me. In forty-eight hours I had managed to piss off my brother, my wife, and my best friend.

"Hey," I replied.

A gym bag lay at his feet. As usual he'd just completed a long strenuous workout. "You haven't missed anything," he said in a droll stage whisper. "They're still rolling the credits." Then he noticed my ruffled appearance. "You okay, man? You look like you've been in an alley fight."

"I didn't even get off a punch," I said.

He continued to glance sidelong at me while Willie Phillips read her ordinance in the strained silence of the meeting chamber. I still wasn't thinking clearly and struggled to follow her points. A municipal Human Relations Commission would be created to investigate discriminatory practices among organizations using city streets or public accommodations. Violators would be fined and possibly sent to jail.

The white contingent sitting up front began to hiss. "*Jail?*" someone blurted. "You gotta be outcher mind, lady!"

The mayor eyed the offender and leaned over into the microphone. "I will ask you to please refrain from responding in that manner," he said. "We will all conduct ourselves this afternoon like ladies and gentlemen."

There was a loud murmur, voices grumbling on both sides of the aisle. The mayor reached for his gavel and pounded it once, emphatically. "I will not allow this assembly to become disrespectful and disruptive," he said, his face stressed beyond its usual seriousness.

"I am aware that several citizens present here today were involved in an altercation at the Liberty Monument this morning, and I will not permit that to happen in *my* meeting. The police have been asked to help maintain an orderly hearing, and I won't hesitate to call on them if I feel that certain individuals are acting inappropriately and need to be removed."

A familiar figure stood up in the audience. Mark Morvant had changed into an expensive pin-striped business suit for the occasion. "I would like to state for the record, Mayor Lalande, that my supporters were engaged in a lawful assembly, with a city permit to conduct our celebration, when we were attacked by an unruly element," he said, turning toward Reverend Frazier and his congregation on the opposite side of the room.

The black audience booed vociferously. Mayor Lalande banged his gavel. "Please take a seat, Representative Morvant. You are *not* recognized to speak! The councilwoman has the floor. Please continue, Miz Phillips."

An imposing figure in her mid-fifties, tall and imperial and fiercely proud, Wilhelmina Phillips had spent most of her life as a high school principal and had served for many years on the state board of education. It was universally understood that she thrived on adversity and had never ducked a fight, physical or verbal, dating back to her activism as a Dillard college student and CORE volunteer during the lunch counter sit-ins on Canal and the boycott of Dryades Street stores in the early 1960s. She was an attractive grandmother now, with a lean, handsome face and gray-streaked hair pulled into an austere bun. Today she was wearing a bright red suit jacket over a white silk shirt buttoned at the collar, with a silver bolo tie matching her earrings.

I listened to the councilwoman read on and began to think she might make it to the end without another disruption, until she stunned everyone with an unexpected addition: "'This anti-discrimination ordinance also applies to the city's private luncheon clubs, where business is conducted on a daily basis.'"

She was unable to utter another word. Half the room exploded in boos and jeering, the other half applauded and cheered. I glanced at Eric. Willie was making her move to open the doors of the Magnolia Club and others like it.

"The woman must have a serious death wish," he said under his breath.

"I'm thinking the food will improve at the club," I said. "You like pickled eggs, don't you, Eric?"

"Very fucking funny."

The mayor gaveled for quiet. Willie Phillips raised her chin defiantly. "Every day there are important business decisions being made in those so-called gentlemen's clubs that affect the entire city, but most of us are excluded from participating. If I'm a black-run construction company, I don't get to make a fair bid when the back-room boys decide who builds a bridge or a highway," she said sharply. "If I'm a female-owned public relations firm, I don't have an equal chance to get the contract when the all-male Magnolia members decide which of their firms is going to produce television ads for the Super Bowl."

Her remarks incited the white audience. The mayor banged the gavel again. "Let's have order, please!" he insisted. "We have a long discussion ahead of us this afternoon and I want to proceed without constant interruption."

Pressing on, he explained that he'd met with several Mardi Gras krewe leaders behind closed doors this morning, trying to find common ground and an agreeable solution, but they had rejected his suggestions and any effort to compromise.

"I asked the krewe captains to help us draft an ordinance that would respect their traditions but at the same time ensure equality and fair practices in the Mardi Gras celebration." He shook his head, clearly disappointed. "I regret to report that there's been no olive branch from the krewes. They refuse to budge on this. They have an all-or-nothing attitude. *So*," he said, lingering over the word, "we will proceed with a public discussion of the ordinance as written by Councilwoman Phillips."

He invited the spokesmen for the opposition to sit at a speakers' table facing the council members. Henry Lesseps, stately and debonair, rose and made his way to the middle chair. He was joined by Basil Parker and Claude Villere.

"O sweet Jesus," Eric said, pressing the flesh between his eyes. "Did he have to bring Laurel and Hardy?"

The mayor greeted the three white gentlemen with lukewarm courtesy and thanked them for volunteering to share their views with the council. "I know this is difficult for you," he said. "I fully understand that the Carnival krewes have always practiced secrecy and protocol and whatnot, and this public appearance is an unprecedented break with more than a century of tradition." He paused and attempted a smile. "We promise not to tell anyone you're here."

His harmless joke was met with audible derision by the white audience. I perused the crowd, counting a dozen of my fellow krewemen from Jove and another handful of Magnolia Club members scattered throughout the left side of the assembly, sitting in pairs but never more than two together. We were such a clever, subversive lot. The White League, indeed. Our people weren't smart enough to undermine a fish fry.

"Gentlemen, the point of this ordinance is to send a signal that New Orleans does not practice discrimination of any kind," the mayor intoned. "We're a big league city in terms of tourism, conventions, and sporting events. We can no longer tolerate segregation and exclusion in the year of Our Lord 1990. It is simply unacceptable. And in the current economic climate," he said, ever the businessman, "we can't risk national boycotts or punitive sanctions from some of the large organizations that may shun this city if we persist in our old ways."

He turned over the microphone to Willie Phillips. "Thank you, Mayor Lalande," she said, "for your valiant effort to meet with the krewe captains this morning. I know you did your best. I'm sorry the krewes were not receptive to reason."

A low, disaffected mumble rolled through the white gathering at slow boil. The councilwoman ignored the reaction.

"I would like to ask our city attorney a question, if I may," she said. "Mr. Marinello, how much does it cost the taxpayers for the city to provide police protection, sanitation facilities, and cleanup services every year during the Carnival season?"

The attorney was marooned at the far end of the council table, a dark-haired man in his mid-forties. "The city subsidizes Carnival to the tune of about three-and-a-half million dollars annually," he responded.

"Subsidizes? Hmm," Willie mused. "White folks call that welfare."

When the boos erupted, the councilwoman threw back her head and laughed, pleased with her provocation. "Did I touch a nerve?" she asked.

"Mr. Mayor," Henry Lesseps interrupted, "may I call on a university economist to respond to that point?"

"Please do."

A gaunt, rheumy-eyed academic who looked as if he'd slept in his tweed jacket shuffled out of the audience and sat before one of the microphones. "My study at UNO indicates that Mardi Gras brings in five hundred million dollars to the city every year, eighty percent of it from out of state," he reported, paging through the notes in front of him. "In taxes, that's twenty-seven million to the city and fifteen million to the state. It's a cash cow, Mr. Mayor. When you balance a deficit of three point five million against revenues of twenty-seven million, that's an incredible exchange. New Orleans is the big winner. In light of the recent oil bust—given that this state's economy is tanking big time—Mardi Gras is the only cash flow we've got going for us right now."

The whites applauded. "Score one for Henry the Fifth," Eric said. "He always knows under which rock to find the math slugs."

Henry addressed the council: "Our krewes put on the best free show in the world," he said proudly. "We think of Carnival as a public service—*pro bono publico*—a gift to the city. If the parades stop rolling, my friends, you'll deny the world its favorite party. And you'll cut off this city's most stable income. It will hurt everyone."

More applause. Morvant rose from his chair, giving Henry a standing ovation, no doubt trying to score points with his future benefactors hiding amongst us in plain sight.

I glanced across the aisle at the quiet, unconvinced black audience and noticed a familiar face in the row behind Reverend Frazier. She had spied me as well and was beaming that radiant smile I had become acquainted with over the past two years. Angelique Thomas, my assistant, patted the empty seat beside her and beckoned me to cross the great divide and join her. It was a dare. I smiled back and patted the unoccupied seat next to me, pantomiming *Come on over.* She wagged her index finger from side to side, *No no,* then crooked it seductively: *You come over here.* We both laughed silently at the absurdity of the situation, two human beings who enjoyed each other's company—who worked together every day—but who couldn't bring themselves to defy the social pressures to stay in our own pews.

There was something about Angie that I found irresistible, and it wasn't just her physical beauty, the willowy figure and strange green eyes and copper waves of hair. Her playfulness was contagious. She kept me interested in showing up at the office every morning, for what that was worth.

I glanced over again and detected a mischievous glimmer in her eyes. She shrugged and made that universal hand gesture, phantom glass to mouth. *Oh hell, let's forget all this bickering and have a drink afterwards,* she seemed to be saying. The New Orleans solution to every problem.

"You make a respectable economic argument, Mr. Lesseps."

At the council table Willie Phillips was leaning forward on her elbows, addressing Henry directly.

"But your position comes down to what I would call the plantation mentality, sir. *Slavery* benefited a lot of people financially, but was it right and morally responsible? Southern society was enjoying a comfortable, stable economic existence, but at the expense of an entire people."

History was her forte. She had taught the subject for years before becoming a school administrator.

"So what I'm asking, Mr. Lesseps, is this: Is it proper to make money through discriminatory practices? Is it okay for the city's leading businesses—most of them run by white people—to reap huge financial rewards during the Mardi Gras season through an antiquated, racially segregated system?"

The hotheaded Basil Parker had decided on his own to field the question himself. "We can't change the economic system in this country, madam, despite your best efforts. But if you push this ordinance down everybody's throat and Mardi Gras goes *dark*," he groused, "you're throwing away good money that benefits your people, too."

The black contingent booed him. By now Eric was practically hiding under his gym bag.

The councilwoman removed her schoolmarm reading glasses and peered down her nose at Basil. "Are you a member of any krewe, sir?" she demanded.

"Yes, I am," he replied defiantly.

"Which one?"

"That's none of your business, madam."

The black audience booed him again. I didn't blame them. If Henry had any hope of salvaging a shred of dignity after this hearing, he would reach over right this minute and unplug Basil's microphone.

"You can't tell us which krewe you belong to?" Willie persisted.

"No, madam, I am sworn to secrecy. It's a tradition I respect."

"Then tell us how you got into this krewe."

"It's like any private organization. Someone puts your name up before a committee, and if they approve, you're voted on by the entire membership. I imagine that Zulu does it the same way."

"Have you ever recommended someone for membership?"

Henry leaned over to say something in Basil's ear, but the younger man blatantly ignored him. "Yes, I have."

"Have you ever recommended a black person, Jew, or Italian?"

"I think not," Basil replied without a moment's hesitation. His chubby fingers interlaced in front of him, he actually seemed to be enjoying himself.

"That sounds like discrimination to me, sir," she said, her

shoulders hunching under the bright red jacket. "Doesn't it sound like discrimination to you?"

Basil shrugged. "I frankly don't give a damn what it sounds like, madam. It's a private organization and we aren't beholden to you or anybody else for our rules and traditions."

To no one's surprise, Mark Morvant rose again and spoke forcefully from his chair. "A point of order here, Mr. Mayor," he said, raising his voice to be heard. "Private clubs have a right to choose their own members as a matter of principle and Constitutional guarantee. Freedom of association is a basic right in this country, Mrs. Phillips. You don't have the authority to take that right away from anyone!"

The mayor banged his gavel. Willie Phillips seized the microphone. "Sit down, Mr. Morvant!" she commanded. "You are not authorized to address this assembly. One more interruption and I will ask the mayor to have you escorted out of here!"

Morvant smiled. He had always loved a belligerent confrontation. "Your ordinance is a blatant attempt to force your personal political agenda on the entire city, Mrs. Phillips," he continued, undeterred. "There's discrimination here today, all right. Against historical tradition, and privacy, and basic American freedoms. And *you're* the guilty party, Mrs. Phillips!"

The Reverend Calvin Frazier lumbered to his feet and wagged his finger at Morvant across the aisle. "What freedoms are you trying to protect, young man? Exclusion? White Supremacy?" he shouted. "You ought to be ashamed of yourself, hiding behind the Constitution!"

Eric sat up straight in his chair. "Hoo, here we go," he said. "We might have an honest-to-God food fight on our hands."

He may have been amused, but I wasn't. I watched the policemen stationed around the room. I didn't relish the idea of getting my skull cracked twice in one day.

"Look at these people!" Like Moses waving his staff, Reverend Frazier waved his arm at everyone sitting on my side of the aisle. "They're the grandchildren of slave owners! This Mardi Gras baloney gives them a false sense of power in a city that's sixty-five percent black! They know the end has come and they're desperate to hold on!"

"Will you please take your seat, Reverend Frazier!" the mayor demanded. "Both you and Representative Morvant are out of order!"

He eyed the policemen positioned nearby, an unspoken signal for alert. The crowds were stirring restlessly on both sides of the aisle.

Amid the chaos, Willie Phillips regained the floor. "I have a few more questions for you gentlemen," she said, addressing Henry, Basil, and Claude seated at the guest table.

"*No,*" Basil said, standing suddenly, causing Henry to stare up at him in disbelief. "We refuse to sit here and be intimidated by you, madam. This is a kangaroo court. You people have already made up your minds about this silly ordinance," he said, raking his finger across the air, singling out the black members of the council.

Henry Lesseps looked mortified. I thought he might grab Basil by the sleeve of his suede sport jacket and pull him down into the empty chair.

"We will not sit here and be lectured or interrogated by you," Basil continued. "If you want to pass this ordinance, go ahead. You've got the numbers. Why don't you just put us all on a boat and send us back to Europe?" he scoffed. "I can guarantee what's going to happen, madam. The krewes will withdraw from Carnival and there will be no parades or costume balls. There will be no twenty-seven million dollars in tax benefits for the city. You will kill the New Orleans Mardi Gras, madam. And that will be on your head for the rest of your life."

The black audience hissed at him. Willie was outraged. "This sounds like a threat, Mr. Parker."

"My great grandfather would've handled this with a *buggy whip,* madam," he said. "*That* was a threat."

"Mr. Parker, that's outrageous," she said.

"End of discussion, madam. We're walking out of this kangaroo court. Good day!"

Basil leaned over and said something to Claude, then to Henry. My father's old friend appeared perplexed by the sudden change of events. He couldn't dissuade his two colleagues from turning heel and storming up the aisle. A smattering of whites applauded them. The blacks stood up to hurl insults. Mark Morvant filed out of his row and joined the exodus in an act of solidarity, followed by Louis Robb and the goon squad from the Liberty Monument. Several young black men stepped into the aisle to confront the entourage with verbal taunts, but the police acted quickly to separate the two sides.

Morvant was enjoying a banner day, the prick. At the battle reenactment he'd come across as a responsible leader with the authority of a city permit. At this hearing he'd emerged as the noble David standing up to unconstitutional Goliath. Both events would grab him more coverage in the evening newscast and the Sunday morning *Times-Picayune*. He had always measured his success by the column inch.

"Sterling performance today, boys," I said, derisively applauding Basil and Claude as they passed our row, their noses raised above the heckling crowd. "With your knack for diplomacy, who needs Jimmy Carter?"

I caught Morvant's eye as he marched past, secure in the center of his thugs. Smiling slyly at me, he pressed his wrists together as if they were handcuffed. I didn't know if he was mocking my arrest or the imminent possibility of his own.

"Hey, where are you going, Blanchard?" Eric asked, clutching my arm as I stood up to follow Morvant's group. I had my own agenda and needed to speak with the man before he disappeared for the rest of the weekend.

"Sit down, Paul," Eric whispered. "You'll give us both away."

The mayor was gaveling for order. A shaken Henry Lesseps stood at his table, watching the cadre of dissenters abandon him. When he saw me sliding down the row, his face collapsed into deeper anguish and he cast his eyes toward the notes in front of him like a seasoned attorney who knew he'd lost his case.

Stepping into the aisle, I glanced over at the black section and met the Reverend Frazier's disappointed stare. He'd recognized me and shook his large old head, the unruly wick of gray hair refusing to wilt even after the wrestling match at the monument. I had let him down. He thought he'd found an ally among the blue bloods, but I had turned out to be like all the rest.

I could have lived with that misperception, I told myself, but not with what I saw in Angie Thomas's eyes. She was also taking note of my departure, and the sense of betrayal on her face left me grasping for a way to account for my actions. How could I explain to her I wasn't leaving because I sided with Morvant and those two buffoons, Basil and Claude? I stopped for a moment and gazed back toward the mayor, who was pounding his gavel and instructing the police to clear the aisle. I looked again at Angie and tried to smile. Her lovely smooth brow was creased, her expression solemn and unforgiving. At that moment a police officer gripped my elbow and suggested in no uncertain terms that I sit down or vacate the chambers immediately.

Chapter twenty

The walkout contingent was greeted with pushing and shoving from the overflow crowd of concerned black citizens amassed just outside the doorway. I arrived in time to watch the police direct several hostile church ladies away from Louis Robb and his associates, who were exchanging insults with everyone around them. Two officers had taken the unfazed Basil and Claude under protective custody and were escorting them toward the stairwell, while Mark Morvant tried to regroup his people at the opposite end of the corridor. Appropriately, considering my day so far, I emerged alone and unprotected into the restless gathering, the last white straggler from the walkout. Several tall, rangy project teenagers came prancing toward me with harm in their eyes. One of them called me a *fat ofay shitbag* and might have roughed me up, but I heard someone say, "This man awright. You boys back off, now. You hear me talkin'?"

At first I didn't recognize Corinne out of uniform—and out of my household. She was suddenly beside me, her hand on my back, a small scrappy aunt-like figure the teenagers didn't dare to sass. "Come on, Mistah Paul," she said. "You in the wrong place at the wrong time, and you best improve your situation."

"Thank you, Corinne," I said as we moved quickly out of the mob into the open corridor. "I appreciate that."

"Nothin' to it," she said, cocking her head sideways with a clever smile. "Now whatchou doin' down here causin' so much trouble?"

"I was about to ask you the same thing."

She glanced down the hallway at Morvant and his men conferring near a water fountain. A local news crew had pursued them with their video cam, and the young reporter was pointing a microphone at the congressman's perfect jaw.

"You not down with that fella, are you, Mistah Paul?"

The microphone and bright lights had animated Morvant. He was turning on the charm, smiling youthfully into the camera as he delivered his sound bite.

"Frankly, Corinne," I said, "I'd like to go kick his ass."

She cackled and patted me on the arm. "I see you back at the house, young man."

"You stay out of trouble yourself, okay?"

I waited for the news crew to shut down and walk away. It didn't take long. As I approached Morvant and his bodyguards, their huddled conversation ceased abruptly and all eyes turned to me. The protection included Louis Robb and four other muscle-bound crackers with mullet haircuts. None of them could have squeezed into a size eighteen collar. It was impossible to guess whether Morvant had met them in some white Southern compound or cane-pole fishing in the swamps of St. Bernard Parish, where they'd no doubt been interbreeding with generations of first cousins. I suspected they were all carrying concealed weapons underneath their sport coats and leather jackets. Watching them close ranks around their boss, I was reminded of Huey Long and his gangster bodyguards. *Morvant*, I thought, *you'd better hope these Goobers are quicker on the draw.*

"Hey there, *cuño*," he said, urging aside Louis Robb with the back of his hand and stepping forward to greet me. He appeared both amused and concerned. "What happened down at the monument? I thought we might have to go drag your butt out of central booking. How'd you end up in those Colored charm bracelets?"

He was referring to the handcuffs.

"As usual," I said, "I got caught 'twixt and 'tween."

"Bad place to be," he observed with a judgmental shake of the head. "You know what the Savior said about being neither hot nor cold, my man. The lukewarm end up as barf chunks on somebody's sandals."

"I'd really like to hear more of your Biblical erudition, Mark," I said, "but we've got to talk."

He glanced over his shoulder at his bodyguards. "You have some information for me?" he asked, sensing the urgency in my voice.

I was still shaky from the nightstick blow, but in a strange way the confrontation had made me feel a little wild and loose, as if some constricting knot had uncoiled deep inside me. "First thing we've got to get straight," I said, edging closer into that uncomfortable personal space between us, "Don't send your goon to spy on my house anymore." I nodded at Louis Robb. "And don't call me at my office. Ever again. Are we clear on that?"

Apparently Louis Robb was jealous of my close encounter with his boss. In three long strides he was all over me, his large hand gripping my bicep like a blood-pressure sleeve pumped to full capacity. I noticed a small bruise on his chin where that protester had punched him.

"It's okay, Louis," Morvant said. "I understand where he's coming from. Our friend here values his privacy."

"Let's talk, Mark," I said, not flinching despite Robb's nasty grip on my arm. "But without the *Hee-Haw* talent."

Morvant seemed to be looking past me. He slipped into that professional smile I'd seen him use on the newswoman. "Whatever you say, *cuño*."

I heard a familiar voice calling my name. "Paul!" she said. "There you are! I was worried sick about you."

I turned to find my sister hurrying toward me. Although it was a casual Saturday afternoon in the city, she was wearing a low-cut, teal green evening dress suitable for dinner at Brennan's, the silky material clinging to her svelte figure. Her blonde hair billowed about her shoulders as she dashed through the stale air of the municipal corridor. She looked radiant, but alarmed by whatever was on her mind.

"Kathleen?" I said. "What are you doing here?"

"Same thing you are, I imagine," she said, gently touching the side of my head. "I came for the hearing. Where did they hit you?"

"In that general area."

So my mind hadn't played tricks on me after all. My sister *had* been present at the Liberty Monument this morning. It had been her face I'd seen peering down at me when I was kneeling on the ground.

"The police wouldn't let me go with you," she said, examining my hair as if I were a six year old with head lice. "I thought they were taking you downtown so I rushed over to the station, but the booking cop told me no whites were arrested. What on earth happened?"

"They let me go. Good old Reverend Frazier," I said directly to Morvant, underscoring the name. "He pulled some strings."

"I called Claire. I called Creed to line up a lawyer. I damn-near called the governor's office," she said in a breathless state I recognized as a carbon copy of our mother's response to crisis. "Are you all right?"

"Well, I—"

Before I could fully respond, she stepped around me and stood up on tiptoe to kiss the taller Morvant on the cheek. "Hello, Mark," she said with a dismaying intimacy. "You certainly seemed to be enjoying yourself in the council chambers."

I was aware that they had known each other in college. Tulane frat boy, Newcomb sorority girl. The same chaperoned dances, 1967.

"If you can't have a little fun," he said, kissing her lightly on the lips, "why get involved?"

As I watched them exchange smiles, I felt my stomach roil— and it wasn't from the blow on the head anymore. The scales suddenly fell from my eyes and everything fit into place. I remembered my conversation with Kathleen two nights ago in the library. *I ran into an old acquaintance at the Upperline,* she'd told me. *I hadn't seen him in years. We talked. He asked for my phone number.*

My sister was dating Mark Morvant.

"*Hey!*" I said, seizing their attention. They both turned and looked at me as if I'd barged into their bedroom with a Polaroid camera.

This wouldn't do. This fucking would not do. I couldn't stand by and let this treacherous son of a bitch take advantage of my sister. Her name, her social status, her money. The idea horrified me. I wanted so bad to tell them something about each other, something that would destroy their preposterous flirtation before it went on an hour longer.

"I hate to break up the love fest," I said, "but I've got to talk to you, Morvant. Right away."

He and Kathleen shared a disappointed glance. "Is this boys against girls?" she sighed. "Don't I get to come along and play, too?"

"I'm sorry, Kathleen," I said.

Morvant pecked her on the lips again. "This evening, right?" he said. "You look positively fetching."

Chapter twenty-one

We sat in the back seat of his Lincoln Town Car, parked on Perdido Street between City Hall and the Civic Center. Municipal government complexes attracted sparse foot traffic on weekends. The landscaped green belt around the buildings created a rare pastoral setting in the inner city, but no one was strolling through the grass, and I suspected that few happy couples had ever spread a picnic lunch under those trees. The volatile Iberville Housing Project was only four blocks away.

"Is this enough privacy for you?" Morvant asked sarcastically. "Maybe you'd feel more comfortable wearing a Rex mask?"

On the sidewalk near the automobile, Morvant's "security force" was circled around Louis Robb, who seemed to be taking a bully's pleasure in his discourse. I doubted that he was holding forth on Ouspensky's theory of the space-time continuum. By their sleazy smiles and furtive glances at my window, I presumed. Robb was making sport of me.

"I talked to Henry Lesseps about the note from my father," I began. "He explained that it was all a joke, Mark. Tongue in cheek. Dad was just venting his frustration with Willie Phillips."

The bodyguards burst into laughter and stepped away from one another. Morvant watched them through the sealed window and smiled. "Is that the best you can do, *cuño*?"

"The White League doesn't exist anymore, Mark. I can see why you thought otherwise, but you're jumping to the wrong conclusion. The League died out in the 1930s. Gone with the wind."

He steepled his long, curiously feminine fingers and stared at the smooth leather upholstery on the seat in front of him. "You disappoint me, Paul," he said in a solemn voice. "I thought we'd come to an understanding, but now you're insulting my intelligence. I'm beginning to question your sincerity. You're not operating in good faith, *cuño*, and that disturbs me."

He reached into his suit jacket and withdrew the earring he'd been holding on to for years. The gift I'd bought at that little shop in the Quarter. He gazed at the object in his open palm as if he were consulting a pocket-watch heirloom willed to him by a doting grandfather.

"If you're calling my bluff, Blanchard, you're making a serious miscalculation. I didn't run my last outfit like a fucking Boy Scout troop." His *last outfit* had been some lunatic white compound up near the Arkansas state line. "I had to pitch 'em high and tight sometimes, I'm sorry to say. I had to punish friends who turned on me. It left a bad taste, but I got used to it."

He tightened his fist around the earring and squeezed until his hand grew bloodless. "I intend to be the next governor of this state," he said, turning his chin to fix me with those cold blue eyes. "I'll do whatever it takes. It's in your best interest, old stick, to help me succeed. Because if I don't get the support I need, I'll go looking for somebody to punish. And your name will be at the top of my list."

I'd always known there was something grudging and sadistic about Mark Morvant, but now it was clear that he was determined to harm me personally, as if that secret wound he'd been carrying around was something I'd inflicted on him myself.

"Look, Mark," I said, feeling desperate, "I'm going to meet with my accountant first thing Monday morning and we'll work out a way to contribute to your campaign. I'm thinking fifty thousand, maybe seventy-five. We'll spread it out however we have to. I'm sure there are creative ways to do this."

He raised one of those carefully tended eyebrows, waiting to hear more.

"You can count on me to go to the wall," I said, despising myself for succumbing to blackmail. "I've got to find a way to cover my tracks, that's all. But I'm good for the goddamned money, man. I said I'd help you out, and I will."

He slipped the earring back into his pocket and extracted a monogrammed handkerchief, the *MM* printed neatly in a corner fold. There was a pinprick of blood in his palm where the hook had jammed in his skin. "Well, *cuño*," he said, a small red dot appearing on the white cloth, "that's a start, isn't it? I appreciate your generosity. I honestly do. But I'm afraid it won't be enough."

I collapsed against the soft leather upholstery and sighed deeply. I had to bite my tongue to keep from telling him how much Henry Lesseps had disparaged him and his incendiary politics, and how unlikely it was that any dignified Bourbon gentleman from Uptown New Orleans would bankroll a working-class kid from Arabi. My instinct told me that the Magnolia crowd didn't trust Mark Morvant any more than they'd trusted redneck Huey Long.

"I know they're out there, Blanchard, planning the way things ought to be, in their infinite wisdom. I don't have a problem with that. They've been at this game a lot longer than I have and I admire their dedication. I'm sure they're even more pissed off than I am about that crazy black bitch and this whole messy Mardi Gras thing. But that's where I can help them. They need a friend in the governor's office and I'm willing to be their man. They've got to hear this, *cuño*. That's where you come in."

He peered out the window at his bodyguards rustling about on the sidewalk like a gang of mischievous schoolboys exchanging dirty jokes. Louis Robb stared back, hands in his pockets, eager to get their motorcade under way. Above the municipal buildings behind him rose a cluster of sleek new skyscrapers near the Superdome, corporate headquarters of the dwindling few companies that hadn't yet moved to Houston or Atlanta.

"Your people have always put their money on the horses they like," Morvant said. "How could they not like a good-looking racehorse like me?"

He was flashing his capped teeth in a self-mocking smile, aware of his irony but more serious than not. He struck me as dangerously well-equipped, his best skill the subtle, chameleon-like manipulation of whatever image suited his surroundings.

"Tell me how this works, Mark. You've had more experience with secret organizations than I have. Am I supposed to walk into the next monthly meeting of the White League and pass the hat?"

I shut my eyes and rested the back of my head against the seat. The pain from the nightstick was still there, a gnawing presence above my ear, and I suspected I needed to go home and recover. "Maybe I should call up the Grand White Pooh-bah and put this on the agenda," I said, unable to control my scorn. "We'll take it up right after the singing of *Dixie* and the Negro castration ceremony."

When I opened my eyes he was staring at me with an ominous smile. "You've got a little less than three weeks to deliver your constituency, *cuño*," he said. "Don't disappoint me again. I shudder to think what could happen to such a fine upstanding pillar of the community." He studied the tiny pinprick in his palm. "Or what his wife and children might think of him if they only knew."

I was tempted to grab Morvant by the throat. I looked out the side glass at the bodyguards bouncing on their toes, smoking Camels like dock workers and gabbing quietly among themselves. If they weren't out there I might have choked the son of a bitch sitting beside me. He may have been in better shape, but I outweighed him by twenty pounds, and I liked my chances in a small closed space like the back seat of a car.

"Leave my family out of this, Mark," I said, taking long deep breaths to slow myself down. I didn't want to do something I would regret for the rest of my life. "This is between you and me."

He inhaled deeply. "Now that's exactly where we disagree," he said. "Family is what this is all about."

Chapter twenty-two

Perry and Nico lived together in a stylishly renovated second-story apartment in the same block as the Court of Two Sisters on Royal Street in the French Quarter. During the colonial era, the street had indeed assumed a regal pretense. Wealthy families lived in elegant residences alongside the shops where well-bred women purchased their parasols and frilled dresses from the Continent. Despite the quaint shabbiness of the street today, with its cluttered antique shops, mildewed rare-book stores, and gaudy t-shirt marts, traces of the old resplendence still remained, arched *portes cochères* and sultry, fern-sprawling interior courtyards with trickling stone fountains on view. The entrance to Perry's address was calculatedly inconspicuous: two steps up from the gray flagstone sidewalk into a narrow alcove, where a door buzzer and intercom plate were the only signs of habitation.

I pushed the button and waited for a response. It was past four o'clock in the afternoon and there was a good chance that Perry was out and about. I pushed again and turned to watch the passersby from the recessed doorway. A tourist family with young children had stopped to ogle the toy soldiers in the shop window across the street.

I thought I recognized the tall man loitering in front of an antique store two doors down. He was wearing a leather jacket and his head was shaved. He kept glancing over his shoulder in my direction.

"Yes, who is it?" To my surprise, the intercom spoke. It sounded like Perry's voice.

"It's Paul," I said. "Is that you, Perry?"

"Did you say Paul or Saul?" It was Perry, all right.

"Let me in," I said.

A long silence fell as I stared at the intercom plate. I thought he might have walked away in a fit of pique, leaving me to ring his doorbell for the rest of the evening, which I was prepared to do if necessary. But then the buzzer sounded and the door released, and I stepped into a small cloakroom area at the foot of the stairs. Perry was standing at the top, peering down at me. He was wearing a forest green turtleneck sweater over corduroys, and his hand gripped a wineglass in an unusual splay of fingers, the eccentric manner of a European theater critic holding a Gauloise. A tad early for cocktails, I thought, but Perry had always made his own rules.

"I see you still haven't changed your pants," he said like a clucking old aunt. "Whatever are we going to do with you?"

I mounted the polished stairs, refinished boards of cypress wood dragged from some nearby swamp two hundred years ago. The walls had been stripped to the stone and lacquered with a clear sealant to prevent the mortar from crumbling. Every inch of renovation bore Nico's careful preservationist touch.

"I want to know what you know, Perry," I said, without introduction. I was in no mood to play cat-and-mouse with my clever brother. "You claim to be an authority on the White League. Spectator and spectacle. So let's hear it, Sherlock. Tell me everything."

We were standing face to face on the landing. He smirked at my urgency and drained the sherry in his glass. The air reeked of its fruity aroma, a freshly uncorked bottle.

"Oh dear, dear," he said. "We're still on *that* subject, are we?"

I persisted, unwilling to let him squirm out of this. "You said Mother and Father always kept me in the dark. What did you mean?"

Avoiding my eyes, he pivoted quickly and ambled across the high-beamed loft toward the wet bar, his heavy tread creaking the long-leaf pinewood floor that gleamed under recessed can lights. Perry and Nico had spent a great deal of time and effort getting everything just right. Cozy white fabric chairs and love seats were arranged for intimate conversation around a bottle-green deco coffee table. The walls had become a gallery of amusing pop icon paintings by Douglas Bourgeois and homoerotic tableaus rendered by a local gay artist beloved by the New Orleans *beau monde*. Prince and the Pointer Sisters watching naked muscular centurions frolicking in Roman baths.

"Your sincerity makes my mouth dry," Perry said with his back to me, pouring sherry at the bar across the room. "I suppose I should offer you something as well. Mother would disapprove if I neglected proper etiquette."

"I'm not here to socialize, Perry. I need some answers."

I walked over to the French doors leading onto the wrought-iron balcony. The long cheerless shadows of late afternoon were overtaking the upper reaches of Royal Street. Back in the 1960s and 1970s these balconies had become the boozy roosts of tattooed merchant marines and their junkie hooker girlfriends, a loud trashy scene replicated all over the Quarter in those days. When Nico bought this place a few years ago, he'd sent the last of the squatters packing and tore out the thin walls that had created a warren of doper crash pads since the Summer of Love. The only residents he couldn't evict were the Formosa termites, a plague now threatening to devour every sliver of wood in the Vieux Carré.

I looked through the glass doors, searching for Louis Robb in the street below. He was no longer standing in front of the antique store.

"Ignorance is bliss, Paulie boy," Perry said, turning to face me. He relaxed against the edge of the bar, tasting the sherry, crossing his sockless penny loafers. "You've lived in the dark this long, why bother with it now? You know what the drag queens always say: 'What you don't know won't hurt you—for the first two inches.' That sounds like pretty good advice in this case."

I wasn't sure whether Nico was on the premises as well, say, wearing a silk kimono and handcuffed to their four-poster bed. I thought it wise to speak to my brother with carefully chosen words.

"I've run into a problem, Perry," I explained, strolling casually toward him with my hands in my pockets. "A personal matter. It's serious, but I won't bore you with the details. I've been told that this mystery group can straighten out my problem, but the thing is, I never heard of them until two days ago. You're right—I'm in the dark about this. And maybe a lot of other things, too. If you could shed some light, I would be deeply indebted to you. I don't know where else to turn."

A familiar wickedness kindled in his eyes. He was beside himself with that perverse, infantile joy I had grown accustomed to. "My word, who did you *kill*?" he asked with a nasty snigger.

With Perry, showing weakness was always a bad idea. Master of the digging remark, he excelled at ridiculing the trivial human flaws in everyone around him. But at this moment I was desperate enough to lay myself at his mercy. I had no other choice.

"If you could just give me a name…a contact," I said, striking a tone somewhere between businesslike and groveling. "A place to begin. That's all I'm asking for."

He sighed and set his glass on the marble surface of the bar. I prepared myself for his sarcasm, but his mood had mellowed and he gave me a considerate smile. "They're hateful people, you know," he said solemnly. "They ruined innocent lives long before the best part of you and me ran down Mother's leg. And they're still at it. I don't want to see you get involved in their ugly business."

There it was again, my brother's concern. Twice in one day. It was a rare occurrence and I wanted to savor the experience as long as possible.

"What kind of trouble are you in, Paul?"

"You're not the only Blanchard with a past. I did something a long time ago that hurt good people and now it's caught up with me."

Thinking about what I'd done left my throat dry and constricted. Perry stared at me, worried. He could see the terrible quandary I was in.

"I'm being blackmailed," I said, lowering my voice. The word left a sour taste in my mouth. "If I don't play ball, I could go to prison, Perry. Lose everything. Claire and the kids. *Everything.*"

He reached for his sherry glass and treated himself to a long relieving drink. His hand looked a little unsteady. He seemed as shaken as I was.

"Can you tell me who it is?" he asked.

I shook my head.

"How much do they want?"

"More than I can produce."

"*Jesu Christi!*" he said in altar boy Latin. "Are you saying there isn't enough Blanchard bean money in a vault somewhere to shut them up?"

"It's more complicated than that. Money isn't the only thing involved."

"Have you talked to the police?"

"I can't do that," I said. "I'm staring down a big-time felony count. There's an old cop who would love to bust me for it."

"Can't we *bribe* the son of a bitch? This is New Orleans, after all."

I shook my head again. "Not this guy. It's gotten personal between us."

My revelation had unnerved him. Two beads of sweat had escaped from under his new hair weave and were racing down his forehead. "Would you like to talk about it?" he asked, using a handkerchief to daub himself dry. "I know I haven't been the greatest older brother in the world, Paul, but maybe I can help."

I smiled at his offer. He was trying hard and I appreciated the effort. "The best way to help," I assured him, "is to give me a name. I need to contact the White League."

What did Morvant expect me to do? Present his case to the League like a lawyer before the Supreme Court? Convince them he was their candidate? Beg for money? These were not skills I had in my repertoire. Anyone close to me knew I lacked the power of persuasion.

"I hate the idea of going to them," I told my brother. "But they're the only ones who can get me out of this jam."

We regarded each other in a state of speechless suspension, two bodies from the same womb, the same shared family history, but with little else in common. Whatever strange unspoken sentiment passed between us, it lasted longer than either of us expected.

"You're not going to…" He downed his sherry, searching for courage. He appeared genuinely afraid for me, his kid brother. "You're not going to have someone killed, are you?"

I laughed nervously. "Is that what they do?"

Pouring too quickly, he clanked the sherry bottle against the lip of his wineglass. "Make yourself a drink and sit down a moment," he said, his upper lip wet with perspiration. "There's something you ought to know."

His bar stock didn't include Bombay Sapphire, so I settled on Tanqueray with a splash of tonic water and two ice cubes. As I sat in one of the armchairs, my brother paced back and forth in front of me like a riled mink in a cage. "Do you know who David Ferrie was?" he asked, finally. It was clearly painful for him to utter the man's name.

"Yes, I know who he was, Perry."

"Has anyone ever told you about my…" He hesitated. "About my friendship with him?"

I didn't want to betray Kathleen's confidence, but under the circumstances I had no choice. "I know about it," I said, nodding gravely. "I also know that your arm wasn't broken in a car accident."

He stopped pacing and stared down at me, his eyes widening in panic. "My God," he said. "Is that story all over town?"

"Not that I'm aware of," I said. "I heard it from Kathleen the other night. She was very worried about you. She said you'd told her years ago."

He touched the back of his head, an unconscious mannerism, the prim Jesuit boy feeling for a hair out of place. "I did," he mumbled, gazing off across the loft. "Yes, I did tell her." And then his eyes settled on me again. "But not everything. Those evil bastards who beat me up were messenger boys, all right. They broke my arm because they knew I'd partied with David Ferrie and they wanted me to keep my mouth shut."

I was deeply confused. "Keep your mouth shut about Ferrie?"

He nodded, avoiding my eyes. "They were afraid I knew too much," he said, his voice drifting off into the fog of history. "The truth is, I didn't know anything."

I had a haunting suspicion of where this was going. "You mean, anything about..." I couldn't force myself to speak the words.

He inhaled a deep shuddering breath. "Yes," he said.

"Are you saying the White League had something to do with—Dallas?"

I felt a shiver run up my spine. I couldn't complete the thought.

"Yes," he repeated. "I'm certain they did. In a roundabout way."

His features had hardened. He appeared angry and hurt and profoundly afraid. For a moment I thought he might cry. And then his entire body shook, like a child after a cold bath, and afterwards there was a tremulous lightness about him, a sudden fragile grace, as if a great burden had lifted somewhere inside him and he'd found the old self presumed lost forever.

"Violence and intimidation, that's their *métier*," he said in a strong clear voice. "Every lynch mob in this town for a hundred years, and every race riot and church bombing has had their name on it. They make the Klan look like vacation Bible school."

Whoever they were, I had no doubt heard their names since childhood. Played with their grandchildren at Christmas parties. It was impossible to picture those gray-haired patricians as calculating killers. Had our father been one of them as well?

"JFK, Martin Luther King," he confessed reluctantly, as though embarrassed by his own dark knowledge. "Trace their assassins, trace the money and their personal associations, and where does it always lead? Right back here to the Big Easy, honey bun."

"And you're saying this League—"

"I am."

I sipped the icy gin in my glass and studied him. A small, spooky smile was slowly transforming his expression. I didn't know if my brother had become a raving paranoid—perhaps a symptom of the deadly disease Kathleen suspected he had contracted—or if there was something to these wild allegations.

"You want to be very careful with them, Paul," he said. "They've brought down greater men than you and I. Don't get too close or they'll destroy you, too."

I understood now, for the first time ever, the extent of Perry's misery. He had lived a hard life, most of it consumed by expectations he couldn't fulfill, passions he couldn't deny, secrets he couldn't reveal. We hadn't talked enough about these things to each other. We had become strangers over the years. But it was clear he was still very fond of me and trying his best to save me from the suffering he'd endured.

"I can see you need a little more convincing," he said, offering an ashen smile. "Finish your drink and let's take a walk to the Cabildo. There's someone who knows a lot more about this than I do."

Chapter twenty-three

We walked down St. Peter Street, passing underneath the shoddy, fern-choked balcony where Tennessee Williams had sweated through his shirtsleeves pecking out *A Streetcar Named Desire* on a manual typewriter. I kept looking over my shoulder to see if Louis Robb was following us. Half a block away, Jackson Square appeared gray and nearly deserted in the waning afternoon light. The sketch artists and tarot readers in front of the Pontalba building had already packed up their wares and were moving on. Four street musicians playing brass, black teenagers from the projects or Tremé, struggled to attract an audience near the wrought-iron fence surrounding the central garden. The horn players' chief rivals were the reckless street-sweepers who had suddenly materialized in small motorized vehicles, a prankish crew spinning wildly over the cobblestones like bumper cars at a carnival, whirling at each other and cutting figure eights while blowing dirt futilely around the square. There was something quintessentially New Orleans about them, showy and daring and ludicrously incompetent. A busload of German tourists had disembarked to applaud the sweepers and take their photographs.

"Such a happy, carefree people," my brother said, observing the young black municipal workers posing vainly atop their vehicles. "Literacy and a living wage will only confuse them."

"The White League would love you if they could only get to *know* you, Perry," I said.

He squeezed the nape of my neck, a rough schoolyard move from our Holy Name days long ago. "Come along," he said, leading me toward the arched colonnade of the stately old museum. "It's time for your history lesson, *mon petit.*"

The Cabildo had been built at the end of the eighteenth century to house the Spanish magistrates during their brief colonial rule in Louisiana. A solid block of stone with a mansard roof and graceful upper gallery overlooking the square, the building matched the ecclesiastical Presbytere on the other side of St. Louis Cathedral, the architectural embodiment of Church and State in early New Orleans. For nearly two centuries the Cabildo had served weighty purpose, most notably as the chamber where the Louisiana Purchase was signed in 1803, transferring Louisiana from France to the United States. Until Father Joe told me the story, I hadn't realized that the building had stationed the Metropolitan Police Force during Reconstruction. The White League had chased them back here after the Battle of Canal Street, forcing them to surrender their headquarters overnight. Three years later, during the election controversy between the Southern Democrats and Republicans, the League had returned with three thousand armed men to again overtake the police station and judicial courtrooms and declare their own winner. I would have bet stacks of U.S. currency that it wasn't the last time white men with weapons had stolen an election in Louisiana.

As soon as we entered the Cabildo lobby, we were quickly surrounded by little old lady volunteers eager to give us brochures, answer our inquiries, accept donations. A pesky blue-haired retiree kept thrusting a pen at our chests, demanding that we sign the registry.

"That's not necessary, ma'am. We're here to see my friend Nico," Perry said with a brisk smile. "He's on the third floor."

"Is he lost?" she asked, somewhat disoriented. "We can make an announcement over the loudspeaker."

"He works here, ma'am. That's where his office is. He's an assistant curator."

"Ohh. That nice Latin boy?"

"If you only knew."

Disdaining official procedure, Perry crashed the gate and headed into the museum. "Hurry up, dear boy," he said over his shoulder, "before these old girls start sticking dollar bills in our waistbands."

He avoided the entry into an exhibit on colonial domestic life in Louisiana—a scintillating collection of dinner plates, coins, and butter churns—and instead ushered me around a corner to the staircase leading to the upper salas, a majestic passageway trod for two centuries by the great spurred boots of statesmen and scoundrels. I followed Perry upstairs like an obedient acolyte trailing his vicar, the museum eerily quiet at this closing hour, with a reverential hush surrounding the portraits of the rakish French explorers and wigged territorial governors that graced the walls along the stairwell. On the third floor we marched through an exhibit room crammed with Civil War artifacts and turned down a long narrow corridor past a row of glass cases displaying uniforms, swords, and tattered flags. When I asked Perry why we were going to visit Nico, he replied somewhat defensively and without breaking stride: "You wanted answers, my brother. This is where you'll find them in spades."

We turned another corner and entered the exhibit on Reconstruction. Halfway to the exit elevators, a twelve-foot oak door was inconspicuously located between two cases filled with memorabilia. A sign on the door declared *Museum Employees Only.*

"Wait here," Perry said before abruptly disappearing behind the door.

I glanced around the hall and noticed only two other visitors in view, an aging couple intensely scrutinizing a floral-patterned carpetbag preserved behind protective glass.

I waited submissively for several minutes. What was taking him so long? To kill time I wandered down the aisle, browsing the Reconstruction exhibits and historical presentations. I shouldn't have been surprised to come upon a case devoted to the Battle of Canal

Street and the White League. But seeing these artifacts on public display, the hard proof that the League had left a large footprint on New Orleans history, gave me an unexpected thrill. I felt like an archeologist who had opened a buried crypt. The objects held a special fascination for me now. A red silk guidon from one of the League's infantry units, powder-stained and ripped by a bullet, was proudly mounted next to a framed certificate of recognition printed with the words *Protector White League* and a list of the men who had fought in the skirmish. There was also a commemorative medal bestowed on the veterans at some later celebration: a ribbon with a bronze cross attached, the letters *W* and *L* and the number *14*—for the 14th of September—embossed on the arms of the cross. By far the most unusual curiosity was the sheet music for a song entitled "The White League Waltz," composed by a zealous follower to honor the fighters and their glorious victory over Yankee tyranny.

And then I spotted the bow. The small black velvet butterfly bow lying on a field of white silk. The exhibit plate stated that nineteenth-century author George Washington Cable had published a short story in 1889 in which he described this bow as the unofficial badge of the White League. Father Joe had been dead right about its secret significance.

When I looked up from the case, I discovered Louis Robb peering into one of the floor displays near the entrance to the exhibition. Hands stuffed into his brown leather jacket, he seemed innocently engrossed in the subject matter, like a small-town history teacher on a weekend tour. A history teacher with a shaved head and a .38 police special tucked into a concealed shoulder holster.

I had had enough of this charade and advanced on him quickly, taking my chances with a public confrontation. "I thought I made it clear to your boss that I don't want you following me, Robb," I said, my words disturbing the hallowed silence of the museum. "Why are you doing this?"

He turned slowly and glared straight through me with those hard cop eyes. His response was unhurried, as if he wanted me to absorb the full force of his size and malicious disposition. "Imagine that," he said, measuring me from head to toe. "Two old friends running into each other at the museum."

"You're wasting your time," I said. "Tell Morvant that bird-dogging me won't make it happen any faster."

"*Paul!*" My brother's voice echoed across the quiet gallery. He was standing in the staff doorway, crabby and restless. "Will you please come on! The place will be closing soon."

When Louis Robb smirked, his chin jutted out, as hard and blunt as a Stone Age ax. "Sounds like your big sister's calling you," he said with a mocking laugh.

"Go fuck yourself, asshole," I said.

As I walked away, proud of myself for daring to insult the man, I could hear him making a nasty sucking noise through his teeth.

The cluttered staff work-room had the air of an old library vault; a repository of ancient damaged volumes and priceless artifacts in need of repair. Two bearded conservators wearing gray lab coats were toiling in silence at their tables, one gluing an ornate vase and the other carefully unscrolling a brittle map. They found a free moment to glower at me, sending a clear signal of disapproval. My presence was an unwanted invasion of their inner sanctum.

Nico was standing beside Perry near a table strewn with musket triggers and other rusted pieces of iron. I could sense they'd had a disagreement, possibly over this intrusion. Nico didn't want us here, either. In a wordless, impatient gesture he motioned for me to follow him. As we crossed the room toward another door, I felt like a trespasser violating the Rule of Order in a cloistered monastery.

Nico's work space was a small, claustrophobic enclosure, more broom closet than office. My first impression was of St. Jerome translating the Gospels. The only missing furnishings were the skull and candles. Otherwise, every square foot of shelving, desk, and worn carpet was piled with books and papers, the slovenly excess of an eccentric, pipe-smoking scholar who had devoted his entire life to a single, all-consuming project. Except that Nico was young, handsome, usually sociable, and without any apparent personality disorder. He was simply a little disorganized. I wondered if his messiness spilled over into their apartment life and how the fastidious Perry could tolerate such a roommate. My brother had no doubt thrown his share of tantrums over underwear left on the bathroom floor.

"This is not a good idea," Nico said, running a hand through his gelled black hair. "It draws too much attention."

Perry leaned toward me with a hand to the side of his mouth. "Naughty Nico is writing his book on the sly," he whispered in mock confidentiality, "stealing an hour here and there on the state's dime. He's supposed to be researching famous canines of the Civil War, or some such thing. Eh, love? The cover is very clever, don't you think?" He gestured theatrically at the cluttered room. "Who would ever guess what the hell he's doing back here?"

"If I lose my job over this," Nico said with a nervous smile, "the Blanchard family will have to take me into the coffee business."

Perry squeezed his companion's shoulder. "Relax, my pet," he said. "Nothing is going to happen."

Nico cleared his swivel chair of several labeled folders and sat down. It was the end of the day and he looked frazzled. His sassy Betty Boop cartoon tie was loose at the neck, his sleeves rolled to the elbows of his sky-blue shirt. A gleaming swatch of dark hair had fallen across his forehead. I had no idea that historical scholarship could be so physically demanding.

"Please sit down, both of you," he said, pointing at a cracked leather sofa that had virtually disappeared under an avalanche of manuscript pages and rolled charts.

I was careful to keep his stacks intact, placing them wherever there was empty floor space, but Perry pawed the loose pages aside like a bull dog digging a hole. "I can't believe anyone can work this way," he complained.

Nico gave him an icy stare, then turned to me. "Perry tells me you have questions about the White League. How much do you know about them?" he asked. "How much do you *want* to know?"

"I'm still learning," I said, glancing at my brother for guidance. "I want to know everything. Are you the resident expert on the subject?"

A solicitous Perry hastened to disclose, "Nico is writing his dissertation on the White League, Paul. He knows more about them than any living soul. He's been working like a busy beaver for four very long, dreary years on this book. Haven't you, doll?"

"It's not as bad as your brother makes it out to be," Nico said, gesturing at the chaos of scholarship all around us. "Just a little tedious at times."

I sensed an ongoing domestic dispute—who was married to his work and who was not.

"I'm very sorry we're barging in like this, Nico," I said. "I'm in a tight jam and need some information. I'd be most grateful for any help you can give me."

He evaluated me for several uncomfortable moments. I suspected he was still chafing from our exchange of two nights ago, when I'd treated him rather brusquely out on the lawn. "I've always thought that if someone like you needed a favor," he said with a cold little smile, "they just pulled out their checkbook and every problem disappeared. Isn't that what Daddy Blanchard would've done?"

Nico clearly had *issues*, as the therapists would say. Resentments no doubt fueled by Perry's own bitterness toward our family. I was pleased to see the young man defend my brother's feelings.

"Let it go, Nico," Perry said with a sad, soft smile. "This isn't the time or place."

Nico glanced at my brother, then swiveled on his chair and shuffled through a ream of typed pages lying on the desk. "I want you to understand that I'm doing this because Perry has asked me to," he said curtly. "That's the sole reason."

"Fair enough," I said.

"We have to do this quickly. You two shouldn't be here, you know," he said, fingering a curl of hair away from his forehead. "Where do you want to begin?"

I shrugged, turning to Perry again. "I'm not really sure," I said. "I've heard bits and pieces, that's all."

"Do you know about the Italian lynchings in 1891?" he asked with a scholar's detachment.

That wasn't exactly where I wanted to begin. I searched my

memory for the newspaper tidbit I'd read many years ago. "Some Italians were dragged out of jail and lynched, right?" I said. "They were accused of killing the police chief, as I recall."

"Somebody shot Chief Dave Hennessy one night in 1890," he said, absently examining his manuscript, "and when his friend found him dying on the sidewalk, the chief told him that dagoes had done it. That was the word he was alleged to have used. *Dagoes,*" he said with a shrewd smile.

He didn't have to remind me that white New Orleans had hated the swarthy Italians who had immigrated here at the end of the nineteenth century to load cargo on the docks. Italians had never been accepted as first-class citizens of our fair city. They were still *personas non grata* in the Uptown social clubs and old-line Carnival krewes.

"So the police rounded up twenty Sicilians and threw them in the parish jail," Nico said. "A group of upstanding civilians called the Committee of Fifty anointed themselves to investigate Hennessy's murder. These were fifty of the city's elite leaders. They were all White League, of course. Most of them had fought in the Battle of Canal Street but were getting long in the tooth."

He explained that nine of the Italians were tried for the murder, but that the evidence was flimsy and the all-white jury acquitted six of the men and deadlocked on the other three. This infuriated the Committee of Fifty. The morning after the verdict, a notice appeared in the newspaper calling for a rally at the Henry Clay statue on Canal Street. It was signed by sixty of the city's civic and business leaders, all of them White League.

"They met at the Magnolia Club to fortify themselves with brandy, then marched out to the statue and preached holy hell. The same place they'd roused the rabble fifteen years earlier, when they'd pumped up their foot soldiers to attack the Metropolitan Police. And pretty much the same thing happened," Nico said, drumming his fingers on a book cover. "A man named Gautier—attorney Russell Gautier's grandfather, I believe—incited the mob to go lynch the Italians, and about a thousand of them stormed over to the parish prison and broke down the doors."

He explained that when the jailers saw the mob approaching, they were humane enough to unlock the cells and let the prisoners flee for their lives. Three Italians were found cowering behind a pillar and were shot to death by gentlemen with pistols, and six others were gunned down in the prison yard. The last two were dragged out to the street, begging to be spared.

"Manuel Polizzi was strung up on a lamppost, but he grabbed the rope and hung on for dear life," he said, his eyes roaming over his notes. "They lowered the poor bastard, tied his hands, and strung him up again. Then they took target practice on his corpse after his neck had broken." He paused and looked at me. "The other *paisan*, Antonio Bagnetto, was kicked and beaten and hanged from a nearby tree."

Perry inhaled a dramatic breath. "Nico is somewhat sensitive about this episode," he said. "His father is Italian."

The young man's dark eyes bore into mine. "My *point* is, Paul," he said, dismissive of Perry's remark, "the White League should not be thought of as a tea club of harmless Don Quixotes fighting imaginary dragons. They've had real blood on their hands from the very beginning. They've beaten and lynched and executed people without mercy. That's why I asked how much you want to know. The story doesn't get any prettier, believe me. Ask your brother."

Perry sagged into the sofa, his knees locked in front of him. "If you don't mind, dear heart," he said in a wounded voice, "I would rather you kept to the history books."

Over the years my brother had obviously learned to protect himself against certain memories and associations, like a soft-bellied sea creature that had evolved a craggy shell.

"Tell me about Kennedy," I said, intimidated by the very sound of this thought expressed aloud. "Were they involved?"

Nico glanced at Perry, then leaned forward in his chair, lowering his voice as if the room were bugged. This did not make me feel any less anxious. "The KGB has always said if you want to know who killed JFK," he mused, "start in New Orleans."

"Well yes, Oswald, of course," I said. "Our hometown boy."

I didn't respect conspiracy theorists, and I didn't want to get caught up in some moldy fringe hypothesis—Assassination Theory #1452—that had been tossed around for twenty-five years.

"Oswald, certainly. And his pals in that whole David Ferrie gang," Nico said, glancing sympathetically at Perry. "But they weren't the only players with a New Orleans connection. James Earl Ray came to town a few months before Martin Luther King was shot. Ray met with people here, took their money. Guess who they were? This was the place in the sixties, Paul. Some sort of confluence of evil shit was going on right here in river city. Racial rage and big money—it made a lethal combination. We were the dark heart of America."

I looked at my brother's earnest intellectual lover. Could there be any truth to this?

"As a rule, the gentlemen of the White League don't dirty their own hands," Nico continued. "They light the fuse and point to a window. There's always some crackpot with a lunatic cause or psychotic obsession who's all too eager to step up and throw. The night riders who bombed Reverend Calvin Frazier's parsonage in 1965. The young clerks who lynched Italians and shot up the Metropolitan police. The thugs who broke Perry's arm."

He sat back in his chair and observed my brother with a concern that was endearing to see. Then smiling ironically, he gestured toward the door to the work lab, saying, "You do something really violent and unforgivable, a hundred years from now you get your own exhibit case."

I could have added Father Joe Dombrowski's story to Nico's list of brutal episodes, but I had too many questions and too little time. The force of so much information was overwhelming me.

"And this is all in your dissertation?" I asked him, my eyes wandering over the mounds of paper on his desk. "The lynchings, Oswald, Reverend Frazier?"

Perry felt the need to answer that question for him. "Dear Jesus, yes, it's all there, Paul," he said, his gaze following mine. "Nico has searched through every library and archive and musty attic from here to Tuscaloosa. He's talked crazy old ladies into letting him read Great Uncle Dickie's diary and Granddad's stack of naughty letters to his mistress. He's cluttered up our hearth and home with hundred-year-old newspapers that crumble all over the carpet. And I can't begin to tell you how many hours of interviews he's got on tape. I've listened to some of these old biddies prattle on till *I'm* blue in the face."

My brother paused and heaved a weary sigh. "We're going to have one doozy of a celebration when Nico completes this masterwork. Am I right, love? I do hope you and Claire will join us, Paul."

Nico seemed embarrassed by Perry's effusive praise.

"After all this work," I said, "you must have a good sense of who the players are, Nico. The White League roster. Surely you have a list of names."

I could see the apprehension in his eyes.

"That's really why I'm here. I need a name. Someone I can talk to."

His smile was slow in forming. Cautious, exploratory. "I can give you names. A whole book full of names, Paul," he said. "But then I'd have to kill you."

Perry snickered. "Not if they kill him first," he said.

They both found this amusing. I did not.

"Nico," I said, "I'm under a lot of pressure. I've got problems you can't imagine. I would appreciate anything you can tell me."

He tapped the edge of a cassette tape against the desk. "The names of the original White Leaguers who fought on Canal Street are well recorded," he said.

I had seen those names listed in the tattered green book. About two thousand entries in all, an overwhelming number.

"But I haven't traced every one of them to the present. I haven't created a family tree, if that's what you're looking for. Something like that would take decades. And besides," he said, "the attrition rate has been considerable. Some didn't have children…some of their children and grandchildren lost interest…and as the years rolled on, some didn't measure up. They didn't make the cut. There have always been men at the top, like General Ogden, who decide which families are worthy to carry on the legacy and which are not."

"Apparently," Perry interjected with a self-accusatory smile, "the

Blanchard boys are *not*, young brother. We flunked the course. But consider their sad dilemma. One reckless faggot, and one, well—I'm not sure what your offense is, Paulie. I imagine that running off to California and living among wanton hippies didn't help your case."

It may not have helped my case, but it had preserved my sanity. Three years of marijuana oblivion in an old Victorian house full of Quakers in the Haight. It may not have improved my social standing, but it kept me out of a Louisiana prison.

"To be honest," Nico said, tapping the cassette tape, "I haven't been able to document any White League activity after the 1960s. That nasty era may've been their swan song. But I keep looking for evidence that they're still around. These are not men who leave a vapor trail. They've spent a hundred years concealing their identities. If their actions were traceable, they'd all be serving time. But since the very beginning, back in Reconstruction, they've always had pull with the newspapers, the police, the courts. Our illustrious public servants owe them. The do-gooders fear them. Everybody plays the game. It's in the city's best interest."

I had the sinking feeling I was going to leave this little pow-wow with nothing solid in my tobacco pouch. Nico must have read the disenchantment on my face because he said, "I'm sorry, Paul. You want me to tell you I've got proof positive that the White League is still going strong and that so-and-so is a member, but I can't do that. It wouldn't be true. There are no bloody fingerprints or smoking guns. These people are elusive, to put it mildly. They cover their tracks. Think about Oswald and James Earl Ray."

What I thought instead was that Nico's dissertation was possibly the most cleverly disguised novel-in-progress of the last decade. It had the potential to rocket up the bestseller list in fiction.

"What are you going to do if your book is published?" I asked him. In spite of my misgivings I was impressed by the snow storm of penciled pages. "If everything you say about them is true, won't that cause some serious problems for you?"

He exchanged worried glances with Perry.

"Yes, well, Nico *is* talking with a small regional publisher about the book," my brother said.

"A *local* publisher?" I asked, hearing an alert siren sound in the back of my head.

"In fact, yes. We've already considered what to do when the book comes out," Perry said, smiling affectionately at his lover. "I haven't discussed it yet with Mother or the rest of you, but Nico and I are planning to leave town as soon as he's done. We don't feel that the climate here will be very—receptive, shall we say."

"Somebody else knows about all this?" I asked, spreading my arms, imagining the potential damage contained in these hillocks of loose notes and labeled folders and half-typed chapters.

There was a knock on the door, insistent and loud. Nico stuck the cassette tape in his shirt pocket and began turning over manuscript pages to their blank sides. "Who is it?" he asked, shoving several books into his desk drawer.

A muffled voice spoke through the door: "May I come in, please?"

Without waiting for permission, the door opened swiftly and we were treated to the tall, angular presence of Claude Villere, Basil's cohort in the council-hearing walkout. The old boy was wearing a dark chalk-striped suit and tie and his silver tuft of hair rose like an egret's plumage. Behind the goggle-like glasses his eyes appeared magnified and triumphant in their detection of something awry. Everything about his bearing suggested the school master with a birch rod concealed behind his back. As chairman of the museum's board of directors, he had every right to intrude, I supposed.

"My, my, who have we here?" he said, his silver mustache a lopsided arch of poorly scissored bristles. "When they complained there were intruders in the work lab, I should have known it would be Charlie Blanchard's boys."

Perry unlocked his knees and stood up from the sofa. "Villere, did your mother forget to teach you how to knock?" he asked in a nasty humor. My brother clearly had nothing but contempt for the man. "We'll be finished in a moment. Why don't you be a good fellow and go nose-polish some Alabama sabers?"

Claude ignored the remark and turned directly to Nico. "Young man," he said, his enlarged eyes surveying the slew of manuscript pages spread across the desk, "I believe you have violated the museum rules, have you not? No visitors are allowed back here. Why don't you please ask your gentlemen friends to meet you elsewhere?"

"I'm sorry, Mr. Villere," Nico said, his hand resting nonchalantly over the notes scribbled on a yellow pad.

I rose to my feet. "This is my fault, Claude," I said, walking toward him. "Nico insisted that our visit was unauthorized, but I'm afraid I twisted his arm." I stopped before my aging Magnolia Club colleague and peered into his ridiculous glasses. "Nico's a special friend of our family and I've always wanted to see where he works."

Claude's eyes darted toward the desk, then back again. "Never listen to a Blanchard, young man, except when it comes to coffee beans," he said, a false smile extending the uneven hairs of his mustache. "That's the lesson here."

Perry was staring at the elderly chairman with a palpable contempt. "Lawdy, lawdy, Miss Claudie," he said. "Isn't there a Cub Scout troop you could be stalking out in the museum? You never know when a little blond boy might wander unchaperoned into the lav."

I clutched my brother's arm and guided him toward the door. "Come along now, Perry," I said, eager to avoid a confrontation. "We've overstayed our visit. Time to leave these gentlemen to the noble work of preserving posterity. Good luck, Nico. Thank you for the tour. Adieu, Claude. See you at the club."

We were hardly out the door when Nico called, "Just a moment, Paul!"

I stopped and turned around, a recalcitrant Perry at my side.

"You forgot your music tape," the young man said, reaching into his shirt pocket. He stepped around Claude Villere and handed the cassette to me. "I enjoyed listening to it. Thanks for the loan."

It was the cassette he'd been tapping against the desk. I glanced at the plastic cover. The name *Ida Benjamin* was hand-printed on the label. My mother-in-law. He had interviewed my mother-in-law for his dissertation on the White League.

"It was definitely a learning experience," Nico said with a suggestive nod at the cassette. "It's always good to hear what other people are listening to. But I'm finished with it—you can have it back. I have a feeling you appreciate it more than I do."

Chapter twenty-four

Perry insisted that I come up to his apartment for a final drink. He couldn't shake his agitation over the arrival of Claude Villere and wanted company while he calmed down. "That smarmy old pedophile," he said, handing me a gin and tonic he'd mixed with an unsteady hand. "He's always sticking his shriveled cock where it doesn't belong."

I wasn't so sure that Claude's intrusion had made any difference. Nico didn't have what I desperately needed. Despite his exhaustive research, he couldn't offer me a single living name.

"Look, I know you're disappointed that we can't point a finger at somebody and say he's White League," Perry said, pouring himself a sherry. "Believe me, if I knew for certain who had me beaten up, the cowardly bastards, I would've clawed their eyes out a long time ago."

"It's kind of like the Mardi Gras floats, isn't it? They can see us but we don't know who *they* are."

His faced darkened. "I have my suspicions, of course. Some of the old boys at the Magnolia Club have never been able to look me straight in the eye. For the longest time I thought they just wanted to bugger me in a pantry closet, like horny Uncle Claude."

Had I heard him correctly? Was he saying that Claude Villere—?

"Don't look so shocked, Paul. He's certainly not the only one I could name."

I didn't want to believe we'd grown up in a world of such despicable secrets and lies. Was it all a masquerade? The people we'd trusted weren't who we thought they were.

The telephone rang. "Hello, doll," Perry said, smiling into the mouthpiece. "I hope we didn't get you fired. Is that big tall Mother Superior going to punish my little school chum?"

Nico said something that made my brother blurt out a high girlish shriek that embarrassed me to hear. The *parrot screech*, as Kathleen and I had labeled his rarest of laughs. It always made us cringe.

I was uncomfortable overhearing their conversation, so I wandered off in search of the toilet. When I returned, the dialogue had turned angry. "Why don't you move a bed into your little cubby hole, pet, and that way you'll never have to come home at all," Perry was complaining.

Within seconds he had slammed down the receiver. "Prick!" he shouted across the empty loft. "He spends half his goddamned nights working on that book. At least that's what he *tells* me he's doing."

I found my gin and tonic and drank it down to the ice. "How did you two meet, anyway?" I asked. "Doin' the White League Waltz?"

He glared at me, unamused. "You're closer than you think, smartass," he said. "Mardi Gras party. I came as a Confederate general and he showed up as a Metropolitan policeman, complete with black face and dashing blue uniform. We staged a spontaneous skirmish in front of eighty people, and I forced him to submit to my authority."

I didn't want to hear any more of the details.

"He'd just started his dissertation," Perry said wistfully. "We had no idea we had so much in common."

I gazed fondly at the ice in my glass. "You know," I said, "I met Claire the same way. The Rex ball, when she was fifteen years old."

My brother sighed with an innocent, reminiscent smile. "I hope you didn't make the darling girl spend the evening on her knees," he said, "like I did poor Nico."

Before leaving Perry's apartment I phoned Touro Infirmary to check on Rosetta's status. The nurse cheerfully assured me that Rosetta had stabilized and was resting comfortably, but she admitted some concern over the elderly woman's disorientation. "She's getting the present mixed up with the past. Her memory's playing tricks on her," the nurse said. "It's fairly common after what she's been through." She explained that the doctors wanted to keep Rosetta under observation until this improved. "Your wife and children are with her right now, Mr. Blanchard. Would you like me to transfer your call to the room?"

Julie answered the phone. "I thought you were grounded for the whole weekend," I said. "Did Mom give you a papal dispensation to visit the sick?"

"Dad!" she squealed. "Are you okay? We've been looking for you!"

"I'm fine, sweetheart. Why wouldn't I be?"

"We heard the police beat you up!"

Claire wrestled the phone away. "Paul, are you all right?" She sounded more angry than sympathetic.

"A little wiser," I said.

"Kathleen called and told me what happened. I tried to get Eric on the line, but he was out. So was Henry Lesseps. Where are all our damned lawyers when we need them?"

"Lynching Italians," I said.

"Beg your pardon?"

"Calm down, Claire. Take a deep breath. I'm okay. They didn't haul me off to jail. I had Jesus right by my side."

Or the next best thing—the Reverend Calvin Frazier.

"What were you *doing*, Paul?" She was even more angry now

that she knew I had survived. "What were you *thinking*? The kids have been worried to death about you all afternoon. Where the hell *are* you?"

"I'm having a drink with Perry." Sherry glass in hand, my brother smiled at me from the wet bar, a churlish grin that showed how much he was enjoying my own nettled predicament. "He sends his love."

"Dammit, Paul, I don't find this as cute as you do. You should have called us to say everything was okay."

"May I speak with my son, please?"

There was a long pause while she breathed fire into the receiver.

"Claire, put Andy on, please. I will explain things to him, and he can explain them to you in a rational manner."

The line crackled again in two audible syllables that I believe added up to the word *bastard*. Then Andy was on the line. "Hi, Dad," he said calmly. "Did you take it to The Man?"

I smiled. I just wanted to hear his soft sweet voice. "I tried," I said, "but his foot came down on my neck."

"Cool," he said. "Did you get tear gassed?"

"Nightstick upside the head."

"Awesome," he said. "Did it hurt?"

"A little. But I'm okay. Really I am, son. Tell the girls to chill. I'll be home for supper. Half hour, max."

"Roger that," he said, my secret co-conspirator.

"How is Rosetta? Is she awake? Have you talked to her?"

He made a long *ehhhh* sound, his voice trailing off as if he were walking away from the receiver. "She comes and goes, Dad. Right now she's sleeping, I think." He whispered, "She thought I was *you*, Dad. She kept calling me *'T Paul*." Short for *Petit Paul*. She hadn't called me that since I was Andy's age. "She asked me if I knew where her son was. Something about how he hadn't come home all night."

I exhaled sadly and stared at Perry across the room.

"By the way, he called looking for you today," Andy said. "Did Mom tell you?"

"Who called?"

"Rosetta's son. That guy in prison. He called twice."

I knew I would have to speak with Jaren sooner or later. I wasn't looking forward to that exchange. "Okay, thanks, pooch," I said. "Tell Mom I'm on my way home."

Perry walked me to the landing at the top of the stairs. This had been the longest time we'd spent together in fifteen years and my leaving seemed to depress him. The mischief had left his eyes and he looked rejected and forlorn, like a man who was going to spend his Saturday night alone.

"Blackmail is a sorry business. I wish I could help you," he said, patting me affectionately on the arm. "Isn't there anything else I can do? You can have my share of the coffee money if you need it."

I smiled at him. It was never too late to be an older brother. "Those things Nico told us about the White League," I said. "They seem a little far-fetched. Do you believe them?"

He smiled sadly. "I've lived through some of it," he said. "The rest I take his word for. Nico is a serious scholar. But he's also a dear sweet boy and we love each other very much. Sometimes I wonder if he's finishing that book just to make me feel better about what happened to me a long time ago."

I could see now that I had underestimated Nico's importance in my brother's life. I was going to have to make amends to both of them.

"I want you and Nico to come over for dinner sometime soon," I said. "Will you do that? I want to introduce him to Claire and the kids."

He smiled and patted the side of my head. "If Dell will serve that bread pudding recipe you stole from Commander's."

We hugged and said good-bye. I took a few steps down the stairs, then gathered my courage and turned around. I should have let this go but I couldn't. "Perry, there's still one thing I've been wondering about all evening," I said.

He shrugged as if to say, *go ahead. Why not?*

"David Ferrie," I said.

His face tightened, a clear warning of danger approaching. "What can I help you with, Paul?"

"When you were hanging out with him," I asked, "did you ever meet Oswald?"

I was risking provocation, but I had to know. To my relief the question didn't offend or incite him. His shoulders sagged, his thoughts turned inward, and he seemed to be searching back nearly thirty years for answers. "He came to some of David's parties," he said matter-of-factly. "I remember he had one of those scraggly beatnik beards, like Maynard G. Krebbs. People called him Leon. He was quiet and intense, and he ran with David's Cuban friends. I never talked to him. He seemed to think he was superior to the rest of us."

"My God, Perry," I said, too stunned to think. "Did you know what they were planning to do?"

He shook his head. "I knew something was in the air. They hated Kennedy and niggers and Communists, especially Castro. Scads of them were playing army in the swamps across the lake, somewhere near Lacombe. I didn't take them seriously. I never imagined…"

I tried very hard to wrap my mind around what my brother was saying. He had been there. He had partied with the usual suspects.

"And afterwards," I said, my heart racing after the truth. "Did anyone question you about what you'd seen? Or who you'd associated with?"

He stared blankly into the maw of history. "I didn't talk to anyone," he said. "I was never asked a word."

I thought I detected disappointment.

He smiled darkly. "I was never given the opportunity to confess."

A scandal of that magnitude would have destroyed our parents. It was difficult enough having a son who was involved with a carpet-headed pedophile. But *this*?

"Henry was working for the D.A. back then," I reminded him. "I'm sure that's why you were never pulled into the investigation."

"Oh yes, loyal Henry the Fifth," he said with a melancholy smile. "Our inside man. One of the perks of growing up in the right family. The other boys in David's posse—Al and Melvin—were dragged through living hell. They've been hounded for what? Twenty-five years now. Every reporter and scandalmonger from here to Timbuktu wants their story. They'll always be under the microscope."

I pitied them, certainly. If they had been anything like my brother, they'd been young and naive and on-the-scene for the flattering attentions and easy physical pleasures. They may not have had a political bone in their bodies.

"They didn't share your good fortune, Perry," I said. "Their folks didn't have the pull to save them."

He regarded me with a cheerless smile. "What you're saying, Paul," he said, "is their folks weren't White League."

Chapter twenty-five

After dinner, while Claire and the children were watching a rented movie in the den, I borrowed Julie's boom box and snuck off down the hall to the library. I didn't want them to hear the cassette labeled *Ida Benjamin* that Nico had given to me. I had no idea what to expect myself.

There was a damp chill in the stately old room, so I lit a fire in the hearth and settled into a straight-backed chair at my father's writing desk. I considered locking the doors, but that would have created suspicion in Claire's mind if for some reason she came looking for me. I was prepared for that eventuality. I would tell her that my assistant had tape-recorded a meeting I'd missed while I was at Angola penitentiary. I needed to hear what the marketing department had discussed about the new gourmet line of coffee.

I slipped the cassette into the recorder and began to listen. It was Ida's voice, all right. Nico was a very charming interviewer, and within a few short minutes he'd enticed my aging mother-in-law into disclosing memories she seldom shared with anyone. Ida spoke expertly about racism in New Orleans when she was growing up in the late 1920s and 1930s, and how a progressive rabbi had challenged all her comfortable childhood assumptions, and what it was like to meet educated black women for the first time in her life and join forces with them to desegregate the city's libraries and the YWCA. I had heard many of these war stories from Claire and Nina, but during our family get-togethers their mother rarely volunteered personal anecdotes and seemed content to ignore her activist past altogether. However, to Nico's credit, there she was, revealing volumes of private material to a young stranger she had only just met.

"Let's talk about S.O.S.," suggested Nico. *"You were the woman who started that movement, weren't you?"*

I vaguely remembered the name. Save Our Schools. Ida's way of fighting back at the venomous Judge Leander Perez and his White Citizens Council, the peckerwoods who had fought to close the New Orleans schools rather than allow them to integrate. Ida had responded by gathering a handful of fearless friends and supporters to keep the schools open and compliant with Fifth Circuit Court decisions.

"That was in 1960, if I'm not mistaken," Nico said, shuffling papers, perhaps looking through his notes.

"Yes, 1960. My Lord, what a year!"

I had only been ten years old at the time, but I could still recall my parents complaining about *that troublemaker Ida Benjamin* and her *holier-than-thou bunch.*

"You were threatened, weren't you?" Nico asked her.

"Oh my goodness, yes. So many times I lost count. Hate mail, obscene telephone calls, vandalism—you name it," she said with a short laugh. *"I often questioned why on earth I was putting myself and my family through such tribulation."*

"But there was one incident that was worse than all the rest. Do you mind discussing it with me?"

A long pause on the tape. I could hear a chair creaking. Ida cleared her throat. She was a sixty-eight-year-old woman with a voice weakened by age and illness, and I imagined her taking a long cleansing drink of water before speaking again. *"How do you know, Mr. Menotti?"* she asked, sounding both surprised and gently annoyed. *"It's never been written about. We kept it out of the newspapers."*

"*The story has been around for years, Mrs. Benjamin,*" he responded politely. "*It's a small town, really. People talk.*"

"*Oh, they do indeed,*" she agreed, laughing. "*They sure as hell do.*"

"*I would like to hear what really happened. But only if you feel comfortable telling me.*"

I searched my memory but couldn't recollect hearing of anything more traumatic than the phone threats and a burning effigy of Ida hanging from an oak tree on St. Charles Avenue.

"*You strike me as a trustworthy young man,*" she said. "*And you come with high recommendations. Will you promise me to write the story accurately and treat what I tell you with the utmost respect?*"

Nico promised her sincerely.

I could picture her fragile, bent frame resting awkwardly on a settee in the parlor of their State Street mansion, the dignity still blazing in those lovely brown eyes, the same eyes she'd passed on to her beautiful daughters.

"*Well then,*" she said, again clearing her throat, "*I assume you're asking about my abduction. Is that correct?*"

"Yes, ma'am."

Her abduction! I leaned forward in my chair. Claire had never mentioned an abduction.

"*My husband had begged me to take a bodyguard with me everywhere I went back in those days. He offered to hire an off-duty policeman, but I wouldn't listen to him. By the way, he's never missed an opportunity to remind me of that every time we have an argument. 'Do it your own way!' he'll say. 'I wasn't right about the bodyguard, either, was I?'*"

They laughed together.

"*But for some silly reason I believed that hiring a bodyguard meant I was acknowledging the hatemongers' power to hurt me, and I didn't want to give them the satisfaction of intimidating me. Sounds ridiculous now, I know. I was a stubborn woman.*"

Nico made a flattering comment I couldn't fully interpret from the tape.

"*So I left an S.O.S. meeting at Reverend Calvin Frazier's church one night and I was only a few blocks away when two cars ran me into*" *a ditch and these white men jumped out and broke my window and dragged me out of the car. They were wearing Mardi Gras masks, so I didn't get a look at their faces."*

Father Joe's abductors had been wearing Carnival masks, too.

"I screamed bloody murder but it was dark and quiet in that neighborhood below Magazine, and nobody came to my rescue."

I wondered if Claire had ever heard this story—if she knew what had happened, but found it too painful to reveal even to a husband. My quick calculation told me that Ida would have been thirty-eight years old at the time, the same age as Claire right now. A mother with three children at home, the youngest still in Newcomb Nursery.

"They taped my mouth and pulled some kind of hood over my head," she explained in an animated voice. *"It was so dark that night. It felt like every star in heaven had disappeared and that God had turned His back on me once and for all."*

The hood again.

Two men held her down in the back seat while they drove off into that hot June night. *"I expected them to molest me and then dump my body out in the swamp somewhere. One of them had busy hands and touched me a lot, but his buddy told him to stop. It could've been worse, I'm sure. They sounded like redneck coon hunters from down in Plaquemines or St. Bernard, and at first I thought they were Leander Perez's men."*

About forty minutes into the ride they stopped the car. She knew they were somewhere far out of the city because the road had been smooth and deadly quiet for many miles, without the sound of a single passing vehicle, and now she could hear crickets singing in the summer woods. Her hands were tied with rope and they kept the hood over her head as they led her like a sacrificial goat up wooden steps to a sagging porch. She sensed that they were at a fishing camp or someone's weekend cabin. She could smell salt in the air and the oily exhaust of outboard motors and suspected they were deep in the wetland marshes south of New Orleans.

The night was heavy and warm. Window units hummed inside the cabin. They seated her in a stiff leather armchair and instructed her not to move. Even with the hood in place she could detect an aroma of chicory coffee and bourbon and the thick choking smoke from many cigars. She felt the presence of several men, their bodies shifting about in the chairs surrounding her, perhaps as many as a dozen of them, watching her silently and toking on their cigars. She waited for what seemed like an eternity before someone finally spoke to her.

"He was an older man with an Uptown accent and it relieved me no end to hear that voice," Ida said. *"Until that moment I thought I was going to be fed to the alligators. But hearing him speak in a cultured way, in that familiar accent I had heard all my life, relaxed me a little, and for the first time since they kidnapped me I thought I might get out of that nightmare in one piece."*

"Did you recognize who he was?" Nico asked her.

She ruminated over the question. *"I've wondered about that man just about every day since it happened, going on thirty years now. After that night I listened very carefully to every older gentleman I spoke with at dinners and Carnival balls and leadership meetings of this and that civic group. I've had my suspicions, of course, but I could never really say for sure who he was. So many of those fellows spoke exactly alike. My husband sounds like them, too, you know. Soft, buttery vowels and dragged-out words. You don't hear their peculiar accent so much any more. They're a dying breed."* She added with a laugh, *"And thank God for that!"*

As she sat in the leather chair surrounded by silent men, her dress in disarray, her wrists bound and her face smothered by the hood, the older gentleman apologized for the abduction. He told her it was the only way to capture her full attention. He hoped she had calmed down sufficiently to listen to what he and his friends had to say to her.

"I chewed him out and told him it was no way to treat a lady and that whoever he was and whatever he had to say, we could discuss this like civilized human beings over coffee in my house, any time he wanted."

The man said that for reasons he couldn't disclose, their group did not make public appearances but had always worked behind the scenes to ensure social harmony in the city of New Orleans.

"*Then I knew who they were,*" Ida declared boldly. "*I had heard about this gang since I was a child, but I never really thought they were real. I considered them another old wives' tale—the white bogeymen of New Orleans. But here I was sitting in front of them, more or less face to face, with my stockings down around my ankles and a sack over my head. They were real, all right.*"

"*And who were they, Mrs. Benjamin?*"

"*The White League, young man. Have you ever heard of them?*"

"Yes, ma'am, I have."

Her words shook me. This was the reason Nico had handed me the tape.

"*The man said, 'We don't disagree with Judge Perez on principle, but we feel he goes about things the wrong way.' They didn't like the rowdy speeches and name-calling and sign-waving mobs. Too much negative publicity for the city. So I said to him, 'No, you just like to kidnap women in the middle of the night. Women with little children waiting for them to come home and kiss them good night. Does that give you the high moral ground over Leander Perez?'*"

Nico was persistent. "*Were they trying to intimidate you into giving up Save Our Schools?*"

The tape spun silently while my mother-in-law considered her response. "*It seemed I had been on their enemy list for a long time—ever since the library desegregation a few years earlier. They hated what I stood for. A liberal Jew rocking the boat in their orderly little world. If I had been a black woman, or a black man, I wouldn't have made it out of there alive that night. I'm sure of that. But I was from a prominent New Orleans family and my husband owned a grocery store chain and rode in Rex every year and they couldn't kill me without causing a big stink.*" She hesitated, collecting her thoughts. "*So the man tried to reason with me. He said that if we integrated the public schools, no white children would attend them anymore. He said that the schools in New Orleans would go from all white to all black in a few short years, because the white kids would transfer to private schools and academies. 'Is that what you want, Mrs. Benjamin?' he asked me. He was a little hot under the collar by then and losing his patience with me. 'You think you're saving our schools, but you're doing just the opposite. White families will withdraw. You're going to make them the poorest, lousiest public schools in the country. The schools won't survive your race-mixing plan, Mrs. Benjamin,' he told me. 'Not in this city. I can guarantee you that.'"*

She paused, as though catching her breath. *"I must admit, Mr. Menotti—his words have haunted me for thirty years. I hate to give that bigot credit, but everything he said has come true. The whites pulled out and left a huge vacuum. The blacks took over. Today the public schools are eighty-five percent black and they're in terrible shape. They're like war zones now."* She issued a deep sigh. *"My friends and I won the battle in the early 1960s,"* she said, sounding discouraged and tired, *"but we lost the war. We changed the laws but we couldn't change the human heart. Do you understand what I'm saying? It's thirty years later and the whites in this town are still unwilling to send their children to school with blacks. And the black leaders don't have the vision or the resources to turn things around."*

A long silence ensued. Nico took his time asking his next question. *"How did it end, Mrs. Benjamin? What happened to you that night?"*

When she spoke again, she did so with a strangled cough, as if the water she'd been drinking was hard to swallow. *"The coon hunters drove me back to the city and dumped me out of their car on the levee road above River Bend,"* she said. *"I stumbled down the bank in the dark and knocked on a door in the Black Pearl neighborhood. Some nice black folks called Hillis and he came to get me."*

This was sounding familiar. The same thing that had happened to Father Joe four years later.

"I was pretty shaken up and cried for three hours straight. Hillis didn't want to call the police because he didn't trust them and he didn't want the story to hit the news. He thought it would bring more crazies out of the woodwork to go after me and others in S.O.S. But I was stubborn and naive, as I've said, and I insisted that we call them in. I should have known better." She laughed. *"The New Orleans Police Department was even more corrupt and incompetent back then than they are now, if you can believe that. They bumble-dicked around for two months and then dropped the case without uncovering a single bone. Does that surprise you, Mr. Menotti?"*

"Not a bit, ma'am."

Another weighty silence, the white noise of a cassette tape rolling.

"There was one other thing," she said, hesitating to finish her thought. *"I didn't tell the police everything about that night. I didn't even tell Hillis. I was too embarrassed. He doesn't know to this day, poor man. In fact, I haven't told a living soul what those men did to me at the very end of their little joyride."*

Nico waited respectfully. When she didn't volunteer to continue, he asked with extreme diplomacy, *"Is there something you would like to add to the record, Mrs. Benjamin?"*

She paused, then inquired again when and where his story would appear. He reiterated that the interview was for his dissertation and that it might never be published at all.

"I'm going to tell you this part, Mr. Menotti, because I want you to understand that those men in the White League were not the gentlemen they pretended to be. True gentlemen would not have done what they did."

Before pushing her out of the car, she explained, one of her abductors had hiked up her dress and slit her underwear with a switchblade knife, ripping the cotton panties off her body.

"I thought, uh-oh, here it comes. They're going to stab and rape me," she said with a nervous quaver in her voice. *"But they seemed content to take my drawers and dump me out in the dark and call me filthy names and laugh like jackals as they drove away. I thought what they did was perverted but not as bad as it could have been. So I didn't tell Hillis. I wanted to spare him that one final humiliation. He was mad enough, as it was, and ready to shoot every Gentile in the Rex Krewe. Which was mostly all of them."*

Nico expressed his own outrage over the incident and then asked, *"Was that the only time you encountered the White League, Mrs. Benjamin? Did you ever hear from them again?"*

"Oh yes," she said. *"I received telephone calls from my dear friend Colonel Mustard, the old fellow who did all the talking that night. He called every few months for quite some time, raising questions and trying to get me to see the light."*

I wondered if it had been the same old man who'd called Perry for years, keeping a jaundiced eye on his behavior.

"Once he even sent me a little package."

"A package?"

"My undies," she laughed. *"Sliced in two, I'm afraid. His note said something like 'You don't want to be caught without these again. Next time could be more embarrassing for you and your family.' The sick old pervert. And there was one other thing in the package, too. A little black velvet bow of some kind. I never understood what that was all about. Some little buttonhole ribbon the gentlemen used to wear to funerals back when I was a child."*

Nico explained the bow's significance to Ida. Thirty years later she seemed more amused than angry.

"Whatever else they were, Colonel Mustard and his White League brethren were no gentlemen, Mr. Menotti. Not by any stretch of the word. I'm certain they were capable of even more serious violence, and I have no doubt that over the years they destroyed a great many decent people in this city."

I clicked off the tape recorder and sat staring at the old cloth-bound book lying on the writing desk next to my father's ancient black telephone. *The White League and the Battle of Canal Street.* I opened the cover and thumbed through the brittle pages, saddened by Ida's trauma and trying to match her story and Father Dombrowski's with these bearded conspirators and the whole dark, buried, secret history of the place I thought I knew. I had always been aware that there were private matters my parents did not discuss with the children, hidden agendas, men-only club meetings, a world of mystery concealed behind the regal Carnival masks. But as I'd grown into adulthood I'd begun to wear the mask myself and sip brandy behind those closed doors and trade social gossip with the brethren, however reluctant and infrequent my interactions had been. Learning that there was another, more exclusive caste within the male mandarins of the city left me feeling deceived and insecure, and strangely offended on some deeper emotional level. I didn't want to participate in such hateful behavior, but I resented being rejected by them. I was a Blanchard, by God. The son of influential businessmen for four generations.

The CEO heir of a hometown coffee fortune. How dare they overlook me? Why hadn't I been tapped on the shoulder and given the wink? Had my own mistake, my vulnerable past, disqualified me from their ranks, as Perry had surmised?

I glanced at the quiet tape recorder and pondered my mother-in-law's disturbing memories of that night in the fishing camp somewhere out in the bayous. I wondered if my father had been present in the circle—if he had sat smoking a cigar with those silent men, ogling the bound and hooded Jewess sitting proudly in her disheveled dress while their senile spokesman prodded her with questions. I despised every man in that room, whoever they were. If my father had been one of them, I was ashamed of him. In my eyes he had dishonored himself beyond forgiveness.

There was a light knock on the library door and Julie stuck her head inside. "Hi, Dad," she said. "You're missing a great movie."

I smiled at her. She was a precious girl and I never wanted to do anything that would bring that kind of shame or dishonor into her dear innocent life.

"Did you guys make popcorn?" I asked with a hungry grin.

"A whole bathtub full. Can't you smell it?"

"Save me some," I said, standing up and slipping the cassette tape into my pocket. "I'm coming, sweetheart. What have I missed?"

"Duh," she said. "Just, like, half the story, Dad. As usual."

Chapter twenty-six

As Claire and I reclined next to each other on our bed, propped against matching husband cushions and watching the ten o'clock news, I held my breath, praying that I had escaped being captured on video. I could foresee how difficult it would be to live this down. CEO *of Blanchard Coffee Beaten and Detained at Confederate Rally.* It pushed all the wrong buttons. This was not the image I wanted to project.

"Oh please, *pleeeze,*" I begged, crossing my fingers as I watched the lead report about the confrontation at the Liberty Monument.

"Is that you on the ground, darling Paul?" Claire asked, glancing up from her *Newsweek.* "I think I recognize your Dockers."

I studied the chaos on the screen. The Reverend Calvin Frazier was being pushed and shoved and locked in a chokehold by the young white cop. The camera cut to Mark Morvant blathering patriotic platitudes into the microphone. Then to a shot of two well-dressed black people, a man and woman in their forties, being escorted to a police car in handcuffs. The story wrapped quickly, the reporter standing in front of the monument and making her sound-bite summation to the camera with a hand-held mike.

"Thank God," I said, exhaling the breath that was burning my lungs. "They didn't get me."

"Not on this channel, anyway," Claire said, turning pages with an air of condescension.

"Oh shit," I said, grabbing the remote and flipping to another channel. "Do you suppose?"

"Let's hope not, Trotsky. You don't want to blow your cover as a secret agent *provocateur.*"

The next channel was covering the anti-discrimination hearing at City Hall. Five seconds of Willie Phillips explaining her position, then a pan of the audience. "There's Angie," I said, noticing my attractive assistant in the row behind Reverend Frazier.

Claire glanced up. "The alluring *Angelique?*" she said in a French accent. "Hmm, good for her. Did you meet her there?"

"No, she was sitting on the other side of the world. You know how these things are. Never the twain shall meet."

The voice-over reported that Mark Morvant and representatives of the Carnival krewes had walked out of the hearing in protest, and I thought I recognized the back of my sport jacket as the white contingent filed through the door. Not enough to clearly identify me. Not enough to associate me with those fools.

"I think I dodged a bullet today," I said, in desperate need of a double Bombay Sapphire on the rocks.

"Has it occurred to you, darling Paul," Claire said, scanning the pages of her magazine distractedly as she spoke, "that someone dodged it for you?"

"What do you mean, darling Claire?"

She studied the full-page photograph of a homeless panhandler sleeping on a street corner in New York City. "You have friends in high places, remember?" she said. "Maybe someone at the TV station is looking after you."

I glanced over at my wife, slumped against the cushion. She was wearing pearl-gray silk pajamas and blue slipper socks with those little balls attached to the heels. Her loose, ample breasts rose and fell in a somnolent rhythm beneath the buttoned shirt. In spite of our glacial drift over the past several years, I was still physically attracted to her. But there was mounting evidence that she didn't feel the same way about me.

I was flipping around for more television coverage when the telephone rang. I reached over to the nightstand and lifted the receiver.

"Are you watching the news?" Eric asked without identifying himself. Whenever he called me in this quasi-alarmed, conspiratorial tone of voice, there were usually several layers of irony to cut through before I could decipher his intent.

"I hope you aren't calling because you saw me making an idiot of myself on one of the channels."

"I'm sure you've heard by now. Willie and her cohorts passed that stupid ordinance," he said. "They're coming after us to pry our cold dead fingers off our Carnival masks."

"Eric," I said, "I don't care if Willie insists on giving Basil and Claude a public prostate exam every Mardi Gras Day."

"Ew," Claire said, abruptly closing the covers of the magazine. "Not an appealing picture, darling Paul."

"Is that Claire?" Eric asked. "Am I disturbing something?"

"We're in bed, Eric. It's kind of late."

"Does this mean she's not sleeping with that Christian Brother?"

In a weak moment at the Athletic Club, while riding stationary bikes side by side, I had confessed my suspicion that my wife was sexually involved with the Brother at the St. Thomas Housing Project.

"We all knew they were going to pass the ordinance," I said, hoping Claire had not overheard his remark. "It should come as no surprise."

"I'm calling because the captain wants us to meet tomorrow afternoon at the den."

The old boys weren't wasting any time. The Mystik Krewe of Jove would decide with all due haste how to respond to the new ordinance that threatened to put us out of business.

"Give them my regrets," I said. "I won't be able to attend. Tell them it's a Jewish holiday I'm spending with my in-laws."

Claire gave me a dark look and swatted me on the thigh with the *Newsweek*.

"You've got to be there, Paul. You and I are the only voices of moderation in that pack of wolves. If we don't stop them, they'll vote to do something incredibly asinine."

"I'm not going to be party to their juvenile plot, whatever it is. I don't care if Willie makes us tattoo a letter on our foreheads, I'm not getting involved in this fight."

There was dead silence on his end. I thought he might have hung up on me. Then, "You're starting to piss me off, Paul," he said in a subdued voice. "I don't know why you always get squirrelly when I try to include you in this stuff. I realize they're a bunch of old buffoons, man. You don't have to remind me. But they're *la famille*, pardner. They're *blood*. Who's gonna throw the beads when they all die off?"

"You will, Eric. You look much better in tights than I do."

After he hung up, Claire and I stared at the television screen for several moments in silence. I was surprised that she didn't offer sarcastic commentary about my conversation with Eric. It wasn't like her to hold her tongue.

"Well," I said finally. "Aren't you going to compliment me for being the last white guy in the city of New Orleans who can pass for a liberal?"

More than anything else I wanted to grab her attention. I wanted her to lean over and hug me, kiss me, the way we used to end our evenings not so long ago.

"Darling Paul, there's a difference between making a choice and avoiding a decision," she said with patronizing sincerity. "I'm not sure you should pat yourself on the back for just not giving a shit."

The hostility that coiled about her remark was as intense as her own sleepy body heat. I was trying to understand what I had done, why our marriage had gone sour, when she rolled out of bed and said, "I'm going to go check on the kids. And then I'd like to get some sleep, if you don't mind."

When the telephone rang again, it was past midnight and I was fast asleep myself. In my fumbling, groggy state I expected to hear Eric once more, or Jaren calling from Angola to curse me out. But it was neither one.

"The Cabildo's on fire and I can't find Nico!" Perry was crying hysterically. "The place has gone up like a match box and fire trucks are spraying water everywhere but Nico isn't home and I think he might be up there in his office. They won't let me near the building!"

"Okay, Perry, calm down. Are you sure he's in the building? Maybe he's having a drink somewhere."

"They've killed him, the murdering bastards! Don't you see what's going on here, Paul? They're burning his work!" He was choking back the tears. "They're on to him and his book and they set his fucking office on fire! I'm going to shoot that pimp Claude Villere. I've got the Ladysmith in my pocket and I'm going to hunt the fucker down!"

"Please calm down, Perry. Don't do anything stupid, okay? Give me fifteen or twenty minutes and I'll be there. Stay in your apartment and remain calm. Do you hear me? Nico is probably hanging around the Quarter somewhere. He'll come home when he hears the commotion."

Claire rolled over and moaned. My excited voice had awakened her. "Whoizzit?" she grumbled.

"Those murdering old cunts!" Perry shrieked into the phone. "They can't take him away from me! I won't let them do this again. I'll put a fucking cap in their heads!"

"Take a deep breath, Perry. Sit down and have a glass of sherry. I'll be there in fifteen minutes and we'll find Nico. Just stay where you are and put that gun away."

"Jesus," Claire said, sitting up and rubbing her eyes, "What the hell's going on?"

Chapter twenty-seven

By the time I reached Lee Circle, sirens were screaming in the distance and a trace of smoke wafted through the damp night air. I crossed Canal into the Quarter, left my BMW with a valet at the Hotel Monteleone, and jogged several blocks up Royal Street toward Perry's apartment. Foot traffic was unusually light for Saturday midnight, and the few revelers I encountered were rushing curiously toward the noise at Jackson Square. Smoke billowed across the rooftops of the old buildings, the acrid, unmistakable smell of scorched timber, and for a moment I wondered if the entire Vieux Carré was on fire. It wouldn't have been the first time the district had burned to the ground.

Breathless and leg-weary, I rang the doorbell of Perry's apartment several times, then tried the handle. The door was unlocked and I stepped inside, calling my brother's name. When he didn't answer, I dashed up the stairs and called again. Although I'd been working out at the Athletic Club of late, my poor fatty heart and lungs were in no condition for this. "Perry, where *are* you?" I shouted, searching the bedrooms beyond the loft space. He hadn't taken my advice to stay put.

I ran down the stairs and out into the street, joining a gang of rowdy Tulane frat boys as they charged around the corner of Royal and St. Peter, following the wail of sirens. A fire truck was parked in front of the Gumbo Shop, its hoses shooting streams of water high onto the flaming mansard roof of the Cabildo. An aluminum barricade had been erected across St. Peter to prevent onlookers from getting too close, and several New Orleans police officers stood guard at the barrier, watching the firefighters at work and keeping the growing audience at bay.

I approached a policewoman stationed at the barricade. "I'm looking for my brother!" I shouted above the din of motors and sirens and hissing water. "Are there any people in the square?"

"Maybe over by the Presbytere," she said, a tall slender black woman built like an Olympic relayer. "We're not letting people any closer."

"How long has it been burning?"

She turned and stared at the water-stained wall of the old museum. "'Bout an hour, I guess," she said. "They're worried the roof might come down."

Nico's office was on the third floor, directly below the roof and the cupola burning against the black sky like a flaming cupcake. I prayed to God, for my brother's sake, that his young friend had not been trapped in the building.

Dark smoke belched downward across the narrow street, leaving a bitter taste in my mouth. A fine spray from the water hoses misted the air. Ash drifted everywhere like large gray snowflakes. My adrenaline was surging wildly now and I set off in a trot along Royal Street, past Pirates Alley and the monastic green garden behind the cathedral, turning down somber St. Ann toward the Presbytere corner of the square. A crowd had gathered at the long curving police barricade, watching two other fire engines pump high arching currents of water onto the Cabildo's roof. Flames were visible in the gabled windows of the third floor, but the lower levels looked dark and untouched by the conflagration. Even to my untrained eye it appeared that the trouble had started at the top. I wondered if there was any truth to what Perry had said on the phone—that someone had deliberately sought to destroy Nico's research.

Several flashing police cars and a red fire supervisor's vehicle were parked haphazardly in front of the cathedral. An EMS van waited ominously close at hand. Firefighters were rushing into the building with heavy tarps, which I assumed were being used to protect the priceless artifacts from fire and water damage. Several men sat exhausted on the cobblestones, helmets and respirators by their sides, resting until their strength returned. I searched for my brother in the crowd milling near the retaining fence. Despite the late hour and their drunken state, the bystanders had grown reverent and eerily quiet as they watched the fire, bright flames reflected on their sweaty faces.

It didn't take long to find him. He was standing where the barricade ended, near the wrought-iron fence of the central garden, waving his arms dramatically and arguing with two policemen at the top of his voice. Perry was trying to enter the square and they were ordering him to remain behind the barrier. I overheard one of the cops saying, "for your own safety, sir. Now please step on back."

"We don't want to cuff you, pod-nuh," the other cop added, "so stop being an asshole and walk away."

"You don't understand!" Perry shouted in their faces. *"My friend is in that building, goddammit! I've got to get him out of there!"*

"It's not your job, pal. Now chill, okay?" the second officer said. "That whole damn roof's about to go."

Perry turned toward the building, his face frozen in horror. Then he noticed something and his features contorted as he screamed in anguish. I turned, too, and discovered what he'd seen. Firemen were carrying a black body bag out the front entrance of the Cabildo, hefting what must have been a human corpse and marching it directly to the waiting EMS van.

"Nico!" Perry cried.

He broke away from the two officers and set out running across the square, the uniformed men in hot pursuit. I struggled over the barricade and joined the chase, yelling, *"Stop, Perry! Don't hurt him, please!"*—but my words were lost in the maelstrom.

The faster cop tackled Perry from behind and their two bodies went sprawling across the hard cobblestones. By the time I arrived, huffing and parched and bending over to grab my knees, they had already forced my brother onto his belly and were kneeling on his buttocks and neck, cuffing his hands behind his back. Perry was crying and attempting to explain himself, but the two policemen were not in a receptive mood.

"Hey, you don't have to treat him that way!" I said, trying not to hyperventilate as I spit out the words. "Let me handle this, please. He's my brother. I'll take him home."

One of the cops stood up and stepped menacingly toward me. "Get the fuck on back behind the fence, pod-nuh," he said, his chest laboring from the struggle, "before I bust yo' ass, too."

"He's my brother," I repeated, backing slowly away with my hands in the air. I couldn't stand to see Perry roughed up like this, his face slammed into the pavement stone, his palms scraped bloody from the fall and a nasty scratch on the side of his face. He was sobbing deliriously and cursing them and calling Nico's name in a heartbreaking lament.

"I can calm him down, officer. Please give me a chance," I said, emotion creeping into my voice. "That might be his best friend they're loading into the ambulance. He was working up there on the third floor tonight and my brother's very upset about this." I took a deep breath. "My name is Paul Blanchard and I own the Blanchard Coffee Company. He's my brother, Perry Blanchard. You've heard of our family, I'm sure. We don't deserve to be treated this way."

The policeman glanced down at Perry, then at me. "Jesus H, Mr. Blanchud," he said, shaking his head. "What y'all actin' like this fuh?"

Three more uniformed officers had appeared out of nowhere to render assistance. "What we got here?" one of them asked.

"Bad boy don't wanna listen to instructions," said the arresting cop, dragging Perry to his feet. He began to pat him down, his nylon bomber jacket, his pant legs. "Had to *pursue* his sorry butt."

I held my breath, praying that Perry wasn't carrying that pistol he owned. He was in enough trouble already.

"Whoa, who dat? What we got *here*?" the cop asked, pulling something out of Perry's pants pocket. "Whatchou doin' with *this* thing, pod-nuh?"

I strained to see in the flickering light of the square.

"Some kinda crack pipe?" one of the new officers surmised, moving in to have a closer look.

"Whatchamacallit," another policeman said. "Musical thing."

"Pitch pipe," Perry mumbled.

"You smoke crack with this thing?"

"I teach music," Perry said, spitting a wad of blood onto the ground.

I was greatly relieved. They hadn't found a gun on him.

"You sure this ain't your crack pipe, Teach?" The officer was examining the pitch pipe very carefully, sniffing the reeds.

"Whose unit we gonna put the Teach in?" the arresting cop asked.

I didn't wait for their permission to walk over and embrace my brother. Tears and blood stained his cheek, and his hair weave had pulled away from his scalp. At first he didn't recognize me and stiffened as I locked my arms around him.

"Paul?" he asked in a weak voice. He was exhausted, disoriented. The chase had left him unsteady on his feet. "Paul, they've got Nico," he said, staring at the men loading the body bag onto a gurney at the back door of the EMS van. "They won't let me see him."

"Who is *this* dude?" asked the cop with a firm grip on Perry's handcuffed wrists.

"I'm his brother," I said, growing more annoyed with his hostile attitude. "The man is upset about his friend, okay? Why don't you cut him some slack?"

"Somebody wanna process Teach's brother here?" the cop asked, looking around at the other officers standing in the circle.

"I've got him," came a deep voice behind me. I turned and saw a large silhouette approaching out of the darkness. He was tall and broad-shouldered and walked with a slight hitch in his step.

"Yo, Lieutenant," somebody said. "Y'ever seen a crack pipe like this one here?"

Lieutenant James Castle was wearing a dark gray sport jacket over a turtleneck sweater. His badge was clipped to his breast pocket. "Come see," he said, taking my arm and walking me away from the group. When we were out of earshot he said, "What's going on here, Blanchard? You keep turning up like a bad onion. What kind of mess you got yourself in now?"

"That's probably my brother's boyfriend they're loading in the wagon," I said, nodding at the vehicle. "And that's my brother they've got in cuffs. Perry Blanchard. Your boys roughed him up when he tried to go over and see if it was his friend."

James Castle stared at the EMS van and sighed, rubbing the back of his thick neck. "What makes him think it's his boyfriend?"

I explained the circumstances.

"You know what the young man looks like?"

"Yeah, sure," I shrugged.

He glanced over at Perry and the platoon of policemen guarding him. My brother was watching the EMS van and had begun to weep again, but he was making no effort to resist his captors.

"Maybe you better come along with me and identify the body," James Castle said. "Your brother doesn't have his shit together."

I expelled a nervous breath. I wasn't prepared to do that.

"You've seen a dead body before, haven't you, Blanchard?"

We both knew I had.

"Let's get this over with, Lieutenant."

"It's over with whenever you're ready for it to be," he said peevishly. He seemed to be talking about something else altogether.

"If we're gonna do it," I said, "let's do it."

James Castle studied me for a moment, then returned to Perry's arresting officers and said something to them. He signaled for me to follow him and we walked toward the burning museum. The firefighters had pumped tons of water onto the building for more than an hour but the flames continued to rage out of control. Sparks whirled like a swarm of sulfurous locusts over the nearby roof of St. Louis Cathedral.

We reached the EMS van as the driver was closing the rear doors.

"Hold on a minute, son," Castle said, showing the young medic his badge. "We need to ID your passenger."

The medic opened the doors obediently and stepped up inside the vehicle, leading the way to the body. "You sure you need to do this, Lieutenant?" he asked. "We've got the man's wallet and his driver's license."

I didn't want to look at a dead burn victim. I didn't want to be the one to tell my brother it was Nico. The three of us stooped over the black bag strapped on the gurney. The odor of burnt flesh turned my stomach. I tried to hold my breath as long as I could. There was a strong possibility that I might lose my dinner before this was over.

"Who is he?" Castle asked, staring at the bag with those small fierce eyes.

"Italian surname, I believe. Murillo, Martino—something like that. Here," he said, locating a clear plastic baggie that contained the wallet. "Have a look yourself. But be careful, the leather's still warm. The heat fused it some."

Castle shook his head. "Unzip the bag," he said. "We'd like to ID the victim ourselves."

The thought of seeing Nico dead made me lightheaded and anxious. I didn't trust my own reaction. "I'm sure this fellow is right, Lieutenant Castle," I interjected. "The driver's license will tell us if it's Nico."

"*Nicholas*," the young medic said. "Yeah, that sounds right."

Castle gave me another hard look, then turned his stony gaze on the medic. "Unzip the bag," he said. "Mr. Blanchard will identify the body."

The young man did as he was told and peeled the bag down to the victim's shoulders. Castle took my arm and forced me to step forward and look. I wasn't prepared for what I saw, or the unleashed odor of charred flesh. I gagged and sat down immediately on a small bench projecting from the van's wall. The only part of Nico I recognized, the detail that would haunt my dreams for years to come, was the knot of his tie and a few inches of a Betty Boop figure that had frayed in a mass of blackened threads.

"Stand up and have another look, Mr. Blanchard," Castle said.

"No," I said, gripping my rubbery knees.

"You're not trying hard enough, Mr. Blanchard. You don't seem to understand your role here. You're gonna have to look the victim's family in the eye and tell them that their boy is dead. Now stand up and face this thing, son. Do what you've got to do."

"Fuck that. I'm getting out of here."

I stood up and moved toward the door but he grabbed my arm before I reached the end of the gurney and muscled me back to the body bag. "This is what death looks like, Mr. Blanchard," he said, squeezing my neck with his powerful hand and forcing me to stare down at Nico's scalded features. "It's awful, I know. The human body is a frail thing. You cain't imagine what a beautiful young girl looks like after she's floated around in a swamp for several days. Bloated and blue and chewed up by God knows whatall. But that's not the hard part, son. The hard part is telling her momma face to face what happened to the sweet child she raised."

I flung his arm away from me. "You sadistic bastard," I said, backing out of the claustrophobic van, desperate to clear my nostrils of that awful stink. But the outside air was dense with smoke and I choked on it as I stumbled my way back to where Perry had remained in the custody of his guards.

The flaring light from the Cabildo strobed my brother's wet face and the dark uniforms around him. They had removed his cuffs, probably on Castle's orders, but he stood rigid and spiritless like a prisoner awaiting his execution by rifle squad. The wavering light revealed his sickly features like an x-ray, outlining sharp bone structure where once there had been soft flesh, and shadowing the cadaverous sockets of his eyes. Seeing him exposed like that, I knew in my heart that Perry wouldn't be with us much longer.

I placed my hands gently on his shoulders and looked into those frightened eyes. "I'm sorry," I said. "It's him."

He nodded, understanding, and clutched my elbows. A strange composure had come over him. Perhaps he had cried himself out. "Thank you for doing that, Paul," he said, his voice hoarse and feeble.

The arresting officer patted him on the back. "Sorry, Teach," he said. "Gawd bless ya."

Suddenly there was a tremendous roar and the policemen around us began retreating toward the garden fence. I turned to see the roof of the Cabildo collapsing in a fiery explosion, the two-hundred-year-old cypress beams crumbling in flames, showering the square with burning embers. Firefighters were shouting and aiming their hoses at the cathedral, struggling to prevent the fire from spreading.

"*Back up, gentlemen!*" someone yelled at Perry and me. "*Get away from there!*"

But we didn't move. We stood together watching the inferno, hypnotized by the blaze, feeling its heat against our bodies. The building was destroyed and Nico was dead. His four years of research had been burned to cinders.

"They did this," Perry said in a raspy whisper, still clutching my arm. "He was going to tell the whole world about them. They knew what he was doing and they had to stop him."

He sounded delusional. Would anyone destroy the city's oldest architectural treasure to protect a few family names and their ancient crimes? I found it hard to believe. But considering what I'd learned from Nico and Ida and Father Joe, I had to at least consider the possibility that my brother might be right.

Chapter twenty-eight

Back at his apartment, Perry sat impassively on a sofa in the open loft while I tended to his scrapes and bruises. There was a nasty scratch on his cheek, and his palms were peeled raw, but he seemed oblivious to physical pain now and remained detached and unflinching when I daubed the damaged skin with hydrogen peroxide and applied an anti-bacterial salve I'd found in the medicine cabinet. My fingers were stained with his blood, and I realized I was putting myself at risk if he had AIDS. I should have been more concerned, but at that moment all I could think of was the time he'd wrapped his t-shirt around my bleeding elbow and walked me home when I was nine years old and had crashed my bike near Audubon Park.

"These pants are a disgrace," I said, pointing to his knees, where the fabric had been torn during the spill across the cobblestones. "What would dear old Dad say if he saw you looking like this in public?"

Perry was lost in a hollow gaze empty of all recognition or human emotion. I wasn't sure he was aware of my presence in the room. I walked over to the sink to wash my hands and noticed the Ladysmith lying near the liquor bottles on the bar. A deadly little stainless steel 9mm handgun Smith & Wesson had created for a woman's purse. Or a suit pocket, as Perry knew all too well. I was greatly relieved that he'd shown the good judgment to leave that weapon behind. At the same time I wondered if I should do him a favor and slip the pistol into my own pocket for safekeeping.

"What time is it?" he asked in a drowsy voice, his first words in half an hour. "I have to call his parents."

I checked my watch. "Almost two o'clock," I said. And then I surprised myself by offering. "Would you like me to call them, Perry?"

"No," he said, staring blankly across the amber-lit loft. "I have to do it."

He didn't move an eyelash for several minutes, his hands resting slackly in his lap. When he finally spoke, he sounded like a patient on thorazine. "They own a little corner grocery in Harahan." Harahan was a working-class neighborhood upriver from the Huey P. Long Bridge. "His mother's side is from Honduras." He appeared to be rapt in consideration. "His old man hates my guts."

I returned to the love seat across the coffee table from him and waited silently, prepared to help any way I could. Time passed. He was in no shape for conversation. I wondered what would become of Perry after this. If he had contracted a deadly disease and his health had begun to slide, who was going to care for him in his final days?

In a short while he stood up with some difficulty and walked stiffly toward the bedroom, carrying himself like a battered boxer after a twelve-round fight. "I'll talk to them in here," he said, shutting the door behind him.

I slouched back in the soft fabric seat and closed my eyes, listening to his faint voice grow louder and more emotional, listening to the sound of his grief. It wasn't a long phone call by the usual standards but it seemed as if an hour had come and gone before I became aware he was no longer speaking behind the door. I may have drifted off to sleep, or into some twilight state where time and thought tease each other in a long, slow, dreamlike seduction. At some point I had stretched out my legs, reclining, with my jacket across my chest like a blanket. Later I struggled to open my eyes and realized that my shoes had been removed and I was swaddled in a thick fluffy quilt. I didn't know I had fallen into a deep sleep until shortly before six A.M., when I woke with a start and read my watch. It was still dark outside the French doors. I pushed aside the quilt and sat up in the chill room, rubbing my face and quickly slipping on my shoes. Perry must have tucked me in while I was fast asleep.

The bedroom door was open now but he wasn't in the room and the covers remained undisturbed, the canopy bed unslept in. I checked the bathroom, the guest room and office and reading parlor, calling his name, but he was nowhere to be found. I returned to the wet bar and poured myself a splash of gin to clear the bad taste from my mouth, and that's when I discovered that wherever he had gone, he had taken the Ladysmith with him.

I phoned home but Claire was sleeping soundly and didn't pick up. My recorded message explained where I was and that I would return home as soon as I could. "If Perry calls, find out where he is and make him stay put until I get there," I instructed.

Then I called my sister.

Although it was six o'clock on a Sunday morning, Kathleen answered the phone before the machine did. Her voice was deep and slurred by sleep, but she sounded neither alarmed nor annoyed to hear from me at this hour. When I told her what had happened to Nico and that Perry had disappeared, I detected rustling movement and the strains of her sitting up in bed, forcing herself awake, trying her best to take this all in.

"Where do you think he went?" she asked in a moaning mumble.

"I have no idea. But you might hear from him first."

"That poor, poor man."

"He has a gun, Kathleen."

"Oh dear. What does he need a gun for?"

"He thinks someone set the fire deliberately. To kill Nico and destroy his work. It's a long story. Bottom line, Perry is out of his gourd and needs to be found before he does something crazy."

"I—I'm not following this, Paul," she said. "Someone set the fire on purpose?"

I heard a man's voice. Close by. In bed next to her. He was asking her a question.

"You have company," I said.

She hesitated, then admitted, "Yeah, I do. Maybe we should talk later."

I recalled that they had made dinner plans for the evening.

"Jesus Christ, Kathleen," I said. "You're sleeping with Mark Morvant."

"This isn't the time for that particular discussion," she said.

"Tell me something. When a night rider sleeps with a woman, does he bring his own sheets?"

She breathed into the receiver. "Okay, I'm going to hang up now, Paul, and give some thought to Perry," she said. "I'll call you back as soon as I hear from him."

"You know what, Kathleen?" I said. "I liked the bald dentist better."

The phone line clicked in my ear.

That son of a bitch, I thought. He'd been after my money, and now my sister's, too. Every dime he could scrounge for his campaign. In his blind ambition he thought money was the only impediment between him and the governor's mansion.

I found a pen and paper and left a note for Perry on the bottle-green deco coffee table, pleading for him to call me as soon as possible. I was seriously concerned that my angry brother was wandering the city of New Orleans with a lethal weapon in his pocket.

Chapter twenty-nine

Before attending Sunday morning Mass with the children, I phoned my mother's apartment in the high security, assisted-living fortress on St. Charles to see if she'd heard from Perry. We'd provided her with round-the-clock care in a comfortable, if increasingly tomb-like suite, surrounded by her favorite mementos and antiques. My call was taken by a black nurse named Oretha, the conscientious but somewhat lethargic woman managing my mother's confined life. They hadn't seen my brother since last Wednesday, Oretha informed me. Without raising alarm, I asked her to get in touch with me as soon as Perry phoned or appeared at their door.

"Yes, sir, Mistah Paul. Is everything all right?"

"Fine—fine. How is my mother?" I asked brightly.

"Doin' good, sir. Real good." The same phrase Rosetta had always used when I asked her about Jaren. "This morning we been practicing on our needlework."

Motor skills, manual dexterity. The stroke had caused permanent damage.

"Let me say hello to her."

I had never been very close to either of my parents, although during the final years of my father's life, he and I had spent a respectable amount of time together at the coffee company and I'd come to appreciate his business acumen and his ability to project authority. Mother, on the other hand, had always remained inscrutable to me, having relinquished all maternal duties to Rosetta while she entertained her women friends at white-gloved luncheons and went about her *errands*, as she called her daily outings at museums and antique auctions and afternoon card games. She had spent more time browsing estate sales, searching for hideous bonnet-wearing dolls to add to her ancient female doll collection, than she had raising her own children.

"Good morning, Mother," I said.

She moaned, trying to form coherent syllables. She could hear and comprehend perfectly, but making herself understood was an exercise in frustration for everyone involved.

"It's okay, dear," I said. "I just wanted to say hello. Have you had a busy morning? Nothing much to report over here. Typical boring weekend at the Blanchards'."

We attended Mass at the Loyola University chapel every Sunday because I wanted Julie and Andy to hear Father Joe Dombrowski's marvelous homilies. I had much to pray for this morning. I could have lit enough votive candles to illuminate a Capuchin monastery. I prayed for the repose of the soul of Nico Menotti. I prayed for my deceased father and my invalid mother, and for Perry to find solace and inner peace. I prayed for my children and Claire, for the misguided Kathleen, and for a speedy recovery for Rosetta. I prayed for Jaren, and I begged God to forgive me. I prayed for Nola Guimont and James Castle. I asked for divine guidance. I asked God to light the way. I asked Him to show me how I could make everything right without bringing shame and disgrace on the lives of those I so dearly loved. I asked Him to show mercy toward me, undeserving though I was. And I apologized for not believing in Him or the Holy Ghost or the heavenly choirs of angels and other mysteries of the One True Faith. I doubted the invisible, I explained to Him in my prayers, although I was beginning to understand that unseen forces did indeed hold sway over more than I was aware.

After Mass, the children and I found Father Joe shaking hands genially with several college students outside the sacristy door. I waited until the last young woman had straggled off and then shook his hand as well.

"Will you do me a great favor this morning, Father?" I said. "Will you hear my confession?"

He smiled at me, the gray brush of his crew cut stiffly waxed into place. "Didn't you get everything off your chest during the silent Act of Contrition, my son?" he asked with mock authority.

"Some sins require more penance, Father."

He seemed amused by my observation. "I haven't sat in a confessional in a couple of years, Paul. We've moved away from that."

My children were playing tug-of-war on the jagged cracks of the sidewalk, which had been heaved up by aged oak roots. "I need this, Joe," I said, watching them grab at each other and laugh—the taller, larger Julie dragging Andy around like a straw dummy. "Please."

The priest cocked his huge head, reading the desperation in my eyes. "It may cost you another bottle of Bombay Sapphire," he said.

"Agreed," I nodded.

Kneeling in the dark, musty enclosure of the confessional, I could hear my children giggling in a nearby pew in the empty chapel. I made the sign of the cross and whispered, "Bless me, Father, for I have sinned. It has been—oh, hell, somewhere around ten years since my last confession."

His face and shoulders were faintly visible through the mesh and violet curtain. He was blessing me in Latin. "Okay, so I've forgotten the translation," he apologized in a stage whisper. "I've never liked the way the English sounds, anyway. Not enough music in the language. But go on, Paul."

I gathered myself together but didn't know where to start. He waited patiently through my awkward silence, asking finally, "Hello, is this thing working? Are you still there?"

"Yes, Father."

"Well, here we are, my friend. Two warts on God's hind leg. Now what's on your mind?"

I took a deep breath and lowered my voice even more. "I've done something unforgivable, Joe. I've ruined the lives of two people I've known all my life and truly care about. But if I come clean and straighten everything out, I'll go to jail. I'll destroy myself and my family."

His chair creaked as he leaned closer to hear me. I had captured his attention. He reflected on my words, then said, "Go ahead, Paul, I'm listening."

Somehow I found the strength to tell him. I inched closer to the screen and in the most cautious of whispers I told him everything. Twenty years of shame. I thought about Rosetta lying helpless in her hospital bed, and my closing utterances to the priest were choked and dry and hard to articulate.

"*Mater Dei*," he said with a troubled exhalation. He rubbed his face as if he needed a shave. "Twenty years, Paul. My God, that's horrible."

He was the first person to ever hear my admission of guilt. Now that the words were spoken aloud, unleashed in the strange gothic dusk of this closed world, I felt dangerously vulnerable, more vulnerable than I'd ever felt in my life. But I knew he was an honorable man who would never break his sacred vow of confidentiality in the confessional.

"Yes, it's unforgivable, Father. I've had nightmares for years. Every day it's eaten at me," I said. "Most of the time I can't look at myself in the mirror. But just listen for a moment. Do you hear that?"

We listened together in silence. Julie and Andy's soft voices echoed in the sepulchral quiet of the chapel.

"They're everything to me, Joe. I'm not going to lose them. I'm not going to disappear from their lives for a single day. Can you understand that?"

He sighed. "Of course I understand, Paul."

"I don't know what to do. I've been supporting Rosetta, making her life as comfortable as I can. I've been trying my best to get Jaren paroled. But the truth is, *trying* is not enough. And it doesn't undo the harm I've caused."

He groped for words, then said, "No, it doesn't, son."

The tension between us was tangible. I could feel his frustration through the violet curtain. He started to say something, then caught himself, exasperated. I remembered how he'd always closed his eyes and shaken his head slowly when trying to make a serious point to his shallow-minded history students at Jesuit High.

"I can give you absolution and penance," he said after a long torturous silence, "but that's the easy part, my friend. God will forgive you, but His forgiveness doesn't mean you're free of this. You've got to find a way to get that poor man out of prison and make amends. You know what they say. 'Without justice there is no peace.' Do you understand that, Paul?"

"Yes, Father."

"I wish I had the answer," he said. "I wish I could tell you how to do this without hurting anybody else. Especially Claire and the children."

I waited on my knees in the darkness for him to give me comfort or relief. Time passed. I couldn't hear my children's voices anymore and I wondered if they'd grown weary of waiting for me and had snuck outside.

"The truth is," Father Joe said, his large face drawn toward the screen, "what you've done makes you no different than the White League."

He was right. I had stood by silently while my old friend was lynched in a court of law. I may as well have shot him in the back.

"*Ego te absolvo,*" the priest mumbled in Latin, blessing me and forgiving my sins. After a string of incomprehensible words he whispered, "Go in peace, Paul. Listen to your heart. Christ will speak to you."

I wasn't so sure of that.

Before going home, the children and I drove down majestic Prytania Street to visit Rosetta in Touro Infirmary. The blinds were open and hazy winter light filled her room, but the dear woman lay silent and despondent, conscious but not fully aware, her sagging eyes fixed on some soft-glowing other world no one else could see or share.

Our presence caused her to stir. She moved her head on the pillow, a sunken smile taking shape as she slowly recognized who it was. "What you doin' here, 'T Paul?" she asked in a croaky voice, grasping my fingers in her cool bony hand.

"We came to see how you're feeling," I said, tugging her hand affectionately. "I brought Julie and Andy. They want to say hello."

Dressed in their Sunday best, the two children waved shyly from the foot of her bed, my obedient private-school brood, Julie in low heels, a dark skirt and a pullover sweater that suggested she would soon have her mother's generous figure. Andy like a miniature banker in blue suit and red-striped tie. What had Claire and I done to these innocent creatures to make them conform so early?

Rosetta stared at them but showed no awareness of who they were. "Did you bring Jaren, too?" she asked. "Where's my boy?"

I glanced at the children. They looked ill at ease.

"No, Jaren isn't here, Rosetta," I said, patting her hand.

She twisted her thin neck to observe me more clearly. "He in some kind of trouble?" she asked, her face darkened with alarm. "You go tell that boy to get hisself over here right now, 'T Paul. I'm gone straighten his li'l tail out if he broke another window."

We didn't stay long. I found the nurse in charge and expressed my concern about Rosetta's mental state.

"We're aware of it, Mr. Blanchard," she assured me. "We're going to run some neurological tests first thing tomorrow morning."

I thanked her and took Julie and Andy by the hands, prepared to leave the floor as an attached trio. This was one of my vestigial manners the children complained about—treating them like toddlers crossing a busy street.

"Mr. Blanchard, there's one other thing," the nurse said, scribbling notes on a chart. "Mrs. Jarboe has received several collect calls from out of town." She raised her eyes from the paperwork. "Her son," she said with a knowing compassion in her voice. "I'm afraid we're not authorized to take those calls. And I'm not sure if Mrs. Jarboe is capable of making that decision for herself."

I knew how upset Jaren must be by now, how desperate to hear the details of his mother's condition. She was the one person who had never abandoned him. I owed my old friend a phone call. I couldn't avoid him forever.

"I'll pay for the calls," I told the nurse without a moment's hesitation. "Let them go through."

"Do you think that's wise, Mr. Blanchard? Considering Mrs. Jarboe's...confusion?"

"Rosetta needs to hear his voice," I said. "Please let the calls go through."

I didn't realize how hard I was squeezing my children's hands until they both deftly shook themselves free.

Chapter thirty

The phone rang during the Sunday meal.

Dell and Corinne had baked an exquisite Morel ham with sweet potatoes, collard greens, and homemade buttery oven-fresh rolls. The two ladies were joining us at the long dining table, as they did every Sunday at noon, and when we heard the ring, Corinne rose to answer the call.

"Let me get it," I said, waving her off.

Eric Gautier was phoning from the Jove den. Their meeting had been disrupted. "Perry showed up with a gun and he's threatening to shoot Claude and just about everybody else in the krewe," he said in a hushed voice, as though he were only an arm's length from the barrel of that Ladysmith 9mm. "You better get down here before somebody calls the cops. Maybe you can talk some sense into him."

The Jove den was in actuality a standard 1960s prefab warehouse located in a rundown black neighborhood on Annunciation Street, one block above industrial Tchoupitoulas and the rail yards along the river. When I pulled up in front of the huge yellow building, I saw that an armed security guard had been posted out front to patrol the array of expensive European automobiles shining under fresh polish. He gave me a diffident wave as I parked, either unaware or unconcerned about the madman wielding a pistol inside the warehouse.

I knocked on the steel reinforced door and was greeted by another uniformed guard, who acted nervous and strangely disappointed. "You the man's bruthah?" he asked, looking past me as if he'd expected someone else, perhaps the SWAT team.

"Yes, I am."

"Better come on inside quick," he said. "They waitin' on you."

There were no windows in the cavernous warehouse, and the interior appeared dark and poorly ventilated, fumes of enamel spray paint and the caustic odor of wet fiberglass hanging heavy despite propeller-like fans turning overhead. Fat Tuesday was only ten days away and the den housed the Jove floats in progress, a secret project on which our master designer and his apprentices toiled for months in advance, coaxing their elaborate creations to life for the parade. The Krewe of Jove didn't reveal its annual theme until the floats rolled out into the gray twilight of Mardi Gras Day, the grand finale of Carnival season.

In the gloomy light I could see a circle of metal folding chairs arranged in a clearing between undecorated float beds, where the krewe must have gathered to discuss Willie Phillips's anti-discrimination ordinance. The chairs were empty and there was no sign of anyone, and for an instant I thought they'd all escaped the building, running for their lives. Then a short lithe figure darted out of the darkness from behind the gigantic fiber-glass head of a laughing Jove, and I heard Eric's voice whisper, "Over here, Paul! Watch yourself! He's not listening to anyone."

Two others were crouched with Eric behind the figurehead, Basil Parker and Creed Brossette, the handsome malpractice attorney married to Claire's sister. Hunkered down like a shell-shocked soldier in bomb wreckage, Creed looked considerably less composed and debonair than he did at family dinners.

"Glad you're here," he said, his face peering up from between his knees. "Perry's lost it completely."

"So I'm told."

"Your brother has finally gone round the bend," Basil Parker whined. His black toupee was slightly askew and he was holding his chest theatrically, as though suffering heart palpitations. "Do something about that crazy fairy before he hurts poor Claude."

I left the protection of mighty Jove and walked toward the float, where heated voices were echoing through the vast reverberant murk. Along the way I made out the bent silhouettes of aged krewemen hiding behind hulking, unassembled parts of this year's mythological pageant. Two old codgers had flattened themselves against a rearing stag with an arrow through its chest. Others cowered beneath a snarling, many-eyed Argus guard dog. Comic, if it weren't for the fact that a deranged intruder was standing on a float twenty yards away with his gun forced into the mouth of a gentleman from one of the city's most prominent families. Claude Villere knelt in front of my brother in a degrading posture, his lanky arms dangling helplessly by his side. From several paces away I could see his long rangy body trembling in fear. Claude was acutely aware that one involuntary twitch of Perry's trigger finger would blow his brains onto the sprawling, tortured frame of Prometheus chained to a rock.

"What's the matter, Claudius my love?" Perry mocked him. "Having trouble swallowing this big hard thing in your mouth? Imagine how I felt that time you shoved yourself down my throat and made me swallow without any noise."

Claude gagged on the gun barrel and Perry laughed darkly, cocking the hammer of the Ladysmith. Ravaged and sleepless, his mind unbalanced, his hollow eyes afire in the looming darkness, my brother towered over his whimpering victim, taunting him without mercy. "I do believe you're slobbering, Claude darling. If you can't handle the load," he said, "I'll have to *punish* you, messy boy."

"Please be decent, Perry." I heard a voice implore him as I approached the float. "Put the gun away and let's discuss this. I'm sure we can all work something out."

Henry Lesseps was standing near the double tires of the float, making no effort to hide like the others. I admired his courage. The old attorney comported himself with the rigor and dignity of a field commander surveying the battle from a distant hill. He alone seemed unfazed by the gun and the appalling behavior of his wayward krewe-mate gone berserk.

"You're a smart lawyer, Henry. Why don't you explain something to me?" Perry said, the pistol pressed firmly between Claude's lips. "Explain how it just so happened that this cunt here comes snooping around my friend's office yesterday, sniffing around the place like a randy old hound, spying on Nico's work, and then lo and behold, a few hours later the office catches fire and my friend is dead. Why don't you explain that merry coincidence to me, Henry, and maybe I won't waste this motherfucker all over your pretty float?"

Henry stood perfectly erect with his hands locked behind his back, a courtroom mannerism. "I'm very sorry about your friend, Perry. The fire was a terrible tragedy for everyone in the city," he said. "But surely you don't believe that Claude had anything to do with something like that."

Perry unleashed his parrot screech, the high shrill laugh—truly a hideous birdlike squawk—that had always raised the hair on the back of my neck. "Dear, noble, Henry the Fifth," he said, "ever the voice of reason. Who could possibly accuse you of being *White League*? Yet here you are, old friend, playing the clever deceiver till the bitter end."

A gruesome harshness eclipsed my brother's smile and he glared down at our father's old companion standing at attention near the wheels. "The game is over, Henry," he said, his words raspy and tense. "I'm going to *out* you and your League once and for all. Starting with lover boy right here. Then everyone in the world will know what murdering shits you all are. They'll know your names and what you've done to me and every poor son of a bitch you've ruined for a hundred years. Are you ready for that, old man? I'm going to fuck things up for your secret sewing circle until only one of us is left standing."

I had never seen my brother so reckless and intimidating. Or so brilliantly convincing. I didn't want to stop him now that he had these bastards by the nasal hairs. But I also didn't want to see him do something horrible that would destroy his life and the lives of everyone who cared about him.

"Perry," I said, walking up out of the shadows, "it's me, Paul. I heard you were causing some trouble and I didn't want to miss it."

He smiled at me, wicked with mischief. "Brother Paul," he said calmly, proud that I had materialized to witness his finest hour. "You're just in time to watch an old pedophile White Leaguer swallow a bullet."

Claude closed his eyes, squeezing them into shriveled pockets of flesh, prepared for the worst. He was breathing shallowly, hyperventilating. I feared he might collapse. Would the gun discharge if he made a sudden, unexpected move?

"Thank God you've come," Henry said, edging toward me. We were face to face now, the old white-haired family friend placing his elegant hand on my sleeve and leaning close to speak in an alarmed whisper. "You've got to get that gun away from him," he said, a trace of scotch on his breath. "He's out of his damned mind."

"Is he, now?" I said.

I glanced up at Perry on the float, then stepped away from Henry's embrace and smiled at the elderly gentleman with a hint of my own malice. He had lied to me at the Magnolia Club. He had been lying for decades.

"I'm not so sure about that, Henry," I said. "He's making perfect sense to me."

Henry looked dumbstruck, but in another instant his surprise transformed into displeasure. His mouth drew tight. There was a measure of cruelty in those thin dry lips.

"I believed your amusing story about my father and you and that plot against Huey Long," I said. "I believed you when you said it was the end of the White League." I smiled wryly at him. "But it wasn't the whole truth and nothing but the truth, was it, counselor? It wasn't the end of the League by a long shot."

His eyes narrowed suspiciously but he held his tongue. I could sense the machinations at work inside his mind, not quite as keen as it once had been, but still calculating and astute and capable of more mental maneuvering than I could manage in a lifetime. There was no way to outwit Henry Lesseps or best him at his own game. My only chance was the full-force preemptive strike.

"What I can do for you, Henry, is walk up there and take that gun out of Perry's hand without anyone getting hurt," I said. "But you're going to have to do something for me in return."

He stared at me impatiently, his expression growing more intolerant. "I'm listening, Paul," he said, sounding a faint note of exasperation.

"Two things," I said, lowering my voice so only he could hear me. "First, no one presses charges against my brother for this. I'll get him some professional help and make sure it doesn't happen again."

Henry raised a single silver eyebrow. "What else?" he said.

"You arrange an audience for me with the White League. Face to face within the next forty-eight hours. No excuses accepted."

His expression didn't change. No one had ever out-bluffed Henry the Fifth. He was the consummate pro at the bargaining table. Forty years in the courtroom, the best in town. Billion-dollar petroleum companies had hired him to save their lying asses.

"You've become a little obsessive about this White League business, Paul," he said flatly. "I don't know what it will take to convince you that you're barking up the wrong tree."

I looked up at Perry holding the gun in Claude Villere's mouth. My brother showed no sign of backing down.

"Give me those two things, Henry," I said, "or we stand here and wait for something very bad to happen to your good friend."

His eyes darted toward the two men on the float platform. "I can't help you, son," he said with a restless sigh. "God knows I would if I could. I've worked some pretty tough deals in my career, but I've never been able to raise the dead. You're asking for the impossible."

I patted him affectionately on the shoulder. "Henry," I said, "I think you're trying to con me, old boy. Bad form, don't you think?"

A stepladder had been set up next to the float frame for access to the platform. I climbed the ladder and saw that Perry was now shaking as badly as Claude, the Ladysmith trembling in his hand, vibrating Claude's concave cheeks. I could hear the air whistling through the poor man's nostrils. He was going to collapse any minute.

"I'm sorry this is happening, Claude," I said, eyeing Perry and praying he wouldn't do anything rash at this very moment. My brother's pale face was awash with sweat, his eyes burning madly. He was a frightening sight, desperate and outraged and beyond all caring.

"I can make this stop," I said to the kneeling man, raising my voice so that everyone could hear my words across the warehouse. "But you and Henry have got to help me out. I've asked him for two simple requests, Claude. Henry nods yes and we can all go home. He knows what they are."

Claude shifted his nervous eyes toward the shadows where Henry Lesseps was standing. The gun barrel was choking him but he snorted once, emphatically, as if to scold Henry for dragging this out. I stared down at the old attorney, waiting for his sign. He made no effort to acknowledge my offer.

"You see, Claude, as things are right now," I said, watching Perry very carefully as I spoke, "the gun may not be loaded."

I looked again at the pitiful figure kneeling on the float bed and pulled the 9mm magazine out of my sport jacket. Unloading the Ladysmith had been the last thing I'd done before falling asleep on Perry's couch.

"There might be a bullet jacked into the chamber, and there might not. But if I hand him this clip," I said, waving the eight-round magazine in the air so that everyone could see it, "the gun will most definitely be ready to fire."

Perry glared at me, his wet face hardening with the slow recognition of my ploy. No one knew for sure if there was a bullet jacked into the chamber. It was certainly possible.

"Two simple requests, Henry," I said loudly, peering out into the dim light of the warehouse. "Or I hand this thing to my brother. What's it going to be, counselor?"

Claude began to blubber, waving his arm frantically in the direction of Henry Lesseps, struggling to express himself with a mouthful of stainless steel. His meaning was perfectly clear. He was entreating his old friend to give me what I wanted.

To my surprise, Perry found the predicament amusing. He flashed me a forgiving smile as his body spasmed with laughter. He sounded delirious, bordering on hysterical, his gun hand wobbling wildly as he tried to steady his grip. Twisting his neck grotesquely, he released the parrot screech once more, a piercing caw that echoed through the gray industrial stillness. My brother was coming unglued.

I looked over my shoulder, finding Henry still standing where he had been from the earliest moments of this farce. He stared back at me with disapproval in his eyes, a troubling look I had often endured from my own father. He didn't appear vengeful or bitter, merely resigned to his own private disappointments. His eyelids contracted slowly until they were closed white shells, as if he could bear no more of this insanity. And then he nodded, a subtle motion of his square chin. He nodded.

At first I didn't believe my own eyes. Henry Lesseps had offered his agreement. I felt my heart beating quicker. "Forty-eight hours, counselor," I insisted in a bold voice. "Face to face."

Claude was still groveling on his knees, gagging painfully, while Perry's body shuddered above him as if he were going into ecstasy. My brother was screeching like a wing-shot jay.

Henry opened his eyes, showed me his soft palms with a yielding grace, and nodded again. *Please end this*, he seemed to be saying.

I turned quickly and approached the two men. "It's over, Perry," I said, covering his damp shivering hand with my own and carefully withdrawing the gun barrel from Claude's puckered mouth. The old boy dropped his head to his knees and began coughing and spitting out strings of collected saliva.

I slipped the Ladysmith into one of my pockets, the magazine in the other. Perry's demented laughter had suddenly become a torrent of tears. He pressed his forehead against my shoulder and locked his arms around me, sobbing uncontrollably. "These dirty bastards," he cried. "They killed that sweet sweet boy I loved."

I let him clutch me for a few awkward moments while the tears poured onto my jacket. When I gazed out across the dusky warehouse, I could see bent old men slowly emerging from their hiding places among the fiber-glass float figures. In the strange muted light they looked like subterranean creatures creeping out of their caves in the underworld.

"Come on, Perry," I said, gripping his arm. "Let's get the fuck out of here before they eat us alive."

Chapter thirty-one

I drove my brother directly to Kathleen's suburban ranchstyle home in deep Metairie, where she was waiting anxiously to take him in. The incident at the Jove den had exhausted him and he fell fast asleep in her guest bedroom, rumpled and unshaven and reeking of sweat. My sister and I sat down at her Scandinavian kitchen table and discussed what to do. We agreed to get him medical attention as soon as possible, together with a grief counselor, and also long-term therapy when he was ready. She phoned a physician friend who promised to drop by after his swim at Tulane.

"Do you think they'll press charges?" she asked, pouring me a cup of bean-ground coffee brewed in a stainless steel dripper. It was not our Blanchard blend. My own sister had gone Euro-trash gourmet.

"Not a chance," I said. "The police report would have to include names and location—and what was going on—and that's the last thing in the world the Mystick Krewe of Jove wants to happen. Can you imagine what the *Times-Pic* would do with this story? 'Rich white man terrorizes his own krewe.'"

As she was walking me to the door, I couldn't resist one final remark. "And how is my old frat brother, the Great White Hope?" I asked.

"Don't start in on that, Paul. I've got too much on my mind right now."

It disturbed me that he'd slept here overnight in an intimate assignation with Kathleen. I didn't trust the bastard's motives. I certainly didn't want him to take advantage of my divorced sister's vulnerable affections or her bank account.

"Are you two planning a church wedding—or a church bombing?"

"You're being a prick, little brother," she said, fingering the messy blonde hair out of her eyes. Without makeup she looked a little washed out and haggard. It must have been a long night for her as well. "Doesn't everyone have a skeleton in their closet?" she asked, cocking her hip and shooting me an accusatory look. "Even you, kiddo."

I froze. My stomach churned. Had Morvant told her something?

"Hmm. I see you're having long-term memory loss," she said with a puckish smile, reading my apprehension.

I couldn't seem to coordinate my brain with my powers of speech.

"California, Paul," she explained, smiling at my clumsy silence. "We all knew what you were doing out there." She raised long elegant fingers to her lips and toked an imaginary joint, the air whistling through her perfect teeth. "But we didn't care, silly. We loved you anyway."

Chapter thirty-two

I waited near the phone all evening for the call. I didn't know what to expect. An anonymous message? A secret password? A summons to a dark address? I had no assurance that Henry Lesseps would keep his word. He was a very clever man. It was conceivable that he'd nodded his agreement as a ruse, acutely aware that I had no bargaining power once the incident was resolved and Perry had safely left the building. How could I force the old attorney's hand now? I realized I was in a precarious position, helplessly dependent on his good faith. On his integrity. On a non-verbal contract with a master of deceit. What made me think I could play this game with the big boys? Lying in bed on Sunday night, sleepless and overwrought, the dark hours drifting slowly by as Claire breathed softly into her pillow, I understood too late that I had been outflanked and outwitted. I felt like hapless Algernon Badger shot from his horse.

The following morning I went to the Blanchard offices on Magazine Street and passed the first hour at my desk listening to a new Neville Brothers tape on my headphones. At around nine o'clock I buzzed old Mr. Mohrman, the company accountant for the past forty years and a close friend of my father, and invited him to my office.

Isaac Mohrman was a small, rat-faced man, always well turned out in suit and tie, his oiled gray hair flecked with bits of dead scalp. He had offered to retire when my father died, but the company needed his expertise and trust, his blind loyalty to the Blanchard name, and I had begged him to stay on a few more years. His book work was flawless if old-fashioned—he steadfastly rejected computers—and I'm certain he would have gallantly swallowed poison before divulging company finances to anyone besides me. A stickler for decorum and convention, Mr. Mohrman couldn't bring himself to call me by my Christian name and always treated me with the deference of a faithful servant, which made me uncomfortable and over compensatory during our infrequent interactions.

As he stood at attention before my desk like an obedient butler, his dandruff-specked shoulders slightly hunched under the Frost Brothers suit jacket, I asked him for $25,000 in cash, deliverable to me by the end of the day. I wanted to placate Mark Morvant as soon as possible, a tidy sum to show my own good faith.

I didn't tell Mr. Mohrman what I wanted the money for, and he didn't ask. "Do whatever you have to do," I instructed him. "My discretionary account, I suppose. Whatever works best."

"As you wish, Mr. Blanchard." You couldn't torture the man and hope for more compliance. I imagined that Dad had made the same sort of request from time to time. It gave me a giddy sense of authority I rarely felt, trying to wear my father's old shoes.

Just before lunch I asked my receptionist to track down Angelique Thomas. I hadn't seen Angie all morning, which was odd. She routinely dropped by around nine o'clock on Mondays to go over my week's responsibilities on a need-to-know basis and to chat about her weekend. I suspected that she was angry at me. I could still see the disappointment in her eyes as I'd walked out of the city council chambers with the Morvant contingent. Among other things I wanted to clear up any misinterpretation.

She took her time appearing at my door. Usually she would knock once on the doorjamb and walk right in with a cheerful smile, chatting away. But today she hesitated, looking uncharacteristically solemn and standoffish.

"Hi, Angie," I said, waving her in. "We must've missed each other earlier."

She was wearing black pleated pants that made her look slender and boyish, and a sleek Mardi Gras purple shirt that accentuated her creamy brown skin. Without its customary animation, her face seemed unremarkable, the gold-rimmed glasses hiding those extraordinary eyes, giving her a bookish aspect. The easy smile, the youthful exuberance, was what transformed her into a beautiful woman. This morning I was staring at a wary stranger who had turned up at my door.

"Come in and sit down," I said, as friendly as I could be. "Let's buzz through a few things."

"Do I need to take notes?" she asked, her attitude sullen and defensive.

"No, come on in. You'll remember anything that's important."

I rose from my desk and joined her at the twin set of cushioned armchairs arranged near a small rosewood conference table. "I want to send over a supply of coffee to the nurses at Touro," I said. "They're taking good care of Rosetta. Could you make sure it happens? Let's do it right away."

She didn't acknowledge my request. "How is Rosetta doing?" she asked instead.

"Not so good," I said. "They're going to run some tests on her today. Her mind seems to be slipping."

Angie's forehead wrinkled. "Poor woman," she said. "She's had a hard time."

I nodded, my chin resting in an *L* of index finger and thumb. "Maybe we should investigate the cost of a permanent coffee donation to the hospital," I said. "They're doing God's work."

She crossed her legs, unresponsive. I had expected her to like the idea.

"In fact," I said, upping the ante, "maybe we should consider supplying free coffee to every nurses' station in the city. Not just Touro."

She glared at me through the oval frames of her glasses. "Are you trying to buy everybody's approval?" she asked after a moment's silence.

I was stunned by her cynicism. I had never seen this side of her. "It's called civic responsibility, Angie," I replied. "Community involvement. Corporate philanthropy. Choose your euphemism. It's the kind of thing Blanchard ought to be doing *more* of. I can't believe you're not embracing the idea with open arms."

She shrugged coolly. "Whatever makes you feel involved, Paul," she said.

Her remark irritated me. "It doesn't matter how I *feel*, Angie," I said with sting to the word. "It matters what I *do*."

"Fine. I'll make sure Touro gets a dump-truck load of coffee today," she said, her fingers laced nonchalantly in her lap. "And I'll ask Mr. Mohrman to run the numbers on what it would cost to supply every hospital in the city."

"Not the cafeterias, please. We'd go broke. Just the nurses' stations."

"Fine," she said again, standing up, obviously eager to conclude our meeting. "Is that it for today?"

I wasn't going to let her get away with such rudeness. "No, it's not," I said, extending my hand toward her armchair. "Please sit down. I want to know what's bothering you."

She wavered, then reluctantly lowered herself again, perching on the edge of the brown leather cushion as if she had no intention of remaining there long. Her long hands were resting on her knees and she stared at me with an unsettling arrogance, refusing to grant my appeal for an explanation.

"If this is about the city council meeting," I said, "I assure you that I do not ally myself with Mark Morvant and his racist goons. You should know me better than that."

Her countenance was as hard and stoic as an obsidian mask.

"I didn't walk out *with* them," I explained. "I walked out to give that asshole a piece of my mind."

A detectable sense of relief crept into her body language. She sank slowly back into the armchair, her shoulders relaxing against the leather. "One thing I've noticed about you, boss—you want it both ways. You want everybody to love you. That's not easy in this town. You're like that camel passing through the eye of a needle," she said with a modicum of sympathy. I was beginning to hear a faint hint of the Angie I knew. "Us colored folks don't expect much, Paul. But just once we'd like to see somebody in your position—somebody with all the right Uptown credentials—walk their camel ass over to *our* side of the aisle. You'd be surprised the way things look from there."

I wondered if this city would ever change. Was there hope for Andy and Julie and their generation?

"Angie, I'm not sure I can turn all that around on a Monday morning," I said with a weak smile. "But let's start with coffee."

She angled her head slightly and squinted through her glasses, a puzzled expression.

"The nurses," I said, gesturing widely with my hands. "Today Touro. Tomorrow the world."

She smiled then, and slowly extricated herself from the enveloping comfort of the armchair. "I hate to tell you this, boss," she said, nudging my fat shoe with the pointy toe of her feminine black strap-ons, "but someday they're all gonna find you out."

Her words left me momentarily perplexed. *Find you out* was not something I wanted to hear. "Who are you talking about, Angie?"

"Both ends and the middle. Everybody you've been playing off—one against the other." She seemed to be enjoying herself at my expense. "They ever figure you out, you won't have a poker buddy left in this whole ridiculous town."

She was right, of course. I didn't know where I stood half the time, or who my friends were. "What about you?" I asked, swallowing dryly. "When I'm found out, are you gonna turn on me, too?"

Her smile blossomed. "I'll have to think about that," she said, pivoting gracefully and striding toward the office door. "In the meantime," she said without looking back, "the nurses. Consider it done. The invisible hand turns the page."

Chapter thirty-three

As the work day wore on, I listened to soothing Johnny Adams for hours on my headphones and gave up all hope of hearing from the White League. I considered contacting Henry Lesseps at home that evening, but I didn't have the temerity to confront him directly. I had no clue what I would say to that revered old dignitary the next time we encountered each other at a dinner party or the Magnolia Club. I wasn't the type to make a scene.

But what was I to do about Mark Morvant? I had stowed the $25,000 in cash in a sturdy Samsonite briefcase, my first installment to his campaign. I intended to quadruple that amount, incrementally, as the weeks rolled on toward the Republican state primary. But it wouldn't be enough. He needed millions in his war chest, and there was a limit to my financial abilities. I didn't know how to tell him I had failed at contacting the White League. He was not a forgiving man and he'd made it clear what would happen if I disappointed him.

Henry's forty-eight-hour deadline passed undramatically on Tuesday afternoon. I was in such a funk I didn't want to speak to anyone in the building. Around three o'clock Angie announced a King Cake party down the hall in the conference room, and when I showed reluctance to attend, she goaded and teased me, removing the headset from my ears during a wonderful Professor Longhair piano rendition and pulling me out of my desk chair by the hand.

"Come on, Muddy Waters," she said, leading me toward the door with sharp nails embedded in my arm. "Your adoring fans await you."

Two dozen employees from the third floor—managers and accountants and office assistants—had gathered around the King Cake while Barbara the receptionist sawed through the purple, gold, and green icing, cutting the oval coffee cake into neat wedges. We performed this ritual every afternoon during Carnival season, washing the cake down with Blanchard medium roast, waiting to see who would find the tiny plastic baby in their slice of cake. Today it was Alex, who extracted the pink baby from his mouth in theatrical horror, as if he'd discovered a roach in his food. Everyone laughed and applauded. The New Orleans tradition called for him to buy tomorrow's King Cake.

As usual it was a festive congregation, except for dour Mr. Mohrman, who stood in a corner and forked up his cake in decorous silence, one jaundiced eye overseeing his young staffers like a disapproving nun. The twenty-somethings always showed up in various states of Mardi Gras disguise. Jane wore a sequined mask with a fluffy red boa feather protruding above her blonde hair. Marcia had sketched cat whiskers on her face with a grease pencil. Big Tom McEnery, our assistant in-house counsel, had strapped a hog snout around his nose and sported a dancing Hula Girl tie. I was in no mood for frivolity and left the room after a few token bites of cake and a round of cordial hellos to everyone present.

I was nearly to my office door at the end of the long corridor when a man appeared from the stairwell exit and strode toward me. He was wearing one of those rosy blank-faced masks that disguised the riders on the Rex floats. His shoulders rolled in a noticeable street swagger and his clothing was more workman than office professional, so I took him for a loader from our warehouse across the street. Did someone invite him to the King Cake party? I was puzzled to see a common bag-handler in the administration building, but even more puzzled that such a man possessed a Rex rider mask. I had one I always wore in the parade, but they were not readily available to the general public.

"They're down the hall where all the noise is coming from," I told him, jerking my thumb in that direction. "Better hurry. The cake's going fast."

He stopped directly in front of me, a stocky figure impeding my path. He made it clear that he was here to address me. "Mistah Blanchud," he said, a white man with a Y'at accent. "Got somethin' fuh yuh, suh."

He handed me an elegant white envelope, the square shape of an invitation. I glanced at his eerie blank mask and tore open the sealed flap. "What's this all about?" I asked.

On a genteel white card with embossed borders, the message was exquisitely rendered in the cursive flourishes of an earlier age:

> *We are pleased to issue this invitation.*
> *Follow your escort's instructions.*

I looked into the mask's hollow sockets at the small, hard eyes staring back at me. For a brief moment I was confused. Then it hit me like a blow to the belly.

"Is this from…?"

Now that the moment had arrived, I was unprepared for my own reaction.

"Let's me 'n' you take a wawk, Mistah Blanchud," the messenger suggested with a shade of menace to his words. "Your transpuhtation is waitin' fuh yuh."

I was suddenly terrified. Perspiration flooded from every pore in my body. What if this was something else? A kidnapping for ransom? It had happened to CEOs in other cities, hadn't it? I turned and gazed back down the corridor toward the conference room. The revelry was at full volume. I knew it was out of the question, but I wanted someone to go with me. Anyone.

"The ride is downstairs, Mistah Blanchud," the masked man said. "You wanna do this uh whut?"

I took a deep breath, struggling to face my fear. I had to take this ride, didn't I? I had to present Morvant's request. Make his case for him. The rest of my life depended on it.

"All right," I said, inhaling another lungful of air. "Let's do it."

An unmarked white service van was parked in the alley between buildings. When we were only a few steps away, the rear door swung open, revealing an interior darkness I hesitated to enter. I had a terrible premonition I might be slammed to the floor and gagged, like Ida and Father Joe.

"Don't worry, Mistah Blanchud," my escort assured me. "We gonna take real good care of yuh."

He waited for me to step up inside the van and then he followed, slam-locking the door behind him. It was too dark to see anything clearly, but I was aware of other bodies drawing breath in the sealed enclosure. "Go 'head and sit down right here," the man said, his rough hands guiding me onto a cushioned bench.

He tapped on the driver's blackened glass and the engine ignited with an explosive roar. My eyes were slowly adjusting to the darkness. I could make out the faint, reflective glow of two other masks opposite me on another bench. Their blank haunting features hovered ghostlike in the black gloom, and I remembered that the men who'd kidnapped my mother-in-law and Father Joe had worn these masks twenty-five, thirty years ago.

"Sorry I gotta do this," my escort said, making a rustling noise beside me. "Jus' anuthuh precawtion, y'unnuhstan."

He found my hands and secured them with hard plastic tie-wrap. I felt a loose cloth hood slipping down over my head. A god-damned *hood*. My collar was damp now, my shirt clinging wetly to my sport jacket. I was fighting for every sharp breath. In the back of my mind I heard a small panicky voice saying not to believe anything he said. Like my crazy brother I had become a nuisance and these men were going to break my bones. Or worse.

Chapter thirty-four

I expected the long drive out into the swamplands, an uninterrupted stretch of liquid asphalt under the tires, the vehicle floating through the dark cold matter of my imagination like a capsule propelled into deep space. My surroundings were sealed tight, erasing all sound except the motor's heavy hum. Minutes passed slowly, the silence oppressive. My escorts didn't speak a word and neither did I. A mouth slit had been cut into the hood to give me air, but there was a gassy leak from the exhaust and my throat grew dry and began to burn. Sweat ran down my face. I could smell terror in the coarse cloth concealing my head, the animal fear of others who had worn this hood before me. I could almost taste the blood in their mouths.

After what seemed an eternity, the van slowed down and turned onto an unpaved road, slipping along over soft terrain, a passage left muddy by the recent rain. Thick foliage scraped the side panels of the vehicle. We were crawling now, ten miles an hour, slogging our way to some remote destination.

"Heh ya go, Mistah Blanchud," the man said once the van had finally rolled to a stop. "That wudn't too bad, wuzzit?"

"Delightful," I mumbled through the slit.

The door opened and I was led out by the two mouth-breathers who'd sucked all the oxygen out of the car. On solid ground again I stretched my legs and inhaled the dank bayou air. I knew immediately we were deep in the wetlands, possibly in Barataria, where Nola Guimont's bundled corpse had been dragged from the black swamp. There was a pervasive odor of decayed vegetation; green tuberous ferns gone to rot, the stink of sulfur and fetid water and dead rodent carcasses half-buried in the prehistoric ooze. I could hear ducks quacking high overhead. This was somebody's weekend fishing camp.

They walked me up wooden steps to the creaking porch, a strong grip on each arm, and I knew instinctively we were at the same place Ida's abductors had taken her all those years ago. I was scared, but I couldn't begin to imagine the panic and intimidation my poor mother-in-law must have felt at the hands of her captors.

Inside the camp, a fire was crackling in a woodstove, taking the February chill out of the damp room. I detected a muffled cough, the faint movement of limbs, and realized there were several people awaiting my arrival.

"Hello, Paul," someone said. "Please have a seat and make yourself comfortable."

Those calloused hands directed me into a soft leather armchair. Then the gentleman speaker quietly dismissed the escorts who had done their muscle work, instructing them to wait outside.

"We're sorry about the inconvenience." He meant the hood and the tie-wrap biting into my wrists. "It's got to be this way, I'm afraid. We have our traditions. They may seem a little crude by modern standards, but we've found that our way works best."

"May I..." My voice cracked. I was incredibly thirsty. "May I have some water, please?"

"Certainly, Paul. Would you like something stronger?"

"No. Just water, if you don't mind."

I smelled their bourbon and Montecristo cigars, just as Ida had described on the tape. Plus a trace of cotton seed oil and kerosene and salty fishing tackle. Male environs, shotguns and casting rods, a weekend escape from the wife and children. Nothing had changed in generations.

"We want to make your visit as pleasant as possible under the circumstances. Please let us know if you need anything."

"Thank you," I said.

I knew that mellifluous old patrician voice, though I couldn't quite put my finger on him. It wasn't Henry or Basil Parker or Claude Villere. But I had heard the voice before. I was sure of it.

"We receive very few petitions, Paul. I can't recall the last time somebody wanted to meet with *us*. It's usually the other way around."

Footsteps crossed the room. Someone leaned close and placed a straw between my lips. I sucked a long soothing mouthful of water, savored it, sipped again. I felt my parched body slowly reviving.

"We respect the Blanchard family and the contributions they've made to the city," he said. "You're good people. Your father was a remarkable man. That's why we're granting you this visitation."

Was he admitting that Charles M. Blanchard had been one of them?

"I appreciate that, sir," I said. "I admired my father very much."

"Is that so?" An unexpected skepticism had crept into his tone. "He left some very big shoes to fill," he said. "You'd do well to value everything he stood for."

His remark struck me as a mild admonition.

"There was some urgency in your request," he said. I could sense the affront my boldness had caused. "So let's dispense with the cordialities and begin, shall we? Why are we here, Paul?"

My mouth was dry again but I didn't dare ask for another sip of water. It would have given away my fear.

"Well, gentlemen," I began by addressing the entire unseen assembly, "I have an old friend who intends to run for governor this year, and I'm here to ask for your support in the race."

A deep silence enveloped the room. It was as if they had all stopped breathing. The only sound was a log sputtering in the woodstove.

"My friend is Mark Morvant," I said, his name rolling painfully off my tongue.

There was a faint murmur among them now, what sounded like faraway voices exchanging a surprised greeting. It did not sound like a positive response.

"He was my fraternity brother at Tulane," I explained. "We've known each other for many years. I intend to support his campaign with my own personal funds. He's quite a charismatic fellow, as you probably know, with die-hard support in his St. Tammany district and St. Bernard and Plaquemines and up in the northern parishes. I think he's got a very good chance to carry the state."

I hated myself for endorsing the man aloud, even to this secret gathering. I hated the bind I had put myself in.

"You'll appreciate him once you get to know him," I continued, exerting my best effort at sounding credible and convincing. "You have the same goals, the same politics. Mark wants a Louisiana that respects everyone's heritage, not just Black History Month. He's a fair man, and you can count on him to represent your interests in Baton Rouge."

I would surely burn in hell for this.

"Who else are we going to put our money on?" I asked. "The guy up there now in the governor's mansion is a granola flake. Do you honestly want him for another term?"

The current governor was a Harvard-educated egghead who often sat off by himself reading Kierkegaard or Martin Buber during fundraisers or in his private Superdome suite at the Saints games. He was out of touch. No one could relate to him. His approval ratings had been plummeting for two years.

"And then there's Edwin Edwards."

The former governor had been indicted twice for racketeering and bribery but had somehow avoided prison. He was a national laughingstock. The New Orleans aristocracy disdained him as much as they'd disdained Huey Long. I was on safe ground criticizing the man as a crude peckerwood sleazebag from backwater Cajun country.

"Edwards is throwing his hat in the ring again," I said. "You know what will happen if he wins another election. He'll spend all his time in Las Vegas. But the schools won't get any better and the streets won't be any safer and the only people making a buck will be his gambling cronies."

I let my words sink in for several moments, waiting for their response. When no one spoke, I nervously filled the silence. "The time is ripe for a candidate like Mark Morvant," I said. "He's transformed himself into a very attractive politician."

I cited his qualities. Intelligent, articulate, charming, mediagenic. I reiterated where he stood. Tough on crime, anti-welfare, anti-affirmative action. The conservative party line.

"He's got all the right stuff to win this election, gentlemen," I said. "All except one thing."

I waited, giving them a chance to consider what that could be.

"Money," I said frankly. "He's not a Kennedy or a Rockefeller. His support has come from working people. Nickels and dimes, a free lunch at the Optimist Club. Poor white folks who are tired of being pushed around by blacks." Christ, I was ashamed of myself. "He needs the financial backing of people like you and me if he hopes to have a prayer against Edwin Edwards and the Democratic Party and all that liberal cash from New York and California."

They had remained uncomfortably silent throughout my presentation. I sat with my bound hands resting slackly over my crotch, wondering if everyone had slipped quietly out of the room.

"I'm in close touch with Representative Morvant and I'll be happy to act as your go-between," I told them. "I would consider it an honor. You won't have to deal with him directly. I can do that for you."

I needed water in the worst way. My mouth was as dry as sackcloth. I was perspiring so heavily I could smell my own body odor. My hair and face, my collar, the blue dress shirt were all soaked in sweat. It was do-or-die time and I wasn't sure I'd made a convincing appeal.

"That's why I'm here, gentlemen. Mark Morvant is our strongest candidate in years and he needs our help. I hope you agree with me," I said, my voice thinning into reedy notes. "These are troubling times. Our enemies are trying to destroy everything we cherish."

They could recite the enemy list in their sleep. Uppity blacks on the city council. A remnant of dying old Jews. A small handful of Tulane liberals. The weekend news had been dominated by their enemies' collective efforts to demolish venerable monuments and age-old Mardi Gras institutions.

"Mark Morvant is the best chance we've got to take back our state," I concluded, on the verge of exhaustion. "I hope you'll work with me to put him in office."

Lightheaded, dehydrated, I sank back in the chair, weak and close to collapsing. The darkness under the hood had left me disoriented and I was experiencing the onset of a panic attack. Beyond my physical discomfort, I felt wretched for saying so many things I didn't believe in—things I had promised myself years ago I would never say. Morvant had forced me into this, the bastard. All I could picture now, in my blind distress, was the hurt and humiliation Claire and the children would experience if I failed here today and he made good on his promise to ruin me.

"Are you all right, Paul?" the spokesman asked. These were his first words since I'd begun my address. "Perhaps a drink, now?"

Who was this man? I knew he couldn't be the same old gentleman Ida had encountered thirty years ago. That son of a bitch must be dead by now. No, this fellow was from the next generation, perhaps his son. He sounded so familiar. I was trying to recall the voice from somewhere in my past.

"Water, please," I said, my throat still unbearably dry. "Another sip, if you don't mind."

Someone bent close again, touching my lips with the straw, an aroma of Scottish blend pipe tobacco on his clothing. I sucked water until I choked, coughing, catching my breath. There was a long indifferent silence while I struggled to calm down. Somewhere in the room a stopper wrenched free of its decanter. I heard a lighter ignite, the soft wet smacking on a cigar. I wondered if Henry Lesseps was sitting here among them. Or others I knew, secretly enjoying my misery.

"We appreciate your convictions, Paul," the spokesman said, "and your generous offer to become involved. We're aware of Mr.

Morvant, as you might imagine. Who could ignore the boy? He's certainly made a name for himself. He's caused quite a stir over the years, hasn't he?"

"Well, sir, he's not the same young firebrand he once was," I was quick to point out. "Mark has changed his image. His views have matured. He's a different man now."

"Yes, yes, we're familiar with all that," the man said. "A step in the right direction. But I'm afraid that stigma will follow him throughout his career. The liberal media will continue to hound him over his past. It's Mr. Morvant's Achilles heel."

I didn't like where this was going. "We're all human," I said. "Many good people made mistakes when they were young."

A slip of the tongue. I regretted revealing something so personal in front of this group.

There was a moment's hesitation, then, "Only the weak and the foolish, Paul. Moral character shows itself at a tender age. The strong offer no excuses. They come out of the blocks quick, and gain strength as they go, and finish at the head of the pack. The weak get left behind, my friend. Sometimes it's only one small stumble early on and their race is over for good."

I had the sudden unquiet feeling he was talking about me.

"Your friend Morvant has caught our eye," he said, "but there's something you need to understand about us. We're not the same hellions our grandfathers were. We've chosen to adapt to the times, Paul. We made a decision many years ago to avoid the cross-burners and placard-wavers. They're crude, uneducated people, and they hurt the cause more often than not. Our methods are more subtle, more effective. Ego and celebrity are not our way. In fact, we consider these things to be counterproductive. In our experience, ego is folly and leads to disaster. Or worse—to discovery. Our problem with Mr. Morvant is that he's an egocentric loudmouth from the sticks, Paul, with too much vanity—and far too much devotion to his air time. We're not convinced he could be a team player." He paused, reflecting. "Frankly, we have grave doubts that Mark Morvant is worthy of our trust."

Worthy of our trust. I took his last remark to heart. Was *I* worthy of their trust? Here I was, Charlie Blanchard's son and the fourth generation CEO of the Blanchard Coffee Company, yet they had never seen fit to invite me into their inner circle. Why? Did they know about my one small stumble early on?

"Tell me something, sir," I said, hoping to sound innocuous and cooperative and not as irritated as I truly felt at this moment. "What does a man have to do to gain your trust?"

Heavy bodies shifted about in their chairs. I could hear an exchange of whispers. How many men were in this room? A half dozen? More? Did I know them all by name?

The spokesman drew a potent breath, an adenoidal draft of air whistling through his nostrils. His reply rang with deadly authority. "It's quite simple, really," he said in a calm, deliberative voice. "To win our trust, a man has to eliminate one of our enemies. That's what it takes, Paul. That's what we've always required."

This should not have shocked me. I had expected something Machiavellian and final. Still, I was unprepared for the raw, resolute nature of his stipulation.

"By *eliminate* you mean—"

"We mean *eliminate*, Paul. That's our tradition. It's been that way from the beginning. One hundred and sixteen years and counting. If someone wants our patronage, he has to demonstrate his loyalty. He has to render the ultimate service. Then he's earned our undivided attention."

The ultimate service. Something they could hold over the man's head for the rest of his life, the cunning bastards. Is that what had happened to Nico? Someone had torched the museum to curry favor with these people.

"And who would Mark Morvant have to eliminate to earn your trust?" I asked, no longer hiding the edginess I was feeling.

I had no choice but to follow this through. If I didn't bring Morvant something tangible, some attainable task, he would happily shatter my comfortable life.

"I'm surprised you have to ask, Paul," the man said.

His colleagues laughed for the first time, a deep rumble of

voices, menacing and damaged by age. Their hoarse laughter chilled me to the bone.

"You know as well as we do who's causing all the trouble these days," the man said. "The smart-mouthed bitch who's ruining Mardi Gras. She's got to be stopped, Paul. She's turning everything upside down. It's been quite a long time since someone like her has come along and raised our ire." He paused for breath, the air again whistling through his nostrils. "If something unfortunate should happen to that gal, your friend Morvant will have our full attention."

The message was loud and clear. Wilhelmina Phillips would have to die.

"Tell your candidate to make us happy," the man said with an icy laugh, "and we'll smile on his gubernatorial aspirations."

Chapter thirty-five

They deposited me back in the alley off Magazine Street, cutting the plastic tie-wrap to free my hands and removing the hood before opening the van door. "You go have yuhseff a nice evenin' now, Mistah Blanchud," the masked escort said as I stood rubbing my wrists in the vacant alley. He slammed the back door and the van roared away.

It was after six o'clock and the Blanchard offices had cleared out for the evening. The cleaning crew was vacuuming the third floor, emptying waste baskets. I trudged to the bar in my office and poured a double Bombay Sapphire over ice. Straight up. Then I poured another. I sat at the tall swivel chair behind my desk, slipped on the headphones, and played a James Booker tape, contemplating my exit strategy. How in God's name could I go through with this? How could I tell Morvant he had to kill someone in order to win their patronage? And if I withheld the truth from him—if I offered no communication from the White League, no proof that I had contacted them—what would he do? My addled brain worked through every scenario, considering the options, searching for an escape route. How would Morvant respond if I told him there was no deal? If I lied and told him I had pleaded his case vehemently, the best I could, but the League had voted to reject his request for support? How would he ever know? What if I told him the absolute truth—that they didn't trust anyone who wasn't born into the right Uptown family? It wasn't my fault, after all, that the White League had no interest in his political career.

My eyes closed, my head resting against the high back of the chair, I was listening to James Booker wail on his piano when I sensed that someone had entered the room. It was Angie Thomas, clad in a full-length overcoat, handbag over her shoulder, crossing the carpet toward me with her mouth moving nonstop as she issued some drowned declaration. She was obviously on her way home.

"Why are you still here?" I asked with a tired smile, lowering the headphones to hang around my neck. "Have you abandoned your husband and child?"

"Back atcha," she said, halting directly in front of the desk. She was studying my appearance with a judgmental eye. "I've never seen you here this late. Is everything okay? You disappeared this afternoon and nobody knew where you went. I checked your parking space and your car hadn't moved."

"Met some old friends for a cold one."

She continued to stare at me as if I had blood on my face. "What did your old friends do?" she asked. "Throw you in a drainage ditch?"

I examined myself and understood her concern. My shirt and tie looked as though they'd been hand-washed in a bayou and sun-dried on a rock.

"You sure you're all right?" she asked. "You don't look all right."

The smile hadn't left my face. "I wouldn't mind some company," I said, raising my tumbler and rattling the ice cubes. "Care to join me? I'm buying."

There was a trace of naughtiness around her expressive mouth. She glanced at her wrist watch. "I'd love to, boss," she said, "but I'm meeting Gary and my old high school history teacher for supper at

Stephen and Martin's." Then she added, "I'd like you to meet her some day. Terrific lady. She changed my life."

"History teacher, hunh?" I thought about Father Joe. "I've taken an interest in Southern history of late. Bring her around for a cordial," I said, shaking my glass again. "We'll discuss the glories of the past and where it all went wrong."

"You'd find her strongly opinionated on that subject," she said, glancing at her watch. "Hey, sorry, I gotta book. See you tomorrow, okay?"

As an afterthought on her way out, she turned and said, "Oh, I almost forgot. Mr. Mohrman crunched the numbers and we can afford the nurses all over town. Let them drink coffee."

"Thank you, Angie," I said, savoring the last drop of gin in my glass. "If I haven't told you lately, you're the best."

She smiled again, the naughtiness still lingering in her eyes. I didn't know how to interpret that smile. "You've told me," she said blithely. "But I always like to hear you say it, anyway."

After she left I sat listening to James Booker and thinking about her. Her and the other beautiful young Creole girl I had known in my life.

Nola. N.O.L.A. New Orleans, Louisiana. A common name for a baby girl in this town. Jaren had pointed her out to me when she was waiting tables at a seedy bar called the Seven Seas on St. Philip Street in the Quarter, around the corner from the fruit and vegetable stands of the French Market. In its day the Seven Seas had been a hangout for hard-core hippies and gutter alcoholics and slumming Tulane frat boys on the prowl. There was an open-air courtyard in the rear, beyond the narrow barroom, where my frat buddies and I competed in loud, drunken dart games and occasionally challenged a reeking resident Dead Head to a match at one of the chess tables. I had noticed Nola long before Jaren told me she was his woman. Who didn't notice her? She was a tall, slender, Creole beauty whose skin was a shade too dark to *passez blanc*, with full wavy hair an unusual copper color and remarkably green eyes. She accentuated her blackness during those Black Is Beautiful times, wearing long dangling earrings and loose African blouses, adorning her thin wrists with exotic bracelets that jangled whenever she set a drink in front of you. I invented excuses to frequent the Seven Seas just to see her, even though my friends preferred other dives in the Vieux Carré, the Sphinx on Decatur or the Dungeon, with its tunnel-like entrance and dance floor in a converted slave quarters. At the Seas I found myself staring shamelessly at Nola night after night, following her graceful movement around the tables, studying that mysterious mélange of features as she smiled and chatted with the customers, many of them Longshoremen from the docks. Later she told me she'd always felt my watchful eyes on her, my strange stalking presence, and suspected that Jaren had sent me there as a spy to make sure she wasn't two-timing him while he was off playing his gigs.

I kissed Nola for the first time on Jaren's party boat in the marina, when we were both stoned out of our minds and he'd gone somewhere to practice with his band. I was young and conceited and naively believed she was attracted to me. But from the outset she made it clear that what she needed from me was money—to support her heroin habit, as I discovered too late—and I had plenty of cash at my disposal. I didn't mind paying for sex with a Creole girl. I had been taught it was an honorable New Orleans tradition.

Nola Guimont and Angelique Foucher Thomas. So many years, so many brain cells demolished by gin and guilt. I realized now that in my mind the two of them had merged. Angie was the young woman Nola would have become had she lived through those dark troubled times. Had she survived life in the Quarter in those days, the hard work on her feet and the all-night parties and heroin and sex with strangers. But for that one deadly armful of scag, Nola might have gone to college, married, given birth to darling children. She might have found her calling, a respectable career, the comforts of a good life. And maybe Jaren would have shared that life with her instead of wasting away in Angola penitentiary. Maybe Rosetta would have become the doting *grandmère* she'd always longed to be, strong and at peace and surrounded by her *own* loving family voices.

I had caused a great deal of grief in this world. I had much to atone for. And now there was one more wretched decision staring me in the face. I sipped my iced gin and listened to James Booker on the headphones and thought about what the old man had said out in the fishing camp in the swamps. *Tell your candidate to make us happy.*

I would have to destroy another life if I wanted to save my own.

Chapter thirty-six

I stopped by Touro Infirmary to visit Rosetta on my way home. Her nurse updated me on the extensive testing performed the day before, blood work and various scopes and scans, more EEGS and EKGs and an interview conducted by a neurologist. The general consensus was that Rosetta was suffering from a chemical imbalance of some sort, which had been corrected for the most part, and that the mental disorientation would eventually dissipate. However, the nurse couldn't rule out latent neurological damage and warned that my old nanny's full faculties might not return.

"Do the doctors know what brought this on?" I asked her.

The nurse shook her head. "The neurologist thought it may've been the result of stress building up over a long period of time. Her cancer recovery. Depression is a natural by-product of chemotherapy, especially in older patients. And of course there's her son." This woman had a natural gift for sympathy and it showed in her soft doughy face. "She talks about him all the time. He seems to weigh heavy on her mind."

Of course, her son. "Thank you, nurse," I said. "We appreciate everything you're doing for her."

When I entered Rosetta's room, her bed had been elevated for supper but she was slipping in and out of awareness while watching *Wheel of Fortune* on the overhead television. The meal remained only half-eaten on the portable tray wheeled over her lap. I patted her slack hand and she smiled at me, sedated and dreamy, a white pasty substance in the corners of her mouth. "I b'lieve he got that girl pregnant," she said in a slurred voice.

I followed her blinking eyes to the television screen. Game show hostess Vanna White, beaming radiant beauty, was large with child. I was amused by Rosetta's suspicion that Pat Sajak had fathered Vanna's baby.

"Thass why I know he wouldn't harm a hair on that girl," Rosetta said. "They having a child together. Jaren wouldn't do no such a thing like they say he done. He wouldn't treat her thataway."

She wasn't talking about Vanna.

"Mistah Paul, you tell them parole men next time you there," she said, her angular face creased with worry. "Tell 'em my boy wouldn't do his woman like that. They bringing a child into this world."

She closed her eyes and soon fell into a restful sleep. I sat down in a chair beside the bed and pondered her disturbing thoughts. My God, could that have been true? Wouldn't the medical examiner have mentioned a fetus during his testimony at the trial? *No, impossible*, I told myself. These were ramblings from the frail mind of a heavily medicated old lady confined too long in a hospital bed.

I sat quietly by her side, savoring a few rare moments of peace. The past few days had taken their toll on my own unraveling nerves and I was beginning to wonder if Paul Blanchard would end up in a straitjacket in some cold white room like this one with an iv rammed in his arm.

After a while longer, I was convinced that Rosetta wouldn't wake anytime soon and stood up to pat her shoulder and leave. The telephone rang on the nightstand. I grabbed the receiver quickly, preventing a second loud ring. The hospital switchboard operator informed me that the call was from the Louisiana State Penitentiary at Angola and that she was authorized to let the call go through.

"Mama, you there?" asked a male voice on the other end of the line.

I considered hanging up the phone and walking out of the room. He would never know it was anything more than a fumbling miscommunication from his ill mother.

"It's me, Mama. Jaren," he said with a filial sweetness I remembered well. "You feelin' all right? Can you talk?"

I took a deep breath and faced what I had to do. "Hello, Jaren, this is Paul," I said. "Rosetta's taking a nap right now. I'm sitting with her."

To fill the awkward void between us, I quickly added, "She's made a lot of progress and seems to be doing better. She'll be back on her feet in no time."

Several heartbeats passed before he finally spoke. "I'm glad we're having this conversation, Speed," he said with a low nasal snigger. "I was beginning to think you were avoiding me."

"It's been a roller coaster ride, Jaren."

"Then you can appreciate what it feels like from my end, sport. You're stuck in lock-up and your mama nearly dies and your cuz says he's gonna call and tell you what's what but then he doesn't call or take your phone calls for five fucking days. You got any idea how messed up that is, man?"

"I'm sorry, Jaren. Lieutenant Castle said he would call you. And Claire said she spoke to you. I thought it was covered."

"Yeah, yeah, that's cool. They did, man. They talked to me. But they ain't *you*, Speed. I wanted to hear all this from you. You're the only one knows my mama good enough to tell me how she really *is*."

I stared down at Rosetta in repose. Her eyelids were twitching slightly but she was fast asleep.

"She's in good hands, Jaren. The very best. I was going to call you as soon as we got all the test results."

This didn't satisfy him. "I talked to her a couple times there in the room and she was out of her head, man," he said, his concern rising. "Talkin' 'bout the old days like it's *now*. What's up with that?"

I explained the stress theory about Rosetta's disorientation. I reported the results of yesterday's tests and repeated what the nurse had told me. "She just needs a little more time to recuperate," I said. "But she's with the A team, believe me. This is the best care money can buy."

"That's what you told me about your lawyer friend. Best mouthpiece money can buy. And look where that got me, man. Fucked up the ass by the parole board one more time. 'Cept now they think they got a confession out of a guilty man." He breathed into the line. "But you know that ain't right, Speed. You and me both know I ain't the guilty party."

My palms began to perspire heavily. Suddenly the cool room felt as stuffy and confined as Jaren's own prison cell.

"I've been talkin' to James Castle," he said. "The brother drove back up here to see me yesterday. He thinks I ought to get me a new lawyer."

So Castle was in the middle of this, as usual.

"That's entirely up to you, Jaren. I wasn't happy with Eric Gautier's presentation, either. I'll hire someone else."

"I don't want your money anymore, man. I don't want you and your people anywhere near my case. Castle says he'll find me a good lawyer. One that's more interested in saving *my* ass than yours."

The phone receiver felt wet and slippery in my hand. I turned my back to the sleeping Rosetta and lowered my voice. "I've been doing everything I can to get you out of there, Jaren," I said.

"Same way your daddy did, I s'pose," he said with a dark laugh. "Don't con a con, old stick. Brother Castle has opened my eyes to the whole scam, y'see. Why I had such a weak-ass lawyer back at the beginning, when your old man was paying the tab. And why this Gautier motherfucker talked me into saying what I didn't want to say. Y'all ought to be real proud of yourself, runnin' that hustle on a dumb niggah that thought the good Blanchard folk was his ticket out."

He uttered a low grunt that sounded somewhere between a sigh and a bitter laugh. "What the niggah never snapped to, m'man, was that all these high-priced lawyers was on the payroll to keep your white ass out of jail."

My God, I thought, could he be right?

"All this time I thought it was some lowlife junkie freak she'd met in the bar," he said. I felt his anger seething through the receiver. "Some shitbag dealer she was balling for the free high. I figured the night it all went wrong, the lowlife motherfucker dumped her body in the swamp." His voice had grown husky and tight. "That's the way I always saw it in my head, Speed. How it musta gone down. My girl and some jailbird rag-ass junkie she didn't really know—getting messed up together while I was out playing my gig. And when her heart popped, he bagged her up like rotten meat and dropped her where the sun don't shine."

I closed my eyes and imagined the last seconds of Nola's life. The heroin must have hit her heart like a mallet. I found myself as choked up as Jaren.

"That's the way I always pictured it happenin', P," he said, a quiet voice rasping in my ear. "Now why don't you tell me how wrong I am?" I withdrew the handkerchief from my pants pocket and mopped my forehead. I was too shaken to continue this conversation.

"I'm going to hang up now, Jaren," I said, turning to study Rosetta's tranquil face, the sharp bone structure at peace but as rigid as a death mask. "I just want you to understand that your mother has the best care in town and is well loved by us all."

I heard him blow air into the phone line. He was trying to pull himself together.

"Takin' care of that sweet woman must be the only thing that lets you sleep at night, Speed. You lose her, ain't nothing left of your soul worth handing to the devil."

"Goodbye, Jaren."

"One of these fine days I'm gittin' out of this place, man, and then you and me are gonna stand toe to toe and look each other in the eye. How bad it gets is up to you. Y'understand where I'm comin' from, old cuz?"

"I'll tell Rosetta you called."

I settled the telephone quietly in its cradle and looked around for something to quench my thirst. There was a glass of lukewarm milk on the food tray and I drank it quickly, panting like a dog after a duck hunt. I sat down in the chair to collect myself and slow the trembling I felt all through my body.

What if Jaren was right about my father and all his lawyers? What if the old man had somehow known the truth about me? It would explain many things. *The weak get left behind, Paul*, that White League spokesman had said to me at the fishing camp. They knew I wasn't worthy of their game.

"Why you and Jaren fussin' at each other?"

At first I thought Rosetta was talking in her sleep. I rose from the chair and saw that her eyes were still closed.

"Don't be tellin' me no lies, child," she said in a familiar maternal scolding I had heard many times as a kid. "I know y'all been fussin' at each other and I want it to stop."

With her eyes shut and her thin, white-robed body stretched out and immobile, she looked like a corpse speaking from an open casket. "I'm sorry, dear," I said, standing over her.

I didn't know which Rosetta I was addressing. A sharp old bird who had overheard our phone conversation, or a feverish dreamer drifting through the faded light of memories long ago.

"Don't blame Jaren," I said. "It's my fault this time."

Chapter thirty-seven

Later that evening I took Julie and Andy to the Tulane campus for a basketball game in the old crackerbox gym where Green Wave teams had been playing since my father was a student. I was a season ticket-holder and a generous supporter of the school, as Charles M. Blanchard and *his* father had been. Two years ago the Tulane president had fired the basketball coach and shut down the program after an ugly point-shaving scandal had exploded in the press, and this was the first season in which the lights had been turned back on the hardwood. Recruiting had vanished and our new team was a dysfunctional group of walk-ons who hadn't won a game all season. Four of the five starters were white, a sure sign that our prospects were hopeless. Sports writers were predicting that Tulane wouldn't score its first victory until the turn of the century.

Tonight Memphis State was pounding us by thirty-four points in the first half. "This game sucks out loud," Andy complained.

"Don't use that kind of language, son," I said, reaching over to grab a handful of his popcorn.

"They oughta let us play six players," he said.

"It's a great crowd, though," I said, scanning the packed gymnasium. The loyal Green Wave fans were restless and searching for anything to cheer about. "Everybody's having a good time. That counts for something. Are you guys having fun?"

The children ignored my question.

"Just because we made one little mistake a hundred years ago," Andy said, "does that mean we deserved the death penalty? It's not fair. Why didn't we just admit it was wrong and say we were sorry and we wouldn't let it happen again?"

The jagged edge of his argument cut deep. I knew what it was like to make one mistake and pay for it the rest of your life.

"It wasn't such a *little* mistake, Andy. It was a felony crime. Somebody should've gone to jail."

"Hey, Dad, do you think I could be a Tulane cheerleader?" Julie asked with her mouth full of popcorn. "I mean right now. Today. Those girls look pretty lame to me. Did cheerleading get the death penalty, too?"

"You know what they say," Andy chimed in, always prepared to deliver a canned one-liner. "'Nine out of ten girls in New Orleans are beautiful and the other one goes to Tulane.'"

"Andy, that's cruel!" I said, suppressing a laugh, squeezing his neck. "Your mother would chew you out for saying something like that."

"She didn't go to Tulane," he retorted, shrinking away from me.

"These Tulane guys are no great hunks either, jerk-o," Julie added, languorously studying the frat boys jeering in the stands.

"Okay, you two. Enough," I said. "Let's enjoy the game."

My eyes wandered down three rows to where Eric Gautier and his family always sat, the same reserved seats season after season. He was there with his lovely dark-haired wife, one of the Behan girls from the Garden District, and their two jock sons. Eric's father often joined them, but not tonight. I had been thinking about the venerable Russell Gautier and his law firm ever since that phone call with Jaren.

"I need to talk to Eric at halftime," I said to Julie and Andy.

"Do you two think you can show some manners and say hello to his boys?"

"Guhhhh," Julie said, making a gagging sound. "They're such A-holes, Dad."

"Julie, do not use that term again until you've been admitted to Yale."

"The girl's got a real potty mouth on her, Dad," Andy said.

"Shut up, dork," Julie said, flinging popcorn at him.

"All right, you guys," I said, "knock it off. At halftime you're going down there to say hello and make nice while I visit with their dad."

At the buzzer the Green Wave team had chiseled the score to 47-21 but the mercurial fans had seen enough and were vacating the gym in droves. I caught up with Eric at the concession stand in the corridor behind the bleachers. He and his twelve-year-old, Matt, were juggling armfuls of soft drinks and popcorn buckets.

"Hey there, Mr. Blanchard," Eric said, smiling cordially as he opened his wallet and handed the concessionaire a wad of bills. "Smelly game, per usual. The alumni should get to vote on whether to cancel the second half."

I had lost my taste for pleasantries. The conversation with Jaren had been troubling me for hours. "Where's Papa tonight, Eric?" I asked him. "He stay out at the camp to get some fishing in?"

He glanced sidelong at me while receiving his change. "What's that supposed to mean?" he asked, slightly hesitant in his reply.

"You were there, too, weren't you, Eric? Sipping a bourbon neat and watching me sweat it out."

His eyes darted at his son, then back to his wallet as he carefully inserted bills. He avoided looking me in the face. "What are you babbling about, Blanchard?" he said, handing two drinks to his son. "Here, Matt, can you hold these?"

"It's taken me all evening to put my finger on that voice, but it finally came to me," I said. "I guess it's been a long time since I've heard your father speak. But it was him, wasn't it, Eric? And my guess is you were there, too."

My accusation cut him to the bone. He looked quickly at his son. "Take those drinks up to Mom and Adrian, please," he instructed the boy. "I'll be along in a minute."

As his son traipsed away, Eric turned to me with a pained scowl. "What the hell are you rattling on about, man?"

He was clutching two heaping tubs of popcorn to his chest as if they were pots of gold.

"You knew that idiotic confession idea would backfire on Jaren, didn't you, Eric?" I said. "But you talked the poor son of a bitch into it and he trusted you. Just like he trusted me to find him a decent lawyer. What he didn't know—and what I didn't know, either—was that you people have been doing your best to keep him where he is for the rest of his stinking life."

Eric walked past me toward the men's room and stopped out of earshot of the casual bystanders queued in the concession line. He turned and waited for me to catch up. "You know what your problem is, Blanchard?" he said in a low angry voice. "You're too fucking dense to know when somebody's doing you a favor."

The old corridor was echoing with loud, excited voices: fans ordering snacks, students hooting and arguing about the game. It was difficult to make myself heard.

"How long has Glynn, Gautier and Lesseps been doing me a favor, Eric?" I asked. "Did my old man put them up to this?"

Light reflected off his wire-rim glasses. "Your old man loved you, dickweed. He was just trying to protect you," he said between clenched teeth. "He didn't want anything to happen to your sorry ass. You're a Blanchard, man. You're *family*, like I keep telling you. When are you going to figure that out? No matter how bad you fucked up, you're still one of us. The old farts don't have to like you—and they don't have to invite you to go duck hunting or sit in their skybox at the Dome. But they'll protect your interests, whether you give a damn or not. That's the way it's always been, dude. They're old and a little out of practice, but when there's an itch, they scratch it. They take care of their own."

Their own. I thought about Jaren and Nico. They didn't fit the family plan. They were disposable. New Orleans had thirty families and everybody else was here to work for them. If you didn't play that game, you didn't stay long.

"I'm disappointed in you, Eric," I said, resisting the urge to knock those tubs of popcorn onto the polished terrazzo floor. "I always thought you and I were different from our daddies. I guess I was wrong about that. You're even worse than they are, man, because you know better."

My remark nettled him. "Grow up, Paul. We are who we are," he said, a vein throbbing in his thin athletic neck. "Run from yourself all you want, but sooner or later you'll end up back where you started. The same prissy white frat boy who got away with murder."

I felt my entire body turn to stone. *Murder.* So that's what they thought I'd done?

"You can listen to funky nigger music day in and day out, but it won't change who you are," he said. "It won't make you one of them. And it won't stop them from frying your ass if they get the chance." He looked past my wide body toward the exit. "Now if you'll excuse me, I've got my family to look after."

The trove of greasy popcorn clasped against his L.L. Bean canvas vest, my old friend Eric Gautier brushed past me and headed for the bleachers. I watched him walk away and wondered how they'd found me out.

Murder. They couldn't take the risk on someone so unstable.

As I stood in line and bought two soft drinks for the kids, a small troubling thought needled its way into the back of my mind. Maybe—just maybe—a young cop named James Castle had put two and two together from things I'd told him in the squad car and he'd gone to my father with his suspicions. Maybe the young cop got a little greedy and tried to shake my old man down. It was the New Orleans way.

Was James Castle the one who had let the cat out of the bag?

Chapter thirty-eight

Another cold front was edging down from the north, the second in a week, and the night air smelled like the first raindrops on a tropical forest. Drink in hand, I opened the French doors at the far end of the library and felt a blast of damp wind in my face, the current blowing my clothes and the heavy drapes at the threshold. Dead magnolia leaves were skittering across the patio by the covered pool. Sipping my gin and tonic, I stepped out onto the flagstones and listened to the tempest creaking the high, heavy limbs of the live oaks on the unlit grounds beyond the flower garden. The children were asleep now and Claire was reading in bed. Standing outside the protective walls of my home fortress, exposed to the dark elements of wind and an imminent, chilling rain, I had never felt so small and insignificant and undeserving of all that I had. This was mine, yes. The loving family, the manse on St. Charles, the name respected throughout the city. But at what price had I acquired these precious gifts? And what would it take to hold onto them?

Thunder rumbled across the starless black sky. The wind sounded like a waterfall swishing through the tangerine trees. I crossed the patio and wandered down the lawn toward the little cottage. The place was unlocked and I stepped inside the dark enclosure, closing the door behind me and sealing out the blustery gale. I didn't turn on the lights. I wasn't sure why I was here, or why I'd chosen to remain in the dark with my back pressed against the door. There was an eerie stillness about the room—a room that had once been filled with so much childish motion and mischief. Mildew was thriving, pungent and damp, and a faint rodent-like odor caused me squeamish concern. I didn't relish the idea of furry, tailed critters gnawing at my argyle socks.

Julie and her hoodlum schoolmates had depleted much of my bar stock and I hadn't taken the time to replenish it. Opening the mini-refrigerator, I found only a half-empty bottle of California white wine and my Bombay Sapphire with less than an inch at the bottom. I drained the gin into my tumbler and studied the area revealed by the meager frosted light of the fridge. No one in this family was using those exercise machines anymore. It was time to remodel the space again, give it another purpose that better suited our collective personality. Or possibly we should consider transforming the structure into a comfortable living quarters for someone who needed our close attention. Someone we could all visit several times a day to share our companionship and prosperity. Rosetta, say. Perry, if he needed special care. Jaren after his release.

Who was I kidding?

The rain had finally struck, a heavy downpour beating the roof and windows. I took my drink and sat on the floor between the treadmill and rowing machine. This was where the old bed had once rested, with its cream-white Irish linen spread we'd used as a shroud. I remembered one rainy spring midnight twenty years ago, making love to her on this very spot, the windows open and a gentle mist wafting across our naked bodies. Her soft lips had tasted smoky and forbidden. The weed relaxed us, heightened every fluttering fingertip and wet drag of tongue. I was intimidated by her experience and raw physical beauty, but I did my best to satisfy her, whatever she wanted. I was under no illusion about love or passion. There was money involved. But she tolerated me and even seemed to enjoy our secret hours together. She made me feel as if there was magic in my touch.

After we'd exhausted each other, usually well after midnight, she would disappear back into the dark streets above St. Charles and I would air the place out, hoping to erase the scent of our secret rendezvous. I was twenty years old and deeply afraid of being caught by my parents. I didn't want to disappoint them. They would not have tolerated their son's drug-addled sexual encounters with a black girl.

The night it happened, we'd fallen asleep together after making love on the old bed. When I woke and reached for her, maybe a half hour later, she wasn't beside me. I noticed the light in the bathroom and called her name. When she didn't respond I thought she'd dressed and slipped away, as she'd done many times before. But I found her lying naked on the bathroom floor, clutching the base of the toilet bowl, a thick string of vomit dangling from her mouth and congealing on the tile. I knelt quickly and shook her. A purple scarf was knotted around her bicep and the syringe still pinched a soft blue vein at the bend of her arm. I hadn't suspected she was a user. The heroin was pure grade Laotian brown, the medical examiner testified at the trial. Junkies were overdosing in housing projects all over town. The new scag on the street was too rich for their blood.

I tried my best to revive her. I shook her hard and splashed water on her face. I wiped off her lips with toilet paper and attempted mouth-to-mouth resuscitation. She tasted sour and foul, unlike her kisses in life, and my stomach heaved from the effort. I didn't know how long she'd been unconscious. Her body was still warm, but there was no pulse. The first rush of heroin had hammered her heart and she was dead before her head thudded against the tile.

I heard a noise outside the cottage door. At first I thought it was wind rattling the knob. Then I realized someone was out there. I downed the rest of the drink and sat up straight. The door groaned open and a human figure stood on the step, backlit by a sudden flash of lightning. It was a woman. She'd been drenched by the deluge.

"Paul?" she said in a small tentative voice diminished by the storm. "Are you in here, darling?"

The overhead light clicked on. Claire was poised in the doorway, staring down at me with dripping hair, her sweatshirt and pajama bottoms clinging limply to her body. I shielded my eyes. The light was blindingly bright.

"Jesus, Claire," I said, "you scared the shit out of me. Do you mind turning that off?"

"I couldn't find you. I figured you must've come out here," she said, running a hand through her short wet hair. "You left the library doors wide open, silly man. What are you doing here, anyway?"

"Please turn off that light, will you? It's giving me a headache."

She switched off the light but left the door open. Lightning flashed again, soundless and bone white, illuminating the lawn and a cluster of banana trees I could make out through the doorway.

"I certainly didn't intend to get caught in the rain," she said, slinging her arms about her with a girlish giggle. "I hope those towels are still in the bathroom cupboard, where I used to keep them. I'm soaked to the bush."

I followed her dark shape as she drifted past the bar.

"Hide your eyes, you sissy," she said. "I've got to turn on the bathroom light."

I could see her rummaging around in the small tiled lavatory where I'd found Nola. Where I'd found Julie vomiting her guts out. Claire located what she was looking for and quickly extinguished the light. I heard the sound of wet clothes peeling off her bare skin like a discarded bathing suit and the soggy smack of each article against the tile floor.

"A *gentleman* would offer me a drink," she said in a merry voice as she dried herself in the dark. "Have you forgotten how this is done, darling Paul? A woman strips for you—you make a romantic gesture before getting her to suck your cock."

"Forgive me," I said, rising quickly to my feet. "I didn't understand what was at stake here."

"Who knows how lucky you'll get if you play nice."

I stumbled my way to the mini-fridge. "May I pour you a glass of white wine, darling Claire?" I asked sweetly. "We don't have many choices, I'm afraid."

"Yes, thank you. Wine would be lovely."

I found a glass on the shelf above the bar, blew away the dust, and poured from the cold bottle. I tasted the wine to make sure it hadn't gone bad.

"Here you are, my dear," I said, reaching out in the dark. "And by the way, you look ravishing tonight." In the light from the small refrigerator I could see the towel wrapped around her body and knotted just above her breasts. "Is that outfit something you picked out from Saks? It's positively *you.*"

"Do you really think so?" she asked. I could hear her take a long drink from the glass as she moved quietly toward me. "It seems a little snug right here," she said, guiding my hand across the terrycloth around the curve of her hips. "What do you think, dear? Would you like to see me in something a little looser?"

I was having difficulty appreciating the moment. My thoughts were elsewhere, haunted by Nola and what had happened that night twenty years ago. I couldn't fully enter Claire's playful mood.

"Let's try this on for size," she said, her fingers deftly untying the knot and letting the towel drop to the floor. "Does this work better for you?"

I touched her cool shoulders and ran my hands down her arms. When I cupped her low heavy breasts, I discovered that her nipples were erect.

"A nice fit, don't you think?" she said.

Surrounding her with my arms, I pulled her supple body to my chest and kissed her tender lips. She tasted wonderful, her tongue slipping slowly into my mouth. It had been months since I'd kissed her this way or caressed her naked skin.

She began to unbutton my shirt and pulled me down onto the musty carpet. I was astonished by this sudden fevered frenzy.

"Darling Paul," she said once her hand had found me in the darkness, "you seem to need a little more persuading."

"I'm sorry," I said. "It's a little nippy in here."

"Don't you want to do this?"

"Of course I do, darling. It's just that it's kind of...strange out here, don't you think?"

The wind and rain battered our dark little hiding place. The strangeness seemed to inspire her.

"Relax. Lie back," she said. "I've never known this to fail."

Her mouth worked its wonders. Soon she crawled on top and rode me in that familiar rhythm that was hers alone. She came quickly, then came again a few moments later. I couldn't remember the last time that had happened. We were like young lovers on the sly, breathless and surreptitious, discovering sex for the first time.

"I want this to work, Paul," she whispered, panting over each word, her mouth close to mine. Those soft pendulous breasts swayed against my chest with each thrust of her hips. "We have too much at stake. Too many years...and the kids. I want us to be okay again."

"I want that too, Claire," I said, panting with her, my hands clutching the smooth damp flesh around her ribcage as I drew closer to my own climax.

"I've been unhappy," she said, her lungs heaving like a sprinter after a hundred-meter dash. "I've been angry at you, Paul."

She didn't seem especially unhappy right now. She was very wet and working toward her third orgasm.

"Why, darling?" I managed to ask. "Tell me what's wrong and I'll fix it."

She raised herself up, straightening her back. Giving birth to two beautiful children had softened her tummy and buttocks and breasts. She hadn't fully recovered the taut muscle tone of her college years, but in my book she was even more sexy and womanly now, at age thirty-eight, after two children. She could still arouse me whenever she chose.

"I've been seeing someone, Paul," she said, her warm hands braced against my sweating chest. "I felt I had to."

This was not exactly the right time to hear this. "Christ," I said, "is it that fucking Christian Brother?"

"No, dear," she moaned, "it's a shrink. A woman. I don't think you know her."

I was very close to coming.

"I thought a woman would be more sympathetic," Claire said.

And then I realized what she was telling me. She'd been going to a psychologist, a counselor. My wife was in therapy.

"I've been seeing her for four months, and…um, are you all right, sweetheart?" she asked. "I think I'm losing you."

"Sorry," I said. "The word *shrink* is so suggestive."

She tried to hold the rhythm but I was contracting rapidly.

"I had to talk to someone about it," she said, rising slightly and reaching underneath herself to fondle my testicles, trying to re-ignite me. "I didn't know how to deal with the public embarrassment, Paul. I couldn't cope with it all by myself. I had to seek professional help. Do you understand that?"

She stopped moving altogether. I was down and out. At this moment, without the thrill of sex to tantalize me, there was simply a hundred and twenty pounds of meat weighing down on my groin.

"I'm sorry, Claire, I'm not following you. Are you saying I'm some kind of public embarrassment to you?"

She sighed deeply, catching her breath. Her body shuddered, and she sounded on the verge of tears. Her hands were no longer embracing me. I reached up to touch her face and found her arms locked tightly across her chest.

"I know about your goddamned Creole girlfriend, Paul," she said in a voice as cold as the rain on the window glass. "I'm not sure I'll ever be able to forgive you."

I lay pinned beneath her, shocked into silence and afraid to move. How could she possibly know about her? *How?* Did everyone in this wretched town know about Paul Blanchard and the dead girl?

I remembered how absolutely terrified I'd been that night in the minutes before I phoned Morvant. Panic and paranoia had overwhelmed me and I was sliding quickly toward an emotional breakdown. I had considered calling an ambulance but I knew what that would mean. Sirens and flashing red lights up and down the street. Cops everywhere, dragging my parents out of bed. A long miserable night of questions and accusations. I couldn't face it. There was a dead black girl on the floor of my family cottage, sex and drugs were involved, and the scandal would have destroyed my future and my family's reputation. And I knew what they did to lily-white college boys in the parish jail. I had heard the stories and I couldn't bear the thought of it. I wasn't going to spend an hour inside that place.

When Morvant arrived in his car at the back gate, I was in pathetic shape and whimpering like a sloppy drunk. It was nearly two A.M. *Get your shit together, man,* was the first thing he'd said to me. *You've got to maintain if we're gonna do this right.*

It had been his idea to wrap her body in the Irish linen bedspread and get rid of her. Before tying it in knots we'd thrown her belongings into the bundle, the sleeveless kente cloth shift she'd worn that night, her leather sandals and strapped cloth handbag and cotton panties and a half-dozen ivory bangles she'd slipped off her slender wrists. The gator hunters had recovered the body and shredded bedspread floating like an ancient white lily in the swamp, but the other items had disappeared into the bottomless, snake-infested murk. The dress, the bag, everything else.

I remembered standing back and watching him kneel over her body sprawled on the bathroom floor. He touched her, ran his hand along her bare ribcage. *Blanchard, you sly dog,* he had said. *How long've you been getting yourself some high yella ass?*

He'd probably removed the earring when I turned away to strip the spread from the old brass bed. The conniving bastard. He was always thinking ahead. Always looking for an opportune moment, an opening, a strategic advantage over friend and foe alike.

I boosted myself up on my elbows. "Claire, I don't know what you've heard," I said, shaken by her knowledge. "I don't know if I can ever really explain—"

The slap was so hard it knocked me flat against the carpet. My jaw was numb, my ears ringing.

"How could you do something like that, you bastard?" she said, warm teardrops falling onto my bare stomach. "Don't you realize you've jeopardized everything we have together?"

"Claire—"

I tried to sit up but she seized my shoulders and pushed me back down.

"Did you think it wouldn't get back to me, you careless shit?

It's a small little circle of gossips, Paul. The same thirty families blah blah. They see two people together, they talk. Especially when it's a colored girl. If you were going to have an affair, why didn't you at least take her to a motel in Bay St. Louis?"

Something wasn't quite right. Something did not compute.

"I've done some checking and I found out she's a married woman, Paul. She has a three-year-old son. You're going to ruin *her* family as well, you prick. Does her husband know about this?"

Now I was hopelessly confused. "What the hell are you talking about, Claire?"

"It's a little late for denial, Paul. My friends have seen you two having drinks together at the Columns. Apparently you've been shameless about it. Cozy lunches at Atchafalaya. How do you think that makes me feel, you asshole? My husband is having an affair with his Creole secretary and everyone Uptown knows about it!"

I began to laugh. She thought I was sleeping with Angie Thomas.

"Oh, yeah, this is hilarious, Paul. You risk losing your wife and children and you think it's all a big joke!"

She slapped me again and this time I grabbed her wrist, trying to restrain her, and we tumbled over in the dark, wrestling and squirming and fighting for position. Using all my strength, I trapped her facedown on the carpet with my one hundred and ninety-five pounds holding her naked body down. We were both exhausted and sweating wildly and gasping for air.

"Listen to me, Claire," I said, my mouth dry, my lungs burning. "I'm not having an affair with Angie Thomas. I haven't slept with anyone but you since we've been married. That's fifteen years of fidelity, in case you haven't been counting."

I shifted my weight off her damp body, gripped her right shoulder, and turned her over on her back. "Are you listening, Claire?"

"Yes, but I don't believe you."

"Why not, darling? It's the absolute truth."

"Because it would mean I've thrown away four fucking months and a lot of fucking money on a fucking wild-goose chase."

"You know better than to listen to Uptown gossip, silly girl. I'm surprised at you. Why didn't you just ask me about this? *Confront* me, or whatever it's called."

"I'm confronting you now, dummy. What do you think this is all about?"

"I thought you just wanted to get wet and naked in a strange place."

We were nose to nose, our mouths only inches apart, breathing each other's labored breaths. I smoothed the wet hair away from her forehead and kissed her deeply. "I'm not having an affair, sweetheart. Whatever's going on between us, it's not about fidelity," I said. "But you're right. We've lost something and we've got to get it back."

She lay still for quite a while, perhaps coming to terms with what I'd said, and then she began to cry. It was a great relief to both of us. We nestled against each other for the first time in many months, Claire's head resting on my chest as we listened to the torrent sweep across the darkness outside.

"I'm feeling a little foolish, Paul. I'm sorry I slapped you."

"It's all right, darling. I'm sure I deserved it for something."

The rain poured down, the wind rattled the panes, and the old cottage groaned and shook in the storm. The air was frosty now, in our spent stillness, and I covered her nude body with my shirt.

Morvant had known about a weekend fishing camp on the bayou below the village of Lafitte, less than an hour's drive south of the city. The shack lay hidden in the dark cypress swamp at the end of a mud road. Using only the flashlight from his glove compartment, we lugged Nola's body to a flatbottom boat roped against a rickety pier and rowed out into the darkness. It was May and the steamy air was alive with croaking frogs and the scream of crickets. There was slow, reptilian movement in the black waters around us. Somewhere deep in the cypress stumps, under ancient beards of Spanish moss, we slid the bound corpse into the lagoon and listened to the low gurgling sound as her body slowly vanished.

Rowing back to the silent camp, I prayed Hail Marys for Nola under my breath and begged for God's forgiveness. But I knew what we'd done was beyond His mercy.

On the drive northward up that desolate two-lane parish road toward the city, I began to weep again. I couldn't control myself. Morvant let me go awhile and then he finally said something. *You're home free, Blanchard. Nobody's going to know a damned thing about this.* And then he turned to me and laughed. *As long as we stay friends. Right, old buddy?*

In twenty years I hadn't forgotten that laugh and the wild look on his face, lit eerie green by the dashboard lights.

"You're shivering, Paul. Are you okay?"

"Just a little cold, I guess."

She curled tightly around my chest and stroked my arms. "We'd better get back to the house," she said, her voice sleepy and deep. "The thunder might wake Andy and he'll wonder where the hell his parents are."

"Claire," I said, holding her close, "I want this to work, too. I love you guys. I want it to work more than anything in the whole world."

"You aren't trying to talk me into a full blow job, are you, darling?"

"I'm serious," I said, giving her a little shake. "Our life is good. I want it to stay that way."

She lifted her head and propped herself on an elbow. "I'm sorry I was so bent out of shape, sweetheart," she said. "You're right—we're fortunate people and we lead a charmed life. Every time I leave the Project I count my many blessings and thank God for what we have. I try to be caring and sympathetic about the things I see down there, but the truth is, I can't imagine living any life other than the one we have together. You and me and the children and our two families. Let's promise each other we won't ever do anything to jeopardize what we have, Paul."

There was a leak somewhere in the room. Ceiling damage. I could hear the slow plops of water dripping onto the carpet.

"Does this mean you aren't sleeping with that Christian Brother?"

She pinched my nipple. "Brother Mike is gay, silly boy. He's got a crush on some guy working in an art gallery on Julia Street," she said. "Come on, let's get back to the house before we're busted by child protective services for abandoning our children."

She crawled to her feet and opened the cottage door. Lightning revealed her naked body staring out at the rain. "Are you coming, doll?" she asked over her shoulder.

"Aren't you forgetting something?"

She giggled cutely. "The clothes are pointless, hon. Leave them here and we'll make a run for it."

I stood up and wrapped my arm around her shoulders. Gusts of cold rain were blowing against our bare skin. We kissed one last time and held hands as we dashed out into the darkness. The rain pelted us and Claire laughed and screeched like a child playing chase. Halfway to the patio, lightning flashed again and the grounds lit up like daytime. We both laughed uncontrollably when we saw each other exposed in the outdoors, pale and awkwardly bobbing and as vulnerable as two featherless hatchlings in a gale. But we kept splashing onward through the blinding downpour and didn't let go of each other even when we'd reached the warm library and raced naked down the hallway and up the stairs, holding hands and praying not to be caught by our children. We didn't let go of each other even when we'd settled warm and dry into the comfort of our own bed.

Chapter thirty-nine

He agreed to meet me in the place we'd always met, the parking lot of the Audubon Zoo. It had stopped raining but the morning sky was heavy and gray, and as usual the standing water was slow to drain from the low city streets. The zoo had been radically redesigned since our encounters twenty years ago—*humanized,* the keepers bragged—and the resurfaced parking area was the driest spot in Uptown New Orleans. This wasn't the same stockade for caged animals I had visited often in my childhood, but I could still hear the old alpha lion roar late at night sometimes, when the air was ripe and the season suited him. It was a fearsome sound, primal and ominous, the shaggy beast staking out his territory, laying down the rules. Come closer at your own peril. His roar was a warning that danger lurked in the darkness beyond our gates.

A maroon Bonneville the size of a Higgins Boat was docked underneath the same live oak tree where he'd parked his squad car back in those days. I rapped on the fogged glass of the passenger door and heard the locks release. He was sitting behind the steering wheel in the suit and tie he'd worn to the parole hearing. I wondered if Lieutenant James Castle was a bachelor, a widower or divorcee, an inveterate loner. Nothing about him suggested a woman's small thoughtful ministrations. He was drinking coffee from a Styrofoam cup and eating a beignet, powdered sugar frosting his large lap.

"Thanks for meeting me on such short notice," I said, inhaling the odors of the closed automobile. Cheap coffee, stale breath, the coil-burning smell of a heater going bad. I could feel the claustrophobia nagging at me like a trick knee. I remembered how trapped I'd felt as a nervous college boy sitting in a hot police car with this slow, deliberate cop close enough to crush my face like a paper napkin.

James Castle shrugged his wide shoulders and took another bite of the beignet. "What's on your mind, son?" He sounded impatient and not altogether hospitable this morning.

"I've spoken to Jaren," I said. "He told me the two of you have been talking."

He looked up from his breakfast for the first time. Those penetrating eyes were capable of instilling instant fear. "I'm gonna get that boy some serious representation, my friend," he said, dropping all pretense of civility. "Don't you think it's about time somebody did?"

It was pointless to tell him I didn't know anything about my father's legal manipulations. It didn't matter to him. Castle had no reason to believe a word I said.

"What's it going to take, Lieutenant?" I asked him.

He stared at me, squinting as he sipped his steaming coffee. I wondered if he was wearing a wire but I truly didn't care. I was ready for it to be over. What was that old blues song about a hell hound on your trail? I didn't want to spend the rest of my life listening for his hell hound footsteps behind me. We had to come to some kind of resolution.

"What's it going to take to end this?"

He stuck the Styrofoam cup in a flimsy plastic holder and tossed the half-eaten beignet on the dashboard, brushing the sugar from his pants. "Your John Hancock on a piece of paper, son," he said with an edge. "That's all it's ever been about. You telling the truth. Sign your name to a piece of paper and an innocent man goes home."

"Aren't you forgetting what he's in there for, Lieutenant? Several counts for the heroin and weed they found on his boat. Dealing drugs. It wasn't just your niece."

He worked his tongue over his teeth, removing bits of dough. "You come clean and at least the negligent homicide rap disappears," he said, searching for the pack of cigarettes in his shirt pocket. "I'll get him a new lawyer and a new trial and he'll walk on the rest of it with time served."

"And what happens to me, Lieutenant?" I asked him. "What's my way out?"

He lit a cigarette and blew the smoke at my face. "You got this far on your name and a prayer, my friend," he said. "Your high-rollin' lawyer pals will figure it out for you. They'll cut a deal with the D.A. and keep your rich white ass out of Angola. That's the way it always works with your people. Just give Daddy's friends a call."

I could breathe his contempt in the smoky air, not just for me but for every white man who had ever wronged him.

"You talked to him about me, didn't you?"

He made a diffident gesture with the cigarette squeezed between his meaty fingers.

"My father," I said. "You went to him and laid out the scenario, didn't you, Lieutenant? You figured *rich old honky*, right? He'll pay to keep his son out of the papers."

He watched me through those small hard eyes as he dragged the cigarette, savoring the taste, and slowly released the smoke through his nostrils. And then he reached over and pressed the glowing tip to my thigh. I jerked my leg away and reached for the door handle but he seized my tie, knotted it in his huge hand, and held me in place.

"You don't know me well enough to make that kind of accusation, motherfucker," he said, twisting the tie until it felt like a noose around my neck. "Now you listen up, frat boy. That was my *niece* you dumped in the bayou, you son of a bitch. If you'd stood up like a man and copped to the crime, you'd prob'ly got off with probation. Assumin' you didn't kill her and it wasn't your smack. But you sat back and let a niggah kid take the fall for you—thirty years hard time—and you didn't say a word. That's gotta cost you, my friend."

I grabbed his massive hand with both of mine and fought to

loosen his grip on my tie. I couldn't breathe and my head was about to explode.

"We're gonna settle this one way or the other," he said, "you and me. You can save yourself some grief and sign something now, or you can keep playing games with me, asshole. But I'm not goin' away—you can bank on that. There's still an old evidence drawer downtown with a chewed-up bedspread and an earring the M.E. found in my niece's ear. Sooner or later it's gonna come together, son. When she's better, I'm gonna ax Two J's mama to take a look at the spread and see if she remembers ever seeing one like it in your household—if one ever went missin'. Who can say, I might even catch a break on the earring some day. I been a cop long enough to know you never can tell when today's gonna be your lucky day."

He released me with a shove and my collar button popped off, falling into my lap. I loosened my tie, coughing and struggling to catch my breath.

"Now git the fuck outta my car, Blanchard, while you still can."

Lightheaded and shaken, I drove around the back of the zoo to the river and parked next to the gazebo perched at the shoreline. My entire body was trembling and I needed to collect myself. The Mississippi narrowed here and its gray waters were flowing rapidly this morning, lapping high on the banks, engorged by the overnight rain. The gazebo was empty, the children's playscape was empty, not another car in view. Bad weather, brisk wind, an ugly day in February. Unfit even for the stalwart Negro fishermen who roamed these grassy slopes with their cane poles.

I sat watching the choppy river through my windshield. There was a small black singe hole near the crease of my pants. My neck was still red like a rope burn and I seriously considered crawling down the bank and sticking my head in the water like a dog in the sweltering summertime. The sadistic son of a bitch.

I sat rubbing my neck and weighing my options and watching a long brown barge with tarp-covered cargo plow its way through the swift waters, steering downriver toward the industrial canal. Did I have the nerve to call Eric now, after our recent hostile confrontation, and persuade him to arrange a plea bargain with the District Attorney? Was I prepared to face this thing after so many years of concealment? Would the consequences be any different today, twenty years later, than they'd been the night I begged Morvant to help me get rid of the body?

Be damned glad I'm loyal to my own kind, he'd said to me as we tied the bedspread around Nola's stiffening limbs. *Now pull yourself together, Blanchard. The world's not gonna miss one more dead nigger junkie.*

I sat behind the wheel for another hour, listening to thunder roll in the distance and stroking the small burn blister on my thigh, wondering what to do. And then I took a deep breath and reached for my car phone.

Chapter forty

Morvant said we should meet at Metairie Cemetery.
Of all the New Orleans cities of the dead, the weather-bleached
marble and granite mausoleums that entombed our dearly departed,
this was the most illustrious, a resting place of stunning grandeur
for the wealthy and socially connected, governors and cotton barons
and celebrity entertainers. My old frat brother had a southerner's flair
for metaphor and melodrama, and he'd no doubt chosen the meeting place for its historical significance. Metairie Cemetery was the
burial ground for more than two thousand Louisiana veterans of the
Civil War, including renowned southern generals P.G.T. Beauregard
and John Bell Hood. When Confederate President Jefferson Davis
died at his home in the Garden District, he was buried for a while
in the cemetery underneath a towering column topped by a statue
of Stonewall Jackson, before Davis's body was eventually re-interred
in Virginia.

I found the Lincoln Town Car parked next to a grassy burial
mound over which Confederate General Albert Sidney Johnston
straddled his prancing steed, saber raised in a call to charge. It was
one of the oldest tombs in the cemetery, and I'd been told as a child

that New Orleanian Beauregard and two other generals were buried inside.

Wearing a dark watchman's cap over his shaved head and a long belted trench coat, Louis Robb loitered outside the rain-spattered black automobile, staring up at the colossal figure of a Confederate soldier caped against the cold and rain, guarding the arched entrance to Beauregard's crypt and reading the roll call of the gray legions that had fallen in battle. When Robb heard my BMW idling to a stop, he turned slowly and smirked in my direction, his contempt for me lacking all subtlety or tact. He strode over to the Town Car, his muscled neck and shoulders swaggering insolently with every step, and opened the back door, nodding for me to get inside. Crawling out of my vehicle I gazed about the grounds, taking precautions to remain unobserved. It was a sodden weekday morning after a rain storm and there wasn't a living soul in sight, only the sprawling acres of proud white sepulchers and their carved statuary signifying quaint heroic virtues. The angels of fortitude, mercy, temperance. The Blanchard family mausoleum loomed a hundred yards away on millionaire's row, as the locals had dubbed the lane, my father and two previous generations, including Great Granddad the White Leaguer. This wasn't a place I visited often. I felt no morbid loyalty to bones and marble.

Ignoring Louis Robb and his surly pose at the car door, I placed my attaché case on the back seat and slid inside, pushing the case toward the man awaiting my arrival. Impeccably attired in a dark gray suit and business tie, Mark Morvant sat reading the newspaper. Even after the door closed and we were alone in the vehicle, he didn't offer a salutation or look up from the paper.

"Did you see what happened last night?" he began as if in mid-conversation. Something on the front page had incensed him. "Those animals vandalized the Liberty Monument!" he said, fuming, the pages crumpled in his clenched fists as if he were gripping an enemy's lapels. "Look at this picture! They sledgehammered one of the altar columns. Smashed it to pieces! And spray-painted all over the names of the dead White Leaguers. '*Racist*,'" he said, reading the graffiti. "'*Tear down hate!*' The ignorant bastards! You see what we're dealing with here, *cuño*? Typical coon emotionalism. They whine about equality and black heritage but they've got no respect for anybody else's heritage. And where were the fucking police when all this vandalism went down? This is exactly what happens when the niggers take over your law enforcement agencies."

I had indeed read the story in the newspaper. The damage was minor: one four-foot decorative column broken, a few phrases of washable graffiti. Frankly, I wouldn't have given a damn if someone had dynamited the thing to the ground.

"Here, Mark," I said, nudging the attaché case closer to him. "I've brought you something."

He glanced at the case as though he hadn't noticed it lying beside him on the leather seat.

"My first campaign contribution," I announced solemnly. "There's more to come."

Peering down at the briefcase, he tossed the newspaper onto the floorboard like a rumpled beach towel and unsnapped the silver latches, slowly raising the cover. His eyes narrowed and a wicked smile shaped his mouth. "Well done, *cuño*," he said, studying the banded stacks of bills arranged neatly inside. He picked up a bundle of greenbacks and thumbed through them like a casino dealer fanning a deck of cards. "How much do we have here?"

"Twenty-five thousand," I said. "It's my gesture of good faith, Mark."

He fit the bundle back into its niche and carefully closed the briefcase. "An impressive start, my man," he said with a respectful nod. "I appreciate your personal commitment. What are friends for? I'm glad you're on board."

It was Mark Morvant the candidate speaking. But he knew the bitter truth behind this charade. He knew I wouldn't have given him a dime unless my back was against the wall.

"But I believe there's other business pending, is there not?" he asked, fixing those Arctic blue contact lenses on me in brutal scrutiny. "Your old family friends. Have you presented my offer to them, Paul?"

I permitted myself a tight smile, enough to let him know I had succeeded. "I think it's time I was very straight with you about all this, Mark," I said, indulging my advantage. "They certainly know who you are. You've made enough noise to catch their attention. But you have to remember that they're *old* school. A closed society. Everything bred in the blood. It's not what a man *does*, Mark—it's who he *is*. You know what I'm talking about. Family name, the proper lineage."

He knew where this was going and it visibly displeased him. He folded his arms, waiting.

"So as you might imagine," I said, enjoying the provocation, "it's not in their nature to embrace or accept a Y'at from downriver, Mark. You're not one of their own."

At this moment it would have been very simple to free myself from his blackmail and a thousand sleepless nights. And to free Jaren Jarboe from Angola prison. All I had to do was leave it at that—*You're not one of their own*—and get out of the car and walk away. Cooperate with that hell hound James Castle, sign a piece of paper, confess. Take what was coming to me. No one had to die.

But then I thought about Julie and Andy and our simple pleasures, sitting together at a basketball game with my arms around their shoulders, loving them more than I'd loved anything in my whole life. And I thought about Claire last night, the passion stirred after our long indifference, the giddy race through the chilling rain. It was still there between us, buried but not yet dead. Laughter and hope and promise. Everything worth saving. I couldn't lose them now. I just couldn't.

"But the gentlemen of the League have always been realists, Mark," I said after a moment's hesitation. "They understand what's in their own best interests. And so they've cut deals over the years. They work with people they know they can trust."

He wagged his foot, projecting impatience. He was waiting irascibly for me to get to the point. I took my time.

"There's just one stipulation they require before they strike a bargain with someone outside the fold," I said, consciously manipulating every chess piece, one move following the other. "It's cold, Mark, but it's the only way they can be certain they have a man's absolute trust."

I didn't want to do this but I'd passed the point of no return. I knew there was a special place reserved for me in hell. Wilhelmina Phillips didn't deserve what was in store for her. She was a good and honorable woman. But it was either my life or hers. And I was willing to fight with everything I had to preserve what was mine.

"You have to eliminate one of their enemies, Mark," I told him, relieved finally to be uttering those fatal words. "That's the way it's always been. And that's the way it's got to be."

I watched his face for signs of shock or astonishment, but there was no surprise whatsoever, only mild amusement in those striking eyes. He'd already anticipated what would be required of him, it seemed, and he was prepared to go the distance. As I sat beside him in the back seat of his Lincoln Town Car, the briefcase full of money resting on the leather between us, it became obvious to me that this was not the first time the man had been called on to do this sort of thing.

"All right, *cuño*, I'm listening," he said, nodding agreeably like a recruit awaiting his orders. "Who do I have to kill?"

Chapter forty-one

Afterwards I picked up Claire at home and we drove to St. Rita's Catholic Church in Harahan to attend Nico's funeral. The church, a 1950s vintage brick structure with a sharp A-frame roof and a prominent bell tower, sat alongside the parish elementary school that Nico had attended as a boy. The pews overflowed with family and friends and devout parishioners who had come to honor one of their own. The mayor and one news camera crew were in attendance, due to the public nature of the Cabildo fire, and so were Nico's coworkers and several dignitaries from the Louisiana State Museum. I didn't see board chairman Claude Villere among them, however. I assumed he was still shaken by Perry's assault at the Jove den and would avoid another confrontation at all costs, even at the risk of appearing disrespectful of the dead. One simulated act of fellatio with a 9mm Ladysmith was probably enough humiliation to last a lifetime.

Claire and I arrived too late to find room in the pew with Perry and his coterie of handsomely dressed male friends, but we noticed my sister waving demurely from two rows back and shuffled in next to her. Claire and Kathleen acknowledged each other with polite but frigid smiles, and I thought it best to position myself between them.

ersaken:

Kathleen was wearing a hat that matched her two-piece outfit, navy blue jacket and skirt, a dated ensemble rarely glimpsed in public after the heyday of Jackie Kennedy. I hugged her and leaned over to whisper, "How's he doing?" I hadn't seen or spoken to Perry since I'd delivered him to Kathleen's house on Sunday.

"Not great," she whispered back, breathing Listerine into my face. "It's going to take some time."

"Did your doctor friend have a look at him?"

She shook her head, disappointed. "Perry refuses to see him. He's being his usual stubborn self. I'm not sure anything I say is getting through that thick skull."

The Menotti family occupied the first two rows beside the closed coffin: Nico's parents and grandparents and four of his siblings and their toddling children. Nico's father was a vigorous greengrocer around sixty years old, with large flat ears and a proud uplifted chin, and dark thinning hair combed straight back Sicilian-style. The mother was small and rotund, a Honduran woman whose moon face was streaked with tears. Throughout the funeral Mass, raw emotion erupted freely among family members at unpredictable moments. I envied their passion. The rest of us listened mutely as the Vietnamese priest struggled through the English service.

I hadn't anticipated that I would feel Nico's loss as well. By giving me that tape, he'd crossed a line he didn't have to cross. He'd tried to help me, despite the danger it had put him in. I was grateful, and touched, and terribly sad for everyone who knew and loved him.

Perhaps it was my own uneasiness with the situation, but I sensed a chasm between Nico's family and Perry's friends, not only in the physical distance in the church but more pointedly in the steadfast refusal of the parents to acknowledge Perry in any way, even with a cursory glance. I recalled my brother's assertion that Mr. Menotti hated him, and it appeared that the death of their loved one had not altered that sentiment. I'm not sure Perry cared at this point. He was surrounded by a dozen true friends who loved and accepted him unconditionally and empathized in this dark hour. By now they had all lost close friends to AIDS, and the death count was far from over. Two of them, Roger and Patrick—I would later come to know them as friends myself—walked Perry to the altar rail for communion. When he returned to his pew, I saw his face for the first time. He had aged a decade in four days. Grief and exhaustion and the nascent virus had taken their toll on his health. Everyone would agree, at the end of these final two years of his life, that the death of his lover Nico Menotti was the beginning of my brother's decline.

Chapter forty-two

I put in an appearance at the office that Wednesday afternoon, had a drink at my desk, and listened to Clarence Gatemouth Brown on the headphones. There were no messages for me, phone or memo. Indifferent to my presence, the invisible hand moved on. Personnel conflicts, shipping snags, broken machinery at the roasting plant, sales and marketing strategies, the daily ebb and flow of running a coffee enterprise—these were best left to Angie and the department managers, and they all knew it. Occasionally an in-house designer would ask my color preference, and that was basically the extent of my participation in company affairs. Now, for the first time in my brief executive career, as I sat at that large empty desk listening to Gatemouth Brown bend the blues on his electric guitar, I considered becoming more involved in the business I had inherited. I wasn't sure if this sudden interest was a sign of maturity or a desperate attempt to hold onto something solid as my ship was going down.

After an hour of listening to Gatemouth and Ernie K-Doe, I was gathering my tapes to leave when Angie appeared at my door wearing a luminous smile. "Knock knock," she said. "Am I disturbing anything?"

"Not possible, Angie," I said. "Please come in."

Her entrance awakened memories of the previous night in the rain-swept cottage and Claire's suspicion that I was having an affair with this lovely young woman. I smiled at my assistant, savoring a brief fantasy that it had been *her* straddling me in the dark playhouse while the wind moaned against the window panes. I imagined her ripe lips tasting smoky and forbidden, like Nola's. And then I did my very best to erase the thought forever.

"I want you to meet someone special in my life," Angie said, stepping into my office to make way for the woman standing behind her in the corridor. "Paul, this is Wilhelmina Phillips, my old history teacher. I don't think you two have been formally introduced."

Startled by the councilwoman's appearance in my building, I tried to recover my poise but managed only to bang against the desk as I rose like a Catholic schoolboy when a priest enters the room. Fortunately there was no gin in my mouth at that moment or I would have choked. Under the circumstances, Willie Phillips was the last person on earth I'd expected to greet today.

"I feel like we've known each other a long time, Mr. Blanchard," she said with a handsome smile. "You wake me up every morning with a nice warm feeling in my tummy."

Angie laughed when she saw the expression on my face. "The coffee, Paul."

I blushed at my own slow, dimwitted response. I was never ready for these coffee jokes.

"Angelique has told me many good things about you, Mr. Blanchard," Willie Phillips said, striding mannishly across the room with her hand extended. "I'm pleased to make your acquaintance."

"Likewise," I said, abandoning the security of my desk to shake her hand. "I admire your courage, Miz Phillips. In fact, I'll tell you a little secret if you promise not to repeat it to a living soul."

At this moment I could think of nothing else but my meeting with Morvant at the cemetery this morning.

"I can keep a secret, Mr. Blanchard," she said, still holding my hand with a firm grip. She was taller than I, a sturdy middle-aged woman with an ardent intensity that shone through the scholarly glasses. She exuded aggressiveness and candor and the strong impression that she would discard her jacket and frilled bow, if necessary, to wrestle my ass on the carpet.

"I voted for you," I said. "*Twice.*"

She laughed and wagged my hand. "Don't worry, young man," she said, "I won't tell your friends you go that way."

I smiled at her, recalling what that old White Leaguer had said in the fishing camp. *You know as well as we do who's causing all the trouble these days. The smart-mouthed bitch who's ruining Mardi Gras. She's got to be stopped, Paul. She's turning everything upside down.*

Angie sauntered over to join the love fest. "I've told Wilhelmina about our new program of free coffee for the city's nurses," she said, "and about some other pro bono work we're considering."

Angie and I exchanged looks. I had no idea what else we'd planned, if anything. But I was willing to take credit.

"That's all fine and good, Mr. Blanchard," Willie Phillips said, "but what really impresses me is your excellent taste. Angelique was one of my star students once upon a time, and I admire a man who knows quality when he sees it. I'm delighted that you've given this young woman a leadership opportunity in your company, and I came by to thank you personally for doing so. Few businesses in this city share your open spirit, I'm sad to say."

Angie's job was not exactly a *leadership opportunity* in the Blanchard operation. She was my assistant, my secretary. But I was willing to play along, if it improved Angie's standing in her history teacher's eyes.

"The truth is," I said, "Angelique runs the company. Everyone close to the top knows that to be the case."

Angie was blushing now, avoiding my eyes, and I didn't know if it was out of a false sense of modesty or because I'd called her *Angelique.*

"I couldn't make it through a single day without her wise counsel," I said, turning my smile on my young assistant. "I really couldn't."

Willie Phillips was smiling at her former student as well. "Mr. Blanchard," she said, "I also came by to extend an invitation to you and your wife."

She handed me a formal white envelope that had somehow materialized from the leather satchel in her left hand.

"I would be very pleased if you and Mrs. Blanchard would be my guests at the Zulu Ball."

I stared at the envelope like a country rube who'd never seen one before, then slowly unsealed the flap. It was a lavishly colorful invitation to the ball with two tickets hand-printed *Admit Mr. and Mrs. Paul Blanchard.* Underneath the calligraphy appeared the standard Mardi Gras line:

Strictly Personal   Present this card at the door   Evening Dress

"This is quite an honor, Miz Phillips," I said, glancing up from the invitation. "I—I'm speechless."

White people had been invited to the Zulu Ball for the past fifteen or twenty years, but the numbers were small and an invitation was considered the highest compliment. Claire's parents had attended one year in the 1970s, but they were the only couple I knew who had ever been asked.

"I really don't deserve your kindness," I said, sweat gushing from every pore in my body. This entire turn of events felt like a bad dream, and yet I had no choice but to accept the invitation or cause grievous insult.

"I'm sure you'll have a chance to return the favor someday, Mr. Blanchard," she said, laughing cavalierly. "I'll be counting on that."

And then I realized what this was all about. Like Mark Morvant, Councilwoman Wilhelmina Phillips had higher political ambitions and would be calling on my support in the future. I studied her strong, confident demeanor—the shrewd laugh and power suit and righteous indignation within easy reach—and foresaw a bid for mayor or state representative. Or perhaps even a campaign for the U.S. Congress. Whatever her aspirations, the controversial black candidate would benefit greatly from a Blanchard endorsement, and Blanchard money, to grant her political cachet among white voters.

I should have seen this coming the moment she handed me the invitation. In New Orleans, no good deed went unpaid for.

"I look forward to meeting your wife as well," Willie Phillips said. "I understand she's the daughter of Ida Benjamin. I worked with Ida back in the bad old days. Library integration and voter drives. She was one tough cookie, I'll tell you for sure. The things she did took intestinal fortitude, especially for a well-to-do white lady. We all thought she was a saint. Is the dear woman still among us?"

"A little bent," I nodded, "but never broken."

"Wonderful," she said with a fond smile. "Please say hello from an old friend."

"I will."

"I'll see you and your wife at the ball, then, Mr. Blanchard," she said, extending her hand again. "I trust this will be the beginning of a long friendship."

Dear Jesus, I thought, shaking her hand one last time before she and Angie left the office. *What had I done? What in God's name had I done?*

Chapter forty-three

Meeting Willie Phillips in the flesh, seeing Angie's affection for her old mentor and hero, had convinced me that what I'd set in motion was horribly wrong. I hadn't killed Nola, even if what I'd done afterwards was unforgivable. But this was cold-blooded murder, no way around it. Was it too late now to stop the wheels from churning? Could I make a phone call and convince Morvant it had all been a misunderstanding? Would he really listen to whatever weak, implausible retraction I had to offer?

But there was a still greater problem for me personally. Even if I did manage to call off the murder, it wouldn't save me from his blackmail and threats. He knew the White League existed now, without any doubt. I had relayed the terms of their agreement. The councilwoman had to die or the White League would remain indifferent to his political ambitions. And if that were the case—if the money didn't arrive in bushel baskets—the vindictive bastard would most certainly fulfill his pledge to make my life a monstrous nightmare.

So still it came down to her or me. Willie's life or mine. I was hopelessly compromised, as usual. Too afraid, too paralyzed, to make the phone call I should have made. And so the death watch began.

For the next few days I followed the evening news with great trepidation. I listened to the local A.M. radio on the hour; I opened the *Times-Picayune* every morning with a queasy feeling in the pit of my stomach and an overpowering sense of dread. I suspected that it would happen sooner rather than later, because Morvant was eager to jumpstart his campaign and desperately needed a quick financial fix from his new benefactors. But I couldn't look at my face in the mirror and I had difficulty hugging my own children. There was a moral taint to everything I touched and I didn't want it to infect their sweet, innocent lives.

To make matters worse, I received a phone call from Lieutenant Castle at my office on Friday afternoon. "I understand you and your wife will be attending Zulu this year," he said with a hint of malice. "I look forward to meeting the lovely lady."

My spirits sank at the prospect of James Castle looking over my shoulder all evening. "I'll be wearing a bow tie, Lieutenant," I said. "They're a little harder to strangle a man with."

"Never underestimate my imagination, son. You have a good afternoon, now. I'll be looking for you at the ball."

On the evening of the Zulu Ball, as I donned my cufflinks and bow tie, watching my beautiful wife apply makeup at the dressing mirror, I was nearly overcome with anxiety and my hands began to shake as I buttoned the studs on my shirt. I felt a nagging premonition that something would happen tonight in the commotion and revelry surrounding the Carnival ball. The premonition was as vivid and certain as it was irrational. But something was telling me that Mark Morvant would seize a moment like this to make his move. Paranoids enjoy their conspiratorial metaphors and secret meanings, and I could easily imagine him sending a symbolic message to his enemies—to the one group that despised everything he stood for and continued to mock his reach for political power. Violently disrupting the premiere black event of the year would certainly endear him to the vengeful gentlemen of the White League.

"Hon, you look as nervous as a rabbi in Idaho," Claire said, curling her long dark lashes at the mirror. "Why don't you go make us both a martini? I could certainly use a drink. This won't exactly be our crowd, will it?"

I went downstairs to the bar and knocked back a stiff gin on the rocks before making two Bombay martinis and returning with them to our bedroom. For some inexplicable reason I decided to slip Perry's 9mm Ladysmith into the tuxedo band at the small of my back. An extra precaution, I told myself. This was what my father-in-law always did whenever he ventured out into the city at night, even when he came to our home for dinner. Many of the older white Uptown CEOs carried handguns with them at all times. Not a single member of the Magnolia Club would have questioned my judgment, given where I was going tonight.

I soon discovered what others had known long before me—that a couple of gins plus a pistol under your belt made a potent tranquilizer. I was relatively relaxed by the time we reached the Convention Center, a modern trade-show arena just upriver from the Riverwalk mall and the recently vandalized Liberty Monument. Despite the brisk weather, there had been a rally of angry white demonstrators at the monument earlier in the evening to decry the desecration of their precious obelisk, and several brazen provocateurs had wandered over to the Center to wave placards and make their annoying presence known to the glamorous black gentry arriving in their limousines for the Zulu Ball.

"You'd think everybody in this town would be tired of picking on each other by now," Claire said as we hurried through the chill February darkness toward the bright glass doors. "When are the smart people going to take over?"

A lumpy middle-aged woman in large glasses was wearing a sweatshirt that said *The Grinch That Stole Mardi Gras* with an unflattering cartoon of Wilhelmina Phillips as the Grinch. Her neighbor was wagging a sign that read RESPECT MY HERITAGE, I'LL RESPECT YOURS. The police were on hand but standing off to the side, keeping a low profile. A confrontation was unlikely beyond a few passing words. The arriving Zulu partygoers were valiantly ignoring the demonstrators and streaming inside the Center amid laughter and an impressive pageantry of French-cut tuxedos and magnificent ball gowns.

To my relief, I saw no sign of Mark Morvant among the protesters. But as we neared the doors I caught a glimpse of a slick white dome rising above the heads in the rear of the group, and I was fairly certain it was Louis Robb.

"Let's move along, dear," Claire said, her arm entwined in mine, tugging gently. "We don't want anyone to think we *know* any of those people."

Louis Robb. The ex-cop from Shreveport. In uniform or not, how many times had he pulled the trigger on a black man on a dark city street or out in the deep piney woods at midnight? He was Morvant's best boy, his perfect pick for the job. But was he stupid enough to try something in front of all these eyewitnesses? I looked back over my shoulder to locate him, but Claire urged me on.

There was a cold industrial vastness to the main exhibit hall of the Convention Center, which had been designed primarily to showcase monster trucks and cutting-edge computer displays. The Krewe of Zulu had made an admirable effort at transforming the inhospitable space into a festive Carnival atmosphere. Dining tables were festooned with Zulu coconuts and palmetto leaves and Mardi Gras streamers of gold, purple, and green. Hundreds of smartly dressed couples were merging into larger parties and searching for their reserved tables. Near the front stage a coronation platform had been erected for the African tribal throne where the Queen of Zulu would be crowned. Two of the krewe's royal guards—the Mighty Soulful Warriors, I'd always heard them called—stood as fearless sentinels near the platform, tall muscle-bound men wearing zebra-skin headdresses and robes and bearing zebra-hide shields imprinted with the letter *Z*. The warriors were painted in black face with exaggerated white lips, their long pointed spears braced at their sides, fierce royal protectors immune to the wisecracks of parading passersby.

"Paul! Mrs. Blanchard!" a female voice shouted from somewhere to our left. Claire and I were not hard to spot, two shrinking white figures lost in a sea of negritude. We had counted only a half-dozen other Caucasians in the entire hall of a thousand people.

"We've been sent out on a scouting party to find you!"

Angie emerged through the crowd with her husband in hand, a handsome dark-skinned man in his early thirties with short-cropped hair and a tidy mustache. I had met Gary Thomas only twice before but knew him to be an articulate Loyola graduate with eclectic intellectual interests. He was completing his internship at Tulane Medical Center and planning a career as a pediatrician.

There was a clumsy moment when Claire and Angie shook hands. Any lingering uncertainties my wife might have had about my relationship with the young woman would certainly not be assuaged by Angie's stunning beauty tonight. She was dressed in a strapless sparkling black ball gown molded to her slender build and slit high up the leg. Her silky brown skin looked tempting enough to drink.

"We're all at Wilhelmina's table," Angie announced, pointing vaguely across the arena floor. "It's over there somewhere."

As we followed our two guides through the throngs of friendly, laughing revelers, Claire leaned close and whispered, "Now I'm disappointed that you *haven't* been sleeping with that gorgeous girl. She's so precious she's giving *me* naughty thoughts."

Willie Phillips was holding court at a large round table set for ten. "Hello, hell-*oooo!*" she gushed, standing to greet us with a delighted smile. "I'm so glad you could join us this evening. Please come meet some of my dearest friends."

She looked ill at ease in her dress, a midnight blue satin affair that covered her tall ungainly body from neck to ankles, the wrist-length sleeves a sheer blue fabric puffing loosely like something from the Elizabethan stage. The dress didn't soften her image, nor did her string of pearls. Willie Phillips was simply not a woman who appeared comfortable in traditional feminine attire.

"Mrs. Blanchard is the daughter of Ida Benjamin," the councilwoman announced, taking Claire's wrist as if to lead her around in circles like a show pony. This proclamation brought lively approval from everyone at the table.

"Your mother is the veritable Lion of Judah, Mrs. Blanchard."

"Please call me Claire, Reverend Frazier," my wife said, smiling graciously at the old gray-haired pastor sitting beside his ancient spouse.

"I understand Ida's righteousness runs in the family," the pastor said, eyeing me with a cagey grin. "I'm told you're helping that Catholic brother in the St. Thomas Project. Working with teenage girls and such. God blesses your good heart, Miz Claire," he said, raising his golden tumbler in salute. It appeared to me that the beloved Reverend Calvin Frazier had started early on the Jack Daniels.

"A little birdie told me a secret about your husband," Willie Phillips said, directing us to our seats. My ears perked up. "I heard he tried to intervene on the Reverend's behalf with an overzealous police officer the other day but ended up in the same sorry soup himself."

Everyone laughed, familiar with the story by now. I was embarrassed. The word had apparently gone around the black community that Paul Blanchard was either a hero or a bumbling fool, and I wasn't comfortable with either interpretation.

"Skull music," said a roguish young man seated next to Angie. "How did it sound to ya, Mr. Coffee? Yo, welcome to the hood," he said, spreading his arms in a mock embrace.

He was the youngest person at the table, with baby dreadlocks and a tuxedo jacket riding up narrow shoulders and a lean neck. Crude blue letters were tattooed across his knuckles, perhaps a girlfriend's name. This was the young blood no one wanted to encounter getting out of their car on a dark Uptown street. As I would later learn, Ahmos was Willie's nephew and her date for the evening. The councilwoman had been a widow for several years.

"Your husband's a hard one to figure, Miz Claire," added the Reverend Frazier, still appraising me with those hooded eyes. "One minute he's saving an old dog from a beating, the next minute he's riding with the dog catcher. You have trouble keeping track of this fella your own self?"

Claire laughed good-naturedly. "He's a man full of surprises, Reverend," she said, glancing at me with an enigmatic smile. "But a little mystery is good for a marriage, don't you think?"

"I'll drink to that," Angie said, lifting her wineglass and smiling at her husband.

A fresh round of drinks arrived and the meal appeared on platters served by attractive black women wearing dark pants and blousy white shirts. Soul food, Creole cooking. Ribs, pork chops, collard and mustard greens, sweet potatoes, hot buttered rolls. Quite a contrast to the anorexic nouvelle cuisine I had eaten too many times at the Jove and Rex balls.

I managed to down two quick gins with dinner and my bladder reminded me that these weren't my first two gins of the evening. Amid the cordial banter at our table I slipped away in search of the men's room, which turned out to be halfway to Chalmette. By the time I found it I didn't care if I had to piss against an alley wall in the driving rain.

The restroom was surprisingly uncrowded. There were three other men present, gray elder statesmen of the Zulu krewe with elaborate tasseled sashes angled across their tuxedo jackets like Knights of Columbus. I was standing at a urinal, relieving myself, when a tall wide-shouldered man unzipped his pants and stepped to the basin next to mine. "Thought I saw you coming this way," he said. I recognized his voice immediately. "You and the missus enjoying yourselves, son?"

"Yes, we are, Lieutenant," I said, my stream going slack. I could feel the Ladysmith snug against my lower back. "And how is your evening so far? Taking a cigarette break?"

I had a small patch of dead skin where his cigarette had burned through my pant leg.

"I always have a good time at this shindig," he said, humming as he relieved himself. "Solid citizens, wall to wall. You sitting at Willie's table?"

I nodded. "She invited us."

"Shrewd lady, Willie Phillips. Politician all the way. Never know what's up her sleeve."

Another man entered the room and stepped up to the urinal on my left. Something about him caught the corner of my eye. He was white. I glanced over and saw that it was Louis Robb.

"That boy Ahmos at your table?"

I was so startled by the situation—Castle on one side, Robb on the other—that I didn't realize the lieutenant was asking me a question.

"Ahmos," he repeated. "He's her nephew. Troubled boy. Gang banger. Willie been trying to straighten him out but he's a hard case."

Louis Robb stood silently facing the wall, a white man conspicuously out of evening dress at the Zulu Ball. I couldn't pee another drop. My earlier premonition was turning into something all too real.

"I know what she's dealing with," Castle went on, his stream loud and forceful against the porcelain bowl. "I once had a *niece* like that. Good kid, down deep. Beautiful child. You shoulda seen her before the heroin tore her up. Tall and beautiful and proud as a princess. But she got mixed up with some sorry son of a bitch that treated her like trash." It was still under his skin, the indignity of that death long ago. "My sister never got over it, rest her soul. And tell you the truth, son," he said, shaking himself before zipping up, "neither have I."

He wasn't going to let this go until one of us was dead and buried.

I dribbled out a few final drops myself, stalling, hoping he would turn and leave without making a scene. I was praying desperately that Louis Robb would keep his mouth shut and not say a word to me. Not while James Castle was still in the facility.

"Expecting trouble tonight?" Castle asked as he washed his hands in front of the wide mirror.

At first I thought he was talking to me. I wondered if he'd noticed the Ladysmith underneath my jacket. But then I realized that Louis Robb had left the urinal and was walking toward the sinks.

"Nothing to it," Robb answered, turning on the faucet next to Castle's. They regarded each other in the mirror. "Everybody's having a high old time."

That's when I realized that Morvant's man was wearing a private security guard uniform with a pistol holstered against his hip.

"You people keeping an eye on those yahoos out at the front

door?" Castle asked him, jabbing the chrome hand-dryer button with a heavy fist.

"They're not a problem," Robb said, watching the lieutenant's movements in the mirror.

His disguise sent volts of panic through me. It was the perfect cover. The bastard was working as a security guard for the ball!

"I'm gratified to hear that," Castle said, giving Robb one last guarded glance before looking my way.

I was slowly approaching the sink area, expecting something terrible to happen at any second. There were three armed men in this tight, enclosed space, and no love wasted between us. I met Louis Robb's eyes for an instant in the mirror. They were hard and calculating and cynical. He seemed to be sizing up the situation. He knew I was wound tight with fear and his terse shadowy smile belittled me. It was clear he wanted me to understand that he could get away with anything tonight, at whatever moment he chose.

"You be careful out there, son," James Castle said to me, chuckling as he straightened his vest and ambled toward the door. "Might be some Zulus looking to roast themselves a white man."

Another group of sashed krewe leaders was filing into the restroom. I left quickly, without acknowledging Robb, the pistol tucked safely in my waistband. Did I have the guts to use this thing to protect myself and Claire if all hell broke loose? I'd been an idiot to bring the gun along. I considered dropping it into a trash bin on my way back to the table, but I couldn't risk someone seeing me do that.

When I sat down again, Willie Phillips was holding forth on the subject of the city council meeting and her Mardi Gras ordinance. "And that pompous little bullfrog had the gall to invoke the *buggy whip*," she explained with a spirited laugh.

I tried to listen politely but my mind was elsewhere. A shooter was in the building, masquerading as a security guard, a stone cold marksman trained to kill. Did he think he could get away with murder in such a large crowd? Or was he stalking his prey, waiting for an isolated moment? *I hadn't counted on sitting next to the woman when the plan unfolded.* I never would have agreed to put my wife in danger.

"Claire darling," I said, leaning over to whisper in her ear. "I'm not feeling very well. Let's make this a short evening, okay?"

She gave me a damning look. "We can't, Paul," she whispered back. "That would be insulting. Just relax, hon. Do you need another drink?"

She ordered me a gin and tonic, my third since we'd arrived, and I began to float away in the airy mists of alcohol. I was only marginally aware that the lights had dimmed and the mayor was issuing a scrolled proclamation while a court of lovely young maids-in-waiting paraded like runway models across the coronation platform. The finer visual details of the ceremony were growing hazy and I couldn't follow the linear flow of things. Before long the beautiful young Queen of Zulu appeared in a shapely sequined gown with thirty pounds of sparkling headdress attached to her like bejeweled antlers and she was crowned by a stooped old grandfather who must've been the Zulu king and then the young woman and her entourage set out across the ballroom floor escorted by a train of those sashed elderly gentlemen and suddenly we were all on our feet applauding and music erupted from huge speakers suspended overhead, Professor Longhair whistling and tickling the ivories, and everyone started New Orleans second-lining behind the queen's court, an endless snaking trail of dancers capering about, waving white handkerchiefs in slow-motion rhythm, and I found myself clinging protectively to Claire as we shuffled along between Reverend Frazier's shriveled wife and Ahmos the gang banger in Liberace tails, and in my gin-legged clumsiness I stumbled against the young blood and he said *Watch your step, cornbread* and shoved me in the back but Gary Thomas grabbed his shoulder, saying *Be cool, Ahmos,* and we slithered along in that long crawling king snake, meandering between tables, dragging everybody into the age-old prancing ritual until the entire ballroom was a writhing cackling handkerchief-waving caravan following some lost Nubian safari single-file through the sweaty humid jungle of coconuts and palmettos toward a shimmering mirage forever out of reach on the distant horizon, forever an illusion no matter how happily we swaggered under the influence of Professor Longhair and his whistling plinking old man's mush-mouthed crooning, *If you go to Noo Aw-leeeens, make sure you go to deh Mahdi Graw.*

In all this dancing buffoonery I noticed three security guards standing off near the bar, but Louis Robb wasn't among them. I was desperate to know his whereabouts, dreading his certain move, the weapon unholstered in crowd cover, a .38 stuck in Willie's ribs at close range, the pistol crack and screaming chaos. I kept Claire within arm's reach, clutching her waist from behind, prepared to throw her to the floor if anything started. She turned with a mischievous smile and yelled in my ear *I think the good Reverend is hitting on me.* I tried to laugh with her and she said *He keeps calling me the Jewess Susanna and asking if he can watch me bathe.* The old pastor swiveled stiffly, waving his handkerchief over his head and giggling *Bring thee oil and soap, daughter!* and we snaked onward through the ballroom, exhausting ourselves until the music ended and the second-line broke down and a thousand stragglers were left roaming the floor like refugees lost and searching for their camps.

"I'm enjoying your undivided attention tonight, darling Paul," Claire said as I escorted her through the crowd, "but you'll leave a bruise if you keep squeezing me like that." I hadn't realized I was gripping her arm so hard. "Are you looking for someone you know?" I hadn't realized I was so obvious in my search for that familiar shaved head. "No, dear," I said, "I'm just a little overwhelmed, I guess."

As soon as we were seated again I ordered another gin. I could hear my speech beginning to slur and my table mates were now looking at me with equal measures of humor and pity. Although I tried to focus and make conversation, my eyes were roaming the floor, looking for signs of anything amiss.

I didn't detect his silent, swift approach from the rear until suddenly he was upon us. I whirled awkwardly in my chair and tried to stand up but his hand pressed my shoulder firmly back down as he said, "No, don't get up on my account," and I realized it wasn't Louis Robb but the overshadowing figure of James Castle glaring down at me as he reached out to shake Claire's hand. "Pleased to meet you at last," he was saying and "I've known your husband since he was a wet-nosed college boy. We go way back, don't we, Mr. Blanchard?"

First Rosetta, and now my wife. He was drawing the circle tighter and tighter around me, like that tie he'd noosed around my neck.

"I hope you didn't meet him in the line of duty, Lieutenant," Claire quipped with a charming smile. "I'm sure my husband hasn't told me everything about his sordid past and those Tulane fraternity pranks they used to play."

Everyone at the table knew the police lieutenant. Cheerful greetings were exchanged. Before moving on, Castle clamped my shoulder even tighter with his huge hand and said, "Someday we'll sit down and have us a little talk, Missus Blanchard, and I'll tell you all his dirty secrets." The others found this devilishly hilarious and I pretended to laugh along in good humor but Castle's hard yellow eyes told me he wasn't joking anymore.

I downed another quick gin after that. Rattled nerves and submissive drinking made a lethal combination. I was deep in the bottle when Claire excused herself to leave the table. "I'll join you, dear," Willie Phillips said, rising tall and imperious. "It may take the two of us to fight our way through the line."

An alarm sounded in my foggy brain. I didn't like the idea of Willie and my wife walking off together into the crowd. "I'd be delighted to escort you," I said, standing unsteadily to slide back Claire's chair.

"Don't be silly, hon," she said. "We know where we're going."

I waited until they were two tables away, walking shoulder to shoulder and engaged in conversation, and then I set off after them. In my graceless condition I bumped into someone's chair, then another, the stylish occupants amused rather than irritated with me. *Easy there, brother,* one fellow said. Still, I managed to keep one eye on the two women strolling toward the ladies room and the other on the periphery of the spreading tables, alert to an armed and dangerous ex-cop marauding somewhere in the hall. I tried to imagine how it would feel to point the sleek Ladysmith at that bald-headed son of a bitch if I saw him stalking the women. The playback in my mind held a sudden daring fascination.

A laughing Claire and Willie Phillips disappeared into the ladies room and I leaned against a white pillar about fifteen yards away, watching the entrance. A growing circle of men, drinks in hand, exchanged jolly male banter at a long food-filled buffet table nearby. I could hear them arguing about Iron Head Heyward and Dalton Hilliard and what the Saints' offense would need next season to win their division. I was tempted to join the conversation when I noticed someone staring at me from the edge of a heavy green curtain draped on the other side of the buffet table. It was Louis Robb, positioned solo, a responsible security guard surveying the frivolity with a cold, implacable gaze. The gin in my stomach soured. He was staring past me toward the door of the ladies room. When he left his post, striding slowly in my direction, I knew he had seen Willie Phillips enter the place where dozens of women were coming and going in a lively bustle. I took a deep breath, my heart thudding wildly beneath my ribcage, and walked out to intercept him.

"Hello, Robb," I said, stepping into his path. I was perspiring heavily and my hands were shaking, but not from drink. I had been scared sober. "We need to talk."

He was visibly annoyed that I had approached him in public. "Make yourself scarce, asshole," he said in a low menacing voice. "My advice, go find an exit door real quick."

"It isn't going to happen tonight," I said, drawing on some deep unknown well of courage to speak to him like this. "Not here. Not now."

He glanced at me with a penetrating coldness. "I've got work to do. Now get the fuck on away from here."

I smiled at him. A calming warmth took hold of me. For the first time in my life I felt as if I had a fair fighting chance against a bully who could break every bone in my body. "You fuck with me, your boss is going to be real unhappy, Louis," I said. "I'm the only guy in this whole goddamned world who can help him get what he wants."

He hesitated, hitching his blunt chin as though to loosen his collar. He'd stored enough information under that thick skull to know I was right.

"I'm calling the whole thing off," I said, my voice gaining strength. "Forget about the councilwoman. I'll tell Morvant myself. I don't want anything to happen to her."

At that instant Claire and Willie Phillips emerged from the restroom with several other women, laughing and jubilant. Louis Robb and I saw them at the same time. He started to step around me but I grabbed his arm. I wasn't going to let him harm a good woman like Wilhelmina Phillips. I wasn't going to put my wife in danger. I was ready to reach back underneath my tux jacket and pull the Ladysmith on him if I had to.

"Do you understand me, Louis? It's off. Tell Morvant I'll take care of this some other way."

He made one swift jerk and my hand was gone from his sleeve. He stared at me through those vicious eyes and I could feel his raging contempt. He hated me as much as he hated everyone in this hall. "My advice to you, Chauncey," he said, lowering his mouth to my ear. "Take the wife and get the fuck out of this shine show. I've got a job to do and unless my boss tells me in person, the deal is sealed."

I had distracted him long enough to throw off the rhythm of the moment. He saw that he'd lost his opportunity and turned and vanished quickly into the crowd near the buffet table. I felt utterly helpless. I had only delayed the inevitable. What was I going to do now? There was no time to contact Morvant and call off his dog.

I braved my way back through the dining tables with fear as my only compass. I could picture the evening unfolding in violence and bedlam. A gunshot at close range, like Sirhan Sirhan. Screams, upturned chairs, a mad scramble for the exits. People had been trampled to death in public panics.

At the far end of the Convention Center, a stage curtain rolled back and a live band blasted horn music rhythm'n'blues across the cavernous showroom, saxophones and trumpets and booming bass, and the people all around me shouted *That's what I'm talkin' about!* Instantly I recognized the growling soulful voice of the legendary Bobby Blue Bland.

"There's your man, Paul!" Claire said with a delighted smile as I reached our table. Willie and her friends were rising exuberantly and scattering off in the direction of that loud heart-pounding brassy sound. "Shall we join them?" she asked.

I was slightly hysterical by then. I grabbed her slender arm a little brusquely, lifting her from the chair, and led her by the hand into the crush of bodies moving toward the dance floor. I realized I probably couldn't save Willie Phillips now but I was determined to flee the building with my wife and put as much distance as I could between the two of us and this impending disaster.

"Why such a hurry, Paul?" Claire asked as I pulled her along. "Mr. Blue Bland's going to be playing all evening."

"Come on," I urged her. "We've gotta get out of here."

We'd reached the open floor where others were dancing ahead of us and she turned and forced herself into my arms. "You're in a peculiar mood tonight, darling Paul. Why don't you relax and dance with me?"

I didn't want to make a spectacle of my resistance so I held her in a tender embrace and maneuvered her slowly toward the exit. "I've had too much to drink, darling Claire," I whispered in her ear. "I think it's time to go home before I embarrass us both."

"You seem remarkably lucid to me, considering," she said as she eased her body closer, pressing those wonderful soft low breasts against my tux jacket and kissing me sweetly on the cheek. "Besides, we can't just leave without saying goodbye to our hostess, silly man."

I gazed over her shoulder toward the outskirts of the dance area. "If anything happens to me, Claire, take the children and move to California," I told her. "San Francisco—it's a decent place to raise them. The private schools are better there."

She giggled nervously and separated from me to look into my face. When she saw I was dead serious, she rested a hand over my heart and said, "Whatever are you babbling about, darling?"

I held her tightly and kissed her bare neck, saying, "If everything goes bad, it won't be worth living in this goddamned town anymore. Take the kids and move away."

"Stop that, now, Paul. You're being a little creepy. Maybe you *have* had too much to drink."

I danced her steadily toward the exit while the big sweating blues man growled about lost love and sorrow, and the ballroom floor filled shoulder to shoulder with swaying couples, not a white face among them except ours. In a few more steps I might have secured our escape, but like some ancient archangel of doom the Reverend Frazier was tapping me on the shoulder, breaking in to dance with my wife. I tried to make excuses but Claire willingly slipped away with the old man and suddenly, as if trapped in a drunkard's nightmare, I was dancing arm in arm with Willie Phillips. She was taller than I and insisted on leading, her long-legged angular movements strong and confident despite the hampering dress and high heels.

"Are you having a good time tonight, Mr. Blanchard?" she asked with a toothy smile.

I caught sight of a security guard slowly patrolling the outer reaches of the dance floor. "Listen, Miz Phillips," I said nervously, "you've got to take precautions. There are men in this town who hate you and will do you harm."

She laughed and said, "I've been dealing with that all my life, young man. Tell me something new."

"Do you have your own security here tonight? A bodyguard or someone who looks out for you?"

Her smile faded. "I can take care of myself, Mr. Blanchard. But thank you all the same."

I thought about Ida, my mother-in-law, uttering those same words just before they kidnapped her thirty years ago.

I felt Willie's long bladelike fingers dig slowly, deeply, into the back of my neck. "Is there something you're trying to tell me, my friend?" she asked.

My eyes swept through the crowd, looking for the assassin in uniform. "Would you like to come to our house for a nightcap?" I asked, a last desperate attempt to get her out of this hall. "Claire and I are leaving now. Why don't you come with us? We would love to have you and your entire table over for drinks."

"Hey, Will-eeeee!" A high screechy female voice behind us. "Happy Mahdi Graw, dawl!"

Several old friends had stopped to greet the councilwoman. She released her fingers from my neck to chat with admiring fans. "It's the Zulu Ball, Mr. Blanchard," she said with a joyous laugh. "The night is young. But I may take you up on that offer later on."

Giving way to her mob of friends, I lurched off into the merry carousel of dancers, searching for Claire and the Reverend Frazier and a tall white man named Louis Robb. Someone touched my arm and I spun around like a dazed prizefighter. The alluring Angie Thomas was smiling at me, her lovely bare shoulders as creamy smooth as a child's coffee milk. "Mr. Blanchard, sir, I've been waiting for you to act like a proper masked gentlemen of Rex and call me out," she said with a daring arch of the eyebrow. "Isn't that how they do it in your krewe?"

The heat of dancing had dampened her face. She was so beautiful, and so familiar, I couldn't find my tongue. An image flashed through my head—the flushed face of that delicious young woman I'd made love to in the cottage on a rainy night long ago.

"Don't tell me you've never danced with a Creole girl before," she teased. "I thought all you Uptown gentlemen had a quadroon mistress tucked away in your attics."

She slipped snugly into my arms and we were dancing to Bobby Blue Bland singing smoky sexy *Somewhere Between Right and Wrong* and in Angie's sweet nursing embrace I lost control of my emotions and began to fight the tears. Something inside me had finally broken. I was overwhelmed now, among these people, with this lovely woman in my arms. My entire adult life had been a lie and it was hard to face the ugly truth square on.

"Are you all right, Paul?" she asked, feeling the catch in my chest.

"I'm sorry," I said hoarsely. "Please forgive me. I've done some terrible things."

"Maybe you should sit down awhile," she suggested, studying my burning face. "You look a little flushed. We'll order you some coffee."

"Just hold me for a minute," I said.

And she did. Like a friend comforting a dying man.

In time I found my voice. "It's hard to realize how terrible it really is until you've been there and seen what you've done to a good man," I said, releasing a string of words I had no power over. "At first you think, 'Okay, I didn't do this. I'm not responsible. It was her fault.' And you try to save yourself…one false step after another…and then you've got to keep making wrong moves even though innocent people are hurt…people you love…and the years go by and you keep trying to protect yourself and everyone you care about but you can't, Angie. It's all built on lies. And the damage is done."

I was babbling now, spilling my guts, and it felt good and cleansing but I knew I was wading deeper into dark waters and I ought to stop before it was too late.

"I've messed up people's lives, Angie, but I'm too much of a fucking coward to do anything about it."

Angie separated herself from me at arm's length and said with grim concern, "I don't think I want to hear any more of this, Paul. I don't know what it's about and I don't think I want to know."

I glanced toward the outer ring of the dance floor and saw her husband Gary smiling politely at me and that young blood Ahmos standing beside him, arms folded gang-sign, glaring with hatred in his eyes. The sight of that angry young man brought me around like a slap to a dream-walker's face. I knew this was no time to stand by feeling sorry for myself when mayhem could break loose at any moment.

"Angie," I said, "you've got to help me get Willie Phillips out of here. Something awful is going to happen if she stays."

She gave me an admonishing little shake. "Jeezum, Paul, I've never seen you like this," she said. "Let's go get you some coffee."

Before I could tell her more, someone tapped me on the shoulder. James Castle was breaking in to dance with Angie. For the first time in my life I was grateful to see that unrelenting old hell hound. How could I persuade him to take care of Willie Phillips without giving myself away?

"You mind if I rescue you from this scamp, Miz Thomas?" the

lieutenant asked with a burly grin. "He's not an entirely trustworthy character around young women like yourself."

Angie was reluctant to release me. Worry lines were etched across her lovely forehead. "He means well, Lieutenant," she said, regarding me with a troubled smile.

"Castle," I said, hesitant and struggling to find the right words, unsure how to begin. But he was absorbed in his own dapper charm and, laughing largely, danced Angie away into the mash of bodies. I saw her craning around his wide frame to watch me with a vexed expression, and then they were gone.

I didn't know what to do next. I stood awkwardly with my hands in my pockets while couples eddied around me. The big sweating blues master was singing *Turn On Your Love Light* and the dancing had assumed a joyous fury. Revelers moved as one in a buoyant tidal flow that caught me up and swept me toward the stage. As I drifted along, controlled by the manic motion of the crowd, I became frantic to know Claire's whereabouts. Grasping onto the stage's purple and gold bunting, I felt a little dizzy and sick to my stomach, panic gurgling inside me. I looked up and saw Bobby Blue Bland scowling down at me as if I was something nasty stuck on the bottom of his shoe. He recognized a sloppy white drunk when he saw one. His horns were shrieking and everyone was dancing smooth soul rhythm and I felt a thousand dark eyes watching me from the dance floor. I had to find Claire and get out of there before the heat smothered me.

When I scanned the ballroom again, I noticed a gray uniform near the opposite wing of the stage, a dutiful security guard covering the perimeter, studying the partygoers, one hand resting on his holster. I squinted through the sweat in my eyes. It was Louis Robb. His attention was fixed on the dancers in the middle of the floor, his head alert, shoulders squared, the body language of a vigilant cop. When I traced his line of sight I saw what had seized his interest. Willie Phillips and Gary Thomas were dancing together out in the center of the crush.

Robb was suddenly on the move. I tracked him weaving through the couples with that hand still gripping his holster. I lost sight of him for a moment, then picked up his slow stealthy zigzag through the shuffling bodies. When I turned again to find Willie, I saw something that stopped my heart. Claire was out there next to them, dancing with the Reverend Frazier and smiling that beautiful brown-eyed smile that had won my love the first time she'd lowered her mask at the Rex Ball. I took a deep diver's breath and shoved off from the stage bunting and jostled my way through the dancers, shouldering people aside, making quick enemies as I stumbled into the fray. I didn't know what I was going to do but I had to prevent Louis Robb from firing a weapon anywhere near the mother of my children. The crowd was so dense I could no longer locate his loping movement but I bulled ahead, raising the ire of every elbowed husband in my wake. *Take it slow, bro',* someone said. And someone else, *Scuse me? Those are my feet you're steppin' on!*

As I broke through one final knot of dance partners I saw that I was too late. Robb had reached Willie Phillips and was inclining his face close enough to kiss her on the mouth. She had stopped dancing and was listening intently to whatever he was telling her. I envisioned the gun slipped from its holster now, the hard nose placed gently against her left breast. *No,* I said aloud, waving my arms frantically and forcing my way toward them. Claire had stopped dancing, too, and was observing the discussion. *Get away from her!* I shouted, my words lost in the din. Robb was drawing Willie aside, leading her somewhere. What had he told her? *You have an emergency phone call, Miz Phillips?* Something like that. *The mayor wants to see you.* He was leading her out of this melee to someplace more private, where he could dispense with her and make his getaway. *Wait!* I yelled. But she was following him obediently now and none of her friends had suspected anything out of place.

"*Hey, Rent-A-Badge!*" I screamed, rushing forward, and this time I was close enough to be heard. Louis Robb turned. He looked surprised by my sudden ruffled appearance and stared at me with an unforgiving anger. Willie Phillips was surprised to see me like this, too. I straightened my cummerbund and smiled at them both. I knew that my only chance of preventing an incident was to make him do his job. So I slowly withdrew the stainless steel Ladysmith from the back of my waistband, raised it high over my head, and started waving the gun around like a deranged drunk.

"*Happy Mardi Gras, every-baahhhdy!*" I barked directly at Louis Robb.

Everyone was pointing at me now and shouting. The crowd had parted, elegant couples backing away, alarmed and offended, pointing at me and warning their friends. Willie Phillips couldn't believe her eyes. James Castle appeared out of nowhere, his stern expression revealing the contempt he'd always felt for me. *What the fuck is this sorry rich cracker doing now?* he seemed to be thinking. I beckoned him with my chin. *You want me? Come and get me, cop.* And then, with my aim raised toward the cavernous ceiling of the Convention Center, I pulled the trigger. The Ladysmith fired and people began screaming throughout the hall. Bodies dove to the floor, husbands covering their wives. A scowling Louis Robb had no choice but to grab my wrist and snatch the gun out of my hand and slam me face down on the terrazzo. My cheek smacked hard against the cold stone and I thought I might have broken a tooth. With his muscled weight piled on top of me, he pinned my arm behind my back and said in my ear, "I ought to beat you bloody, you stupid motherfucker."

I offered no resistance. Amid the chaos of voices, strong arms dragged me to my feet. James Castle had collared my tuxedo jacket. "Are you out of your goddamned mind, Blanchard?" he said, shaking me like a naughty child.

Within seconds we were surrounded by those Zulu warriors in zebra-skin robes, their faces painted fiercely black. One of them gripped my neck and said, "What the fuck you doin' in here strapped like that, Dirty Harry?"

"Let's get him outside," someone insisted.

But I wiggled free and threw myself on James Castle, locking onto his barrel chest in a sweaty bear hug. "Don't leave Willie," I said in his ear. I could smell his perspiration fighting with a woody cologne. "You hear me, Castle? Don't leave her side. They're gonna kill her tonight."

He shoved me away with a strange, indignant look. Louis Robb and the Zulus had seized my arms now and began hustling me out through the frightened crowd. I fought my captors, hoping to catch Castle's attention one last time. He was still staring at me, puzzled and alarmed, and I didn't know if he'd understood what I said.

"Believe me, man," I shouted back at him, nodding toward a dismayed Willie Phillips. "Don't leave her side."

The security force dragged me along at a breathless pace. I felt like a boxer in the middle of his entourage, bouncing down the ramp toward the ring. Claire was jogging alongside our troupe now, pleading with them not to hurt me. Angie and Gary Thomas were interceding, too, appealing for mercy. Once we were out in the cold night air of the parking lot, Gary convinced the Zulu guards to release me into his custody.

"We oughta kick his fat white ass," one of them said. "Doin' us like that."

I looked around but couldn't find Louis Robb. In all the confusion he had slipped away.

"Take your husband on home, Mrs. Blanchard," another Zulu said. "He's not welcome here anymore."

"I'm terribly sorry," Claire said on the verge of tears. She seemed overwhelmed by the awful scene but relieved that I wouldn't be beaten or arrested. "I apologize for my husband's behavior. I didn't even know he owned a gun."

"He's had way too much to drink," Angie explained, keeping her distance, appalled by what I'd done.

"Let me help you get him into your car," Gary volunteered. "Maybe we should follow you home."

"That won't be necessary," I said, patting Gary gratefully on the shoulder and straightening my tux jacket. I watched the tall robed warriors retreat toward the Convention Center in a gabble of laughter and incredulity. "I'm sober as a Mormon, Gary. I just needed a little air. We can take it from here."

Claire drove us back home to St. Charles Avenue in an icy silence. She refused to speak to me as she left the garage and huffed across the pool patio with her heels clacking angrily against the flagstones.

Upstairs I found her dragging sheets and blankets out of the guest room closet.

"Come on, Claire," I said apologetically. "You don't have to do this. I'll sleep in here if you want."

She whirled quickly and hit me in the chest with a pillow. "What the hell were you *thinking*, Paul? What were you doing bringing a gun to a Carnival ball? Especially to *that* ball! We may have to move to California after all, thanks to you!"

"I'm sorry, darling. I wish I could explain."

"You certainly made a fool of yourself. And you embarrassed *me*, goddammit. Aren't you ashamed of your behavior?"

"Of course I'm ashamed, Claire. I feel awful about it."

"A *gun*, Paul? A wealthy white man carrying a *gun* to the Zulu Ball! What kind of message will that send to our black friends?"

"Try to forgive me, Claire. There's more to it than you know." Stopping Louis Robb was the only decent thing I'd done in twenty years.

"Are the police going to show up on our doorstep tomorrow morning and arrest you, Paul? Won't that be a jolly sight? The children will be so proud to see their father being led away in handcuffs."

"That's never going to happen," I said.

I hoped James Castle had taken my words seriously. I didn't want to read about Willie's murder in tomorrow's headlines.

Claire pulled a duvet out of the closet. "I'm going to sleep right now and I hope this will all have been a bad dream when I wake up in the morning," she said. "I'm going to pray that my husband didn't really destroy his reputation and mine on one of the rare occasions we were invited to socialize with black New Orleans."

Yes, I knew it was only a matter of time before eyewitnesses gossiped to their office coworkers and white neighbors and the story made its inevitable journey to the hoary gentlemen of the Magnolia Club and my fellow krewe mates in Jove. What happened to that drunken fool Paul Blanchard at the Zulu Ball would become a juicy hors d'oeuvre to chew on at Garden District cocktail parties for the next ten years. It was a reputation I would not live down easily, if at all.

"On second thought, you *will* sleep in here, Paul. I'm not the one who should be punished," Claire said, stuffing the duvet and an armful of sheets against my chest. "If I'm not at breakfast in the morning, it's because I'm out consulting with my divorce attorney."

"Claire—" I mumbled through the linen.

"Rosetta isn't here to hold your hand on this one," she said before storming out of the room. "Make your own bed for a change."

Chapter forty-four

I woke alone in the guest bed with a nagging hangover. Someone was knocking on the door. Julie ventured into the room with coffee and toast on a tray. "Mom told me to bring this to you," she said, looking around the room as if she'd never been here before. "I guess you're grounded now too, Dad."

If I didn't gain control of the situation, I might be grounded for a long, long stretch.

"What were you busted for?" she asked, setting the tray beside me on the rumpled covers.

I sat up and took a sip of black coffee. It scorched the back of my throat like kerosene. "Possession of a firearm," I croaked.

"That's so totally redneck," she said.

"It's in the blood, honey."

"I didn't think we were rednecks, Dad. Does that mean my children will have rickets?"

After a long shower I spent the remainder of the morning trying to reach Mark Morvant by phone. I left messages at his home and office, coding my words in careful tones. "I have to speak with you right away, Mark. I want to cancel our contract as presently agreed upon. Is that clear?" I didn't know what I was going to do, but I did not want a murder on my hands. "I'm sure you've discussed this subject with Louis Robb. Do not proceed. We've got to talk."

Claire and I managed to avoid each other the entire day. The tension in the house reached a toxic level, like the silent, invisible effects of radon. Shortly before dinner I couldn't bear it any longer, so I went out for a drive and decided to visit my mother in the walled fortress she lived in near Lee Circle. I hadn't been to her apartment in several weeks. I had always found the place to be too dark and oppressively confining for my taste, but mother had chosen it because two of her sisters and several friends had landed there in their old age. Unfortunately, all of them had passed on by now, leaving her without companionship in the waning days of her hobbled life.

The apartment building was as fortified as a Moorish castle, and I had always suspected there were catapults and vats of boiling oil atop the massive white stucco walls. I drove into the shadowed archway, identified myself by driver's license to the guard sitting behind bulletproof glass, and rolled into the courtyard after the barred electronic gate was raised like a drawbridge. The complex had been strongly buttressed to ward off those bands of young black street thugs that roved through the imagination of every aging white person in New Orleans. Frankly, I wasn't secure enough in my own feelings to ridicule anyone else's fears. I was glad that my mother was out of harm's way, contented and well cared for. That was all that mattered.

Nurse Oretha answered the door and led me into the living room, where Mother was sitting in her wheelchair in front of a loud television program, trying to crochet a single stitch on a small crisscross of yarn that had little chance of becoming a pot holder before Andy graduated from high school. Mother was alert and smiling that ironic smile permanently affixed to her mouth. I was pleased to see her dressed properly in a cotton gown, her meringue of white hair washed and styled for the Sabbath. When she saw me enter the room her eyes danced brightly and she moaned a tortured greeting, buzzing toward me in her motorized chair. I kissed her clammy forehead, patted her shoulder. She was excited and trying to talk, but the attempt was painful to hear.

The sad truth was, something essential had been missing between my mother and me for as long as I could remember, and it took some effort now to maintain the pretense of closeness. When I was growing up she'd been like one of those idealized statues of the Virgin Mary in church, a splendid abstraction of motherhood, but cold to the touch. I couldn't recall her ever holding me in her arms.

"If you don't mind, Oretha, I would like to spend a little time with my mother alone," I said to the nurse, whose corpulence seemed to increase day by day even as my mother shrank smaller and smaller into oblivion. "Are there any errands you could run for an hour or two?"

Oretha was clearly irritated by my request, which would uproot her from her cozy nest on the couch, from which she held forth with a dog-eared Bible, needlework, and a jumbo bag of potato chips. But she slowly complied, throwing on her winter coat and rattling car keys on her way out the door.

I sat down in an armchair that had once occupied a corner of the visitors' parlor in our home on St. Charles. The lacy antimacassar was still in place across the back, yellowed now by age and the stains of decades-old Brylcreem.

"I came to talk with you about something that's been bothering me, Mother," I began without ceremony. "The White League," I said, lowering my voice. I spoke these words cautiously, as if the walls had hidden microphones. "You were married to Dad for forty-five years and you must've known what was going on."

Her countenance remained fixed with that eerie, eternal smile, but I could read the sudden alarm in her eyes.

"I don't really know how to communicate with you—or how we're going to get through this. But I'm in serious trouble, Mother, and you may be the only person in this whole stinking world who can help me."

Her eyes darkened and she tried to express herself, but as usual she couldn't be understood. Her good hand floated from her lap and she reached toward me. I leaned forward and grasped her cool fingers, a rare physical moment between us. She still had strength in that hand, which she demonstrated with a healthy squeeze, as if to prove she was listening closely. *Go ahead*, she seemed to be saying.

"I did a terrible thing that could destroy me," I told her. "And if it comes to light—if I'm found out—it would destroy Claire and the kids, too, and probably ruin the Blanchard name forever. Do you understand what I'm saying, dear? I've got myself in an unbelievable mess that could send me to prison for a long time."

She sighed, a long mournful rattle in her throat. Her head sagged to one side and she shut her eyes, the body language of disappointment.

"I know, Mother. I'm sorry. The more I try to save myself and the family, the worse it gets. I wish I didn't have to tell you these things."

She inhaled deeply, pulling herself together, summoning emotional strength. I could feel her apprehension but also her desire to hear why I had come. A change had taken hold in her. When she looked at me now, there was a penetrating intelligence behind those eyes.

"The White League is my last hope," I said.

In a very real sense, this was true. If the League decided to lend its financial support to Morvant, I was out of the quicksand. But how could I force their hand without following through with their demand for blood?

"They can erase all my problems if they want to. I'll walk free, Mother, if the League chooses to wave its magic wand. The trouble is, they don't take me seriously. When I went to them and asked for help, they treated me like some chump door-to-door brush salesman with mud on his shoes."

Her eyes hardened. Hearing this visibly displeased her.

"I'm not one of them and I never have been. I guess being Charlie Blanchard's son doesn't count for much anymore."

She raised her chin, a familiar imperious gesture I had seen all my life. I detected the faint glow of pride in those powdered cheeks. Someone had slighted her husband and the family name, and that was unacceptable to her.

"I don't know where to turn, Mother," I said, slumping back into the soft embrace of the armchair. I rested my head against the stained antimacassar and studied her regal posture. "I'm tired and worn down and running out of time. I thought you might be able to give me some advice. Something I could use. Christ, you must've dealt with these people when Dad was alive. How the hell can I get their undivided attention?"

I was indeed weary and slightly hung over, and my final words degenerated into an unmanly whimper. I looked at the impaired figure sitting in front of me and realized I was placing my life, my entire future, in the hands of a wheelchair-bound stroke victim who may not have understood a single word I'd uttered for the past half hour. Exhausted, and longing for some semblance of inner peace, I closed my eyes and thought about the many times I'd curled up in this old chair with an adventure book when I was a child, escaping the real world outside St. Charles Avenue and the stern authority of those two strangers who ruled our private world within. But now I needed her. There was no escape from this nightmare I was facing. I needed my mother to become flesh for once in her life, a hand to hold and lead me out of the darkness.

I heard the electric motor whine and opened my eyes. Mother was rolling toward a gloomy doorway beyond Oretha's couch. Where the hell was she going? Before leaving the room she stopped and maneuvered the wheelchair around to face me. She said something incomprehensible and waved her good hand, beckoning me to follow.

I couldn't recall being in her bedroom more than once or twice since she'd moved in. It was a stuffy chamber, overheated, the organdy drapes drawn against the winter light. The four-poster bed was the same one she and my father had slept in their entire married life. And those sinister baby dolls were everywhere—her prized antique dolls she'd collected since before I was born. Three dozen, four dozen. A creepy assortment of hideous little creatures dressed in frills and lace bonnets, sitting like sullen cats on her vanity and chiffonier and the top of a mammoth armoire. For years Perry and I had plotted to heap those macabre demons into a funeral pyre out on our lawn and set them ablaze. Their malevolent smiles had haunted my childhood dreams.

I watched Mother wheel into her huge cedar-lined closet, and soon I could hear her thick voice babbling for my attention. There was an old steamer trunk in the closet that she wanted me to pull out into the bedroom. It was an arch-topped monstrosity with rusted hasps, heavy as a lead coffin and dark with age. I nearly twisted my back dragging that thing out of its hiding place behind the dresses. Mother kept pointing at the trunk and trying to tell me something, her efforts like a deaf mute attempting to mimic real speech. I paused to catch my breath and mop my forehead with a handkerchief before unbuckling the leather straps. Slowly, patiently, I was able to free the corroded latches and lift the old lid. A peculiar odor emanated from it like invisible smoke, an acrid ferment of mildew and moth balls and something indescribably corporeal, perhaps the lingering residue of human salt. Rose petals had been scattered over the top layer of the trunk's contents, but the petals were now brown, shriveled, and without fragrance.

Underneath the dry petals, a Confederate battle sword lay across a gray wool uniform jacket folded neatly by expert hands. Mother reached down and grasped a shoulder of the jacket, muttering excitedly, indicating for me to take it out of the trunk. I gingerly placed the sword on the carpet and lifted the jacket from its ancient repository, sizing it against my chest. CSA officer's dress issue. It must have belonged to Great Granddad, or more likely to his father. The left breast was pinned with a silk ribbon like the one I'd seen in the Cabildo museum display, its metal piece a bronze cross imprinted with the letters *W* and *L* and a large number *14* in the center—the battle date, the hallowed 14th of September.

And then I noticed something else.

Through the top button hole of the jacket blossomed a small black velvet butterfly bow with a dotting of white silk on each wing. Discreet, enigmatic, it suggested a secret meaning, like a cryptic handshake offered by a passing stranger. The same kind of bow that Father Joe Dombrowski had shown me in his parlor. The calling card of the White League.

This trunk had belonged to my father, and to the Blanchard men before him. Why hadn't he ever opened it for Perry and me—shared its many secrets? At this point I'd given up searching for a convenient explanation that would spare my feelings. I truly didn't care anymore.

"Okay, I understand," I said, examining the empty pockets of the uniform jacket. "You want me to wear this thing the next time I meet with the White League. Yeah, that should get their attention."

She rapped my knee with the back of her frail hand, chiding me for my sarcasm, and pointed into the trunk, jabbering instructions. Digging deeper, I found one of those red silk battle guidons and a framed crumbling certificate that proclaimed *Protector White League* with the inscription, *"This is to certify that Adam D. Blanchard was present for duty and in action in the charge of the White League on the Metropolitan Police on the 14th of September 1874."*

"Great Granddaddy himself," I said aloud, studying the certificate. "Did you know he stopped his buddies from executing that Police Chief Algernon Badger right there on the street?"

But Mother wasn't interested in historical anecdote, she was engaged in the single-minded pursuit of something buried deep in the trunk and continued to point and jabber and grab at things she couldn't move. I came across family photographs I'd never seen before and three bundles of ribbon-bound letters and a tattered velvet jewel box full of gaudy necklaces and earrings, but none of these mementos claimed my mother's attention. She waved them off as if they were spoiled meat.

And then I found it. Settled near the bottom of the trunk. What appeared to be an old family album as thick as a monk's manuscript, large paper sheets pressed between leather covers. When I extracted the book from the clutter, Mother grew excited and began patting the thing with the flat of her hand.

"This is what we've been looking for?"

She nodded and calmly uttered the word *yuh*. It was the clearest syllable she'd spoken all afternoon. A strange tranquility overtook her and she straightened herself in the wheelchair, smiling that eerie smile and watching my reaction through solemn eyes.

"Well, let's see what we've got here, then," I mumbled to myself as I walked over and sat on the edge of her four-poster bed. I placed the album in my lap and carefully opened the worn cover.

For the next hour I sat reading on the bed, mesmerized and lost to my surroundings. I perused page after page of that long record, the brittle paper threatening to tear with every turn. It was a kind of annotated scrapbook, part handwritten journal and part portfolio of newspaper clippings dating back to 1874. All the stories related to the White League. They seemed to be arranged in chronological order, and I browsed the early entries with some haste. Original accounts of the Battle of Canal Street published in the *Picayune* and bygone newspapers called the *New Orleans Times* and the *Bulletin*. Accounts of the storming of the Cabildo police station and the instatement of Confederate General Francis T. Nicholls as governor of Louisiana. But what seized my attention was not so much the newspaper articles themselves, their yellow corners waxed to the pages, but the handwritten inscriptions penned next to each story. Below an article about a white man stabbed to death during a scuffle with a group of *"negro instigators"* guarding black children at an integrated school, the inscription said, *"WL brother killed in action while purifying the schools; took forceful steps same night against nigger perpetrators. Three shacks burned back of town."*

This sent a chill through me, but I read on.

"Last two dagoes resisted their fate," noted the journal entry beside a clipping about the lynching of the eleven Italians at the parish jail in 1891. *"Had to hang one of them twice, for he refused to go peacefully to his Maker. WL brothers administered several pistol rounds to necktied prisoner to ensure his proper disposal."*

And on the next page, *"Dragged his body out and burned the black devil in the street."* These words accompanied an article about a black nationalist named Robert Charles who had murdered a policeman and gone on a shooting spree in the summer of 1900. *"Duty performed by WL brothers—"* followed by a list of eight men, their surnames all familiar to me. According to the entry, these upright citizens had dragged Robert Charles's body out of the boardinghouse where he'd been killed by police, and then they set the corpse aflame with kerosene as a public warning to *"other insolent niggers with dark intentions in their savage hearts."*

Yes, I knew their surnames, all eight of those men. Their families were very much among us.

And so I continued to scan the pages of the album and read each handwritten entry, an appalling record of White League activity for a hundred and fifteen years, their murderous secret underworld machinations, explicit names given proud credit for arranging or taking part in lynchings, beatings, bombings, arson, disappearances, strikebreaking, and even the occasional destruction of a white opponent's political career. I was astonished by what I was reading. I could scarcely absorb it all. This scrapbook was potentially devastating to every family mentioned. And not because of ancient skeletons in the closet or some misty Old South pride at stake, but because the journal entries ranged well into the modern era, claiming responsibility for unsolved crimes involving men who were still alive. The examples were astounding:

> 1960: *"Jew troublemaker Ida Benjamin warned in no uncertain terms."* The note identified half a dozen men who were present at her kidnapping interrogation. Henry Lesseps. Russell Gautier and his father. My father, as I had feared. Jack Lacoste, whose children swam in our pool for many summers. A doctor named Morrison, now retired and near death.

> 1963: *"Money well spent on G. Banister and D. Ferrie and their Cuban recruits."* Two men from our parish church, Messieurs Ricks and Bordelon, had funneled White League cash to the anti-JFK people.

> 1965: *"More incompetence by subcommittee. Preacher not home when bomb detonated."* The subcommittee in charge of murdering Reverend Frazier included a man who still ran an oil drilling company headquartered in town.

1968: *"Deposited funds in Galt's (J. Ray) NOLA account
per discussion after he drove in from Los Angeles."* The contact with James Earl Ray had been a local department
store owner whose son was in my class at Jesuit.

These incidents had all taken place in my lifetime, and the involved
parties were carefully recorded in my father's distinct, elegant handwriting. He had obviously taken over the record in middle age, anno-
tating the latter pages of the scrapbook after his father and grandfather
had passed it down to him. As I turned back through those final leaves,
reading them closer now that the shock had worn off, I struggled to
accept what I was seeing before me in black and white. This was my
own father's hand confirming money paid to assassins and church
bombers and the kidnappers of my future mother-in-law. I raised
my eyes from the book and stared at my mother, who had remained
perfectly silent in her wheelchair for nearly an hour. She must have
sensed my horror and revulsion as I read these passages, because when
I studied her now, I could see trepidation in those aging eyes and a
slight tremble in her good hand.

"You had to know this was happening, Mother," I said, unable
to veil my indignation. "You knew what was going on for years and
you didn't lift a finger to stop it."

Her rigid body stiffened even more and her breathing grew
shallow and labored.

"They dragged Ida out of her car one night, threw a hood over
her head, and drove her out to a fishing camp to humiliate her," I
said. "Did you know they did that, Mother? Claire was just a child,
maybe nine years old. What if they'd killed her mother? Ida was a
proper Uptown lady and Dad's goons fondled her in the car and
committed an indecency I won't describe. I'm sure the noble southern
gentlemen of the White League neglected to tell their wives about the
brutality and blood and begging for mercy. They murdered people,
Mother. Tortured some of them first. They weren't the Kiwanis Club,
for Christ sake. Didn't you realize that?"

I could see this was upsetting her but I didn't care. It was time
she faced the bitter truth. It was time for both of us.

"I can*not* understand how you lived with this for all those years, Mother. I'm sorry you can't defend yourself right now, because I would like to hear how you justified this evil behavior. The White League is worse than I ever imagined, and I'm ashamed to be from one of their families." My voice had turned shrill. "It hurts me to say this, Mother, but I'm ashamed of being your son."

Tears had gathered in her eyes. I wasn't proud of myself. I had managed to badger a frail shut-in to the point of tears.

"I'm sorry," I said. "I have no right to be sanctimonious. It's not like I can speak from any high moral ground myself. I'm no better than anyone else in our goddamned miserable family."

The tears spilled down her cheeks and she fought to catch her breath. I tucked the heavy scrapbook under my arm and walked over to her wheelchair and did something I couldn't remember ever doing before. I touched my mother's face. Her skin was as furrowed and leathery as the straps on the steamer trunk.

"I suppose you want me to have this book," I said, smiling kindly at her and thumbing away the tears, "or you wouldn't have dragged it out of mothballs."

I should have shown more gratitude for what she'd done for me. I had come here pleading for her help and she'd given me something very precious, and very dangerous, and in return I had accused her of terrible things and made her cry.

"Understand something, Mother," I said, dropping to one knee in front of her chair and peering into those sad damp eyes. "I don't intend to keep this going. I won't be adding any new stories to the book. And neither will my son. The old hatred stops here," I said, pounding the center of my chest with a closed fist.

At that moment I saw something ignite within her, a glowing satisfaction I hadn't seen since her stroke.

I saw elation.

I saw hope.

Maybe I was only imagining it, or projecting what I wanted to believe, but suddenly I thought I understood for the first time why my father hadn't invited Perry and me to join the White League. Mother wouldn't let him. It may have been her only avenue of insubordination, the only place she could say *No, Charles.* However removed she'd been from our childhood lives, however shallow and self-absorbed and seemingly indifferent, perhaps my mother had found the temerity to say *No, Charles, you can't have my boys. This is where it ends.*

I squeezed her hand fondly and she squeezed back, showing me the strength that remained. "Thank you, sweetheart," I said, patting her knee. "You may have saved a life."

Chapter forty-five

I knew I could find them at the Magnolia Club on Mardi Gras Day. They were men who cherished their traditions. They had all ridden in the Rex parade that morning, imperially costumed and hurling beads to the screaming multitudes, and then repaired to the club with their families in the afternoon, dining on the lavish buffet and drinking themselves senseless before the final Jove parade and the evening balls. I had done this myself as far back as I could remember, first with my parents and then as a young masked kreweman playing the game. But I wasn't going to play that game anymore.

As I entered the rear of the building and passed through the portrait gallery of dead presidents, I heard the reverberant drone of voices punctuated by a little girl's shriek. Fat Tuesday was the only day of the year that women and children were invited into this private sanctum. Throughout our fifteen years of marriage, Claire had steadfastly refused to accompany me or to allow Julie and Andy to attend. As a Jew she was offended by Magnolia's exclusionary by-laws and the fact that her father had been denied membership. I had never challenged her on this. Now I was certain that she was right. I didn't want Andy to ever set foot in this ridiculous old tomb.

I greeted a group of frosty wives chattering at the foot of the polished oak stairwell. A tiny girl wearing white ballet tights underneath her petticoat was spinning around them like a miniature airplane.

"My goodness, Paul Blanchard, don't you know it's against the rules to drag your work with you on Mardi Gras?" said the dark-haired Violet Gautier, Eric's wife.

I smiled and mounted the stairs with the briefcase at my side. It was usually filled with blues tapes, but not today. "A little Carnival surprise for the boys," I told her, patting the leather.

"Smutty pictures, I imagine," laughed one of the other women. "Don't we get a peek, dawl?"

"*Brrrrooooommmmm*," buzzed the little girl, her arms stretched wide like airplane wings banking around her mother's skirt.

I found them in one of the small smoking parlors on the second floor. When I opened the door and dared to walk in on them, their heads snapped around abruptly and they all stared at me from the ring of armchairs arranged around a mahogany coffee table. Surprise registered on their faces. Surprise, and indignation.

"Pardon me for crashing your little circle jerk," I said, studying each man in turn. "Did I hear someone mention my name?"

There were only five of them present, but it was a strong five. As good as it would get. Henry Lesseps, Basil Parker, and a sheepish Claude Villere, who glanced at my briefcase and began to squirm in his seat. I imagined he didn't want another confrontation with the Blanchard family and whatever I was concealing. He could probably still taste the oily steel in his mouth.

"Hello, Eric," I said, staring hard at my old schoolmate. He was sitting next to his father, the distinguished attorney Russell Gautier, the two men clouding the air with cigar smoke. I recognized that distinctive brand from the fishing camp. Cuban Montecristos. "I suppose I should've known you'd be here with the rest of them."

Is this how they'd decided Nico's fate? And Ida's, thirty years ago? Brandy and cigars in the club room?

Basil Parker leaned over to tap his cigar into a shell-shaped ash tray. His Magnolia Club medallion was pinned to the breast pocket of his blue club blazer, and like the other gentlemen in the room, he was sporting the blue and green striped club tie. "Well, well, Blanchard *fils*," he said in a mocking tone. "We were wondering why you didn't ride in Rex this morning. Have you decided to wear a bone through your nose and join the Zulus?"

His colleagues laughed.

"Very likely you Blanchard boys feel more at home with the bullet heads," Basil added with a snicker.

I was almost certain he was wearing eyeliner and a little lipstick. Mardi Gras had provided his cover today.

"Some friendly advice for you, young duck. If you ever drop your gun in front of those big Zulu bucks, don't bend over and try to pick it up, white boy."

I walked over and set my briefcase on the coffee table between them. "I've got a little advice of my own," I said, resting my hand on the leather. "You might want to spread out today, gentlemen. Separate rooms. Willie's anti-discrimination ordinance has given the crazies new hope. One well-placed satchel of c-4 will take you all out."

The men fell silent. Their eyes were riveted on my briefcase.

"Have a seat, Paul," Henry Lesseps said, ever the avuncular voice of calm. "Would you like a cigar? They're number two's, courtesy of Fidel."

"Thank you all the same, Henry, but no," I said, slowly unzipping the case. "Cigars have never been my style."

"We've been concerned about you," he said. "You seem awfully stirred up about things lately. Is everything all right with you and your family?"

"No, Henry, everything is not all right."

I looked at Russell Gautier, who had remained silent and vigilant throughout these tense moments. "It took me awhile to put a face and name to your voice, Mr. Gautier," I said, "but it finally came to me. Are you the bull moose leader of this outfit now?"

He was Henry's age, mid-seventies, another balding gray-haired man with slack jowls and horn-rimmed glasses, as nondescript as the rest of his brethren. He hadn't been especially close to my father, as I recalled, but Dad had never uttered a critical word against him. I had few memories of Eric's father. In fact, I couldn't recollect a single cordial exchange between Russell Gautier and myself at any point during the past forty years.

"What's on your mind, Paul?" he asked, his sonorous courtroom voice bristling the hairs on the back of my neck. It was the voice from the fishing camp.

I glanced at Eric, who was blowing smoke, aloof and with an infuriating self-composure. He seemed to be enjoying himself, sitting at the right hand of God the Father Almighty.

"Let's all take a moment to look at some family pictures together, shall we?" I said, opening the briefcase and carefully extracting the old scrapbook. I placed the dark leather-bound volume on the coffee table before them. And then I pulled out my father's pearl-engraved .22 Banker's Special and set it on the table near my knee, within easy reach. "I brought my little friend along in case someone decides to do something stupid," I said, prepared to shoot anyone who made a sudden move toward the book. "I'm sure you've all heard by now that I've become very fond of pistols and have no problem using them in public."

They all stared at the gun in horror. I began to slowly turn the pages of the scrapbook. "I think you'll be acquainted with most of these Kodak moments," I said. A century of meticulously recorded history, handwritten and intimate, names and incidents and boastful claims. The secret life of the city. Their fathers and grandfathers, and the casual listing of Henry Lesseps and Russell Gautier and Basil Parker when they were younger men earning their stripes. What I had here would make Nico's four hard years of research pale by comparison.

"Let's take a long stroll down memory lane, gentlemen. It's a perfect day for it," I said, continuing to slowly turn the pages. "And then we're going to kick back in our chairs and have a nice friendly chat."

Chapter forty-six

That evening I finally heard from Mark Morvant. The wild background noise told me he was partying somewhere down in the Quarter. I wondered if Kathleen was with him. "Sorry, *cuño*, I've been out in Evangeline Parish for a couple of days," he said, "scaring up support. Got your messages. Louis told me you were a very bad boy at the Darktown Strutters' Ball."

"We've got to talk, Mark."

We set the meeting for noon the next day, Ash Wednesday. The cemetery again, near the burial mound of the Confederate generals.

The sky was as heavy and somber as it should always be on that grim holy day of obligation, with a wintry rawness and the smell of rain in the air. There were more automobiles today, a respectable turnout of church-dressed visitors milling about their family crypts with wreaths and tall glass votive candles. The long black Town Car was parked next to the statue of the CSA soldier reading the roll call of the dead. As I approached in my BMW I could see a trench-coated Louis Robb chucking rocks at the fat seagulls hovering and screeching overhead. When I edged to a stop alongside the Lincoln, Robb opened my door with a functionary seriousness. I thought twice about getting out of the car. He didn't look happy to see me.

"What you got there?" he asked, nodding at the attaché case in my lap. He was still bristling from our encounter at the Zulu Ball.

"Same thing as last time," I said.

His bone-white hand gripped the top of the door as he leaned in to breathe in my face. "You packing a piece again, killer?"

I opened the attaché case and showed him the money. Another $25,000 in cash. "My wife was out there on the dance floor," I told him. "I didn't like what was going to happen."

He grabbed the case and set it on the wet ground. Then he seized my arm and pulled me roughly out of the car, shoving me against the back door and patting down my overcoat. A hump-shouldered *grandmère*, her hair covered by a scarf, was watching us from her family plot.

"You might wanna think twice," Robb said, working his stern jaw, "about letting your old lady dance with niggers."

When he opened the rear door of the Town Car, Mark Morvant was sitting with his ankles crossed in the spacious back seat and calmly reading the *Times-Picayune*. He was wearing a dark suit and tie and his high forehead bore the distinctive cross of ashes administered by a priest at the morning's Mass.

"So when did you become a Catholic, Mark?" I asked, amused to see him smeared with that age-old reminder of Ash Wednesday.

"I haven't gone papal, *cuño*," he said, "but I'm an ecumenical kind of guy. There are rooms and rooms in my heart for all God's chilluns. Haven't you heard about the new Mark Morvant? I share the common faith in Jesus with my brothers and sisters across the land. I'll even eat gefilte fish if you promise me it tastes like pussy. I'm all things to all people, baby. Ain't nothin' but blue skies from now on."

I opened the attaché case and displayed the contents. "Here's another basket for Jesus," I said.

His striking blue eyes brightened as he stared at the banded stacks of bills. "And who is this offering from today, Brother Blanchard?" he asked, casually reaching toward the money.

I shut the lid so fast his manicured nails were nearly clipped. Surprised, he squared his shoulders and shot me an angry look.

"It's from me again, Mark," I said, "but that's going to change."

He wasn't as tough and street smart as he imagined himself. I had always known that about him. I caught his eyes wandering out my window, nervously searching for his bodyguard.

"I talked it over with my old friends in the garden club," I told him, "and I persuaded them that it was in their best interest to support you for governor."

He relaxed and slowly smiled that winning mediagenic smile. There was a triumphant glow about him.

"They agreed to suspend their rules," I said. "You don't have to kill anyone."

My old frat brother shrugged. "Somebody's gonna do that bitch sooner or later," he said. "I don't much care one way or the other."

The Blanchard scrapbook had made quite an impression on the five men smoking cigars in the club room. I savored watching their faces as I showed them page after page. They understood that I would turn the book over to a journalist or a federal prosecutor without the slightest hesitation if they didn't cooperate. Supporting Morvant was only one of my demands.

"But let me make something perfectly clear. They don't really like you, Mark," I said. "It wasn't an easy sell. They've got their standards, I'm afraid, and you don't fit the profile. I had to twist their arms a little, but they're pragmatists and they respond to the harsh realities of history when it's rubbed in their faces."

For an instant I thought I saw something akin to hurt flash across that flawlessly sculpted face, a buried uncertainty that surfaced and then just as quickly disappeared beneath the surgeon's handiwork.

"They've laid down conditions," I informed him, "and there's no negotiation on this."

He braced himself. "Let's have it," he said, nodding, creasing his brow.

"I'm their go-between," I said. "You deal with me and me alone.

I bring you the money in cash. There won't be any paper trail to banks or account names, so don't ask. They don't want to meet you, Mark. They don't want this to be misunderstood as social acceptance. You won't be invited to join their clubs or krewes or any of the usual Uptown horseshit, so put that out of your head. It's not going to happen. Do you understand that? This is about representation in Baton Rouge, pure and simple. You'll get their money and their votes, but you won't ever sit down at their all-night poker table. Try not to be offended. It's the way they are, man. Take it or leave it."

There was the hurt look again. A lifetime of social rejection in that one fragile moment of self doubt, the working class boy from the wrong side of the tracks scorned by his betters, overlooked, dismissed. I had to admit there was something about the bastard I appreciated, however grudging. He could have settled for a life of quiet defeat, like a hundred thousand others from Arabi and the boondocks, damned to dragging tools around a petrochemical plant or selling insurance. But after all these years of fierce defiance he still hadn't surrendered or taken the easy way out, by God. He had backbone. He was out there on the public stump every day, defending his beliefs, love him or hate him. He wasn't hiding behind a desk in his daddy's coffee company.

"I can live with that," he said after long consideration. There was no bottom to his ambition.

"Good, then," I said. "The first installments should start coming in next week. I've seen to that."

He reached over to take hold of the attaché case but I gripped the corners firmly with both hands and held him in check. "Those were *their* conditions, Mark," I said, refusing to let go. "I have my own."

We stared at each other, man to man. He was clearly losing patience with me. He wasn't used to someone else setting the terms.

"This is the end of it, my friend," I told him. "When this race is over in November, we won't be seeing each other again. The debt is paid. Final curtain. Are we clear on that? Don't ever come knocking on my door again."

He pursed his lips, slightly amused by my intensity. "And I thought we were just starting to get past the foreplay, *cuño*," he said.

I was in my own zone now, focused and uncompromising. "There's one more thing," I said, still unwilling to relinquish the attaché case just yet. "You've got something I want back."

He regarded me with a perverse, gnomish smile, as if I'd uncovered his deepest secret. Something distracted his thoughts—a memory, perhaps—and he drifted off like a schoolboy daydreaming at his desk. I didn't know where he'd gone. He was slow to respond, dreamy and reluctant.

"'Parting is such sweet sorrow'," he said with a sad smile. He reached into his suit pocket and found the cowry shell earring I'd given to Nola. "You know, Blanchard, she was truly a beautiful girl. I could see that even when she was stone cold dead with vomit smeared across her tits. I can't believe you let her die on you, you dumb prick."

I stared at him, too angry to speak.

"I can't believe you threw away a perfectly good fuck."

He studied the earring in his palm, a tarnished object now, cracked and misshapen, more talisman than adornment. "I've been hanging on to this thing for twenty years," he said solemnly. "I still dream about that girl. I can see her naked body, all brown and smooth and…." He closed his eyes, savoring the memory. "You were one lucky son of a bitch. But like everything with you candy-ass Uptown boys—easy come, easy go."

He handed me the earring, settling it gingerly in my opened palm as though it were a sacred amulet. "If she'd been my high yella squeeze," he said, "I would've taken better care of her."

I examined the small delicate shells and wooden beads. Clear recollections of Nola had faded with the years, but I could still see this earring against her long noble neck.

"I'll contact you next week," I said, sliding the attaché case at him. "Don't call me, I'll call you. Is that understood? The others should have their first contributions by then."

He had me, I had him. The perfect stalemate. His dark knowledge, my leverage with the White League. His power to reveal, my power to deny. It was a delicate balance, a vicious deathlock. Chang and Eng, forever attached, forever dependent. One false move and we were both doomed. I opened the car door to leave and then stopped myself. "By the way, Mark, I'd be careful with my sister, if I were you. I love her dearly, but she's got a serious weakness," I said. "She likes black cock, my friend. The first boy she ever sucked off was Jaren Jarboe, and she developed a taste for it. You know what they say—'Once you go black….' Her husband tried his best for years, poor bastard, but he couldn't make her give it up. I hope you're using protection, Mark. You never know where Kathleen's mouth has been."

He tried to conceal his disgust but it was there, a small hard tumor of doubt behind those cornflower blue eyes. Racists were such predictable people. The same hot buttons always worked on them.

"Have a safe day," I said, offering him a tepid smile. He didn't look very happy for a man who'd just received $25,000 in spendable cash. "I'll be in touch."

I drove down millionaires' row to the Blanchard family mausoleum and parked in front of the white temple where my father and three generations of forebears *reposed in eternal slumber*, as the saying went. It had begun to rain again and I sat watching the cloudburst wash the Roman columns and bleached marble walls of that durable old crypt. I remained there for nearly an hour while the cold rain hammered my car and the family vault and the cemetery grounds all around me. Ash Wednesday, I thought. Dust to dust, ashes to ashes. Our final destination. We would all end up here soon enough.

As I slumped behind the wheel that day, listening to Irma Thomas on the earphones and waiting out the downpour, my thoughts wended their way back to California. I had rarely allowed myself to conjure up memories of that far-off time and place, partly because it was too painful to dwell on Paradise Lost. My life there had been so sweet. I missed those days and would never get them back. I'd drifted around San Francisco perpetually stoned and hopelessly in love with a half-dozen wild young women and as carefree and broke and irresponsible as everyone else I'd met out there. I remembered feeling that I'd discovered Nirvana and would never leave. I would never go back to the prim, claustrophobic, stultifying life of sad old New Orleans, the city of the dead. The South I'd grown up in was rotting and backward and doomed by its hatreds and intractable, small-minded ways. Yes, I had done wrong—something terribly wrong—but I had come to the Promised Land to find my better self and start anew. At least that's what I'd convinced myself at the time.

So why had I returned to New Orleans? After three years of absolute freedom on the West Coast, why had I stumbled my way home like the prodigal son returning to his father's table?

There was an official version of the story that I'd kept on ice in the back of my mind and I almost believed it myself. The three years of reckless living had caught up with me. My physical endurance had collapsed. I was penniless and sick with hepatitis and had whimpered back home like a mangy dog, counting on my family to take care of me for a few months until I recovered. It was only a temporary respite. I had planned to return to San Francisco as soon as I regained my strength. But then I'd come upon a young and stunningly beautiful Claire Benjamin at the F&M Patio Bar that night on Tchoupitoulas Street and fell in love with her as I'd always known I would and within a year or two we were marching down the aisle in holy matrimony.

Somewhere along that twisted road I'd been ambushed by children, formal family dinners at the house on St. Charles Avenue, the inherited coffee company. How had that happened? I'd wanted out, hadn't I? I'd escaped to the Land of Milk and Honey. Why was I still here?

There were rationales within rationales, but the bitter truth was something every New Orleans child of wealth and privilege understood. We *always* came back home and remained here for the rest of our days. We couldn't survive out there. For a few years, maybe, until the newness wore off. But not forever. We missed the favors, the dispensations, the exclusive memberships, the many small indulgences that attended who we were. Everyone else was here to work for us.

And so I never went back to California. And to no great surprise, I never heard from anyone I knew out there. Not one phone call or postcard. It was as if they'd never existed. As if those three years had been a fever dream. Like Shangri-la, the way back had disappeared.

It was just as well. I had everything I wanted now. Claire and the children, the mansion on the Avenue. Love was a blessing and a trap. It made us happy and it drove us mad. It made us beholden and it caused us to do things we would forever regret. There was no end to what we would do to hold on to those things we truly loved. My father knew that better than anyone.

And so I sat in my sturdy BMW listening to Irma Thomas's moody, soulful voice while the winter rain lashed the windshield. And I thought about my loved ones and all they meant to me. I pulled the old White League scrapbook out of my leather briefcase and opened it awkwardly in my lap, turning the brittle pages to that place near the end where my father had written one of his last journal entries. They were the words of an aging paterfamilias who had spent his entire lifetime safeguarding what was his. I studied the fussy cursive script that the schoolchildren of his generation had learned like a secret catechism:

"Must protect him at all cost!" the entry said.

The tone was different here than it was in the notations he'd penned next to other newspaper articles. The exclamation point and the word *Must.* He was showing emotion, spontaneity, desperation. And a firm resolve to do something. The story had become personal. It had flown off the news page and entered his home.

Love wore strange guises, expressed itself in peculiar ways. Sometimes pride was mistaken for love. In my father's case he didn't separate the two. His love was manifested as an alpha male's instinct to save his offspring. And the family reputation, of course. *Must protect him at all cost!* Which also meant must protect myself.

There were many things I could not have predicted as I sat staring at Dad's exasperated notation that rainy Ash Wednesday afternoon. I could not have known that my brother would die in less than two years, and my mother a year after him. I could not have imagined what would happen between Jaren and me. But on that rainy Ash Wednesday afternoon I sat listening forlornly to the voice of Irma Thomas coiling like cigarette smoke through my head as the BMW rocked in the windy thunderstorm, its heavy rains cleansing the name BLANCHARD etched in marble above the mausoleum door.

And for maybe the third or fourth time I re-read the *Times-Picayune* article pasted to the page of the White League scrapbook: *Man on Trial for Drug-Related Death, Disposal of Body in Swamp.*

Somehow my father had known it should have been me on trial instead of Jaren. Somehow Dad had known the truth and had used his considerable influence to rescue my unworthy ass. He had been my guardian angel, but also the unforgiving judge who had diminished me forever in the eyes of his friends. I owed him my gratitude, but not my affection. I owed him my freedom, but not my devotion.

Protector White League, Great Granddad's framed certificate had declared.

Must protect him at all cost!

The cost, as usual, had been the price of someone else's life.

Chapter forty-seven

In May I received a call from Eric. I hadn't spoken to him since Mardi Gras and wasn't sure I would ever hear from him again. I assumed that our friendship had suffered a lethal blow. But he was cordial over the phone and acted as if nothing serious had transpired between us. He was my old schoolyard chum calling to invite me to lunch at Antoine's.

"I have good news about Jaren," he said. "The Parole Board has agreed to convene a special session."

You bastard, I thought. You could have made this happen years ago.

"Let's have lunch and mend fences," he suggested. "I miss beating your ass on the racquetball court."

I met him the following day at Antoine's in the Quarter. The bent old Italian maitre d' was the same gentleman who'd known my parents by name for forty years. He smiled and greeted me with "Aftuhnoon, Mistah B.," just as he'd always greeted my father, and showed me to the small corner table where Eric sat nursing a martini. My friend's hair was still wet from his morning workout and he was wearing a tie and white Panama jacket. White between Easter and

Labor Day. In this city, red traffic lights were merely a suggestion but dress codes were chiseled in stone.

"Hello, Paul," he said, saluting me with his drink and a warm smile. "I'm really glad you could make it."

I ordered a Bombay gin on the rocks and we toasted each other across the lily vase. The venerable restaurant was filling quickly with New Orleans regulars who'd been lunching here since my friend and I were in diapers, the men wearing business jackets and slant-striped ties, the women clad in dresses and heels. Withering offspring of the thirty families. This somber place of dark oak and hushed tones, these timeless daily rituals, had jelled us all in our own social aspic.

There was a crusted chill between Eric and me, as I'd expected, but we did our best to make small talk and find our way back to civility. We talked about the safe matters of the heart, wives and children, the Tulane freshman pitcher from Texas who could throw a ninety-mile-an-hour fast ball. After Eric's second martini he had relaxed enough to reach inside his jacket and withdraw a fat white envelope.

"I'd like to make a contribution to your candidate," he said. He was the last hold-out of that group from the Magnolia Club smoking parlor. Everyone else had given generously and promised more as the campaign progressed. "Our boy seems to be on his way. Who'da thunk it."

Mark Morvant had just won the Republican nomination for governor and had captured the attention of the national media.

"I suppose you've got your reasons for backing this yahoo," he said with a puzzled smile, "but frankly I'm a little surprised, Paul. I've never figured you for a closet Klansman."

He slid the cash offering across the white table cloth without the slightest regard for how this might look to our neighbors at the next table. I tucked the bulging envelope into my jacket. Another healthy grand or two for Candidate Morvant.

"We've all learned to make compromises, Eric. Some things we do because we want to," I said, "and some things because we have to."

His eyes wandered toward his briefcase resting on the empty

chair beside him. "Let's erase any doubts about this, Paul," he said, shifting into that pious lawyerly tone I had come to know and distrust. "We're going to get Jaren out of there."

I studied him and finished my gin down to the ice. Winning Jaren's parole had been my strongest demand. I knew those gentlemen in the smoking circle could pull the right strings if they wanted to.

"That's mighty white of you, Eric. You mean you're finally going to do the job I've been paying you for."

He was clearly stung by my sarcasm. "I never liked fucking you around, man," he admitted. "But as you say—some things we do because we have to."

I was still too angry at him to let him off. "Why don't you grow a pair, Eric, and start thinking for yourself instead of always doing what Daddy wants?"

We stared at each for several uncertain moments and then he said in a calm, determined voice, "You're more like the rest of us than you think, Paul."

He was right, of course, but I didn't want to argue anymore. I had suddenly lost my enthusiasm for it. I was emotionally drained and ready for lunch and suggested we look over the menus.

"I reserved a room for us," he said, nodding toward the rear of the establishment and the warren of small private rooms used for parties and banquets. My parents had sometimes booked our family into one of those airless, claustrophobic chambers for birthdays and New Year's Eve celebrations. Social gatherings at Antoine's were the top of my list as the most boring affairs of my childhood.

"I figured if we ended up having a fistfight, it would be better not to wake the mummies," he said, his eyes scanning the aged patrons seated at tables all around us.

We left the dining area and ventured down a narrow hallway where a waiter emerged from a closed door with an empty tray floating on his fingertips. It was the room Eric had reserved.

"Let's see what's behind door number three," he said, trying the handle with a confident smile.

I followed him in. Chairs shifted around a long cloth-draped banquet table as a score of men stood to greet us. I froze, studying their faces and the watchful expressions each one returned. Henry Lesseps was there, and Basil and Claude and old Mr. Mohrman, my father's accountant. Creed Brossette stood next to my former brother-in-law, Kathleen's ex-husband. The men all raised their wineglasses and offered me a silent toast. I could feel the hair rising on the back of my neck.

"Welcome, Paul," said Eric's father. His words broke the tension in the room and there was a sudden involuntary mutter of voices.

I turned to Eric, who beamed in proud triumph. He was the best friend who hadn't given up on his wayward schoolmate. I was speechless and torn between enduring the moment with polite restraint or turning and walking out the door.

"We've decided it's finally time, my friend," Russell Gautier said as he approached me with a small ivory box placed in both of his outstretched hands like a liturgical vessel. He presented the box to me and I had little choice but to open it. The black velvet bow lay on a bed of purple silk like a dead insect pinned to a cushion.

"Welcome to the White League, Paul," he said, grasping both of my shoulders with his long bony hands and giving me a manly embrace. I could smell the aroma of Montecristos in the fabric of his suit.

The group applauded. Eric clapped me affectionately on the back. Someone brought me a glass of wine.

Chapter forty-eight

A month later, Eric drove Rosetta and me up to the Louisiana State Penitentiary at Angola. Once we had entered the woodlands north of Baton Rouge and the Tunica Hills overlooking the green river valley, we were surrounded by blooming dogwoods and azaleas in what felt like the lush primordial garden from which Cain had been banished for slaying his brother. A vengeful God had exiled him to those relentless riverbottom cotton fields with a hoe and a tote sack to drag his heavy burden, life without parole.

It was a visitation Sunday and we joined the line of silent cars backed up for miles along the two-lane country road, patiently waiting our turn to pass through the inspection point at the main gate of the prison. Nailed to the telephone poles were those crude hand-painted signs offering hymnlike solace. I imagined some poor old black church-lady toiling away with a paintbrush on her back porch at a nearby farm, fulfilling her Christian duty to comfort the afflicted. I could imagine Rosetta painting these messages if she lived a short piece down the road. The last sign before the guard station said:

> *Be no weeper*
> *Your brothers keeper*
> *Open the gate*
> *Before its too late*
> *Jesus is coming*
> *Let Him in*

Rosetta had fully recovered from her illness by now and seemed elated on the drive up through the dark swamplands. She chattered and napped and told stories about Jaren and me as children. The time we'd got in trouble breaking windows at a vacant house on Coliseum Street. The time we'd stolen someone's golf ball off the course in Audubon Park. I had heard these stories many times, but I listened attentively and smiled at her cheerful recounting. This was the most animated I'd seen Rosetta since she'd undergone chemotherapy last year. We were bringing her son home today and she was delirious with joy.

"I'll have to speak with the warden and sign some papers," Eric said as we pulled into the gravel parking lot in front of the administration building. "It shouldn't take long."

"You make sure you dot every *i* and cross every *t*, Mistah Gautier," Rosetta said, staring out the window at the families milling toward the Visitors Shed. "'Cause we never crossing back to this part of hell ever again."

I shouldn't have been surprised to find that familiar maroon Bonneville occupying two spaces near the entrance. When James Castle saw us arrive, he crawled out of the imposing vehicle, dropped a cigarette to the crushed gravel, and worked the butt under his dusty wingtip shoe. He was dressed in a dapper blue suit and tie and grinned at Rosetta as they made their way toward each other for a fond embrace.

"Thank you, Lord Jesus, for the good angels you have sent to help me and my boy," Rosetta wailed. She began to cry in Castle's arms.

"It's a righteous day, Miz Jarboe," he said, glaring over her head directly at me. "Righteous at last."

I waited next to Eric's bug-spattered Mercedes while he escorted Rosetta into the administration building to negotiate the formalities that would release Jaren under his parole supervision. I made excuses about being in the way, but the truth was I needed to collect myself before facing Two J as a free man. I hadn't had any contact with him since our hostile phone call in February, and I was worried that our first encounter might be awkward and confrontational. I wouldn't have made this trip at all had it not been for Rosetta's plea that I accompany her.

I expected Castle to join them in the warden's office, but he left Rosetta and Eric near the front doors and doubled back along the sidewalk, as if he'd forgotten something in his car. "I suppose you're looking for a pat on the back for finally doing the right thing," he said, lumbering toward me and pausing to light another cigarette.

I folded my arms and shrugged. "Nothing I do will change your mind about me, Lieutenant," I said. "Maybe we ought to leave it at that and move on."

He smiled through the plume of smoke surrounding his large head. "That's way too easy, my friend. You gotta feel some hurt before this is all over with."

Hurt, the man said. I almost laughed. I had been clubbed by a nightstick and slammed against a hard terrazzo floor in front of two thousand people and hustled out to the swamps with bound hands and a sweat-stained hood over my head. That wasn't exactly the routine appointment calendar for gentlemen in my circle. I could still taste the blood and fear.

"You want what's left of me, Lieutenant, take your best shot. I've been knocked around pretty good, but I'm still walking."

He found my comment amusing. "You're a strange cat, Blanchard," he said with a broad smile. "I don't think I'm ever gonna figure you out."

I let that pass. It was a warm, humid summer day at the worst prison farm in America and the sun was beating down on the dry fields sloping off toward the river. I couldn't imagine how any man could endure this wretched place for twenty years. Especially someone who was innocent.

"One thing I can't figure out about you, either, Lieutenant," I said, the tension building as I waited for Jaren to walk out into the bright sunshine in civilian clothes. "Why didn't you bust me for firing a weapon in public?"

He flicked cigarette ash onto the green lawn. "I believed you," he said, canting his huge head to give me a probing look. "I knew you were telling me the truth about Willie Phillips that night. You got my attention. I've made damn sure she's had security ever since."

We stared at each other. "Why'd you do it?" he asked. "Take up for Willie like that."

I shrugged. "I like her. I didn't want to see her get hurt."

He shook his head, studying me as a doctor studies a strain of virus he's never encountered before. "You are one strange cat, Blanchard. But maybe there's hope for you yet."

We had reached another impasse. There was little left to say to each other. It was pointless to stand around in the brutal sunshine, sweating through our suits, so we both retreated to our automobiles to sit behind smeared windshields and wait.

After half an hour, the three figures emerged from the administration building. A euphoric Rosetta was crying jubilantly and clutching Jaren with both her arms like a needy child dragging at a father's waist. My old friend was wearing a tan shirt and tie and brown shoes so polished they gleamed in the sunlight. He had put on several pounds since the parole hearing in February and his face looked bloated, his trim mustache showing more signs of gray. In the natural light there was an unhealthy yellowish tinge to his skin. The eyes that followed me, as I got out of the car, appeared puffy and lethargic. I had expected to confront Jaren's usual proud defiance but instead was witnessing the countenance and carriage of a damaged man.

James Castle stood beside me, waiting for mother and son to complete their emotional reunion as they stopped to embrace. Rosetta hugged Jaren even harder and praised Jesus at the top of her lungs.

"I hope you realize that when you ratted me out to my father," I said, watching Eric rub Rosetta's back affectionately, "you made it worse on Two J. The old man circled the wagons to save my sorry ass."

Castle made a grunting noise deep in his throat, something that sounded belittling and final. After a moment's silence he said, "He's riding back with me."

I turned to look at him.

"His mama, too. They're both riding back with me, Blanchard. I don't want you anywhere near these good people. You and your lawyer pal can crawl back in your hole now that the job is done."

I felt the heat rising in my face. "Rosetta will have something to say about that," I countered.

"You're finished here, podnuh," he said. "Go on home before I change my mind about you. As it stands right now, I'm going to forget you exist. That's probably the best thing for both of us."

He walked over to the Bonneville and graciously opened the door for Rosetta. She looked a little puzzled, but Jaren didn't. He followed Castle's lead as if every gesture had been rehearsed. As if he'd practiced this departure in his mind every day for twenty years. He didn't say a word to me as he helped his mother into the car. He didn't have to. The slow, simmering look he gave me said it all.

Chapter forty-nine

It was a three-hour trip back down through hardwood timber and the concrete outskirts of Baton Rouge and deeper into the verdant bayous of nowhere land. My companion and I had much to reflect upon and we drove in silence. At some point near the outlying thicket of St. John the Baptist Parish he sighed and said, "Well, man, we got what we came for. Take a little consolation in that."

"Sure, Eric. We ought to be proud of ourselves."

He stared at the highway before us and scratched his tailored beard. "I realize that nothing about this is ever going to make you happy, Paul," he said.

"I'll try to live with myself. I suggest you do the same."

We sped onward across the elevated interstate above the fertile green delta of the Mississippi River. The marshes revealed a summertime bloom of lily pads and submerged cypress trunks and long winding trails of algae spread like emerald carpet across the still surface of the waterscape. The sun burned high and bright, reflecting off the glassy lagoons, and I was relieved to be returning back home to loved ones waiting for me. Tonight the Blanchards and Benjamins would gather for dinner, drink merrily, and exchange the latest horror stories of muggings and gunshot wounds and rape in our doomed city. Tomorrow I would sit behind my desk at the office, content that the invisible hand was guiding the company as it always had. An orderly, well managed life was important to my people. Structure, assignments, proper procedures. A delicate mosaic, all the pieces aligned correctly. This was the way things would forever be in the world I had grown up in.

As Kathleen had once put it, *in the end we are who we are.* Did we ever escape that fate? Did we ever shed the skin we'd been born with? I had tried, in my way, and failed. The big dreams had died with age and indifference. So from now on I would seek comfort in the smaller pleasures I could manage within the walls of my own prison. Claire and the children. Bombay Sapphire on the rocks. Walter Wolfman Washington growling the blues in my headphones. And Tulane basketball, even if the team didn't win a game until the turn of the century.

On our way back to New Orleans that Sunday afternoon I looked out the side window of the Mercedes and noticed two swarthy Cajun fishermen in a flatbottom skiff puttering across the swamp toward an island of tangled cypresses. I could see the rifle in their boat. They were pelt hunters, hide merchants. Muskrat and nutria, the occasional alligator. Their thick laughter drifted on the wind as they cut the small motor and disappeared into the trees. What are you going to find out there in deep water, *mes amis?* A beautiful black girl unfurling from her white linen shroud like a water lily opening in the moonlight?

Somewhere out in that desolate bayou of dead flesh and razor-sharp teeth, a group of white men was packing up their fishing camp, closing the storm shutters, loading gear into their four-wheel trucks, prepared for the drive back to the city. The weekend was over and the cigars were all smoked, the decanters empty now until the next trip out. They had discussed the grave matters of the day and the warp of things to come. Who should live and who should not. They had always done this, and they always would.

I recalled what Eric had said to me. *You're more like the rest of us than you think, Paul.* That was undeniable. They didn't need to

initiate me with hoods and strange ceremony. I had borne the mark
of the White League my entire adult life. A dead lover disposed of
in a swamp. A black man buried in prison. The legacy had lived on
in me.

But I had not accepted the glass of wine offered to me in the
back room at Antoine's that day. I no longer sought their recognition
or approval. I had possession of the scrapbook that could destroy
them and they were trying to pacify me with their ludicrous offering of membership. It was a nasty bit of subversion and everyone
in the room knew it. I had handed the ivory box and small black
bow back to Russell Gautier and said, *I can't accept this, Mr. Gautier.
I'm sorry, sir, but this kind of thing is not for me.* And I'd walked out
of the dining room with the enmity of two dozen powerful men
following me like the crosshairs in a rifle scope. But I was thinking
about my brother and poor Nico and what they'd done to Ida and
Father Dombrowski and so many others I couldn't begin to name.
I was thinking about my mother and how she'd tried to keep their
odious circle apart from Perry and me. And I was thinking about
my own children. With the last shreds of my dignity all but gone, I
had pledged in my heart that Julie and Andy would never know the
hateful world I had grown up in.

Chapter fifty

The dinner party at our home that evening was abbreviated and flat. Kathleen, Mother, and Perry were missing from my side, and Nina and Creed canceled at the last minute. I suspected that family members had sensed the growing tension between Claire and me since the Zulu Ball and were avoiding our table. Which left us to contend with the oppressive personality of Dr. Marty Benjamin, blowhard orthopedic surgeon, who dominated dinner conversation with his usual pronouncements. These days, however, Marty had become downright liberal on his views of the Mardi Gras anti-discrimination ordinance. "I *love* to see those anti-Semitic bastards sweating through their leotards," he'd said with bellowing laughter after his third Scotch.

In the late hours after the party I lay awake in bed, regretting everything that had happened since Mark Morvant appeared at our doorstep. My life had imploded. The quiet assurances were gone, the tidy measures I had clung to for many years. The worst part was that Claire and I had been sleeping separately since the incident with the gun. My temporary residence in the guest bedroom had turned into a four-month exile. She hadn't forgiven me and our marriage was steadily disintegrating. I had suggested counseling but she ignored me altogether and chose instead to go about her daily routines as if she were a melancholy widow and I the lingering ghost who appeared from time to time to scatter newspapers in the breakfast nook.

You gotta feel some hurt before this is all over with, James Castle had told me. Losing Claire's affection and respect was the deepest hurt of all.

Around two in the morning I gave in to my aching thirst and rose from bed to go downstairs and mix myself a drink. But as I passed the bedroom window and glanced out at the giant oak limbs standing guard against the house, I noticed a light in the cottage below. At first I thought it was the full moon playing tricks on my eyes. But no, a square of light was burning dimly within the dark stone wall of the little structure in the back acre. Had Claire or one of the kids forgotten to turn off the switch? Or had Julie snuck out there with her school friends again to carouse and drink my gin? I marched down the hall to her bedroom, opened the door quietly, and found her sound asleep. Andy was asleep in his room as well. Relieved that there were no shenanigans afoot, I threw on a bathrobe and my slippers and trotted downstairs to the library and out the French doors onto the dark patio. The bright moonlight reflected off the still water of the swimming pool and bathed the flower gardens and tall spreading trees in a gentle pale incandescence.

It occurred to me, as I approached the dark cottage and its soft-glowing window, that I should have brought a baseball bat for protection. I stopped before the door and listened, as I'd done when Julie and her friends had invaded the premises, but there was no sound whatsoever, only the warm summer night alive with crickets chirping in a single loud rhythm and the lonely nocturnal moan of the old stud lion pacing in his cage at the Audubon Zoo.

I opened the cottage door with caution and stuck my head inside, making sure there were no intruders. Nothing had been disturbed. The bar was wiped clean, the bottles neatly arranged, the workout equipment hadn't been touched in months. "Anyone here?" I asked timidly as I stepped into the room to look around. The air held a stuffy closeness, like trapped attic heat, and the usual mildew odor of disuse. I made a mental note to ask Corinne to ventilate the place tomorrow during the day, then turned off the switch by the door and started to leave. But I remembered I'd restocked the mini-fridge not long ago with tonic water and a fresh bottle of Bombay Sapphire, so I turned the light back on and found a clean glass in the cupboard and a full ice tray in the small freezer. I was carefully measuring gin over the crackle of ice when a shadowy figure stepped out of the dark bathroom and came toward me. I gasped and dropped the glass, spewing cold liquid across my bare ankles.

"What's the matter, Speed?" the man said, grabbing my throat with one powerful hand. "You seeing ghosts tonight?"

He could have crushed my windpipe but instead let up and gave me a forceful shove that snapped my head against the cupboard. Light flashed through my brain. My body shook all over.

"This where you brought her, man?" he asked in a voice that sounded old and slurred. He was either drunk or stoned or under heavy medication. "This the place y'all went fucking behind my back?"

I rubbed my throat, remembering how thin and vulnerable Nola had looked, curled on the bathroom floor.

"Go ahead and do what you're going to do, Jaren," I said, my hands falling to my sides. I'd had this coming for a long, long time. "But make it quick for old time's sake. I don't have the stomach for fighting anymore."

He slapped the side of my head, something a cruel mother might have done to her unruly son. I thought about the ragged little boy with the scabs on his ears.

"You some kind of punk, boy. Lettin' your old running buddy take the fall fuh yuh."

His face appeared swollen, his skin that unnatural jaundiced color I'd noticed in the harsh sunlight of Angola. He was wearing a cutoff t-shirt and the prison muscle had gone slack in his bare arms.

"Nothing I do or say can ever make it up to you, Jaren. But I want you to know I tried my best. I made Rosetta's life as comfortable as I could. And I thought I was hiring a good lawyer to get you out of there."

He had no patience for my apology. He seized my shoulder and forced me to kneel down in front of him. "You and me were inside right now, I'd have to make you my bitch, Speed," he said, "for what you done."

I lowered my head, staring at the carpet, expecting him to hit me again. Or something worse.

"Stand up," he said. There was a frightening serenity in his voice. "Come on, get up, goddammit. I'm not gonna hurt you."

I hesitated, then stood up slowly.

"I need money, man. I'm going away," he said. Something had changed in him. He spoke to me like an old friend. "I need about twenty large and I'll be out of this fucking place. You won't ever have to worry about ol' Two J for the rest of your sorry life."

I let out a deep breath. "Where are you going, Jaren?"

"California, most likely. Got some buddies out there—graduates of the state. They know how to treat a man right."

"You can't leave Louisiana. You know that. They'll send you back to Angola."

He gave me that sad old Two J smile. "Chance I'll take, Speed. I've only got six months, maybe a year left. I came down with Hepatitis C in that shithole and it's got a hold of me real bad."

I bit my lip. I could find no words to speak.

"I don't have the heart to tell mama about it. And I don't have the strength to hate you anymore. I'm not gonna make it, man. My liver's fucked and it could shut down on me any day."

He may as well have beaten me senseless. I could have taken that more than hearing this.

"I want you to tell her for me, Paul. After I'm gone. Do me this one last favor and it's squared between us."

It was impossible to feel any lower, or to loathe myself more than I did at that moment.

"Let me get you a doctor, Jaren. We'll find the best one in New Orleans."

When he smiled now, he resembled his aging mother smiling at something I'd said to make her laugh when I was a boy. "It don't matter anymore," he said in that damaged voice. "I'd rather get shut of this fucking state and spend the rest of my days living the good life on a beach somewhere."

I took another deep breath, searching for oxygen. The room was stifling and the air tasted bitter and stale. "Don't screw around with this thing, Jaren," I said. "I'll find you a whole goddamn hospital full of doctors that'll take care of you."

I choked up, fighting tears. He crossed his arms, leaned back against the bar, and studied me with a patronizing smile. I remembered that expression from when we were boys and he'd beaten me in *horse* for maybe the hundredth straight time. I couldn't recall ever winning a single game against him. He was the best at everything we'd ever done together. Basketball, Chinese checkers, fishing in the river behind the zoo. He'd always caught the biggest fish, flown the highest box kite. And when the fun was over and he'd bested me once again, he'd pat me on the shoulder and show me this same smile that meant, *You've got a lot to learn, kid.*

"A man spends twenty years inside, he earns some head time to work things out with himself," he said, watching me through those sickly eyes. "These last few months, staring ol' Mistuh Bones in the face, I've had to deal with some heavy shit, man. It may surprise you to hear I finally learned how to pray."

He laughed at my reaction, then shrugged.

"It was time to get right with the Man Upstairs, since I'm due to meet the cold motherfucker soon enough. So I been working on forgiveness, Speed, and it ain't been a cakewalk for the Two J. I had a lot of ground to cover. I had my own debts to pay. I've done a shitload of praying here lately, and one fine day I realized something. It came to me like a Holy Jesus revelation," he said, smiling and spreading his fingers as if to create a puff of smoke. "I realized *you* were locked up same as me. All this time you been banging your head against the bars you built around yourself. I'm betting you're pretty skinned up by now, P. And you never could take a hit worth a damn. You a little too candy smooth for a male child."

His smile was affectionate now.

"So in my hour of forgiveness I'm gonna do you a favor, Inmate P. I'm gonna set you free from those walls that been closin' in around your worried mind for twenty years." He paused, blinking, his expression turning suddenly intense. "I'm the only one that can do this, y'understand. I'm your judge, jury, and parole board man."

He seemed to be working through the substance of that thought.

"Knowledge is power, m'man, and I've got the power to give you freedom or hold it back. That's the one thing I been keeping under my cuff since the day I walked the long cold walk into Cellblock G. You had your little secret, I had mine."

Listening carefully to every word he spoke, I waited for him to go on.

"I killed her, Paul. Simple as that. I gave her that scag—the Laotian brown *H*." He said this in a calm, lifeless voice. "The word was on the street. Nasty scag, don't go near it. I knew it would pop her heart."

I stared at him, too paralyzed to move or speak.

"I was strung out real bad myself back then and could barely put one foot in front of the other. All I knew was that my old lady was foxing somebody on the sly and she thought she might be knocked up. I was so pissed I wanted to kill them both. Typical junkie bullshit," he said, shaking his head, disgusted with the person he had once been. "I didn't have a clue she was banging my old childhood cuz."

I couldn't bear to hear this. I tried to focus on the faucet dripping in the bathroom.

"I got what was coming to me," he said. "Twenty years for killing a girl. So go in peace, Brother Paul. Sleep a little sounder tonight. Your parole officer is releasing you from that weight you been carrying." He reached for the Bombay Sapphire resting on the bar and drank straight from the bottle. "But always remember this, m'man. It was my call to make. And I chose to free your worthless ass. You can thank Jesus for that. Sing hallelujah, motherfucker."

He gave me that familiar old pat on the shoulder, then took the bottle with him as he walked toward the door. "Get me that twenty grand by tomorrow afternoon," he said. "I don't want to spend another week in this fucking state."

He stopped and looked around the room. "We had some good

times out here, didn't we, Speed? You and me and Kathleen. That soft old bed used to sit right over there."

I nodded yes, I remembered.

He stared at the silent treadmill and the place where the bed had once rested on iron legs. "I hope she taught you something," he said in a distant voice. I knew who he was talking about. It wasn't Kathleen. "She had a way about her, man. You and me, we were fucked up to treat her like we did. She deserved better than us."

He took another long drink from the gin bottle, staring at the space where the bed had been, and then he opened the cottage door and disappeared into the warm humid night.

After he left, I slid to the floor in my bathrobe and sat crying for a little while, remembering the days before my parents told Rosetta she couldn't bring her son to our home anymore. Those long-ago days of fresh mowed grass and sweet iced tea under the oaks and children running free in blissful ignorance. And I remembered the later years, too. This cottage and Nola and the night my innocence was lost in a dark swamp. And possibly my soul as well.

Jaren, what happened to us? How could we have done such things?

It was already deep into the morning hours when I left the cottage and crossed the dark lawn, reentering the house through the unlocked French doors. I trod up the stairs to Claire's bedroom, our bedroom, until I stood over her sleeping body. The room was filled with her magnificent scent. I missed this woman. I longed for her. I wanted our life back.

She stirred slightly and I pulled back the sheets and crawled into bed with her. "My God," she said, waking with a start. "You scared me, Paul."

It was the first time I'd lain next to my wife in four months. I wrapped my arms around her warm body and held her close. She offered no resistance, so I kissed her sticky lips.

"Shouldn't we talk about this?" she asked in a sleepy moan.

"We will," I said, and slipped my hand underneath her pajama shirt to feel her skin.

Epilogue

Republican candidate Mark Morvant fought a hard and bitter fight against the incumbent in November. The national media was both mocking and fascinated by his popularity in our state. But despite a sizable war chest from my personal contacts and sixty percent of the white male vote in Louisiana, Morvant lost the election. Black voters registered in unprecedented numbers and sealed the small margin of victory against the one-time white supremacist. He vowed to run again, of course, and grabbed headlines however he could. On Christmas Eve he married the daughter of a prominent Fifth Circuit judge in an elaborate wedding ceremony at St. Louis Cathedral. It didn't surprise me. When I finally got around to asking Kathleen what had happened between her and her manicured lover boy, she admitted that she herself had broken off the relationship when he refused to have sex with her anymore. "One day he was going down on me like a lesbian sailor, the next day he wouldn't even shake my hand," she confided after a few drinks one night during the holidays. "I don't fully understand what went wrong, Paul. But trust me on this—you know it's over when a man turns down your blow job."

Three months after the heated November election, Wilhelmina

Phillips declared that she would run for state representative from
Orleans Parish. She continued to be hated and admired, depending on
the color of your skin. Her anti-discrimination ordinance had taken
effect by then and the three oldest Carnival krewes refused to comply,
choosing instead to cancel their parades through the streets of New
Orleans, ending a tradition dating back more than a hundred years.
Mardi Gras would never be the same again. The magic was gone.

Willie called on me privately for my support and I gave her
as much money as I'd given to Mark Morvant. I liked the woman,
as I'd always said, even though she eventually lured Angie Foucher
Thomas away from me. In the years ahead, Angie would become
Willie's chief aide and public relations director and an articulate
spokesperson for their issues. I was proud of my former assistant. And
filled with unbounded gratitude. Before she left the company, Angie
had spearheaded the campaign that brought gourmet coffee to the
city. She had breathed new life into a bedraggled old firm and had
made me an obscenely rich man. A few months after her departure,
an ambitious young entrepreneur from Seattle spent a week down
here observing the Blanchard operations and was inspired to create
his own gourmet coffee franchise, and now there is one on every street
corner in the country. I fronted him thirty percent of his start-up
capital in exchange for a quarter of his profits. It worked out well
for both of us.

Over the course of another year, Perry shed weight down to
skin and bone and lost control of his bodily functions. He ranged in
and out of lucidity. Eventually he moved in with his friends Patrick
and Roger in their exquisitely renovated corner apartment building
farther down Royal Street. They doted over him like hospital nuns.
I paid all the medical expenses and visited Perry every day during
those last months and brought Claire and the children as often as
possible. Kathleen wheeled Mother in to see him on two occasions,
but it was difficult for both of them. Mother couldn't speak, and Perry
couldn't focus his attention or express himself in a linear fashion. I'm
not sure that Mother fully understood what was happening to her
oldest child.

In his sick bed Perry became cheerfully dreamy and free of all cynicism. Perhaps it was the medication. He tried to sit at the piano stool and play for us, but toward the end he was unable to do even that. The news of his final hour came while Claire and I were eating cheeseburgers in the Camellia Grill. Somehow Roger had tracked us down and appeared in a taxi to summon us to the hospital. Perry was already unconscious when we arrived at Touro, and I didn't get to say a proper goodbye. I bent down and kissed his still-warm forehead. He was the only brother I would ever have, and I had always loved him.

In accordance with Perry's wishes, we buried him next to Nico in Greenwood Cemetery, across the interstate from the Blanchard crypt on millionaire's row. My brother had made peace with many things by the end of his life, but he hadn't forgiven my father, whom he believed had willfully ruined him because of his gay lifestyle. Till his dying day Perry contended that Nico had been murdered by the White League, and I was in no position to argue otherwise.

A few days before he passed away, I was sitting at his bedside, reading aloud from a novel he'd always wanted to read: *Answered Prayers* by Truman Capote. Perry found the book wickedly amusing and I enjoyed the sound of his laughter, no matter how tortured and dry.

"He called last night," he said at one point, out of the blue, interrupting my animated performance.

I didn't understand what he was referring to, but that was not unusual. Perry's memory was unreliable by then, his powers of recall intermittent.

"My old friend from the Columns," he persisted, a little annoyed that I had not immediately understood.

"My guardian angel, Paulie," he said with a hollow smile. "The old boy who's been calling me for years."

And then I knew what he meant. It had been the elderly gentleman who had phoned him from time to time, admonishing him for his wicked ways, keeping close watch on his behavior.

"My God, Perry," I said. "Are you sure it was him?"

He laughed, baring his teeth. They were discolored now and too large for his sunken mouth. "Do you know what the bastard had the stones to say to me?" he said, giggling dementedly. "He said he was sorry for any *inconvenience* he'd caused." He was beside himself with laughter. "And he asked me not to hold a grudge."

I was amused to hear this as well, but for a different reason. "And what did you say to him?"

"I told him to suck my bleeding urethra," Perry said, attempting a diminished version of the parrot screech. He was laughing so hard he began to cough, his face blossoming red from the strain. I sat him forward and patted his back, trying to calm him.

"Can you believe…that fucking…White League, Paulie?" he managed to say between choking coughs. "They want me to…forgive them…now that I'm…on my way out and…can't embarrass the family name…anymore."

I gently rubbed his back. "Maybe they want you to put in a good word for them with the Great White Father upstairs."

He was almost breathless but composed enough to speak now without coughing. "Too late for them, I'm afraid. The Great White Father tried to join Jove and the Magnolia Club," he said with a twisted smile, "but they found out His son's a Jew."

I was happy that Perry got the last laugh. The incident seemed to vindicate him, at least in his own mind. It pulled a very old thorn out of his claw and brought him enormous satisfaction. Such a simple gesture, that apology. I didn't have the heart to tell him it was I who had insisted on the phone call from the elderly gentleman.

I still had the scrapbook tucked away securely in a bank vault downtown. Along with the earring. Artifact, talisman, ancient burial relics. Someone will find these things after I'm gone and wonder what manner of man I was.

Not long after Perry's death, I invited Eric Gautier to lunch at Antoine's. I enjoyed the irony of my choice. We still saw each other occasionally, played racquetball at the Athletic Club. Something was missing from our friendship, or perhaps something darker had crept in to replace what had once been genuine. But we tolerated each other's company. There was guilty knowledge between us.

I told him at the outset that I was picking up the tab for lunch.

"To what do I owe this unexpected treat?"

"I've got a favor to ask."

He looked up from the menu. "I don't have any more tickets for the playoffs," he said.

I shook my head. "I want you to be my campaign manager."

He uttered a small laugh, reached for his glass of wine. He was waiting for me to explain the joke.

"I'm going to run for political office," I said.

He nearly choked on the wine. "That's good, Paul. That's very good."

"I'm serious," I said. "I'm considering the governor's race."

He didn't move a muscle for nearly two minutes. Then he said, "Hmm, let's examine that idea," leaning forward and lowering his voice. He glanced at the nearby tables to make sure no one was listening. "You dumped a black girl in a swamp and let her boyfriend rot in prison for twenty years. You blackmailed the city's most influential citizens into making campaign contributions. You fired a lethal weapon at a public event. You've never worked an honest day in your life. You don't know a damned thing about the legislative process. And you've probably never voted in a national election."

"Well, yes, I've certainly got the qualifications to be governor of this state."

He sat back in his chair and studied me, then downed the rest of the chardonnay in his glass. His smile had transformed from bemusement to a daffy, ruffled perplexity. "Jesus on a pogo stick. I think you're halfway serious," he said.

"You're overlooking the other part of my résumé, Eric. I run a highly successful business—the third largest private employer in New Orleans—and I make generous charitable contributions all over the parish. I'm a practicing Catholic. Married, two lovely children. No gambling addiction, lynchings, or prior convictions. That puts me way ahead of the pack."

He was laughing now, tears pooling in his eyes. "What party are you going to run in, my friend?"

"It's Louisiana," I said. "What difference does it make?"

He daubed his eyes with the white napkin from his lap. "This is choice," he said, giggling. "Thank you, Paul. I needed a good laugh."

"And one more thing in my favor," I said. "I'm personally acquainted with the city's most influential citizens. I'm certain they'll want to support my campaign."

That's when he stopped laughing and his suntanned face revealed a pained expression of disbelief. "No," he said, catching his breath. "Please, no."

I smiled at him.

"Please tell me you're kidding, Paul."

"I want you to be my campaign manager, Eric. I know how good you'll be at raising money from all the right people."

He stared at me in silence for several awkward moments, then filled his glass to the brim with wine. "Oh, dear God. You're absolutely serious."

I smiled at him again. "I need to put some meaning in my life," I said.

He swallowed air, wet his lips with wine. "Couldn't you do that by building a nice big community center for disadvantaged youth?" he asked.

I took my time, read the menu twice, sipped my gin and tonic. "Okay," I said. "I'll put up most of the money for the center, but I want significant contributions from everyone in the League."

He looked enormously relieved. "And you'll give up the idea of politics?"

"For now," I shrugged.

"That's a wise decision, my friend."

I wasn't serious about running for governor. I just wanted to see the man squirm a little. I needed his undivided attention.

"You'll still have to be the point man on this project, Eric. You'll be the one to solicit their contributions. I expect results."

"Fine," he said, mopping his brow with the napkin. "Not a problem. I can handle that."

"We're going to call it the Rosetta Jarboe Community Recreation Center. We'll build it right next to the St. Thomas Housing Project. Tell the brethren it will benefit young black kids," I said.

"Tell them it's the beginning of many civic-minded projects that will help the youth and elderly of New Orleans. I expect your boys to be silent partners in every one of these ventures."

Eric set his menu aside and waved to the waiter. He ordered another bottle of wine. It was one of those stressful days that required adequate lubrication.

"Okay, I get the point, Paul. But when is this going to end? We know you've got the scrapbook and all that. Obviously you're still pissed. But how long are you going to squeeze our nuts in a wringer?"

"Until there's atonement, Eric. For all of us."

"Reparations?" he said snidely.

"Call it what you want."

Something darkened in his eyes. "As your attorney I advise you not to push them too hard, man. They're not going to play this game with you forever. Do I need to remind you that bad things have happened to people who displease them?"

It was the price I was willing to pay. "I advise your friends not to fuck with me, Eric."

We ate a quiet lunch together, the heavy cuisine served by a dying breed of Old World chefs. Our conversation suffered. I could feel his resentment; he could sense my lingering hostility. It would be this way from now on. I had more enemies than friends. More money than respect. But I could sleep soundly at night with my wife again. I could look my children in the eye.

Many strange new acquaintances passed through my personal orbit during those seasons long ago. For some there was justice and vindication, for others there was only more loss and uncertainty. I gave my old friend Jaren the twenty thousand dollars he'd asked for and drove him to the airport one sweltering summer day. He avoided any emotion as he shook my hand and told me to take care of his mother. I implored him to reconsider his decision, but he smiled and hoisted his tote bag onto his shoulder and said, "Stay away from trouble, Speed. It follows you around." That was the last time I would ever see him.

I visited Rosetta that evening and told her that her son had left for California. She cried for a week and I seriously considered readmitting her to the hospital for rest. But soon Jaren began to call her every night, and that revived her drooping spirits.

Claire and I had planned to raze the cottage in our back acre and build Rosetta a comfortable apartment with a convenient kitchen and state-of-the-art handicap accessories. We were willing to do whatever was required to make her happy. But Rosetta loved her bungalow on Arabella Street, a place she'd bought and paid for, a place of her own. She still lives there today, retired now from her duties in our household but active in her church and always busy tending her garden of periwinkles and hydrangeas and sweet olive. She will outlive us all.

As the months rolled by, Jaren's phone calls to his mother became less and less frequent, and one day they stopped altogether. I contacted the police in Oakland, where he had told us he was living, and they made a perfunctory attempt to locate him, but reported no luck. An Oakland police sergeant assured me that they had higher priorities than searching for a street-wise ex con who didn't want to be found. I even hired a private investigator to look for Jaren, but after six months of taking my money he admitted there were no solid leads. It was nearly impossible to track down a hard-timer who was living in the margins, he informed me. There was no evidence that a man named Jaren Jarboe had ever spent a day in Oakland, California.

A few years have come and gone but I still have hope that we will bring my old friend home someday. I will bury him in the Blanchard crypt on millionaire's row. I don't give a damn what anyone says.

Author's Note

The Crescent City White League did indeed exist. The formation of the League and call to arms by its leaders, the Battle of Canal Street and its aftermath, the written response by General Philip Sheridan to the actions of September 1874, and the details of Reconstruction New Orleans are all historically accurate. The Liberty Monument is still intact, though removed at some distance from its original prominence. White League survivors of the battle lived well into the 1930s and were present for various dedications and celebrations at the monument. The rest of the story is the product of my imagination.

Acknowledgments

A great many people contributed to the creation and enrichment of this book. I am grateful to Professor Lawrence Powell of Tulane University, who introduced me to the Crescent City White League. His student Jenny Lawrence graciously allowed me to read her honors thesis on the subject. I am indebted to several writers whose books and articles informed my writing, especially James Gill, Carol Flake, Kim Lacy Rogers, Joe Gray Taylor, Adam Fairclough, Edward F. Haas, James Conaway, Wilbert Rideau, Charles Y.W. Chai, Sanford Levinson, and the charming apologist Stuart O. Landry. Tulane law professor Oliver Houck directed me to Betty Cole, Laurie White, and Allen Karger, all of whom provided invaluable insight into the ethos and procedures of Louisiana State Penitentiary at Angola. I also consulted attorney David Anderson and my old friends Scott Turow, Baine Kerr, and Cynthia Bryant on matters of law, and they generously shared their expertise. To these good people, and to all my sources for this story, I offer my sincerest appreciation.

I am most thankful to my friends Stephanie Bruno and the poet Ken Fontenot, native New Orleanians who supplied dozens of crucial details about life in the Crescent City in the 1950s and 1960s.

And I am grateful to former New Orleanian Jane Shumate, who schooled me in mythology.

Early drafts of the novel benefited from the careful reading and criticism of many good friends and exceptional writers: Jim Magnuson, Sarah Bird, Annette Carlozzi, Geoff Leavenworth, Dick Holland, Michael Hurd, Lynda Gonzales, Maria Nehring, and Carol Dawson. Jim Kunetka was especially supportive and encouraging. My old compadre April Smith suggested a plot adjustment that made an enormous difference. And Robin Jamail's advice proved miraculous.

Bill Contardi of Brandt & Hochman was tireless in his support and perseverance. He gave me hope, and I thank him for that.

My editor, Deborah Meghnagi, was as perceptive as she was patient. The story is stronger because of her thoroughness and care.

I have dedicated this book to my late friend Rick Roderick, because he never stopped believing in me. He read the manuscript shortly before his death and responded with his usual insight and wisdom. His friendship will stay with me all the days of my life.

Finally, I want to thank the many wonderful friends I have made in New Orleans over the years. I see their faces and remember their names and cherish *les bontemps* with them all.

About the Author

Thomas Zigal

Thomas Zigal is the author of the critically acclaimed Kurt Muller mystery series set in Aspen, Colorado. He is a graduate of the Stanford Writing Program and has published short stories and book reviews in literary magazines and fiction anthologies for the past thirty years. He grew up on the Texas Gulf Coast and in Louisiana and now lives in Austin, Texas.

The fonts used in this book are from the Garamond family

The Toby Press publishes fine writing, available at leading bookstores everywhere. For more information, please visit www.tobypress.com